BEYOND

THE

FLAME

ESSENCE OF OHR
Book 3

PARRIS SHEETS

BEYOND THE FLAME
Essence of Ohr – Book 3
Copyright © 2022 by Parris Sheets

FIRST EDITION SOFTCOVER
ISBN: 1622536576
ISBN-13: 978-1-62253-657-3

Editor: Darren Todd
Cover Artist: Samuel Keiser
Interior Designer: Lane Diamond

EVOLVED PUBLISHING™

www.EvolvedPub.com
Evolved Publishing LLC
Butler, Wisconsin, USA

Printed in Book Antiqua font.

BOOKS BY PARRIS SHEETS

DEDICATION

To my sister for letting me talk on and on about my made-up worlds and her immense patience when I bounce 'what if' plot points off her. For my brother who has encouraged and celebrated my writing achievements. And to my bonus brother, I don't know why you have so much faith in me — or that I deserve it — but I'm grateful for it. I couldn't have hoped for better siblings.

BEYOND
THE FLAME

ESSENCE OF OHR
Book 3

PARRIS SHEETS

CHAPTER 1

Gray plains. Gray winds. Gray skies. It had become Kole's least favorite color. The Ashland Plains proved so dreary, the dullness of it all had managed to bleed into his dreams. He longed for bright blossoms and vivid sunsets. One thing he wanted more than color? Water. They'd run out last night, and though the late morning hours only just leaned toward noon, his nose, throat, and mouth felt as dry as bark.

Kole, Felix, and Vienna clung to the trunk of the rambler. The walking tree provided little relief from the ash-filled winds tugging at Kole's dusty clothes, but having a ride helped slow his spiral into dehydration. Trudging through knee-high soot would do no good for any of them. Kole squeezed his hands around the roots of the tree, which he used as reins to control the behemoth, and urged it faster. The rambler's roots below, long and lean like spider legs, picked up the pace at his command.

"How much longer till this bloody plain ends?" Felix groaned beside Kole. His brown curls, dusted in ash, bounced at the tree's heightened gait.

"Vienna?" Kole asked. "Where do you suppose we are now?"

With an exacerbated sigh, Vienna fetched the map from her belt and unfurled it. "I don't know why you two keep making me pull this thing out. The volcano is long gone. No landmarks, no telling."

"At this point, just lie ta me, Sis." Felix wiped his eyes. They matched his sister's perfectly. Brilliant green—jewel-like against the dreary landscape. "Say we'll be outta here by dinner, and I won't peep a word the rest the day. Swears it."

"I'm not going to lie to make you feel better. Here. Look for yourself." Vienna offered the map to her brother, but he swatted it away.

"I've got the rambler going as fast as it can," said Kole.

A strained feeling emanated from the roots poised in Kole's hands. The tree needed water. Usually, the rambler got its nutrients from the soil when anchored. The roots would sink into the earth like any normal tree. The morning after, the rambler would pull free and stand tall, energized. But the first morning the rambler had emerged from its slumber here in the Ashland Plains, it appeared drained. Since then, the bark had taken on a brittle texture. No stretch to assume the same poisonous gases spewing from the volcano nestled at the heart of the Ashland Plains tainted the surrounding earth as well. Kole refused to anchor the rambler again for fear the toxins would render their only ride useless.

"Well, it ain't fast enough for me, mate."

"Felix," Vienna scolded with a punch to his gut. "He's doing the best he can. So is the rambler. It's just as weary as us, I imagine. Sorry, Kole."

"It's fine." He was grateful for the conversation no matter what it entailed. Anything to provide a distraction.

"I didn't mean ta blame him; just lettin' ya know what's all in our heads right now. Outta food, outta water. How long ya reckon we'll make it 'fore one of us collapses?"

"It's not the food that'll do it," Kole said. "We need water soon—sooner because of my...." His eyes fell to the frayed hem of his sleeve. The red sheen of scar tissue stared back. Cords of thick flesh maimed his hands. He flexed his fingers. The scars hindered full movement. The fire disfigured more than his hands. Every inch of him held the same marks—the same resistance. Due to his permanent injuries, his need for water had grown exponentially. His body no longer self-regulated his internal temperature. No sweating meant overheating. And if he overheated....

Vienna's freckled face turned to him. "We'll find water." A promise held in her voice, one that made Kole believe it true.

Heat rose in Kole's cheeks, and he turned away. Though he'd known the siblings for a while now, she still had a way of rousing his anxiety. He blamed the feelings on his scars—told himself the nerves came because he still found it hard to fully accept his new appearance. No matter how much he tried to push the thoughts out of his head, he knew what some might think at first glance. Monster. Freak. Someone to be pitied. With Vienna, everything felt different. She'd been the first one since the accident who looked at him and didn't so much as flinch.

"Wish we had Fiona." Felix leaned back and propped his hands behind his head. "That little bird coulda scouted out a pond or somethin'. I'd drink from a puddle. Too bad someone had ta send her off." A harsh side-eye to his sister.

Whatever encouraging warmth Vienna held in her gaze dropped as she set her sights back to her brother. "And leave Leo blind to what's been going on? Maybe *this* is why he didn't pick you for the mission."

"Ugh, that hurts, V." With a closed fist, Felix mimicked stabbing himself in the heart. "But the more I been thinkin', the less I think we really know. I mean, Pipes is alive and working with Savairo."

"It's more complicated than that," Kole said. The mere mention of her name brought forth unpleasant memories. When Piper had disappeared during the battle for Socren, Kole and the Liberation believed her dead, or fated so. Savairo had taken her, after all—the blood crazed warden who murdered any in his path to create monstrous servants. Kole never guessed he'd reunite with their beloved Liberation member on the side of an erupting volcano. *With* her supposed captor.

"Is it really that complicated?" Vienna posed. Fidgeting fingers playing with the frayed thread of her sleeve revealed her scrutiny on the matter. "She force-fed you Soul's blood. She connected you to... you know."

Aterus. The god responsible for the whole mess that was Kole's life, who'd broken the pact of the Seven Souls for his own selfish gain. Aterus' betrayal cast destruction and death upon all of Ohr. Because of him, the Black Wall consumed the land, little by little. Those flames—those black flames—had burned away not just Kole's skin a few months ago but his identity.

"Good or bad, or somewhere between, it doesn't matter what Piper is," Kole said. "She's saved me too many times to count. It was a mercy giving me that blood."

"You can't be serious." A violent cough took Vienna. She hid her face in her elbow until it passed, then cleared her throat.

"Better than what Savairo had in mind. He wanted to take me straight to Aterus." In that scenario, Kole's choices would've surely been severed. His fate would lay in Aterus' hands. But the way Piper had played it—feeding him blood to spark a connection between their minds—let Kole retain his choice. There was only so much the god could do to Kole from a distance. "Least through the mind-link, I could escape."

"Blondie's gotta point." Felix arched his back. A pained brow tucked down over his eyes as he rubbed where he'd been leaning against the rough bark of the trunk. "If Kole's a prisoner, how's he gonna free the Souls?"

Vienna silenced at that.

"It was a good call with Fiona." Kole nodded to Vienna. "Sure, we could have used a bird out here, but Leo should stay up with what's going on. He'll know what to do."

"Well, if he *does* know what ta do next, there's no way in hell he's gonna find us out here. *We* can't even find us. And we gotta map."

"There is another way to get our bearings." Kole nodded to Felix's wrists.

Tilting his head back onto the trunk of the rambler, Felix sighed and said, "Yeah, I know."

"You don't have to if you—"

"Dontcha worry, Blondie. I know it's time I start using it." Felix rubbed his wrists, where small wisps of smoke danced from the seamed scars of his skin. Felix had his own permanent reminders of the horrors of their journey. But his hadn't come from fire. "Tonight. I'll do it tonight, eh?"

Vienna rested a hand on her brother's shoulder. "Whatever you think is best."

The afternoon passed quietly. Kole focused on steering the rambler, while the siblings leaned back with eyes on the horizon in case unwelcome company found them. Few words were shared until the bright light of day dwindled. Ash thickened the air, blocking out the sun's outline. The only way of knowing the time of day was when the brightness grew and faded, marking sunrise and sunset. Otherwise, Kole and his friends could only guess the hour.

The sky took on a terracotta hue. Night grew near. Kole marched the tree on for a little while longer, then stopped to set up camp.

The three companions slid down the roots of the gargantuan tree to the powdered floor. They must have been closing in on the Ashland boundaries because the buildup of soot had thinned. Where it had been knee-deep before, now it topped Kole's ankles.

Kole set his hand on a root. The rambler shook in response. "Sorry, big guy. You have to go another day without rooting." The groan of wood answered him. "It's for the best. You remember last time." Hand still on the tree, Kole closed his eyes and dove into his head. He took a deep breath and reached his mind out to the rambler. Though the brute relayed a bit of resistance, the tree complied.

Roots stretched out, whipping to and froe, as if stretching and shaking away the strain from the day's travel, then tapped back down to the ground in an arced shape. The rambler created cage-like walls with its tendrils all around the trunk. A small gap emerged before Kole, which acted as a doorway. The idea had dawned on Kole to use the tree as shelter the night before last, when the winds kicked up so much dust, they'd all tossed and turned, congested and coughing. The small room under the rambler offered protection from more than the wind, though.

"Any minute now," Felix followed Kole in but refused to sit. Instead, he paced the short length of the shelter repeatedly. His fingers combed through his curls, which had grown so long, they grazed his shoulders. "Know I should be used ta it by now—I mean—I know it's comin', but the thing always pops up all creepy like. Makes me jump every time."

"It'll be all right. Remember, *you* control it. Sort of like me and the rambler," Kole said.

His friend's eyes glanced up at the bottom of the trunk hovering overhead. "'Cept trees don't have claws. And their species haven't killed thousands of innocent people. There's a bit of a gap in the evil meter, wouldn't ya say, mate?"

No arguing with that. Sure, the forest where Kole had lived, filled with walking trees, had been dangerous—getting in the way of a stampeding rambler meant getting trampled—but few had died in comparison to Felix's burden. The trees proved as deadly as any wild beast. And when tamed, they became less feared.

"The sun is down," Vienna called from outside. A rustle as she ducked through the doorway and settled a worried gaze on Felix. "Don't send it away this time. At least not without—"

"Yeah, yeah, I know. Gotta make it useful, gotta—for the love of Souls!" Felix jumped when a shadow swept across the wall. A humanoid figure appeared in the corner. It swayed, head trained on its master. "First off, no more of that, ya hear," he scolded with a wagging finger.

The shadow's long claws twitched. The resemblance was uncanny. The demon shared Felix's short stature, the same hip-favored lean, which gave off an aura of mischief, and even the silhouette of the hair—*Souls!*—it had grown to touch the Kayetan's shoulder. It truly was Felix's shadow.

"Well, go on," Vienna said expectantly, yet she hugged the wall as she rounded the room to Kole. "Talk to it."

"Don't always work that way, Sis. For the more complicated commands, I gotta do Kole's thing and use my mind."

A touch to his hip made Kole flinch. He caught Vienna pulling the sunstone dagger from his belt. Apparently, she still held her fear of the shadow. For good reason. Kayetans had tormented their city for decades, killing and massacring innocent people at the warden's command. The siblings' parents had been slaughtered by these very demons. Kole gave her a look of warning but let her take the weapon.

"I'm in control," she whispered, eyeing the penumbra.

"Kole?" When Felix's attention turned to him, Vienna hid the dagger behind her back. "Could use yer help, mate."

Kole moved to the center of the room and sat, cross-legged. A wave of his hand encouraged Felix to join.

"I can hear him whisperin'." Felix lowered across from Kole with his thumb pointed to his head. "That's good, right?"

"I'm not an expert on Kayetan communication," Kole lifted one side of his mouth in a teasing grin, "but, yes, it's probably good. It— *he?* —is open to you. What do we call it anyway?"

Felix shrugged. "It's my shadow, so he, I guess. Ya want me ta ask him that instead of findin' us water?"

Good to know Felix's humor remained. Felix had lost it at first when he'd returned from his time with Savairo. The warden had abducted Felix and forced him through the blood ritual, which had severed the shadow from his friend's body. Felix had barely survived the encounter. The aftermath, physically and mentally, from that horror had morphed Felix into something unrecognizable. No longer the happy-go-lucky thief from the city. That part of him still shined through every now and then, giving Kole hope that one day Felix might make a full recovery. Mostly now, Felix held a blank stare, and his smile lines grew less severe.

The ritual had left Felix with a long, continuous scar outlining the sides of his body, yet his mobility remained, something Kole wished he could say about himself. No one should have to bear the burden of such wounds, least of all a friend. Though happy, it would be a lie to say Kole harbored no envy. *If I could move like the days before my own accident....* A dream that would never come to pass.

Kole removed the thought from his mind and focused on Felix. "I'll take you through the strategy Russé taught me. Close your eyes." When Felix obeyed, he too fell into the peace of darkness. He hoped to keep things light and extend Felix's peppy demeanor for as long as possible. "What do you see?"

"Vienna," Felix said. "He's lookin' at her."

Kole had heard Felix mention it before. When night came and the Kayetan emerged, Felix had this strange ability to see through the eyes of his detached shadow. Unsure of why or how, they assumed it had something to do with the smoke dancing from Felix's wrists. Something had gone wrong, or at least *different*, during the blood ritual that created the demon.

"Are you in control of the vision?" Kole asked. "Can you make him look somewhere else?

"No. Just see what he sees. It's kinda like when ya have a dream, I guess—watchin' in on it."

Interesting. They share sight but not control. Kole assumed they'd be more bonded, since the ritual had stopped before completion. Truthfully, they all stood blind to Felix's situation. The only other person they'd know who had control of their Kayetan had died a couple days ago. Shikar had meant to train Felix before her passing. Now Kole, Felix, and Vienna had to go it alone.

"Give it a command. Something simple." Kole opened his eyes to find Felix's face contorted in concentration, his bottom lip clenched between his teeth. Slowly turning to get sight on the Kayetan, Kole waited for it to heed its master's secret command.

The shadow folded its arms and tapped an impatient foot.

"For the love of Souls, mate," Felix erupted. "Do what I say." He jumped to his feet and shook a fist at his Kayetan. "It just keeps lookin' at Vienna."

Vienna tensed at that and lowered in her stance as if readying to pounce.

Kole climbed to his feet and held his arms out between them. He studied the devil for a moment. If this truly was Felix's shadow, he might be able to read the physical cues. The tapping foot stood out as a clear sign of agitation. Something else about its posture sparked a cue in Kole. *What is it?* The shadowed chin gave it away, tilted down and slightly angled. Felix did the same when he sensed danger.

"He doesn't trust her." Immediately, he guessed why. Kole pointed to Vienna's arm wrapped around her back. "Hand it over."

She dropped her arm, revealing the dagger clenched in her fist.

Felix turned on her. "Why ya got that? Thought we got past tryin' ta murder it."

"I'm not actively hunting it. It's... for protection in case—"

"In case I go on a rampage?" Felix mimicked his shadow's agitated posture. "May not be able ta make it do things, but I can keep it from... *doing* things."

Kole scrunched his mouth at that. Didn't quite makes sense, but he knew where Felix was coming from. He approached Vienna with an open hand. "It's a block. If Felix is going to make any progress, we need to trust him. Which means his shadow, too. No more commandeering my dagger."

Vienna twirled the hilt in her palm as she stared past Kole's shoulder. When her eyes came back to him, she handed over the weapon, saying, "Technically it's mine." Then she walked straight up to the Kayetan. "Let's be clear here. If you so much as scratch my brother or Kole, I will find a way to vanquish you, with or without that dagger."

Kole's jaw dropped when the shadow held out a clawed hand. An offering of peace?

A long moment passed while Vienna stared at the hovering hand. Finally, she lifted her own—trembling as if unsure—and curled her fingers between the smoke-like claws. She didn't squeeze, for her touch would pass straight through the creature, but she held herself there, stiff as a tree, confirming the pact.

In a blink, the Kayetan swirled away, leaving a trail of smoke through the roots where it escaped.

Vienna turned. "Where did it go?"

"Guess it was you." A smirk set on Felix's face. "I told it ta find us some water."

As if on cue, Vienna's cough returned. She nodded to her brother, then hunched against the bark until her fit subsided.

The night dragged on. Felix and Vienna had long passed into their dreams, snuggled up in the soot, while Kole spent another night restless. Less ash sifted to their lungs with the roots acting as walls. No need for a watch since the rambler would rouse the group if danger approached, Kole leaned against the tree and stared blankly into the darkness. Quiet should bring peace. *Should.* Yet all it brought was images of the past.

This crazy quest—*more like death mission*—had started a little over a month ago, when Kole learned he had a connection to the lost gods of Ohr. The Seven Souls, as they called them, each had a part in creating the world. His lifelong mentor, Russé, who'd disguised himself as an old man throughout Kole's youth, revealed his true identity as the Green Soul, creator of all plant life. Russé was the reason Kole could steer and control a tree as easily as a horse. Hell, the Green Soul had given the ramblers the ability to walk in the first place.

Apparently Kole had released Russé from his prison at the young age of five, though he held no memories of the event. Before Kole learned of all this, he—and everyone else in Ohr—believed the Souls had abandoned them. The truth? One of the Seven, Aterus, had betrayed the gods for his own gain and banished his kin from the land. But the Souls were a perfectly balanced petal propped on the tip of a finger. The absence of one Soul sent that petal whirling and allowed chaos to consume the land. That chaos came in the form of the Black Wall: the dark fire that had left Kole maimed and had slaughtered his family and closest friends.

"Niko." Kole thought the name so vividly, he had said it aloud. *If only you were here.... I need help.*

A way existed to return Niko from the grave—one that had recently presented itself to Kole. At the time, he'd refused the offer, but things changed when he had reached his limit back at the volcano. The moment he released Obell, the Red Soul, something within Kole's spirit surrendered. He alone bore the pain. He alone bore the burden of returning peace to Ohr. And what did he get in return? A *chance* that it would work—that his efforts would destroy the Black Wall. But a great penalty loomed over such a victory: Kole may die in the process.

How much more would he have to endure for Ohr? Why *him*? A fifteen-year-old boy. Why was *he* meant to suffer for the mistakes of others?

Death. *Is that what I'm running toward?* Kole squeezed his hands into half-balled fists. The taut scars pulled sharply against his knuckles, preventing them from fully closing. *Haven't I suffered enough?*

But there was another way.... A way out.

Kole's eyes scanned his sleeping companions. Neither stirred as he snuck through the cage of roots into the dark, open plains. He walked far enough so that the wind would conceal his voice, but he maintained full sight of the rambler.

He struggled to swallow the dried lump spreading in his throat. Even the thought of what he intended to do next made his hands tremble. *There's no other way. There isn't.* The thoughts did little to subdue his fear.

With closed eyes, he reached into the depths of his mind and followed the roads to where the Souls lay like parasites in his brain. He could feel the doors leading to each one. The ones he'd already released,

Russé, Issira, and Obell, no longer held fortifications against him. Their doors, if pushed, would open at will, he knew. They offered easy connection. The others lay dormant, forever waiting for release. But he searched for one Soul in particular. The one which frightened him the most.

He found no door, but Kole knew the god lived within him somewhere, for they had connected before.

"*Aterus.*" Kole let the name ring through his body, then waited.

No answer.

After a shivering inhale, Kole clenched his fists. "*I want to make a deal.*"

A tingle ignited in his fingertips. Subtle first, then it built in his veins. He felt the throb of his heart pulse through his arteries like strikes against a war drum.

The voice came clear in his head. The voice of Aterus. "*I'm listening.*"

CHAPTER 2

The face of Piper's enemy stirred in her head. She replayed the death—the murder she'd committed a day ago—over and over again. Not out of guilt; she carried no remorse. Piper reveled in the act. The kill strengthened her. The image of the flesh melting off Savairo's face as she pushed his head into the boiling lava... she closed her eyes and welcomed the goosebumps. Too long had the blood sorcerer held power over her. Too long had he tormented Socren and the people of Ohr. No doubt anyone who learned of Savairo's demise would celebrate. If they'd seen it, though—the way it'd all played out—would they deem her savior or monster?

"Piper."

The sweet voice stilled her thoughts and brought Piper back to reality. She sat knee-deep in ash. The remnants of the exploded volcano lay at her back.

"We need to know what happened. Will you talk now?" The woman knelt beside her. The stained blue silk of her gown along with the ash smeared across her face made her seem almost human.

How interesting they'd take the forms of the species that marked their end. Piper took in the god's eyes; the color of thunderclouds, and they swirled, too, like skies birthing a twister. The Blue Soul, as the people of Ohr had come to know her. "Like you don't know, *Issira.* What you saw is what happened."

Issira leaned back, angular brows soft over her unreadable expression. "You would have burned with him. You would've met the same fate had I not doused your pride. But the lava didn't affect you. Why is that?"

"Feigning ignorance? Or do you just want to hear me say it?" Piper rose and faced the cooling streaks of lava draping the volcano. A few bright veins of orange remained. Mostly, the rivers of fire glowed dull, like dying coals.

Two other Souls stood around her, staring, waiting. One, she'd met before. Russé, the Green Soul. The one responsible for enchanting the trees of the forest north of the mountains. His power over plants made the trees of the forest a menace, walking on their roots and bumbling about like cattle. But here, in the desolate plains, he held little threat.

And the other god who stood beside Russé? A new face. Freshly released from the volcano, no doubt, which meant he could be no other than Obell, the Red Soul. Despite having three gods in her company, she only felt their weakness. *Dried up powers. Fallen divine. Pity.*

Piper surveyed the volcano. "Look at this mess. I thought you'd handle things subtly. Were you surprised I found you, Russé? You left a clumsy trail from the beginning."

"Freeing my kin felt more important than covering our tracks at the time," Russé answered. "The only surprise was learning you traveled with Savairo. Are you working for him?"

A laugh escaped her. She smiled, replaying the blooming fear in the blood sorcerer's eyes the moment he realized she had the upper hand. "Not anymore."

"Aterus, then?" Russé leaned against his gnarled staff. The old man's persona was almost believable. He'd thought of everything: the beard, the hunched back, even a weapon that served as a "walking stick." The form might have fooled humans, but not her.

"No. I left my father's graces a long time ago. By my own choosing."

Russé stepped back. "Father?"

Even Obell clenched his fists with palpable confusion. The behemoth man's muscles flexed and twitched beneath rich, deep skin. "Aterus had a child? Impossible."

The shock on their faces pleased her. Save for Issira's, which never flinched.

"What are you talking about?" Russé asked.

Piper swung her head to the Blue Soul. "Why don't you ask Issira?"

Belches from the cooling volcano filled the tense air between them.

"Issira?" Russé turned to his kin. "You know something about this?"

Issira brushed back her pin-straight black hair and lifted to her full height. "I know of her."

"You *knew* of a child?" The wrinkles of Russé's face deepened. "Yet you kept it hidden all this time."

"It's an abomination. Human and god together. Diluted power," said Obell. As his fury intensified, so did the light of the lava behind him.

Piper rolled her eyes. "This *abomination*," she pointed a thumb at herself, "is more powerful than any of *you* at the moment. I'd show a little more respect for the person who is single-handedly going to pull this world out of the destruction you all created."

"Aterus created this!" Obell roared. The volcano rumbled at his anger.

"*All* the Seven Souls are responsible," Piper snapped. "With your quarreling and need for control, even now."

"Enough." Issira flung a hand toward Obell. A jet of water burst from her palm and soaked his skin. On contact, the water sizzled and steamed away. Obell's shoulders fell forward, more composed than before. "Before the calamity," Issira began, "Aterus and I made a deal. My end was to keep the pregnancy a secret. I never met the mother, nor did I ever see the newborn." A quick nod Piper's way. "After I realized my error, I confessed."

"You never mentioned a child," Russé accused, his fingers wrapped tightly around the gnarled top of his staff.

"And what of it?" Issira's sweet voice held a sour note. "What does her existence have to do with finding the rest of our kin?"

Russé rubbed his temples and sighed. "We don't know the complications."

"Honestly, neither do I," Piper admitted. Beyond the few otherworldly gifts she possessed, she never fully grasped what it meant being the offspring of a Soul. A curse? Blessing? *Depends on the day.* "That's not important for now. What we need to do is stop bickering and find Kole. Where is he?"

"I sent him away," Russé answered.

"What?" The annoyance in her voice wouldn't be reined in. "Are you insane?"

"It was too dangerous for him on the volcano, and I needed to ensure Issira and Obell escaped unharmed, so I told him to run the rambler as far from here as he could." Russé glanced to his kin, who, other than a few scuffs and bruises, seemed in good shape. "He'll sit tight until we find him."

"He'll *sit tight*," Piper mocked. "When has Kole ever *sat tight*? For claiming to know him so well, I seem to have a better grasp on him." She waved a hand at the dense winds of ash swirling over the plains. "How are we going to find him in all of this?"

"The ash will settle once the volcano sleeps. Soon, the air will clear," Obell said.

"I can sense him through our connection." Russé closed his eyes for a moment, leaving Piper and the two other Souls to stare at one another.

She snuck a peek at Issira. A part of her felt indebted to the Soul for keeping her deal with Aterus all this time. Even when her father captured and imprisoned his kin, the Blue Soul never faltered. Piper held a bit of admiration based solely on that. *Who knows what the gods would have done to me or my mother had they discovered us. Probably killed us both.* Still, whatever budding trust was forming came with scrutiny. The Souls had moved against one another before, and Piper held no doubts they'd do the same before the end.

Issira caught her stare and held it. The few seconds felt like minutes under the Soul's gaze. Something squirmed in the back of Piper's mind. Not a thought or feeling. Something simpler. A presence—foreign, yet oddly familiar. Was Issira trying to breach her thoughts? Piper shook it away. *No one's getting in my head if I can help it.*

"They've gone north," said Russé. "I can sense him and the rambler."

"No use wasting time." Piper trudged through the ash away from the three Souls, knowing full well they would follow. Though she preferred to continue alone, she lacked the skills to track Kole now. No. Not lacked. Piper chewed her bottom lip. She had one way to find Kole. But what she'd have to do... the mere thought made her shudder. One slipup and it could ruin her. *A last resort. Only as a last resort.*

CHAPTER 3

When Kole opened his eyes, the Ashland Plains had gone. The mind-link showed him a wide, bare landscape weighed heavy with hills of golden sand. No heat or cold touched his skin. The place seemed void of temperature and wind. Somehow, the sky shone clear and bright without a sun.

"This is... unexpected. Much more pleasing than the ocean of blood."

Kole clenched his teeth, then turned to the voice.

Aterus walked down a nearby dune. Each step sent a small river of sand rushing down with him. The Soul looked just as Kole remembered from the previous mind-link: salt-and-pepper hair, hard features, and broad shoulders, which stretched his white tunic tight across his chest. "It seems as though your opinion of me has shifted." Those dark eyes glinted as he approached.

Kole waved to the desert scene. "I'm not controlling any of this." He'd never even seen one before, merely heard of them through childhood stories. None existed within the confines of the the Black Wall and hadn't since the wall of fire had consumed the lands far south a couple decades before he was born. How could such an unfamiliar landscape show itself so clearly to him?

One side of the god's mouth lifted. "Maybe not direct control. But it is you."

Three days ago, when they'd spoken in the last mind-link, they'd stood on a red sea and the pink sky had rained blood. Aterus claimed the gruesome scene represented Kole's opinion of him. A murderer. If the Soul assumed correctly, what did a desert mean?

Aterus slid his hand down the sleeve of his white tunic. Brows raised. When his eyes trained back on Kole, something sparked behind them, and his tense posture softened. "I'm glad to see you safe."

"You know why I'm here," Kole blurted. Every passing moment offered another chance to second guess himself or the siblings to discover his absence. He wanted this done.

"I told you last time; *that* deal was gone the moment you denied it."

Kole chewed his corded lip. "Then I'm here to make a different one."

Aterus folded his arms and studied him but continued his silence.

"I know what I want now. I'm not clouded by the wills of others."

"The will of *your Souls*," Aterus corrected.

"Yes."

"What is it you desire, Kole? I will not give you your refugees back if that's what you're asking. I've already offered that, and I refuse to be so kind again."

Why had he been so stupid before? Dozens of children, the orphaned refugees of his camp who'd died in the Black wall, could've had their lives back if he'd agreed last time instead of listening to Russé.

"I want Niko." Kole's mind raced. Was that all he wanted? No, but should he risk too many demands? Negotiations always dwindled the price. Might as well lay it all out and cut where he could. "I want my body back."

Aterus lowered his head like a wolf stalking prey. "No."

A shiver of anger ravaged Kole's body, trembling his hands. He balled his fists to hide it, though he knew his efforts were in vain. A feverish heat swept through the desert at his shifting temper. It seemed his emotions controlled more than he thought.

"If that's all...." Aterus started to turn. No doubt he felt the morphing climate—could read Kole's every emotion.

"Wait!"

The Soul ignored his cries and walked back up the dune. His bare feet shimmered, fading away like a mirage.

"Niko. Just Niko." A portion of his heart sank at the admission. The part which longed to become whole again—to break free of the bars that were his burns.

Mid-step, Aterus paused.

"Please. That's all I want. I'll make your deal. I'll free the rest of the Souls and give them to you."

A stubbled chin turned over the Soul's shoulder. "Your friend? That's all you want?"

Kole swallowed, fighting back the protests clawing up his throat, which begged and pleaded to take back his words. "Yes," he forced.

"How generous you are." Aterus turned back to Kole. "Willing to live crippled till the end of your days."

"I'm not crippled," Kole roared. Things had shifted since the last mind-link. Before, Aterus had come to Kole with a deal. The Soul had been the weak one. Now *Kole* begged for a compromise. Aterus held the control here, and he knew it.

"No. I guess you're not." The Soul straightened and closed the distance between them. "You will give my kin to me. Convince the imprisoned to transfer their essence to me so they can ascend, and I will remain over Ohr as the one and only god. With the strength of four, I will be able to overpower Russé, Issira, and Obell. They will concede in the end. If not on their own, after a few more millennia back in their prisons."

"Millennia?"

"Don't fret, Kole. I doubt it will take that long. Niko will be returned to you as soon as I have the three you've promised me. As for the Black Wall... I will have enough power from those you give me to keep it at bay — even restore half of Ohr. But the wall will not burn out completely until all seven are merged. It's the only way balance can be restored. Russé will give up when he knows the key won't be sacrificed. Obell and Issira will follow shortly after."

When the key won't be sacrificed....

He means me. A shred of doubt reared up, but Kole forced it down. He held no pity for Russé, who would have Kole die for the cause... and many times over again.

Kole's hand went to the pendant resting on his chest. He pulled it free and stared at the symbol of the Seven Souls. "What if I can't convince them? What if they refuse?"

The sand shimmered despite the absent sun as Aterus bent and grabbed a handful. "We may be gods, but our will is as fragile as your own. At first, we put up walls. Hope is strong." The sand slipped through his fingers in thin streams, but he closed his other hand over the leaks and the sand ceased flowing. "Isolated for so long, our will — our sanity — begins to fade." Aterus' second hand, cupped around his first, only acted as a temporary solution to the leak. Soon the sand slipped through the cracks in his fingers once more. When the stream finally slowed, he opened his palm to Kole. Small granules remained tucked in the creases of his skin. "The time to act is when they still hold reason — still hope for a way out. Too much reason and they will deny you. Too little, and they will have turned mad from isolation. The time to prey is now, Kole. They are ripe."

Gods dwindling into madness. The thought frightened Kole. With all their power, one wrong word could sour his mission. *More than Ohr is at stake. I have skin here. I will* make *them agree.* The thought made him pause. Those words compelled him to see himself in a new light. The Kole from a month ago would've called out such greed, but he knew better now. He would act for himself, yes, *and* for others. If claiming control over his fate labeled him as heartless, then so be it. Better than accepting death.

Kole thumbed the pendant he'd inherited from his old camp leader after his home had burned. Seven jewels encircled the black center stone. *He* was that black stone. His spirit was a conglomerate of borrowed life force. Kole possessed a piece of life from each god. *That* was the way it worked. Aterus had locked his kin in a different plane, and Kole—linked to them—acted as the anchor, which allowed them to return to Ohr in their fully powered form. The god had to take back their piece of life force from Kole in order to be freed, but the act killed Kole. Kole only survived the encounter if the Soul, once freed, returned the fragment to him. Thus far, Issira and Obell had agreed with the terms. They had Kole, their key to finding and releasing the rest of their kin, in exchange for dwindled powers. The Souls came back as half-gods. But once Kole had released the final Soul, how long would they allow him to live before taking back their powers?

"You hesitate," said Aterus.

Kole shook the complications from his mind. "I keep trying to think of another way."

"Why?" Aterus dusted the sand from his palms.

"I... It doesn't feel right."

"To you? Or is it what Russé and my kin want you to think."

Kole tucked the pendant under his shirt. "I don't know anymore. They speak to me. They give me their pain... but also protection. I don't know who to believe anymore."

"Their words are poison. You cannot trust a Soul."

Kole narrowed his gaze. "You're a Soul."

"But my essence isn't connected to you. You are free of my burden." Aterus let his hands fall to his sides. "You believe the others because that it what their influence wishes. Kole, you must never forget, your mind is not your own. And it never will be as long as you remain their host."

"You think they tell me how to feel?"

Aterus scoffed. He turned to the dunes and clasped his hands behind his back. "More than how you feel. Everything you do and say."

The idea had never crossed Kole's mind. Sure, a small part of six gods dwelled inside his spirit, but he knew when they spoke or reached out. *Every action? Impossible. I'd feel it.*

Aterus spied him. He must have detected Kole's doubt because he shook his head and ran a hand through his gray-peppered hair. "Have you ever thought about *why* you fight my word? My ideas? Instinctually you believe them to be wrong. Part is because my brothers and sisters pose influence over you. The other is because I *do not* reside in your head as they do. My words have no rule over you." With a wave of his hand, the symbol of the Seven materialized in thin air, hanging in the space between them. Prongs led out from the center stone to all, save for the gray circle—Aterus' color. With a snap of his finger, a new prong grew out from the center black stone to reach the gray one. "If a piece of my essence were in you, you would be more inclined to agree with it. That is why you battle with me so. The others' thoughts of me have turned into your own. Drown them out—free yourself from their corruption, and you can find truth." He thrust his palms at the image and severed the connection of all seven stones seeping into the center. "You can decide and think and act of your own free will. It is as I intended humanity to be."

All this time Kole had sought a singular solution. But this way— Aterus' way—Kole would live out his full life with Niko. He'd live to become an adult. But would it be *right*?

"What happens to Ohr when the Souls are gone?"

The gray stone faded away. "I rule."

"Will you kill as you've done before?"

"I have never killed." Aterus' eyes narrowed. "Those deaths came from the spread of the Black Wall."

Kole threw an accusing finger. "Which *you* created when you imprisoned the Souls."

"The wall wasn't my fault. Even now I keep it at bay for you and everyone within. Had I have known the outcome...." Aterus shook his head after a brief moment of consideration. "No, that wouldn't have stopped me. But I would've prepared. Figured out a way to combat it and to control its destruction before I imprisoned my kin."

"You'd really do it all again because of some woman?"

"You are young. Love eludes you, but yes, because of her."

"One life?" Kole scoffed. "You broke the peace of Ohr for one life?"

"Is one life not worthy?" Aterus turned and steadily walked around Kole, circling him. "A bit unfair to judge me, is it not? Niko is one life, and you seem ready to risk everything for him. And you yourself seek this path because you fear your own death in the end if you follow Russé's way. Am I right? If you call me selfish, you label yourself the same."

"That's... it's different." Kole's thoughts scrambled to make sense of everything, especially while Aterus slowly rounded him.

Is it different?

True, Niko was one life, but Kole worked to save Ohr, not blindly act on his desires and bring about destruction in the process. *That* was the distinction between them. Why was it so hard to come to that conclusion? Was it *really* different, or was Kole grasping at any justification he could scrounge up? "I wouldn't bring him back at the risk of Ohr—of others. Niko wouldn't want that. You said you would've prepared. That's what I'm doing. I need to know how things will be if I give you the Souls."

While Kole struggled to deny his and Aterus' similarities, the Soul paused at his side.

"How best to say this?" Aterus tilted his head and tapped a finger on his chin. "The Seven worked for a time. We balanced out one another. But *so many* voices begin to stagnate. After a time, nothing changes—nothing is done for lack of agreement. They deemed one life, my Evangeline, insignificant, yet every life is important to someone. Something you seem to understand."

Aterus closed in. The wind of his breath brushed Kole's forehead.

The proximity of the Soul riled Kole's nerves. At his full height, Kole only came up to Aterus' chest. No matter if the Soul meant to intimidate or not, it felt as if the god loomed over him. Kole swore he could feel his ankles twitching to run.

"What right did my kin have to challenge my love? Because they are gods? How is my opinion less potent than theirs when we are all divine? I feel it is time for *one* to rule. One who can invoke change. Just as I have done for Evangeline, I will do for Niko. And you. I will save Ohr and undo the horrors of the past."

It all sounded good. Too good? If Kole were to take the deal, he had to check every end. "The Black Wall won't take any more lives while it stands?"

"I can't promise that until I get my Souls, the three I've tasked you with. I won't have the resources otherwise. If it does move before then, it won't be my doing." He rounded to Kole's front. "Any other questions? This feels like an interrogation."

"You told me to think on my own. I need to learn everything I can if I'm to trust you."

"You don't need to trust *me;* you need to trust the arrangement."

The way Aterus spoke came off so different than Russé. The Gray Soul spoke freely and bluntly, yet his words felt coated. Something still hung there, unsaid.

"You need me as much as I need you," Kole said. "Don't pretend otherwise."

Aterus leaned in. "You brought me here for a reason." The gravel in his voice made Kole's head buzz. "Clearly, you've lost faith in Russé and see me as a viable substitute. Let's not waste time." He straightened and backed away. Arms open wide, he said, "Make your choice."

We both understand, then. There's no way out of this alone. At least Aterus laid his crimes out in the open, unlike Russé, who revealed a new twist and lie at every turn.

"Just know, I will not entertain this deal again," said the Soul. "If you leave this time without an agreement, you are on your own to figure out your role in this. And I will be forced to take my own steps to secure Evangeline and myself."

Kole chewed his lip. He'd have Niko. The Black Wall would be contained or destroyed. Disagreements between gods wouldn't ravage the land again. And he'd have his *life*. What else could he possibly want? But he had another card to play.

"What happens to one happens to all. That's what you said. Is it true?"

"It is the only law that cannot be avoided."

"That's what I thought." Kole failed to hide his blooming smirk. There was one thing Aterus kept close — something he wished to hide — and Kole had found it. "Then you are broken, too."

Aterus' leer confirmed Kole's suspicions.

"Fragments of the other six Souls merged into me. And you said you are not connected in the same way. But you *were* fragmented. And I know who holds that piece of you." Kole felt the power of this advantage grow within his bones. Something Aterus never counted on him discovering. "The very person who fed me your blood and forced this new link between us. Our mind-link. Your daughter, Piper."

The Soul's body kept stone still. Maybe out of shock, or maybe something brewed in his head: a way to squirm out of this. Kole refused to allow that.

"A family secret, I suspect." Kole folded his arms. "I can keep it that way if you'd like. For my own price."

At that, Aterus' lips pulled back in a toothy grin. "Would that price include your body back?"

"Glad you can keep up."

Aterus clasped his hands. "What makes you think she's worth anything to me?"

A bluff. Well, if he wanted to deny it, Kole would play along. "If not love, then the reason why you've kept her alive all this time." It was something Kole had speculated over the last few days. A small seed of revelation that had only just began to sprout. The reason why the simplest and quickest of solutions to all of the Soul's problems had been abandoned. Kole held the pieces of the Souls within him, so why not kill him and be done with it? Release the essences inside of him to go back to their proper places. With Russé and the others, it was more complicated. Even if their kin had full power, they'd still be locked away with no way to trace them. They needed Kole alive to locate their trapped kin. But Aterus... he didn't need that. So why would Piper live? Either because of a father's love for his daughter, or death of the vessel meant death of the fragment. In the latter case, Aterus would never reach his former full power again.

As the two stared at each other, Kole finally witnessed the cogs churning behind the god's eyes, and he sensed weakness.

Before the moment could pass, Kole held out his hand. "My body, Niko, and Ohr for your kin."

The sand crunched under Aterus' feet as he approached. His fingers curled around Kole's and shook, binding the deal. When he pulled away, a smile appeared. Kole never expected someone like him to smile like that—full and genuine. Amused. But the expression fit his face. Suited him.

"I have something for you. A gift for your assurance." Aterus stepped back, and the sand swirled up from the ground like a small tornado. The golden granules clumped together near the ground then built up.

Feet appeared. Then legs. The sand built tall into a humanoid shape. A man. Kole stepped back. His instincts flared with unease. A gift? What sort of gift would Aterus bestow? Some sand monster?

The sand settled into the body. Grains smoothed and softened into skin—a deep tan. Plain clothes draped the body. Clothes Kole *knew*. His mouth opened as granules sank and grew, forming a hard jaw line and sculpted physique. A perfect replica of his childhood friend, who'd burned in the Black Wall, stood before him.

"Niko," Kole breathed. He risked a hesitant step forward. Close enough to reach, Kole held out a hand and grazed his finger down the statue's arm. It felt real, flesh-like, but the figure kept still like an oversized doll. Kole studied the face. Everything—every detail exactly how he remembered. The shadow of stubble around Niko's cheek Kole had always envied, and the disheveled hair that always seemed to fall in just the right place. The brown eyes stared blankly ahead—not toward Kole, but through him.

Kole reined in his excitement. The awe of seeing his friend shifted to seething bitterness. "I've already seen this trick." Last time Kole had talked with Aterus, the god had dangled Niko before him like a puppet—a tool—to soften Kole. He wouldn't waste any more emotion on a visage.

As Niko stared, an inner light danced in the pupil. Like a birthing flame, the eyes came alive. They narrowed.

"Kole?"

The voice sent a shiver through Kole's core as old memories of the past rushed him like a bull. His best friend—no, his *brother*—stood before him once again. Seeing him felt like no time had passed. It could've been yesterday, when he and Niko snuck out of camp to wander the walking forest, pretending they were great shepherds commanding the trees around.

But it hadn't been yesterday. A month he'd been dead, and yet here he stood. "Enough of this, Aterus. I don't want to see it."

Aterus leaned back and folded his arms.

Niko's mouth opened as he lowered his gaze to his body, lifting his arms and patting his clothes. At last, his hands brushed the stubble of his chin. "How? How is this—where are we, Kole? What's going on?"

Something in the voice sent off an alarm in Kole. This seemed different than the last time. More real. Either Aterus had improved or.... "Niko?" It took all Kole's effort to pull his eyes from his friend and find Aterus quietly watching them. "What did you do?"

Aterus shifted. "Exactly what you asked. I've brought back your friend."

"Brought me back?" Niko asked. He turned to Aterus then stepped behind Kole. "Who is that?"

"Well, not fully. Not yet," said Aterus.

Kole's heart pounded at the possibility. "What do you mean?"

"I've brought back Niko's spirit. It's all the energy I can currently spare without weakening my hold on the wall. I did make a promise to you, did I not? No more deaths on my account." Aterus' fingers tapped his bicep. "His full revival will have to wait until I get my Souls. But it's him with all his memories... and he can learn and retain anything you share in this state. Everything but the body. He's tethered to you, Kole. No one else can see or hear him. They won't know he exists unless you tell them."

"I'm a ghost?" Niko asked meekly behind Kole.

"Call yourself what you like," Aterus waved a disinterested hand Niko's way, then focused back on Kole. "I hope my generosity will encourage a hasty delivery. I await the next Soul. And if you aren't aware, you are being tailed by Russé and your old company. Deal with it how you wish, but if I sense our arrangement is faltering," Aterus jutted his chin to Niko, "*he* will be ripped from you again."

Within a blink, Aterus vanished.

A sinkhole appeared where the Soul had stood. Sand spiraled down. The nearby dunes flattened, all falling to the depths. Kole tumbled back as the sand beneath his feet slid out from under him. He landed on his backside, but still he moved, carried forward by the shifting ground.

He kicked and thrashed to no avail. As if caught in an undertow, Kole's body slipped beneath the sand's surface and sped through the desert. With his final effort, he punched his head above the surface in time to see the lip of the sink hole rise over him. Darkness rushed up as the desert swallowed him.

CHAPTER 4

Kole scrambled up. He whipped his head left and right. The Ashland Plains surrounded him. A look down at his soot-covered clothes told him he'd fallen asleep in the ash. He patted the layer from his body and wiped his face and eyes.

Memories of the mind-link sobered him. Had it been real? *One way to find out.* "Niko?" he called into the dying wind. He held his breath, waiting.

"I'm here." Like a solidifying mirage, Niko appeared before him.

Kole couldn't help the smile overtaking his face. The muscles in his cheeks felt stiff from underuse. "It is real!"

A light sparked in Niko's eyes, then extinguished as a puff of drifting ash passed through his torso. "Well, not... *real.*"

"It's just the first step. I'll get you back, I swear it."

Niko eyed him, worry clouding his features. "Kole, what happened to you?"

Kole lost his smile. Instinctually, he touched the scars riddling the skin of his face. The last thing Niko must remember was separating in the winds of the Black Wall. He'd yet to see the aftermath. "I survived the flames." A sense of pride underlined Kole's tone—to his surprise. For the first time, confidence swelled in his chest as he thought of the past. No longer a victim. *No, I'm a fighter.*

"You've missed so much, Niko."

The tales of the last month filled the hours leading to dawn. Kole shared everything—no secrets left hidden to his childhood friend. Mostly, Niko remained silent, taking it all in, but when Kole spoke of the refugee massacre, his friend cried. Speaking about that night brought back Kole's own anger and grief. He thought the pain had left him—healed—but it had only scabbed over. Kole continued, hoping the change of subject would stall the pain.

He spoke of the victories—all the good that had come from his journey thus far. The shift seemed to work. Niko's eyes dried, and his mouth pursed in a slight smile the way it always had in the years before when Kole spoke of his grand adventures as a shepherd's apprentice. Every now and then, Niko would ask for details or clarifications, especially when it came to Socren and Savairo.

"I wish my family could see Socren," said Niko. "Wish I could."

Neither Kole nor Niko had seen the city at peace. Sure, Kole had stayed a couple days after the battle, but those days had been filled with digging graves for the fallen. "Leo—he's the head of the Liberation—he's sorting everything out. Trying to get it back to something relatively normal. I couldn't tell you what's going on now."

News of the Souls' existence on Ohr came as a happy surprise. Of course, Niko had known *of* the Souls. They'd heard stories about them throughout childhood. The shocking part came when Kole mentioned their old camp leader's involvement and how Goren had used Kole as a sacrifice to bring the Souls back as flesh and blood.

When Kole finally finished, Niko turned to the first dim light of morning and stared. "It's a lot."

Kole nodded. He never really stopped to think about everything that had happened. It had all come fast and complicated. He gave Niko a moment to think, then asked. "Do you think I'm a monster?"

Niko whipped his head around. "Why would I think that?"

"I made the deal with Aterus. I've shifted to the other side of this whole mess. He's the bad guy." A familiar emotion swirled his stomach. Guilt. In the past, he'd been a slave to it. But here, standing beside Niko's spirit, he quelled the burdensome feeling through sheer will.

"That night the Black Wall came for us... I was so scared." Niko's eyes glazed over. No doubt the memory of that night replayed in his head. Even his hands shook. "All I remember was holding on to you, wishing for another way for it to end. The moment we separated, I knew what waited for me. I would've done anything to change it. I wanted to live, Kole."

"I know. I couldn't help you then, but I can now. Aterus will bring you back once I free the rest of the Souls."

Niko turned to him. His hard jaw twitched, and he gave a half smile. "I understand why you made the deal. I can see both sides, Kole. Russé isn't completely right, and neither is Aterus. It just sounds like you're lost in all of this. Everyone's priority is to use you. Saving you is an afterthought. You're looking out for yourself, and there's no shame in that." His fingers raked his scalp, ruffling tight black curls. "It's your choice. I'm already dead, so I really don't have a say in the matter."

"We're going to reverse that."

"Don't do that," Niko scolded with a finger. "Don't use me as this bargaining chip in your head. Do this for yourself—because *you* want to live and believe Aterus *will* hold to his word when it comes to Ohr. Only those two things matter because they still exist in the world. I'm old news and—"

"Niko, stop—"

"No, listen!" He held out a firm hand meant to touch Kole on the shoulder. His touch passed through. Niko pulled back and studied his hand in the pre-dawn light. "I'm a ghost." He wiggled his fingers. "You say you can bring me back, and I won't lie, I want that too, but until then, I can't be the reason for you taking the deal. You understand that don't you, Kole?"

As much as Kole wanted to resist the logic, it seeped through. Niko's time—his natural timeline—had passed. Letting something from the past interfere with the future may be a bad idea. He sighed. And he thought the day he'd learned Russé's identity as a Soul was confusing. This day topped any other. If only things could be easy. A simple choice. That's all he wanted—one where everyone ended up getting what they wanted. *Well, maybe not everyone....*

"Deal or not, you're Aterus' pawn too. Just promise me one thing." As Niko's eyes trailed down, Kole caught a glint of worry within. "Be careful?"

Kole nodded then took a long, deep breath. He had Niko back. Peace filled him. No longer would he do this alone. Niko understood. *He always has.* His friend's acceptance gave Kole hope that Felix and Vienna would feel the same. "Shit."

Niko raised a brow.

"I need to get back before they wake up. I don't want them to know yet." Kole broke into a jog toward the rambler perched tall on its roots in the distance.

Niko matched his pace. "Woah! Look at the size of that thing. You can control it?"

"Sure can. I'm a shepherd, after all. Even if the whole apprenticeship thing was some cover for Russé to keep an eye on me."

"I've *got* to see this in action. You'll teach me, right?"

"I told you I would. Kole and Niko, the greatest shepherds ever to walk Ohr."

"No way we'll beat Russé, but I like the sound of that. I can't believe he's a Soul."

Kole groaned at the name and stopped. "Speaking of Russé, he's tracking us as we speak. I have to block him."

"How are you going to do that?"

"I'm not exactly sure. This whole connection with the Souls is a bit complicated. I usually seek them out. I feel them in my head and open a door to communicate."

"Then do the opposite. Close the door and barricade it."

Kole nodded. "Worth a shot." After a breath, he closed his eyes. Even now, he felt Niko's presence beside him, which comforted him. With new confidence, he dove into the deep cavity of his mind where the Souls resided. A simpler task now. Fewer headaches plagued him the more he practiced, and he swiftly navigated to the source of their connection. He found Russé easier than the others. Kole credited this to the time they'd spent together—familiarity seemed to thin the veil between them. But a thin veil, though useful if he sought to speak with the Soul, could make his task more difficult. Kole needed to seal the door—hide from a god.

Niko must've sensed Kole's concern because he whispered, "You can do this, Kole."

The reassurance strengthened him. Homing in on the portal to Russé's essence, a thought came to him. *I need to block them all. Issira and Obell, too, or they'll try to get through when Russé fails.* An idea sprouted. *Risky, but it may work.* He'd tear down the walls of the other Souls, the ones he had yet to release, and use those defenses against Russé and his companions. It'd leave him more vulnerable to the imprisoned Souls, but he had nothing else as an alternative. He couldn't create energy from nothing. The best bet was using the Souls against one another. Whatever the consequences, he'd face them when they arose. So he got to work, shifting the defenses to those who sought to track him. When he finished, Russé, Issira, and Obell's presence felt distant, unreachable. A pang of sadness passed him, but Kole shrugged it away. *They had their chance. It's time I fight for myself.*

Silent, Kole and Niko returned to the rambler and slipped between the cage of roots. Kole jumped at the sight of the Kayetan standing over Felix. The demon lifted his head at Kole's presence. Two sunken indents indicated where the eyes should have been; instead, voids of black smoke lay in the depths. The otherwise featureless face trained on Kole. Though Kayetans possessed no eyes, Kole always felt a chill when their faces turned his way.

"Bloody hell, what's a Kayetan doing here?" Niko squealed.

"It's fine. He's one of us. Sort of."

Felix's Kayetan shifted his gaze to Niko.

Kole froze.

"He's looking at me," Niko said, voice quaking. "Like, *directly* at me."

"No way, you're a ghost, remember? No one can see or hear you."

"Of course I remember. I'm the one who's dead."

Kole waved a hand to call back the creature's attention. "It's just a coincidence."

Niko tiptoed behind Kole, and the shadow's head followed. "Nope. It *definitely* sees me."

"I hope not." If the Kayetan knew of Niko, then there was a solid chance Felix would know too. Except, Kole didn't quite understand how the whole human-Kayetan connection thing worked. *This might complicate things.* "Maybe you should go for now."

Niko's ghost vanished at Kole's request.

The moment passed as the first light of day speared through the cracks in the roots, banishing the Kayetan until the next night. Felix stirred. His hand swatted at the light as if were a buzzing mosquito.

"Felix. Vienna. Wake up. It's time to move."

Vienna rolled up at her name. Her eyes locked with Kole's for a moment, distant as if still stuck in a dream. Her chest heaved, and a bout of coughs took her. Deep, throaty gasps and wheezes.

The fit sprung Felix to his feet. He crossed to his sister. "You all right?"

One hand hid her face as she coughed into her elbow while the other kept Felix from approaching. After clearing her throat, she croaked, "I'm fine. Just need some water."

Kole cursed himself. The Kayetan had hovered over his sleeping master probably waiting to report back. Instead of worrying about Niko, Kole should've roused Felix. "I saw your shadow before the sun rose. I didn't think to wake you, sorry."

Felix turned away. His head tilted to one side as if recounting a secret whisper. "I may've been sleepin', but... my dreams were bonkers. I think... I think I know where ta go."

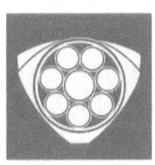

The day passed quick and silent. Kole ran the rambler into the ground, following Felix's directions. Like some invisible map, his friend pointed out landmarks so vague, Kole and his companions surely would've missed them. Before long, the dreary Ashland Plains diminished, giving way to blades of green which popped through the thinned layer of soot like new spring growth in late winter. Color at last. *I hope I never see gray again.*

"We're close, mate," Felix said with a wink. "I'm gonna drink my weight of it."

Kole's thirst ran so deep, every breath pained him. Even his ravenous hunger seemed a meager problem in comparison. "First Vienna."

Felix looked over his shoulder toward his sister, who'd been curled up next to the trunk all day. "Yeah, you and Vienna."

The deepening gold sun glinted off something in the distance. A reflection? "Look. I think that's it."

"Coroko River," said Felix.

In his excitement, Kole tugged too hard on the rambler, and the tree jerked right. Felix braced himself on the trunk, but an unaware Vienna rolled off. Instinctively, Kole sent another command through the tree. Roots shot out to catch Vienna before she fell fifty feet to the ground. "Sorry," Kole said meekly.

"What's going on? Have we found it?" Vienna said, apparently her annoyance at Kole's careless act forgotten by the hope of water.

"A river," Kole said. "And that means fish, too." On cue, his stomach rumbled with such force it shook his arms and legs.

The sprint to the river ensued. Wind brought the smell of water to Kole's nose as the rambler barreled on. He clenched the roots in anticipation, imagining the trickle of cool liquid down his throat. For as fast as the tree stampeded, the mile journey felt longer than the entire day behind them.

Kole charged the rambler straight into the shallows. Felix whooped and hollered, and even Vienna let out a gasp of joy as the mist off the trudging roots splashed their faces. Kole swore his very skin sucked in the moisture. Though he meant to push further into the current, the rambler halted and drilled its roots into the mud of the riverbed, anchoring on its own. "I don't blame you," Kole whispered to the exhausted tree.

A deep rumble came from the wood in response. Relief, no doubt.

Kole wanted nothing more than to swan dive into the clear water. He reigned in his urge and switched his full attention to Vienna, who hid her head in the nook of her elbow as he climbed around the trunk.

"Let's get you down." Kole offered a hand. When she peeked up from her arm, her face had flushed so pale, her freckles stood out dark, more prominent than he'd seen before. Sickly. Before he could question her, she set a smile on him and took his hand.

Felix aided him, thankfully, for Kole lacked the strength to get her down by himself. Since the rambler proved too preoccupied to follow orders anytime soon, they took the easy way of dismounting and slid down the length of a thick root. All three shoved off and splashed into the cool river water.

Kole stood waist high in the rushing current. It was enough to push him off balance, but he waded closer to the river's edge and found traction. They all cupped their hands and drank deeply.

The water invigorated him, washing away the exhaustion of the last few days. Pure relief. Pure joy. The feeling radiated from his companions as well. After minutes of drinking, they smiled at each other.

Felix's vulpine eyes glinted mischievously. Then, before Kole could realize his next move, Felix sent an open palm across the water's surface and sent a wave directly at Vienna, who blocked her face in shock, then smiled. A second later, another spray of water shot toward Kole.

The water fight continued, no one really winning as all three ended up soaked to the core. With their energy spent, they waddled out of the river and set up camp.

Vienna had caught a fish for each of them. It had been easier than expected. The fish seemed curious about the hundreds of new roots plunged in their home. Little did they know, those same roots acted as a maze for trapping them. Vienna caught them with her bare hands. Their dinner, which had roasted over the fire Felix had managed to get going, tasted glorious.

Vienna's cough broke the ravaging sounds of eating. She cleared her throat when Felix and Kole glanced up in concern. "It's nothing. Choked is all."

Kole picked at the bones, searching for more meat, then finally discarded the rest.

"Kole?" Vienna asked.

He met her eyes. It felt like days since he looked at her — really looked at her. The majority of their journey out of the Ashland Plains, she'd been curled up by the trunk. Immediately, he warmed and nodded in response.

"I'm concerned about the Souls. Has Russé reached out to you?"

Kole swallowed the forming lump in his throat, except this one wasn't from thirst. "I haven't been in direct contact. It's not like talking really, more like sensing." Her perplexed gaze told him she needed more convincing. "He knows which way we went." Which was the truth. Actually, Russé could probably pinpoint their exact location—well, where they had camped last night—*before* he blocked him. *We need to move soon.*

"I feel like they should've caught up by now. What if something's wrong?"

"You know Russé." He shrugged it off casually. "He wouldn't tell us either way."

"So what's the plan then, eh?" Felix gagged, then spit out a bone. "Little sucker," he muttered in annoyance at the needle-like bone, then continued. "We gonna wait 'em out here? Seems like a good spot. Got all the stuff we need, anyway."

Vienna nodded in agreement.

"Actually, I've been thinking about searching for the next Soul."

"On our own?" Vienna asked. Her quizzical frown vanished after a moment. "Not that I don't think you can't do it, I...." She cleared her throat again, took a deep breath, and restarted. "I know you are capable of it, Kole—finding the Soul—but what about the ritual? Don't you need Russé?"

This was exactly what he was afraid of: the questions. "I've never done it on my own, but I can try, at least," he batted back. "If I can't do it, well, then we'll know where the Soul is if nothing else, and when Russé *does* catch up to us, it'll be all the easier."

"Keepin' a step ahead. I like it." Felix raised his half-eaten fish in salute.

Vienna went quiet, though Kole knew it'd be foolish to assume she'd swept all concern aside.

"Ya gonna try tonight?" Felix asked.

"That's the plan."

"All right, Blondie. You and me. We'll do our mind things." Felix glanced to the sinking sun. His Kayetan would show soon. "Hey, V," he called as she rose from the grass.

"I'll keep an eye out, of course. Just give me a minute. I need more water." She left, hand clutched to her chest.

CHAPTER 5

Piper tapped her fingers impatiently on her bicep. *We'd sooner find Aterus at this rate.*

"I can't sense him." Russé rubbed his temples, clearly vexed.

"An entire hour wasted," Piper muttered under her breath. They'd traveled north for a full day with no sign of Kole or the rambler. "He isn't following your orders. I knew he wouldn't. *You* should've expected the same and never let him leave your side."

Russé's face went stone still.

"Where would the child go?" Obell asked. Even through the simple act of conversation, his muscles flexed and shifted beneath his skin. Piper would be lying to herself if she thought she could best him. "You know him, Russé."

"Last I sensed him, he was heading west. If he's moving, it means something is wrong. Looking for something or running from something."

"Water, probably—food. Did you expect him to wait in a desolate wasteland?" The wind pulled loose a strain of her red hair. Piper forcefully tucked it back in place. If they spent much more time in the plains, she'd be tempted to cut her whole head of hair off. Another piece found its way out of her braid and tickled her cheek. *For the love of Souls.*

"The demigod is right," Obell said.

"*Don't* call me that," she growled before she realized who'd said it.

Obell's fiery eyes danced as they landed on her. One side of his mouth lifted at her aggressive tone. "Wait until tomorrow to link with him again. My bet is they will stay put when they've found sustenance."

"Doubtful, though he does have a point." Piper neglected Obell's side eye. "The closest water source west is the Coroko River. We should start there. But I guarantee we'll find a cold campsite."

"You think he's looking for the next Soul?" Russé fidgeted with his staff at his own words.

"I know it."

Issira whirled to Obell. Like opposites in their powers, their appearances promised the same distinction. The gentleness and grace of the Blue Soul clashed against the utter brawn of the fire god. "Obell," Issira's voice sang, "do you know which of our brethren was after you? Next to contact Kole? If we knew who was next in line, we might be able to predict where they'll end up."

His black brows, thick and wild like licking flames, sunk as if troubled. "I couldn't tell."

Russé perked up. Both hands gripped his staff now and ground the end into the soil. "What do you mean by that?"

"The Soul did not communicate directly. I did, however, sense the presence readying itself as Kole freed me, anxious to move to the front of the line. Whoever it was felt strange."

"Strange how?" Russé probed Obell.

"I did not recognize them. They were unfamiliar and alien. I don't know what to compare it to." As he thought, the air around him grew warm and then hot. "Scattered. Incoherent."

Piper stepped back, retreating to cooler air. "The isolation has driven them mad." All three Souls looked on her as if she'd spoken the vilest of words. "Don't be so surprised. The roots of madness can find fertile soil in the minds of gods. Easier now that you're broken." Piper could have sworn she heard a growl from Obell over the hissing wind.

"Even so," Issira stepped between her brothers, "we must figure out who it is. We can't allow one of our kin to spiral beyond salvation."

"Braxus, Caradin, and Vara... hmm." Russé stabbed his staff into the ground as he paced, leaving punctures in the soft layer of ash. "There has to be something you heard to narrow this down?" He looked hopefully to Obell.

"Search my mind if you think it best, Russé." Obell offered up his hand. "What I told you is all I know."

Piper's laugh came out as a snort. "I have an easier solution." A sneer came easily. "Who was the weakest minded?" They all look appalled, maybe by her words, or more from the smile she refused to contain. It pleased Piper to see them squirm. "There's a hierarchy to everything and everyone. Even if you never admitted it outright, I know you all have your kin ranked in your mind. The cleverest. Wisest. Most benevolent. Most powerful," she said, letting a darker tone slither around the last one. "Who's at the bottom of the list for... " she paused a moment to find the right words, "*mental fortitude*."

The three Souls gazed at one another as if none wanted to be the first to speak.

Piper stroked her braid, waiting. "A bit odd, don't you think? That when you all reigned in full godhood, there were so many secrets and squabbles." She let her eyes linger on Issira. "Backstabbing."

The Blue Soul turned up her chin at the accusation. Maybe she wouldn't admit it now, but the secret was out. Issira had made a deal with Aterus in exchange for power. The Blue Soul was supposed to protect Evangeline, Piper's mother, and keep the forbidden relationship hidden, which she had managed for a time. Then, for some reason unknown to Piper, Issira had a change of heart. She informed the other souls of the illegitimate love between Aterus and one of his creations, and in that decision, condemned Ohr to its current fate. That was what Aterus claimed, anyhow. Her father always refused to take full blame. Piper knew better.

Piper ground her teeth, frustration growing, then said, "Now, when your biases could actually be of use, you hide behind what? Good manners?" She held up her hands in disbelief. "For Ohr's sake, speak up."

"Braxus." Russé's chest swelled. His kin set solemn gazes on him. Both nodded in agreement. "It would be he who broke first."

"Thank you, shepherd," Piper said, letting venom lace her respects. She tilted forward in a half-hearted bow. "Now we are getting somewhere."

Braxus, huh? Soul of earth and moon. At first guess, she'd think he'd be the strongest. The Souls' temperaments seemed to match their creation; Issira, calm and intuitive like water, Russé, honest as nature, and of course Obell, fierce as his flames. Shouldn't Braxus be solid? Unbreakable as the stone he forged? She brushed away her questions. Clearly, by the Souls' unanimous answer, Piper had assumed wrong. Still, earth and moon held little clues to Braxus' whereabouts. "He could be anywhere," she finally said.

"Anywhere west," Obell corrected. He looked to Russé for confirmation. "Isn't that where Kole was heading?"

"Yes, but there's nothing of note in that direction. Nothing that makes sense with earth. I would guess Braxus' prison to be a natural landmark, like a mountain or canyon." As Russé frowned, his wrinkles deepened.

"Maybe Kole headed west to the river then. For water rather than the Soul," Piper offered. "The tip of the Poleer range is north of that. Those peaks could be hiding the god."

Issira gave a grin; one that touched her eyes in a way that sparked a jealous tinge in Piper. "We can gain ground by the river," the Blue Soul said. "I'll make sure of that."

Though Piper didn't quite know what that entailed, she'd take the god's word for it if it meant catching up to Kole. Whether he knew it or not, Kole was in more peril without his Souls to guard him. "Then it's settled. Unless Russé gets in contact with Kole, we head upstream."

CHAPTER 6

Kole opened his eyes. "I got an image."

Night had fallen, and with it came Felix's Kayetan. Kole had been nervous when the shadowy fiend first materialized, wondering if the creature would tell his master about Niko—if the thing truly *had* seen the ghost last night. Either way, the news never reached Felix. Kole could tell by the liberation member's unaltered mood.

At his words, Felix spun. He stood a dozen paces away, where he'd been running communication drills with his Kayetan alongside the riverbank. "That was fast. Was expectin' it ta take all night, honestly."

"Don't get too excited, yet. It's just an image."

"Better than nothin', I say." Felix placed his hands on his hips. His Kayetan copied him. "Whatcha got?"

"A marsh." Kole climbed to his feet and pushed through the tall cattail reeds that brushed and tickled his skin. He'd opted to go inland a bit to sit among the grass. It had been so long since he'd been around anything green, other than the rambler of course, and the feel of the blades gave him a sense of home.

"Not just a marsh," Niko said. A frown appeared on his face as if he remembered that no one but Kole could hear him. "This is going to get really annoying really fast." He sighed, then said, "Tell him what you told me."

"I will," Kole whispered.

"Huh?" Felix asked. The Kayetan behind him tilted his head toward Niko again.

Surely at some point, the Kayetan's stare would raise suspicion, so Kole swiftly stepped in front of Niko. Maybe it had been a bad idea to call on his dead friend while the Kayetan hovered around. Though Niko's presence calmed him and had made it easier to search for the Soul, he figured it best to summon him when he had a moment alone from now on. "Uh, I was just saying I noticed something strange about it."

Felix nodded his head, waiting. "Well, what is it, Blondie? Wait." He cupped his hands around his mouth and called for his sister. "She'll wanna hear this."

Kole heard her before he saw her. She came from the river's edge coughing and hacking.

"What is it?" she croaked.

The paleness of her face alarmed Kole. His small cough and scratchy throat had left him after a few handfuls of water. Vienna seemed worse—the ferocity strengthened, shaking her whole body.

"You look—"

"I'm fine," she said too quickly. The waning moon gave off just enough light to make out her guarded expression. "What is it?" she snapped, cutting off Kole's chance to question her further.

"I made contact." Kole made a mental note to check on her later. "Usually when I see an image, it's like looking down on it from above. A frozen moment. But this...." He recalled the vision. Two separate pictures of the same scene. Yet they were off somehow. Slightly apart from each other. Like looking left, then right at the landscape. The whole thing left him a bit dizzy. "I saw a marsh. That's not the weird part though. It was a moving image—two of them. I'm not sure what it means."

"I can't believe you can actually speak with them," Niko mused behind him.

Kole glanced back at his unseen friend but held his tongue while Vienna and Felix stood present.

"I guess that is strange." Vienna folded her arms—less of a casual movement and more like she was clutching her torso. "But we know where to go now. There's a marsh northwest of here. I'm sure we'll figure out the rest on the way." Then she spun on her heel and stalked off to the water, leaving Kole, Felix, and ghost Niko to stare after her.

"Something's wrong," Kole warned.

"I'll say," Felix gave a low whistle. "She's had a bum mood for days. Whatcha think's botherin' her?"

"She's sick, Felix. I think it's the ash. She's been breathing it in since we ditched our masks back at the volcano."

"But it's only been a few days," Felix gazed after his sister's retreating silhouette.

"Toxic fumes, remember?" Kole and his companions had all been warned before they went searching for Obell that the Ashland Plains lay empty for good reason. The very air and falling ash came from the depths of the belching volcano, poisoned and tainted. They had acquired masks to combat the toxicity on the journey *to* the volcano. Since releasing Obell, though, they'd been breathing it raw. "Maybe Shikar was right about her masks. Maybe they really *were* broken."

A heaviness passed between them when Kole mentioned the Yamani's name. Shikar, a creature of rock, had aided them in their search for the Red Soul. Not only that. She'd watched over Felix after he'd survived the ritual that turned his shadow into a Kayetan. Shikar promised to train Felix and help him adapt through his transition—teach him to use his Kayetan for good instead of as one of the death tools which had terrorized northern Ohr for the last decade. No one was better suited for the job than Shikar, for she stood as the only other survivor of Savairo's blood spell. That plan was gone now. The injuries she'd sustained escaping the volcano had claimed the Yamani's life.

"I dunno about that. We've all been walkin' in this ash. I feel fine. How 'bout you?"

Kole nodded. His rasps had come from dehydration. "Fine after the water."

"Same. So why's it only her, then?"

"I'm not sure. It has to be the ash, though. We'd both have the same sickness if it wasn't. We should keep an eye on her. I don't think she'll tell if things get worse. Wouldn't surprise me if she's already concealing how bad it is."

"That's Vienna for ya," Felix agreed. He turned back to his Kayetan slightly, then paused and looked back to Kole. "Mind givin' me some pointers, mate?"

Cold air brushed next to Kole's shoulder. Niko hugged close, his face skimming Kole's peripheral vision. "Still don't like the whole Kayetan thing. Don't tell me you actually trust it?"

"Sure," Kole said, answering them both. When Niko went silent, Kole crossed to Felix. "What are you trying to do?"

"Call it what ya want, but I think I got somethin' goin' here." Felix moved to the side so Kole had line of sight on both him and his creature. "Watch this, Blondie." He held out his arms, soft side up, to his Kayetan. The demon mimicked the position. "Wait for it...."

Kole stared for a moment, impatience wrinkling his nose. Then he spotted something. He cocked his head as the ends of the Kayetan's gaseous claws lengthened. The smoke drifted toward Felix and slithered to his wrists, where the botched ritual had left Felix with strange scars — rings of smoke seeped from his wrists, like dark, ethereal manacles. Both master and servant stood, linked together by their smoke.

"What is it?" Kole took a step forward, inspecting. "Do you feel anything?"

"It's the craziest feeling," said a voice. Felix spoke, but a strange echo underlined his words.

The rasp alarmed Kole. He glanced up at Felix, whose green eyes had faded black. "Felix...your eyes."

"I can see through both ours eyes at the same time. It's kinda trippy." Felix swiveled his head to Kole, and as he did, so did his Kayetan. "There's two Blondies." A gurgling laugh erupted from Felix.

Strange. Their minds must be more linked than I imagined. "Can you hear your Kayetan? His thoughts?"

"I hear 'em. *Feel* 'em."

Maybe Felix's connection was less like the one Kole shared with the Souls. It definitely seemed stronger than the link he'd seen between Shikar and her Kayetan; *they'd* been completely separated. Sure, they had still communicated between minds, but it appeared as a master-servant relationship. Felix had something more here. Anyone could see that. "What's it saying, Felix?"

A note of curiosity shaded Felix's voice. "It wants ta try somethin'."

Before Kole could ask more, the Kayetan leaned in. The demon shrunk, its body siphoning into the smoke that danced around Felix's wrists. Kole went rigid as an awful gurgle bubbled from Felix's throat. "Felix?" He stared.

Finally, the Kayetan completely gone, Felix raised his head. The dark color of his eyes had spread from the iris and engulfed the surrounding white. Eyes darker than clear midnight meet Kole. Smoke wisped from Felix's eyes, nose, and mouth.

"Felix?" Kole tried again.

"Told you they can't be trusted," Niko said sourly over Kole's shoulder. "It's possessing him!"

Recognition flickered in those demonic eyes. Freckled cheeks lifted, and a toothy smile greeted him. "I feel incredible." Though rasp still laced the voice, the intonation told Kole that Felix was still there—not changed, just merged somehow. Felix swung his head side to side. "Everthin's so clear. Bright, like when the suns out and stuff."

"That could be useful." Despite the encouragement he forced into his tone, Kole backed away a few steps, just as unsure of this new transition as his ghostly friend. "What else?"

"Well, there's these weird floatin' lights in the distance. Not sure what those buggers are, but they sure are pretty."

Odd. "Floating lights? What do they look like?"

"There's not many. They're too far away ta see. Wait—" Felix pointed a finger toward Kole. "One's right next ta ya."

Heat drained from Kole's face when it clicked. The merge between Kayetan and master let Felix see the way the creature did. Kole followed the direction of Felix's pointed, smoking finger, and it led exactly where Kole thought it would. Niko. *The light is Niko.* He put up his arms up, trying to shield the ghost.

"Aww, Blondie, don't ya be scared. It's just a floatin' light. It's not gonna hurt ya or nothin'... least I think."

The tension Kole'd been carrying in his shoulders relaxed. Felix couldn't *see* Niko. Not really. Felix may figure it out before too long. Those lights had to be spirits. Ghosts. The dead wandering the land....

The thought sent a violent shudder down his limbs. Is that what happened when death came? The spirits forever roamed Ohr. Lost? The old saying he'd been taught leapt to his thoughts. *May the lost find their way.* The refugees had said those words when someone passed in the camps as if the words had meaning. As if they *did* something. Now Kole knew for certain what those lights were, but why were they here? And if they truly belonged to the deceased, why so few? Why not thousands—one for every person who'd lived? It meant some found peace. Yet, others found a reason to stay.

"Ya look pale, mate. Am I scarin' ya?"

"A little," Kole admitted. True, but more so, he just wanted the Kayetan out of Felix before either caught on. "Do you know how to get it out?"

Felix shrugged. A blink later, shadow trickled from Felix's wrists and the Kayetan fell back into its original, disconnected form. "Maybe let's not tell V just yet, eh? Wait till she's got less ta worry about."

Kole nodded. When she had to know, he secretly volunteered Felix to do it. With the Kayetan released, the creature returned its stare to Niko's ghost. Kole sidestepped again to block his friend. "Maybe you should practice sending it on some errands." *Anything to get it away.* "Find us a safe path to the marsh?"

"Good idea."

While Felix turned to commune with his living shadow, Kole took the chance to escape back to the rambler. Despite his best efforts to bring the tree out of the water, it refused to budge. The whole ordeal left him a little embarrassed when he noticed Vienna eyed him from the shore. Her gaze lasted for a brief moment, then fell back to the river. As he waded back through the waist-deep water, he shrugged off his failed attempt. "Tired is all. Needs to recoup."

Niko nodded encouragingly beside him, while Vienna sat perfectly still, either unaware of his words or purposefully ignoring him.

Kole moved out of earshot, then turned on Niko. "You should go for now. I'll have to call on you once everyone is asleep and Felix's Kayetan is away; otherwise, they might start asking questions. It was a close call tonight."

With one final wave, Niko swirled away.

CHAPTER 7

It took three days traveling upriver to reach the spot on Vienna's map where they had planned to cross. Apparently, the river narrowed here. Kole took her word for it, though the river seemed just as daunting as the previous days. Each passing day of rest sent new energy through the rambler. The abundance of fresh water had caused new growth. Green buds unfurled into wide leaves. At this rate, the canopy would rebound from the damage the volcano had dealt in a few more days.

"I'm sure it's here." Vienna, curled up in her usual spot next to the trunk, slid a finger up the tan paper of the map. "Yes, this is the bend. If we go much farther, we'll hit Lake Galen."

"Think this guy can handle it?" Felix nodded to the current. His wrinkled brows emphasized his skepticism.

Kole felt that same uncertainty. The river roared, cutting out all sound from the outside world. An intimidating feat, to say the least. "We have to try."

He squeezed the roots in his hands. With a gentle nudge of his mind, he prodded the rambler's reaction to the raging current. He sensed a hesitance at first, but then the tree lifted higher on its roots in boastful pride. The rambler had grown stronger these last few days because of the full nights of anchored rest. Despite its ballooned strength, it still heeded Kole's every call. He felt a connection with the tree, stronger than he'd ever felt before. Then again, back in his shepherd apprenticing days, he'd never worked with the same rambler twice. Training had been about learning the variation in the trees and working to adapt to each one if he hoped to tame them. This one, he was quite fond of. During the last few nights after anchoring the rambler, he'd climb up and prune the dead or burned twigs, remnants of the Ashland Plains, and care for the tree's budding leaves while speaking in secret with Niko.

Kole asked the rambler once more if it was prepared to cross the river, ensuring to communicate that they'd find another way over if this plan failed. The overwhelming urge to please radiated from the rambler, and Kole smiled.

"Secure the loose items, and grab a root," Kole instructed. "We're crossing."

Felix and Vienna heeded Kole's command as the rambler stomped toward the shallows. With the weapons they'd brought over from Grayfall wedged into the nook of a branch and their packs hoisted over their shoulders, Felix and Vienna made their way back to Kole, who instructed the rambler to coil a root around all three of them. They sat snug, backs pressed into the rough bark of the trunk, as Kole tightened his grip around the reins and urged the rambler into the river.

Water splashed high from the puncturing roots. The icy spray hit Kole head on, dampening his black uniform. He shivered as the late fall air caught his skin.

Lower and lower the rambler sank. Each step put them deeper in the current, and with it, the hidden ferocity of the current made itself known. The rambler shuddered as the roots battled through. Soon, the tree edged into a lean upstream to combat against it. If the rambler toppled over, they'd all be at the current's mercy.

Not even midway and already the water level lay within an arm's reach from the base of the trunk.

"Climb!" Kole yelled to the siblings over the river's cacophony.

Felix and Vienna reacted obediently. By the time they'd reached the lowest bough, cold water seeped through Kole's boots. He looked up and caught both their concerned gazes when they finally noticed Kole hadn't followed them.

"Whatcha doin', Blondie? Get up here."

"I can wait a little longer," he mumbled to himself as the river lapped at his ankles, overtaking the base of the trunk. A smile tugged on Kole's lips. So close to danger, and yet, fear had no hold on his heart. On the contrary, he'd never felt such control in his life. The rambler's strength seemed to fill his spirit — his courage.

Kole clamped his eyes shut, focusing on the rambler's movements. The longer he held onto the reins, the longer he could keep things under absolute control. Sure, steering from the branches was possible, and he would take that option in a moment, but the roots... *they* were the life source. Shepherds only had *full* command when they linked through the roots. Kole was determined to stay and aid the rambler as long as he dared.

Unintelligible shouts echoed down from Felix and Vienna, but he refused to budge. If he could just make it to the center—the strongest part of the river—then he'd join them.

Kole cleared his mind and focused on the link with the rambler. Their bond intertwined so closely, Kole's legs felt like the roots—shoving step by step through the battering current. The hundreds of roots felt weak on their own. Each one ran cold to the core and drained of strength. Kole knew what to do.

A roll of his wrists, and the tree understood. Kole had used this technique before. He felt the many tendrils braid and twist with their neighbors. Singular strands may have little power, but together they could withstand this. A dozen or so thick roots formed. Immediately, the rambler gained ground and held its own against the river.

Pleased, Kole opened his eyes and gasped as he was suddenly aware of his own body again. The water leveled with his chin. *Time to go.* With one final command, Kole released the reins. The roots coiled around his waist and lifted him out of the water. They gave him a short ride to the bough, where Vienna and Felix sat, then sunk back into the water like diving sea snakes.

Kole clung to the limb, completely drenched, and peeked up to the siblings, who glared back in a mix of awe and fury.

Vienna held a rope in her hands. It dangled halfway down the trunk above Kole's previous position. Kole guessed they'd thought of their own plan to yank him up. He smiled at them, but only Felix returned the expression: a full toothy grin.

All while shaking her head, Vienna pulled the rope back up, wrapped it, then reattached it to her beltloop.

With new strength, the rambler marched against the river. The journey proved all too easy after they'd passed the deepest waters, and slowly, the trunk emerged as it found the shallows of the western side of the river.

"Bloody hell, Blondie. Didn't know ya could do that." Felix gave a rough pat to Kole's back.

"Neither did I." When Kole settled his pride, pleased he was able to showcase his shepherd skills, he caught Vienna peering at him from over Felix's shoulder. Kole quickly looked away.

"Hey, would ya look at that?" Felix said between them, unaware. He pointed to something on the bank.

Kole followed Felix's finger to the thin trees. Too sparse to be called a forest. Then again, the only forest Kole had laid eyes on was Solpate—so dense and lush, the sun never touched the ground. This seemed bleak in comparison. After a quick scan, Kole realized Felix hadn't been talking about the trees but rather, its occupants.

Dozens of dull-colored birds perched on the branches. Usually, it wouldn't cause Kole to take a second glance, yet every beady eye focused on the rambler crawling onto the shore. Same with the next tree in line—filled with an array of birds and squirrels, all paused with their attention intent on the walking tree.

"Strange," Kole whispered.

"More than strange, mate. I've seen some crazy stuff livin' the last few years with a sorcerer and all, but this is... there's somethin' wrong with them. They got eyes like... I dunno. Think it's rabies or somethin'?"

Vienna and Kole exchanged a quick, amused glance before she said, "Yeah, Felix, maybe it's rabies."

Felix must've picked up on her dry tone because he placed his hands on his hips with his brows scrunched in the middle of his forehead. "Ya gotta better idea, eh? I'd like to hear it. Go on, then."

Vienna reached over and flicked her brother's earlobe. They teased each other back and forth while Kole slipped down to the base of the trunk, took the offered reins, and commanded the rambler further ashore. The animals' heads turned in unison, watching the gargantuan tree and its occupants go. Kole urged ahead, hoping to put distance between them and the unsettling fauna.

Every tree they passed held the same scene, only now Kole noticed some rabbits and a fox had stopped on the ground to peer in the same unsettling way. The fox bared its canines and stalked them at a distance for a brief while until scampering back into the depths of the forest.

The roots in Kole's loose grip twitched. Unbeknownst to him, while his attention had been on the curious creatures, the rambler had swerved closer to the river. The tree relayed its wish to re-enter the shallows. Not just re-enter, but cross back.

"Something's going on," Kole said. "The rambler is scared of the forest for some reason."

"*Some* reason?" Felix scoffed as he climbed down from the bough. His hair had been ruffled into a massive pouf, no doubt the work of Vienna's teasing. "Bet I can guess." He jumped the remainder of the way, then patted the trunk. "I feel ya, big guy. This place is givin' me the creeps. Still think it's rabies."

"They're intelligent," Vienna's raspy voice came from above. She let her feet dangle from her spot on the bough but made no move to join Kole and her brother.

"Whaddya mean, V?"

"Like Fiona. Leo has that spell on her." Her arms wrapped tight around her chest as she held back a string of coughs. Once it settled, she cleared her throat. "It's how she can understand spoken commands."

Kole squinted at a blur in the distance. Something fast, going the same direction as them. "You think these animals are under a spell?"

"No. I don't know. Maybe" She stopped to breathe, hiding her face in the bark. Talking seemed to take a great deal of energy. "It just reminded me of Fiona is all."

"It would take a ton of energy and time to cast something on all of the animals, wouldn't it?" Kole was no expert on magic, but he knew sorcerers needed ingredients or components for a spell. He'd seen Leo, the liberation leader back in Socren, pull off wide-ranged spells before in the heat of the rebellion, but who out here would have that sort of power? And what was the purpose? Besides, the particular feat Kole had witnessed covered half an army. This seemed to be something of a larger scale. And that left one option left. "It's got to be the Soul."

Another shapeless blur streaked between the trees, but it remained too far to make out any details. All Kole knew for sure was it seemed to be tailing them. *The fox? No, too big for that.*

"But we're days away from the marsh, right V?" Felix glanced up to Vienna, who nodded. "That's what ya saw in yer vision anyway. If the Soul's all the way out there, how's it doin' stuff over here?"

Kole shrugged. "Same way Russé affected all of Solpate. The whole region north of Poleer is rambler territory—well, was." It pained him to know the moment he and Russé had departed the forest, the colossal walking trees and nature-touched animals began reverting to normal. He wondered what his home looked like now after two months away. Had it been that long? Kole had given up counting the days.

"Least we know we're goin' in the right direction, then, eh?"

They stuck close to the bank for the days' journey. The thought of nightfall sent a wave of dread to Kole's stomach. Yet nothing could stop the sun's slow creep toward the frail treetops, which looked like overgrown weeds in the shadow of their rambler. The sky turned into a watercolor of vivid pinks and oranges, deepening by the minute. Such beauty acted as a reminder that the last week Kole and his companions had trekked through nothing but gray-hued landscape. These colors seemed foreign. The fresh scenery and water-tinged scent of the air rejuvenated Kole while his thoughts wandered away from the curiosities of the flanking forest.

A faint howl punctured any serenity he'd found in the last few hours. Dusk fast approached. Apparently, wolves held a concern here. *Nothing in its right mind would close in on the rambler.* He just hoped these animals *were* of sound mind. And any other *creature* who may have dwelled there.

They settled on making camp on the bank, straying just far enough from the river until they found dry land. No way they would ditch beds of ash for soggy sands. Kole anchored the rambler, allowing its roots to reach the water beneath the soil yet retain a small cave-like space beneath the trunk for him and the siblings to wriggle in for protection. It made for tight quarters that night, but he preferred that to lying out in the open. Who knew what sort of prying eyes might crawl from the western lands?

With Felix's Kayetan patrolling the tree line and he and his sister settled under the rambler for the night, Kole called on Niko in this rare moment of privacy. For once, Kole wasn't tired, so he sat on the edge of the trunk and used his extra energy toward linking with the next Soul again.

"Anything new?" Niko's question broke Kole's concentration.

"Sort of. I still see the marsh, but it's a completely different place than before. I think deeper in."

"The Soul is giving you a trail to follow? A map to its prison?"

"I hadn't thought of that. I guess it makes sense." He chewed his lip, mulling the thought in his head. It seemed too easy.

"What's wrong?" Niko asked.

"Issira and Obell only gave vague hints to their location." Kole remembered the blurred images he'd gotten from the Blue Soul. Eventually he'd sharpened the image to identify a distinct set of hills that led him to the pool where Issira had lain imprisoned at the bottom. And Obell—the only hint Kole had with that one was the searing agony of fire, which they later guessed meant the volcano. Even then, they'd only followed a hunch.

Niko cocked his head. "You're upset it isn't harder?"

"It's concerning is all." Kole shrugged. "Maybe it's nothing, but it feels different than the last two."

"Have you ever thought that's because of you?"

"How do you mean?"

"You're improving," Niko said as if the conclusion were obvious. "That's what happens when you practice. Just look at how you handle the rambler now. Shepherding is a mind thing too, right? Strengthening that skill is bound to affect your other abilities."

Kole chewed on his lower lip for a moment. Niko had a point. In the last few days, he'd come far with the rambler, more so than he ever had with Russé's guidance. The question was why, though? Had Kole been relying too much on the Soul? Maybe he'd always been this capable and only needed the pressure of having no one to fall back on. With shepherding *and* communicating with the Souls.

"All I'm saying is, why fight it? It's a good thing," Niko said.

Going off on my own is *a good thing*. Kole's usual stresses had lessened. No headaches for days. Sure, sleep still evaded him most nights, but lately, it'd grown rather tolerable. Kole enjoyed calling the shots — enjoyed the control he had over his own fate. But to obtain this newfound freedom, he'd had to lie to his only friends.

"I broke a promise, Niko."

Niko glanced over, face neutral, ready to listen. It was what Kole enjoyed most about his old friend. He listened without judgment. The afterlife — if there was such a thing — hadn't changed that.

Kole leaned forward enough to spot the sleeping forms of the siblings below. "We made a pact back in Grayfall. With all the deceiving between Russé and the Souls about my fate, we decided no more lies. Promised it." Kole held out his pinky, remembering when he had curled it around his friends' to fulfill the pact. "But I'm lying to them about... well, the *new* pact I made."

"Aterus," Niko whispered. He looked up at Kole. "Are you thinking about telling them?"

"That's the thing. I *want* to."

"But you don't think they'll understand," Niko finished for him.

"I know it." All this time he'd been giving grief to Russé for the same thing he was doing now. "Aterus is the enemy. I can't blame them for thinking that way. Hell, I still think it too."

Niko frowned at that. "An enemy who has common goals."

"Exactly."

"Listen, Kole, I'm not going to tell you what to do. Tell them. Don't tell them. That's up to you. Just...." Niko pursed his lips as if trying to find the right words. "It's your life in the balance here. Make sure you do what's best for you too, you know? Never feel guilty about trying to save your own skin."

Kole pictured how the talk would go. He went through the scenario, playing out different ways to justify the pact he'd made. In his mind, though, all of them ended with fury. Abandonment. If only he could make them understand.

"I wish I could sense how they'd react before I told them. If I knew there was no way they'd see my side, I wouldn't bother bringing it up."

Niko's head lifted. His features perked into a sly smile. "You can. Lure them to the subject — hypothetically. Test their reactions. That should — "

"Kole?" Vienna's raspy voice interrupted them. "Who are you talking to?"

Kole stiffened as she crawled out from beneath the rambler and braced herself on a root. Her wandering eyes landed on the trunk next to Kole, where Niko hovered.

"Just myself," he lied, resisting the urge to shoo Niko away in case it worsened Vienna's suspicion. Luckily, Niko caught on and faded away but not before mouthing "good luck," to which Kole sighed through his teeth.

A fog hung over her eyes, whether from grogginess or her growing cough, Kole couldn't tell. "You said something about 'not bothering to bring it up,'" she pressed.

"I, uh." What else had she heard? He could tell her now. Lay out his secret. Was he ready for that? The answer made him give an exaggerated sigh. "It's the Soul."

She stared at him with a sour expression for a long moment — so long, Kole wondered if she believed his words. Then, her face relaxed, and in that moment, under the thin veil of moonlight, he realized her cheeks held a deep shadow. She'd always had prominent cheek bones, but now it held a sunken quality.

"Are you all right, Vienna? You look...."

"What did the Soul say to you?" she asked, clearly avoiding his concerns.

"Nothing. I'm just a bit frustrated, I guess." *That* he could sell. "No progress, you know?"

She only nodded. Her glazed-over eyes took in the empty space around him. "You've been acting strange, Kole."

That look she'd given. She'd seen him while he had been talking with Niko's ghost. Kole bit the inside of his cheek wondering how to respond. He couldn't bring himself to lie to her again and again. It pained him as much as it would pain her if she found out. All he could do was nod.

Vienna blinked slowly and dipped her head. "I can't imagine what it must be like. All this burden on you. Everything swimming around in your head."

"I can barely keep track of it all." The truth.

"You know I'm here if you need me," Vienna said. "My brother and I promised to protect you. Not that we can do much about the whole...." She tapped her temple. "Russé will find us soon. He'll help sort it all out."

Kole refused to talk about this further. One moment of vulnerability and he'd slip. He always seemed to want to spill all his secrets when he talked with her. In search for a distraction, his fingers passed the pouch at his side. He fiddled with the object inside. "I have something for you. Close your eyes and hold out your hand."

Vienna peered at him but held out her open palm.

"Eyes closed," he urged.

After a lift of her arched brow, she obeyed.

Careful not to cut his fragile skin on the broken teeth of crystal, he pulled out the necklace he'd swiped in an abandoned shop back in Grayfall. Blue crystal petals stretched out from the opal set at the center. Despite all the chaos the pendant had gone through the last several days, only a few of the edges were chipped and splintered. He held the chain and let the jeweled pendant fall gently into Vienna's open palm, who opened her eyes before Kole could say anything.

She stared at it, a mix of confusion and admiration playing back and forth on her expression. "Where did you get this?"

A red-hot wave flushed through him: a feeling he hadn't been expecting. He ran his hand through his short blond hair. "One of the buildings in Grayfall. It was abandoned, so it wasn't really stealing." He paused a second, weighing her everchanging features. *Maybe she doesn't like it.* "I just thought of you when I saw it. You said you wanted to be a florist when you were a kid," he said, backtracking.

"I did tell you that," she said, face still unreadable.

His heart felt like a sinking rock in his chest. "You don't have to take it if you don't want to. It's impractical out here."

Finally, her eyes lifted from the blue flower and landed on Kole. He looked away, the intensity and fear of refusal too much for him to take.

"It's lovely, Kole. Thank you."

Vienna leaned in and his heart thumped in his chest. Her closeness made him want to retreat, but his muscles defied him, froze in place. Lips pressed lightly against his cheek. A soft peck and they were gone, but the spot where they had touched his skin flared with a burning heat. Suddenly, he was all too grateful for the cloud blocking the moon in this brief second. His blood pulsed through his veins with the same force as his previous near-death encounters. No doubt his already red-hued face was the color of a cherry. The lump in his throat blocked his "you're welcome," and it came out as a grunt.

Vienna held up the chain. "Will you put it on?"

Throat still useless, he nodded frantically and fumbled for the clasp. She turned around and swept her golden braid to the side. The scent of her hair, faintly of honey and sweat, slammed into Kole's nose. The aroma, mixed with his pattering heart, made his fingers clumsy. Kole bit down on his lip as he tried to get his scarred skin to cooperate. The tiny clasp proved too difficult for his blundering fingers. The thick scar tissue prevented his digits from bending in the way they needed to open the damn thing.

After a prolonged minute, Kole sagged in defeat. "I can't. It's too... it's too small for my hands."

She turned back around, not a tinge of disappointment on her face, and took the chain from Kole. "Don't worry about it." Her long fingers delicately locked the chain around her neck, and she pulled away, lifting her chin to show it off. "How does it look?"

"Good." He realized he'd almost barked the answer, so he said it again more softly. "It looks nice." A gulp.

She smiled. The first one he'd seen from her in days. It was infectious. He found himself smiling back. A dumb grin. *Like an idiot. Stop that.* But his muscles acted on their own accord, unwilling to obey.

Then, panic filled her eyes. She twisted away just as her back snapped up, arching so violently, Kole knew it had to pain her. She coughed into her hands. No, too vicious for a cough. It sounded as if her lungs were trying to force themselves out her throat. Vienna swayed. The force sent her falling toward the trunk.

Kole reached out. Without the strength to stop her fall, he merely softened her way down, careful to keep her head from hitting the bark too hard. Nothing could stop the fit, so he waited it out, keeping a hand on her arm for support.

"Vienna?" he said softly when the attack subsided. "Are you okay?"

"Fine." She kept her face hidden.

"It's the fumes, isn't it? From the volcano? We don't know why it's affecting you when we were all in it. But we are going to find out and we are going to fix this, okay?"

"Don't worry about me. It's not that bad. Really."

When she rose, Kole gasped. Speckles of blood dotted her hands. A smear of red lined her lower lip where she had attempted to wipe it clean.

Vienna recoiled at his reaction and hid her face in her arms, then quickly wiped away the leftover residue.

"What's with all the racket?" Felix grumbled. Noises of his shuffling set Vienna into a panic. Kole could tell she was trying to rid the evidence before her brother appeared.

"Vienna's getting worse," Kole said.

She paused her scrambling and cast him a pained look.

Felix popped out from below and studied his sister in the dark.

"I can handle this," she croaked.

"Like hell ya can." His eyes narrowed on the pendant around her neck. "Where'd ya get that?"

"Nowhere," she snapped, then tucked the crystal under her collar. The top petals shown above the hem.

"We should find a town in the morning. Maybe someone will know something. Have medicine or a remedy of some kind," Kole said.

"We shouldn't abandon the hunt for the Soul on my account. I promise you, I'm fine."

"We won't," Kole assured even though he didn't fully mean it — or rather, had a way around it. Her health came first. Even if finding help took them miles off course. "We still have a ways to go before we get to the heart of the marsh. We'll just keep an eye out for help. Besides, we need supplies anyway for when we veer from the river."

A good compromise. She would accept it because they had nothing left in their packs. No water or food supply except the river.

"C'mon, V. You're no use ta Kole if you're too sick ta walk."

She leaned away from the trunk, balancing herself to prove a point. "I'm quite capable of that."

"The blood though...." Felix frowned.

"All right, I get it," she silenced him with a hand. "We'll ask when we get supplies."

With that, the conversation was over.

CHAPTER 8

Felix's Kayetan brought ill news before morning broke. Apparently while canvasing the thin woods, the animals had tailed the shadow wherever it went. Kole was uncertain what the behavior meant, but the small voice of his instincts warned against wandering too far from the river.

Kole parked Vienna at the top of the canopy. A pair of eyes and ears that high up might prove beneficial in their new surroundings. Normally, Kole would have been hesitant to prop anyone up that high in the rambler, but after his success crossing the river, no doubts preyed on his mind when it came to his capabilities with the tree. If anything should happen, he had access to every extremity and power the rambler possessed. A strange feeling. For once he felt in control.

Though Kole's sleep left him groggy, the moment he rose the great tree from the earth, a new strength flowed from the roots and through Kole's touch. His core tightened at the burst of energy pulsing between their connection. He felt... invigorated. Russé had never mentioned such a relation between shepherd and tree before.

The sun hung straight overhead when Vienna called down. "I see smoke up the river. A couple miles off."

"A town?" Kole looked up. The thick canopy blocked sight of her.

"There's nothing on the map, but I doubt Leo would know anything of smaller villages," her voice echoed down.

"They gotta have somethin'." Felix had been distracted, playing with the smoke furling from the scars on his wrists. "Worth a shot ta stop by at least."

Before long, Kole made out a cluster of houses and buildings along the bank, each constructed of thin logs. A dock jutted out over the edge of the river flanked with boats, which bobbed with the current. No movement between buildings. No one on the dock or in boats. Beyond that, nothing stood out as odd—merely a riverside town. *If you can call it that.* The only proof the village lay inhabited was the stream of smoke drifting from the largest building at the far end. As Kole studied the building, he spotted a face in an open window. The thought of leaving the rambler behind came too late as a scream carried from the wide-eyed child.

Kole pulled on the roots, stopping the rambler with a jerk. Somehow, though she remained unseen, he sensed Vienna wobbling in the canopy and commanded a branch to steady her.

The screaming child cut off abruptly with the slamming of the window. Kole's eyes flicked to the double doors as they burst open, and a crowd nearly two dozen strong marched down the steps. A handful held weapons; a couple bows, an axe, and one held a hammer. They wore plain clothes of a woven material. Kole expected pelts from a place so isolated in the wilderness.

Beside him, Felix reached for his weapon. Kole cast a root around Felix' wrist to prevent them from looking any more hostile than the villagers already imagined. "Don't. If it comes to a fight, we'll just run."

The villagers stood their ground, eyeing the rambler in horror. None had yet seemed to notice Kole and his companions on the massive tree. He lowered the trunk, letting the roots splay out over the soil rather than anchor. He needed them free in preparation for a speedy retreat. Only when the bottom of the trunk touched down did Kole spot recognition in their eyes, yet their faces twisted with more confusion than relief.

No one moved as Kole stepped from the trunk, Felix on his heels. Kole willed the rambler to lower Vienna. Leaves rustled as the boughs carried her down.

Closer now, the villagers huddled together, forming tighter ranks. It seemed they harbored too much fear to approach. When no leader revealed themselves, Kole decided to speak to the group.

"We didn't mean to scare you. We aren't here to harm anyone."

Their horror-filled eyes bored into Kole.

"Some kind of demon," a whisper rose over the group.

"The boy is one of them," came another.

Kole clenched his jaw. The shock of humiliation hit his gut hard when he realized the comment had been about him. His scars always had a way of crippling his confidence. The moment he got caught up in happiness or fear or anger—the moment he forgot about them, even if only briefly—a reminder always came. *A freak. No wonder the child screamed. I am nightmare inducing.* Kole took in a sharp, shaky breath and stepped back. "You should take this, Felix," he murmured, trying to keep the pain from his voice.

"Sure thing, boss." Felix cast him a worried glance, then stepped around him and added a cheery note to his tone. "The tree ain't gonna hurt ya, I swear it. We've only come ta get supplies."

His mind half on the conversation, half buried in his own shame, Kole dug the balaclava from his waistband and pulled it on so only his eyes showed just as Vienna walked up. She squeezed his wrist in... sympathy? Encouragement? But he slipped away. Her unfazed expression told him she hadn't taken it personally.

After a few minutes of explanation, all lies that Felix made up on the spot, the villagers seemed to relax their postures, though no one abandoned their weapons. The agreement had been made: waterskins, a change of clothes, and whatever food they could spare in exchange for the rambler's assistance.

Kole returned to the tree while Vienna and Felix went with a woman to collect the supplies. The armed villagers surrounded the rambler, keeping a safe distance when it reared up at Kole's command, then led Kole just west of the houses. There, surrounded by piles of dirt and mud, sat a deep hole. Shovels speared the earth, stored upright and ready.

"Floods destroyed the last well. We built it too close to the river," said a voice.

Kole scanned the people below, searching for the source. He had expected an older villager to act as spokesman—which is why it took so long to pinpoint the speaker. A young man—though older than Kole by the looks of it— with sandy-blond hair and a short beard to match. He clutched a carpenter's hammer. A poor choice for a weapon if the lad meant to protect himself against a rambler.

The young man faced the great tree, chin directed to Kole's position, but his eyes flicked around, never landing directly on Kole.

Kole instinctually pulled his mask up further. His very presence made them uncomfortable. *Demon*, they'd said. *That's what I am.* Who could blame them?

"We've been working on it, but progress has been slow." A look to his people. "We've had an accident or two."

"You want me to dig it." Kole gripped the reins before the man could answer. He was unfamiliar with the construction of wells. Back home in *his* forest, Solpate, the refugees drank straight from the streams. "How deep?"

After a quick briefing of the dimensions, the other villagers scattered. Not far. They kept close enough to see Kole.

Drilling up dirt; an easy task for roots. After a few instructions, Kole let the rambler work on its own. He merely stood on the trunk to supervise, using the spare time to study the village. Only houses. A few workshops, maybe. The building the villagers had been holed up in when Kole and his friends first arrived seemed to be a town hall of some kind. Upon closer inspection, a small marking above the door caught his eye. Why hadn't he noticed it before? The symbol of the Seven Souls. It was a place of worship. Kole pulled his pendant, baring the same symbol, from beneath his shirt and let it hang open on his chest. Maybe if they saw it on him, they'd relax.

The rambler had reached fifty feet deep. The mud thinned the deeper the roots dug. A little more to go.

Another passive gander at his surroundings made Kole pause. Even here, the animals in the trees eyed him. Too attentive for normal wild behavior.

"You get used to it," the man said, jerking his chin to the forest. "Probably the same thing you'd say about that tree of yours."

Kole gave a half smile, but his mask covered it. "Have the animals always been... odd?"

"In the marsh? Yeah." The man sat back on a pile of dirt, still never fully reaching Kole's gaze. "I assume you've never been this far west?"

"Never." Kole shifted his body so it faced away from the villager. It seemed to ease the man's tension.

"The farther west you go—deeper into the marsh-- the stranger they get. We don't hunt there if we can help it. Stick to fish, mostly. There's something about killing the animals in there that seems wrong."

"Their eyes," Kole said.

"Yeah. It's too real. Human-like. Least here by the river they're calm—well, calmer. The animals way out there?" He waved west. "They get aggressive. They'll attack anything. Day or night. Hungry or full. Even birds and what not. Rabbits, too."

An oddity for sure. Kole had never heard of a rabbit attack. It sounded comical. "What do you think it is?"

A snorted laugh. "Depends on who you ask. Either some kind of rabies outbreak or they are protecting something."

Kole pursed his lips at the rabies idea. Had Felix come along, he'd be wagging a finger at Kole saying "I told ya so."

"What kind of something?" Kole asked.

The lad shrugged. "Legends of a silver elk so beautiful and pure, its coat shines like the moon. That's just old stories though."

Old stories. The phrase sparked a memory of something Russé had once said to him. He thought back, trying to recall it. "Stories, no matter how outlandish, always hold a seed of truth." That is what the old Soul had said about the cursed city of Grayfall, which ended up very real. It may be well worth it to pry into whatever folktale the man knew. After all, it hit all the marks. Legend of a mysterious beast? The environment around it shifted in a particular way? Check and check. The Soul. It had to be.

"Have you seen it?" Kole asked.

"The elk? 'Course not. You'd have to go deep into the wild territory to find it. Besides, I'm not so sure about the legend anyway. The whole 'those who go never make it back' part of the legend makes no sense at all. If no one comes back, how do we know it's there in the first place? People just don't want kids going in there. It's dangerous and the warning works, so people keep telling it. The cycle continues."

"You've never wondered if it's real?"

"Not enough to risk my life."

If a stag stood as the focal point for the eerie forest, then Kole knew without a doubt which god his visions were about now. Caradin. The Orange Soul. Creator of beasts.

As Kole opened his mouth to question the villager again, the rambler pulled mud-crusted roots from the well, finished.

The young man whistled in awe. "Impressive. Would have taken us weeks. Guess we should start laying stone before it caves." A signal to his fellow villagers and they all gathered around. "We appreciate you holding up your end of the barter. Unfortunately, we'll have to ask you and your tree to wait on the outskirts while we finish gathering your supplies. We'll send your buddies back to you when we've finished."

Kole's stomach sunk at that. Even after the conversation, he was unwelcome here. Be it him or the rambler. Or both. Either way, Kole dipped his head then gave the tree a pat and left without complaint. He'd learned what he needed.

While Kole waited along the bank, a good half mile from the village, he withdrew inside his head and focused on the next Soul, just to test his theory. The connection came easily enough. Somehow, things proved simpler while he maintained contact with the rambler. The tree gave him strength.

Dual pictures, once more. The scenery had changed a bit. Less marshy. The vision swept from side to side. Far off, blurred, stood thin trees like the ones that grew close to the river. A quick flash of black. The vision disappeared for a second then came back again in an instant.

A smile pulled at Kole's lips. He knew exactly what to look for.

Chapter 9

"Eyes. I'm seeing through the Soul's eyes. *That's* what the double vision is." Kole leaned his head back against the roots. The rambler's trunk blocked the sun while its roots sloped and intertwined to form makeshift reclined chairs for the three of them.

"And Caradin is this silver elk that guy was talkin' 'bout?" Felix scratched his brow. "And ya think that's the reason the animals are all shifty?"

"I *know* that's the reason." Kole had never been more certain about anything. The only problem his revelation posed was how to get to the god through lands filled with hostile beasts.

"Will we be safe on the rambler?" Vienna asked, as if sensing Kole's concern.

Felix patted the root he lounged on. "This bugger'll take out anythin' that gets in the way."

"Felix is right. I don't think any animal — super aggressive or not — can stand up to us. Long as we stay on the rambler, this should be easier than the other Souls." Kole shrugged despite Vienna's unconvinced frown. "No erupting volcano or killer water. A simple hunt for once."

"Too simple," she muttered.

Both Vienna and Felix had seen firsthand how dangerous releasing a Soul could be. The water of Issira's pond, where the Blue Soul had been trapped, attempted to drown anyone who entered. Vienna herself had pulled Kole free when he thought death had surely claimed him. And then Obell. That encounter lay fresh in all their minds: fleeing from streams of lava and the fiery rocks raining down from the eruption. Were they all dangerous, though? He'd released Russé, too — well, he'd been five years old at the time, so he didn't remember much. The only thing he knew came from the journal entries his old camp leader, Goren, had written. He touched the pouch that held the book, fingering the edges of the cover through the leather canvas. The more he thought back to the journal entries, the less confident he became. He *had* died from that. Maybe Vienna had a point.

Kole chewed his tongue, lost in thought, then finally decided. "I don't know what we're walking into, but we have to do it anyway. The best we can do is be on our guard and have a plan." The moment he shifted from his lounged position on the roots and climbed to his feet, the tendrils slithered and twisted, creating a walkway to the riverbank. Kole followed it down. "I'll keep track of Caradin on the way."

Before leaving the river to track inland, they all took turns washing off in the water, using a curtain of roots for privacy, then pulled on their fresh clothes from the village. Solid green and brown tunics paired with trousers of thick, rough fabric. Something more suitable for the cooling days of late fall. The cloth itched against Kole's scars, agitating them, unlike the soft, worn material of his Liberation uniform. Still, that outfit stank, and no matter how thoroughly he scrubbed it in the river, some of the ash buildup wouldn't come off. They hung their old clothes over a branch to dry, though Kole kept the soggy mask from his uniform and hung it around his neck for safekeeping. Then they wedged their supplies between branches in the canopy.

With the help of the rambler corralling several fish for Felix to catch, Kole and his friends filled their bellies with as much water and meat as their stomachs could handle before setting off. He hoped the massive meal would hold them over for a day, maybe two, before they had to break into the food in their sacks. No telling when they'd run into another village out here. The slosh of the full waterskin on his hip eased his mind.

Kole drove the rambler west. The villagers had shown Vienna where their encampment lay on her map. She'd marked it and guided Kole as they traveled. All the while, the animals watched. Soon, firm soil gave way to sludge. Roots sunk into the thick, goopy earth that marked the edge of the marsh. Each time the rambler pulled a leg free, the ground made a sucking sound. Progress slowed.

The western sky turned a hot shade of red. The color reflected off the standing water in the distance, looking very much like a landscape drenched in blood. The scene reminded Kole of the red ocean in his first mind-link with Aterus. His thoughts pinpointed on the deal he'd made with the Soul. A punch of guilt pained him. He pushed his friends toward something they didn't fully understand. Tonight. He'd try Niko's plan tonight.

The mire made sleeping on the ground out of the question. They'd sleep in the canopy for the night. Thankfully, Kole's stomach remained content with their late-afternoon gorge, which meant no need for hunting or dwindling their reserves.

While Felix and Vienna found branches to settle in, Kole called for Niko. The ghost whirled before him a second later. Kole's worry must've been plastered to his face because Niko drifted closer and hovered a hand on his shoulder.

"You'll do all right. If you can handle a rambler, you can handle a little talk, right?"

Kole peered over at his companions. "I hope so."

"I'll give you some space. Call for me if you need me."

"Wait." Kole reached toward him, then snapped his hand back to his side in case Vienna and Felix looked his way. "Will you scout ahead? Take a look at the animals. See if they're...."

"Plotting your murder?" Amusement glittered in his eyes. "Sure."

His friend's indifference to the danger surprised him. During their time in Solpate, Niko had always been careful and quick to resist Kole when he dove headfirst into danger. The responsible one, as Russé would call him. "I thought you'd need more convincing."

Niko gave a drawn-out eye roll. "You realize I'm dead, right? There's no need for caution anymore. I finally get a taste of what it's like to be the fearless Shepherd Kole, and I'm going to enjoy it while it lasts."

Niko left a moment before true night fell and the Kayetan reappeared. Under Kole's suggestion, Felix sent his shadow to scout the perimeter. Kole wanted to be alone for this.

The building anticipation of the talk made Kole's hands tremble. He wanted to lay everything out just as they all promised they would. He needed support. Encouragement. With his friends on his side, he knew he could do this. *And what if they don't understand?* The negative thought irritated him, and he forced his efforts on ways to explain his decision. A plan in mind, he had a root lift him up to the canopy, where the siblings had already secured a blanket between two boughs for him. A hammock tonight, like how he slept back in Solpate with Niko.

"I keep thinking about that mind-link with Aterus," Kole blurted.

Felix and Vienna, who'd been shifting around, trying to get comfortable, paused and looked over to him from their branches.

"I noticed you've been restless when you do manage to sleep," Vienna said, clearing her throat every few words. Clearly in an effort to suppress an oncoming coughing fit. Unfortunately, the villagers only offered honey and ale for her worsening symptoms. She drizzled a portion of honey into her waterskin, refusing the ale when Felix insisted. Felix returned the bottle to his pack.

"I've had a few nightmares, but that's not what I've been thinking about."

They waited silent and patient.

Kole fiddled his thumbs. *Say it carefully. Make them understand.* "I don't want to die."

Their matching furrowed brows made their relation all too obvious. It seemed the statement had taken them off guard.

"We won't let that happen," Vienna said.

"How? What plan do we have? There's no guarantee for any of this. And *I'm* the one who's in the balance here."

"Russé's not gonna let ya die, mate. You've got all the gods on yer side. And the Liberation. And us."

"With all of that, there's still no solution." He took in a deep breath then said, "If you had one wish to ask for anything at all, what would it be?"

Felix scratched his head, nose wrinkled. "Ta get Ohr safe, I guess."

They both looked to Vienna for her answer.

"Ask for anything?" She cocked her head, eyes scrutinizing Kole. "What powers are granting such a wish? What strings are attached? Everything has a cost. Magic... even wishes."

Kole figured Vienna would be the one to convince. Back in Socren, she'd been the thinker of the Liberation—the leader, and Leo's right hand. With such a position came a responsibility for others. Self-preservation might not have a place in her head. Something Kole could understand. He'd believed the same for a very long time. Up until he realized the ones he'd lay his life down for would not do the same for him.

"That answer's no fun, V," Felix huffed. "What about you, Kole?"

"I'd want to live," Kole said pointblank. He couldn't bring himself to look at them. "The only one who's offered a plan to save me is Aterus."

Vienna leaned forward. "The Souls want to save you. *We* do, too," she whispered fiercely. "Aterus will say whatever you want to hear. This is what he wants—for you to second-guess yourself. To divide us. You have to stay strong. I know your trust in Russé and the others is frail, but Felix and I will find a way. Have faith in us."

How can you two hope to find a solution when the god can't? That was what he wanted to say, but he settled for, "You're right."

The plan had succeeded. He'd gotten his answer, but it came as a loss. He'd keep the deal to himself, though there was no denying he needed someone to hold the burden with him. Caradin. Once Kole released the next Soul, he'd have an ally. A forced one, but it would do.

"Thanks for letting me vent," Kole said.

"Anytime, mate."

Vienna offered a pinky to the group. Felix smiled and curled his around his sister's.

Hesitant, Kole crawled over, his heart screaming at him for deceiving them. He forced a smile that matched Felix's, then added his wrinkled and scarred pinky to theirs, mimicking the last promise they'd made back in Grayfall. *Honesty? Truth? What does it all mean anymore?*

A violent heave and blood splattered over their hands. Vienna yanked her hand from theirs and covered her mouth. A bead of blood slipped between her fingers.

"V?" Felix moved to her side in an instant, but she kept him at arm's length.

Kole snatched one of the dried shirts from the branch and handed it off to Felix.

Vienna refused it, all the while heaving and hacking. Then she spun away and clutched her arms and legs around the thick branch. Head over the side, hidden behind the bough, she vomited. Streaks of red rained down and splashed the roots below. The fit lasted for a long, drawn-out minute until the coughs lessened, then stopped altogether.

She reached a hand out, face still hidden.

"Her water," Kole instructed.

Felix handed it over, but she slapped it away.

"Ale," Vienna wheezed.

Her brother obeyed. She shifted and sat up, keeping her back to them as she guzzled the bottle.

"Ya might need some tomorrow, Sis." Felix reached for the bottle, but his hand waited there until she'd had her fill. They swapped the ale for the shirt Kole had retrieved.

Once Vienna finished cleaning up, she turned back to them.

Kole bit his tongue to stop his gasp. The vessels in her eyes had burst, leaving them pink and bloodshot.

"Don't take this the wrong way, V, but ya look like death," Felix said.

"I feel like it." Every breath sounded strained and shallow and her back arched as if the effort to sit up straight had become too much.

"We should go back to the village," Kole suggested. "We need to get you help."

"They have no medicine. There's no use going back." Vienna leaned against the trunk, her skin left sickly pale and thin from the coughing spell. "There's more villages on the edge of the marsh, but I think their supplies will be similar."

"Does the ale work?" Kole asked. "If nothing else, we might be able to get more."

"It numbs my throat, which is nice. I won't know the full effect for a few minutes."

"It's gonna hit ya hard." Felix helped lay her down on the forked branch where her blanket draped. "She's never touched the stuff," he explained to Kole.

Kole thought back to his first sip of ale. Felix had offered it back in the Liberation hideout, claiming it would calm his nerves. So it had. He remembered the radiating warmth slowly reaching out from his stomach to his tense muscles. That memory seemed so long ago.

After Felix wrapped the blanket over his sister, who closed her eyes to rest, he caught Kole's attention with an adamant wave.

They climbed down the trunk, out of earshot, then Felix whispered, "She's burning up."

"A fever?" Kole mumbled, more to himself. "We need to keep her cool." He was suddenly grateful for the changing season. The last warmth of autumn faded by the day. He hadn't overheated in days thanks to the growing winter chill. But what more could he do for her? Kole rested his palm on the anchored rambler and sent a message through their connection. On cue, the tree gently swayed its branches, causing a bit of a breeze in the canopy. The tree safely rocked Vienna back and forth, though she looked as though she'd already passed out from the ale. "That'll help for now, but we need to find a city. Someplace that has the resources to help her."

"Zeal's somewhere on this side of the Coroko River. I dunno how far, though," Felix said. "Remember Leo talkin' 'bout it. The geography lessons I was suppose ta be listenin' to." He rubbed the back of his neck, inadvertently pushing the hair aside so the Seven Souls tattoo on his earlobe peeked out for a brief second. "Wish I woulda paid more attention, now. 'Course it bites me in the ass."

"We'll look at the map when she wakes. But if you're sure it's east, we should travel through the night."

"What about Caradin?"

"The Soul is east, too. With any luck we can knock this out quick and continue to Zeal."

Felix nodded. "I just don't get it, mate. How'd we get outta this without a scrape?"

Kole thought for a moment. There had to be a reason only Vienna contracted the poisoned lung, as their late Yamani friend had called it. Maybe the answer came from Felix and Kole rather than Vienna.

"We have something in common," Kole said, trying to piece the solution together. "I just don't know what it is."

"We're both boys."

Kole dismissed it with a shake of his head. "That volcano has been spewing out ash for centuries. Something *that* obvious would've been easy to figure out long before us. It's something else. A power. Magic. Some sort of protection."

"What would we have that V doesn't?"

An idea kindled in his head. "Vienna is normal—well, human and... unscathed. We've both been injured."

"Don't ya think that'd make us *more* open ta sickness?"

Kole considered it for a moment. They had both donned the scars that had nearly killed them. It made them weaker than most. *Near death, but we didn't die because....*

"No, Felix, don't you see? That's *exactly* it. We were both healed by Souls." Kole touched his chest. "Russé saved me, and Issira did the same to you after your shadow had been removed. There must be some lingering effect. A heightened immunity or something."

"Think you're on ta somethin', Blondie." Though they had found the link, Felix remained morose.

"They'll have answers in Zeal. It's a big city like Socren, right?" Kole asked.

"Bigger."

"The more likely they'll have someone there with answers." Kole glanced up to the blanket the siblings had set up for him, sighed, then hunkered down on the ledge of the trunk, letting his feet dangle over. A pair of roots slid to his open palms. "You should get some sleep. One of us should be at full strength."

"Sure, mate. 'Sides, my Kayetan'll wake me up if things get interestin'." Felix closed his eyes for a moment. The vein on his forehead grew prominent as he concentrated. "Looks like he spotted a pack of wolves a few miles straight west." His green eyes flashed open again. "Maybe head more north for a little ways first."

"Will do." Kole shifted the rambler around and pushed the tree accordingly.

Midnight came and went. The hoarse, tempoed breaths of Vienna sleeping high above lulled Kole in and out of a shallow sleep. The weight of his head falling forward every now and then snapped him awake, but the alarm only lasted for a moment before his eyes rolled back once more.

A long, drawn-out howl alerted him. Nothing but dark marsh lay ahead. The rambler, he found, had moved its roots from Kole's hands during his phasing slumber and slipped around his waist to prevent him from falling off the lip of the trunk. All this the tree had done on its own accord, protecting Kole. Gratitude swelled in him. He leaned his head back against the bark. Although the tree offered no actual warmth, a seed of heat met his skin on contact. Internal, he realized, as the rambler poured some of its energy into its shepherd. He suddenly felt the refreshed sense of a full night's sleep without actually acquiring one.

Another howl interrupted his tranquil moment. He squinted his eyes and peered ahead, though the added effort proved useless in the pitch night. The crescent moon lay hidden behind a thick cover of clouds, only showing itself for a moment when the billows thinned.

Kole remembered Felix's warning about the wolves to the east. But Kole had steered far north to avoid them. They seemed to come from behind them and each call sounded no closer or farther than the last.

Keeping pace....

"They're following us," Kole whispered into the night. The rambler shook its leaves at his realization in clear agreement. But did that mean they would refrain from attacking? Kole hurried the rambler's pace with a thought, and it obeyed, though the noise of slurping roots in the deep mud grew so loud, Kole was convinced every animal within a mile could hear them now. Urgency outweighed subtlety. He wished to speak with Niko and see if he had found out anything more during his scouting mission, but he'd yet to return.

"What's goin' on?" Felix's slurred speech gave away his half-awake state.

"The wolves are following us."

Shuffles sounded overhead as Felix clambered down the trunk. A muttered curse drew Kole's attention. Felix's grip must've slipped on the bark because he fell down, clipping the length of the trunk as he descended.

Kole moved to grab a root. Before he could grasp the vine to give the command, the rambler acted and caught his falling companion, then placed him safely on the trunk base alongside Kole. The moment gave Kole a sense of awe. The rambler had acted on his will without instruction, as if it had simply read his mind. He placed his palm on the bark and thanked the rambler. Groaning wood answered him.

"Are you all right?" Kole asked.

Felix perked right up. "Sure. Nothin' better than a near-death experience ta wake ya up." He tucked his disheveled curls behind his ears. His eyes flashed black.

Communing with his Kayetan, Kole realized. Sure enough, the shadowed silhouette appeared mid-air, floating along with the trudging rambler.

"He's seen them up close," Felix confirmed. His transformed eyes stayed distant.

Kole glanced between Felix and the Kayetan. "What is he showing you?"

"They're on ta us, all right. Not like a hunt, though. Just... watchin'." The normal emerald shade returned to Felix's eyes, severing his connection.

Kole surveyed the landscape as another howl called. "They don't like us in their territory. But they won't attack us on the rambler. At least we were right about that part."

"What's the plan then, boss?"

The nickname only deteriorated Kole's confidence. Felix and Vienna put too much faith in him. "We stick to the plan. We should cut west now. No need to avoid the pack anymore, and it's a quicker route to Zeal. I'm sure they'll fall back when we leave the marsh."

When the rambler changed course, fierce growls and snipped barks echoed in the night. The quick change sent a ripple of goosebumps down Kole's arms.

"Or maybe not," Felix whispered.

The answer came to Kole in an instant. The silver elk. The hyper-aggressive animals. The shifting temperament of the wolves. The pack wasn't protecting their territory, they were making sure Kole and his friends left... stayed away....

Away from the very thing that changed them. Caradin.

"They're protecting the elk, Felix," Kole said so suddenly, Felix jumped in his seat. A smile sprang to Kole's lips. "That means the Soul is close."

With a quick touch to the trunk Kole relayed his wishes to the rambler. The roots halted in the mud then turned around and proceeded back the way they'd come.

"What are ya doin', Blondie? Goin' straight toward them? Ya crazy?"

"This is our chance. Keep watch with your Kayetan. I need a second to concentrate." Before Felix could protest, Kole plopped himself on the ledge of the trunk and closed his eyes. Slow, controlled breaths allowed him to block out the surrounding distractions. He connected to Caradin in an instant. Maybe he was getting better at this thing.

In his mind's eye, Kole found himself staring out from the double vision of the stag's eyes like he had before. The dual pictures disoriented him. He struggled to find a landmark to focus on and hopefully give him a hint of the Soul's whereabouts. The inky dark night only made things more difficult.

Then it came. Not from his linked vision with the Soul but the howl of a wolf and from a completely different direction. North. But it made no sense. The wolves never could have caught up and circled their rambler so quickly. How did —

The howl came again a split second later. Same tone. Same wolf.

A delay in the sound. That's when he realized he shared more than just the stag's vision. He'd heard the howl first from Caradin's ears, then from his own.

Now he knew exactly where to go.

Kole jerked up, complete certainty firing in his core. It only took a passing thought and the rambler gained speed, readying a charge.

"I hope ya know what yer doin'," Felix said. He braced the trunk, eyes fully black once more as he linked with his Kayetan. "They've picked up speed. Comin' in fast from the front and sides."

Kole never thought he'd be grateful for their Kayetan ally. Where Felix's and Kole's eyes came up useless through the moonless night, their shadowed companion thrived. Without the Kayetan, they'd be charging blind.

"Should I have him attack?" Felix asked.

"No. I don't want to anger them any more than we already have; we just need to get past and we can outrun them to Caradin. He's close. I can feel it."

No more than five minutes passed when Kole spotted the first four-legged blur. The wolf launched at a root. Teeth snapped. Kole felt a jab of pain jolt through the rambler. The beast clung on, whipping back and forth as the tree tried to slip free of the sharp hold.

Kole pulled his slingshot from his hip and loaded a pellet. Between the jarring stride of the rambler and the flinging root, he couldn't quite narrow in on the wolf. He sent a shot out, but it missed. Another pellet, another miss. *Hold still,* Kole urged the tree. A split second to aim. That's all he needed. The root paused as commanded. A thud came, then a whimper. He'd finally landed a shot. The beast released its vice grip on the root and fell into the sludge below.

The victory proved brief. When Kole finally looked around, two more wolves had taken hold of other roots.

"Felix," Kole called. "Knock them off."

"On it." Swift streams of smoke zoomed over the canines.

Another pierce of pain shot from the tree. Kole winced after noticing the Kayetan had missed the dog and severed one of the roots instead. "Careful, Felix."

"I've told him," Felix answered.

The other wolf fell without a hitch.

The sound of gnashing teeth and growls now came from the rear. It seemed they had passed through the center of the pack. And once through, the rambler's massive stride easily outran the wolves.

Kole sighed and let the pent-up stress roll off him. Through his connection with the tree, he could feel Vienna still perched in the canopy, passed out from the ale.

"Ya know where ta go from here?"

After focusing, he rejoined with Caradin. This time, he ignored the double vision and listened. He heard the distant slurp of roots pushing through mud: the sounds of their own rambler closing in on the Soul. A dark mass moved in the stag's vision, catching Kole's attention. He laid eyes on the shape of a massive walking tree closing in. Suddenly, the stag snapped its head around. The marsh rushed by as the Soul retreated.

Kole shook off the link between them. "He's running. Felix, get up to the canopy. Use your Kayetan to tail it. Tell me which way to go.

It only took a minute for Felix to scale the trunk. The tree parted its branches, giving a clear path to the highest point, and boosted Felix here and there when he faltered.

Kole kept the rambler on course. His fingers twitched on the roots, waiting anxiously for Felix's command. Even the rambler pulsed with exhilaration from the chase.

Thus far, they had stuck to the edge of the marsh, where the trees and plant life grew scarce, mostly a plain of mud. But now they ran into the thicket. The sludge thinned and gave way to more watery ground. Obstacles of tangled roots, trees, and bushes lay in their path. The rambler towered well above everything out here, favorable for sight, but mobility remained a problem. The breeze racing past Kole's cheek died, telling him their pace had slowed significantly.

"I see it!" Felix shouted high above. "Turn right."

The rambler felt Kole's intention and shifted course quicker than Kole could pull on the rein. They bounded off, following Felix's small adjustments.

There.

Something shimmered in the distance. A slip of light through the boscage. Then it vanished. Kole scanned the marsh before him, eyes darting around trying to catch another glimpse. Wood crunched under the rambler's steps, breaking and snapping the plants that stood in their path.

"Can't this thing go any faster?" Felix asked. "We're fallin' behind."

Kole chewed his bottom lip. The rambler was already pushing as hard as it could.

"I can have my Kayetan—"

"No. We'll use it as a last resort. I have an idea." He transferred control to the rambler and instructed it to follow Felix's direction, then braced himself against the trunk and closed his eyes.

"Caradin." He reached out to the Soul with his mind. "Slow."

A presence flickered in his head, responding to the name. No words came. Only an overwhelming sense of fear. Kole's heart hastened to a dangerous pace when the feeling touched him. His lungs ached, and he choked as an involuntary urge to pant overtook him. The alien feeling came from the Soul, he knew, for something similar had happened when he had linked to Obell.

"Don't be scared," Kole formed the words in his head. "I'm here to help you. I can free you from this form."

Confusion mingled with the terror. Still the Soul gave no hint of acknowledgement. If Caradin ignored reason, Kole had no other option left. He pulled his mind from the Soul's, and immediately his body calmed, their connection broken.

"Do it," Kole yelled.

Felix nodded then closed his eyes.

A bleat echoed through the night. The Kayetan had struck it.

Before long, bright spots of light dotted the underbrush. Flecks at first, here and there, then thickening stripes appeared painted across the leaves. The strange, luminous substance led away from them. It finally triggered an understanding in Kole's head. This was blood. The elk's blood.

Kole made the rambler slow as they closed in on the frantic cries of pain.

Angry howls of the wolfpack, still in pursuit somewhere behind them, seemed to answer the stag. Only a matter of time before they caught up. Kole had to make this quick. He climbed down to the roots and jumped into the knee-deep water. His boots soaked through and chilled him straight to his bones.

"Kole," Felix called from the canopy. Concern laced his voice.

Kole waved a hand at him. "Watch for the wolves. I won't be long." He swatted through the tall reeds and trudged through the murk, all the while keeping a close eye on the path of flecked silver leading the way.

Dim light glowed through the thicket. One final pull and he parted the marsh stalks standing between him and the downed elk. He squinted his eyes against the intensity. The color and raw light blinded him. It was as if the moon itself had dropped from the sky and landed at his feet. He held out his hands like shields and peeked through the small gaps between his fingers until his eyes adjusted. But they never did.

Only when the stag moved could he differentiate the outline of the animal against the silver radiance. Kole rounded to Caradin's head, where a grand crown of antlers reached long and wise from the beast's skull. Merely staring at the beast sent a deep-rooted pain through his eyes like a migraine. Kole jumped when something moved beside him. Felix's Kayetan swayed, head trained on Kole. Pearly liquid dripped from one of its claws.

Kole scanned the elk for an injury. A puddle of what looked like molten metal spread from one of the back legs. Assuming Caradin possessed the same unnatural healing abilities as his kin, the stag would regain its strength soon. Already the stream of blood pouring from the haunch lightened to a drip.

When Kole moved closer to the stag's face, its black eyes widened. Caradin bleated and flipped over on his back. Kole stumbled. The wind of a swiping hoof ruffled his hair. A near miss. Kole needed to calm the animal before Caradin hurt himself or those powerful hooves and sharp antlers actually landed on their intended target.

He closed his eyes and reached his mind out to the Soul. *"Caradin, calm down I—"*

Pure, wild energy cut him off. Kole's head spun with the emotions pulsing through the animal. His own leg ached as if it had been sliced by the Kayetan's claw. Swirling panic jumbled Kole's thoughts. The fear he'd felt earlier when he'd reached out to the Soul during the chase had risen to dangerous levels. It compelled Kole's own emotions... made him lose all clarity.

Kole ripped his mind from the Soul before it completely overtook him. His heart pounded so hard in his chest, he thought the frail organ might explode. And his lungs—he gasped for air like a landed fish, yet his body burned for more, unsatisfied. It took a moment for his mind to desync from the Soul and regulate.

"Incoming, Blondie!" Felix shouted from his vantage point.

Dammit. Out of time. Caradin may have blocked him out, but Kole would have another chance. He refused to set out on another hunt when they had the Soul so close.

At Kole's will, the rambler approached. Roots reached past Kole for the stag. He let his hand brush the slime-slickened tendril as it passed and urged the rambler to proceed gently.

Caradin flailed when the roots curled around him. Bucking hooves clipped the restraints, and a few of the roots split and were sliced open. Splinters rained down and sank into the murky marsh water.

More tendrils joined the first wave and pulled the elk in by the legs. The rambler formed a cage beneath the thick trunk and set the buck inside. It reminded Kole of a mother cradling her womb.

"We gotta go, mate."

The tree grabbed Kole and positioned him on the trunk. "Northeast," Kole mumbled. The rambler bolted at his command. They kept pace until the howls faded away, and soon after, the marsh too. All the while, soft bleats came from the bottom side of the trunk until finally they subsided, and the stag passed out.

CHAPTER 10

"Ya think it needs food? Water?"

Kole shrugged.

"Can't ya ask him? It's a *him*, right? Caradin?"

"As far as I know."

Kole had stopped the rambler and climbed down the roots with Felix when the sounds of the restless stag signaled the Soul had woken. Traveling through the night had gotten them safely away from the marsh. Though the water-soaked land lay far off on the horizon, hints of the sour smell lingered in the air. Kole was glad to have drier land below them. He stood barefoot, now; his boots and socks hung over a branch, still drying.

"Guess it wouldn't hurt to lower him down. Maybe it'll calm him." Kole had the rambler drill its roots into the soil, forming a cage to prevent the Soul from fleeing. Only then did the small root enclosure tucked up beneath the heart of the trunk lower and set the buck onto the ground.

Dawn's light gave them a better look at the creature. Kole's breath caught in his throat as the roots slithered away.

The elk's body had changed. No longer a shining star of light, the Soul's form held a ghostly, faded quality that reminded him of the moon during the day. Almost as if some translucent cloud stood between Kole and the buck.

Kole grabbed the roots, which stood as bars for the imprisoned stag, and pushed his face through a pair, trying to look closer.

Caradin bounded up, alert. His dark eyes focused on the two boys. The moment they locked onto him, Kole felt like he was seeing the beast for the first time. Kole had seen plenty of stags before. They'd tamed dozens for riding back home in Solpate forest, but their size and their grace paled in comparison to the creature before him.

The antlers, tall and wide, elegantly bent and swirled upward like a lavish crown. Too symmetrical, like artwork. The sheer size of them seemed far too heavy for such a neck to carry them, yet the buck stood heads taller than the creatures he was familiar with. Every muscle bulged with pure strength. The girth and power of the beast would surely surpass any bear. Kole shuddered to think what would have happened if one of those anvil-like hooves had struck him last night.

"Well... go on, mate. Talk ta it," Felix whispered with a nudge to Kole's back.

Kole cast a glare over his shoulder. "It's not as easy as it looks."

"Whaddya mean? You've talked to it before, haven't ya?"

Kole frowned. "Not exactly."

"Well now's yer chance." Felix tapped one of the roots with his knuckle. "Deal with the Soul, and I'll check on V."

Kole huffed then gave the word for the rambler to pull Felix up to his sister in the canopy. With Felix gone, Caradin shifted his swelling chest toward Kole as if showing off his size, trying to intimidate. *No need for that. You've already got me uneasy.*

The two stared each other down for a long moment, neither willing to make the first move.

"Niko?" Kole called meekly from the side of his mouth. He hadn't seen Niko since he'd sent him scouting ahead the previous night. *What could possibly be taking him this long?* Worry befell him, but he promptly shook it away. What trouble could his already dead friend get into? Still, though, he'd prefer company while he took this next step.

He gulped, then slid his leg through the crack in the roots.

"Is that him?" Came Niko's voice.

Kole jumped, then spun to find Niko floating by his shoulder. The quick movement made the stag drop its head and charge. Kole stumbled and scrambled backward as Caradin closed in on the root cage.

Antlers pierced one of the wooden bars. Kole shielded his face from the spray of splinters, and a groan reverberated from the trunk at the attack. When Kole looked back at the raging animal, who huffed and snorted, pawing the ground, he realized the antlers had caught in the roots.

"Not very smart, is he?" Niko flew closer, inspecting the creature, who didn't seem to notice him. "This can't really be Caradin."

"It is." Kole carefully stood, hands open and outstretched as he moved toward the sharp tips of the antlers, hoping the gesture would convey to the elk that he posed no threat.

"Have you talked to him yet?"

Kole rolled his eyes. Felix and Niko seemed to think this job was simple. "Not exactly," he repeated the answer he'd given a moment before through gritted teeth. With a strategic push, and a little help from a bending root, Kole freed the buck. Caradin staggered away, then trotted around the circular pen snorting, head held high and aloof.

"What are you waiting for?"

"Well, you," Kole said flatly. "Where have you been?"

Niko rubbed his stubbled chin. "Actually, I went to Zeal to check out the place."

"All the way to Zeal?"

"You said to check ahead," Niko said defensively.

"I didn't mean that far."

"Well, now I know the fastest way there. Looks like the girl will need it."

Kole sighed. After he filled Niko in on the events of last night, he motioned back to Caradin, who stood against the opposite side of the cage, hoof pawing the ground again. "I have to figure this out before we get to Zeal or we'll draw too much attention. Rumors of a shining stag will lead Russé straight to us."

"What do you need me to do?" Niko asked.

"Just stay with me."

Niko nodded then hovered by Kole's side. Even with his eyes closed, Kole felt the buzz of his presence on his arm, and it gave him a boost of confidence.

Kole rolled his shoulders, then dove into Caradin's head. He was ready this time. The Soul's terror and confusion had morphed to anger. Nothing but solid anger and determination to flee its confinements.

"Caradin."

A sense of acknowledgement came at the name. Still no words.

"I can set you free, but I need to speak with you first. We need to make a deal."

Kole expected to feel something. Understanding or anything telling Kole that Caradin was listening. Instead, a wall of dominance surrounded Kole's consciousness as if the stag were trying to claim rule over him.

"Careful, Kole," Niko said. "Looks like he's ready to charge again."

Kole's eyes flew open, but he kept his mind linked with the Soul's. Caradin slowly lowered his head, dark eyes fixed on Kole. "He's not saying anything. You'd think he'd want to be free after a millennium stuck in this form. Honestly, I don't think he even understands me. I'm just getting like... feral emotions."

"Then play to that. Think like a stag."

The words sparked a thought. *All these centuries... trapped in this form.* He thought back to the last Souls he'd released. Issira and Obell had reacted very differently to the prolonged imprisonment; Issira had maintained a calm clarity, while Obell built with fury. *Is this how Caradin has coped? Giving in to the animal nature?*

If it were true, Kole had no hope at explaining his deal with Aterus, let alone convincing Caradin to refrain from killing him outright when he tried to free the Soul. But he had to give it a go, so he went with the only strategy he thought might work.

Kole clenched his jaw and made a show of stomping his foot on the ground. Though it felt ridiculous—the thought of *him* looking intimidating—he knew the elk wouldn't see scarred skin or a disfigured face and mark it as weakness. If he made his body big enough, he could pull off a threatening charade. Niko had given him the idea, thinking like an animal. Kole had seen the forest stags back home tussle for higher rankings in the herds. The knowledge never crossed his mind as useful. Now, he'd put it into play. But boy was he glad Felix and Vienna were too preoccupied to witness this. Felix would never let him live it down.

Caradin pulled back his head, ever so slightly, taking in Kole's new behavior.

Chest puffed, Kole zeroed in on the Soul's mind. Dominance stood firm against Kole, but a hint of calculation kept the elk still. Kole used it to his advantage. No small show would convince the stag to back down. Submission would only be granted to Kole through a great act of power and will. One last breath, then Kole grabbed the roots and slipped into the cage with the mighty animal.

"What are you doing?" Niko had followed him in. Concern furrowed his brows as he glided alongside Kole.

Kole made sure his focus stayed on Caradin. Any break in concentration might alarm the stag and give him an opening to charge. "I'm taking your advice. Think like a stag, right?"

"Right, well, in *my* version, I pictured you doing that from *outside* the cage," Niko said, voice hysterical. "You're going to turn yourself into a human kabob."

Every step Kole took, slow, steady, yet intent, brought him farther from the roots—farther from safety. At this point, Kole would never make it back behind the cage in time if Caradin called Kole's bluff. *No turning back.*

"I can do this." The words meant to ease Niko's worry doubled as a mantra for Kole as he halted little more than an arm's length from the points of those antlers.

"Caradin," Kole projected the name in the buck's head.

The ears flicked forward. If nothing else, it solidified that the Soul knew his own name.

He projected the faces of Issira, Russé, and Obell into the Orange Soul's head, but the stag only stared, unblinking. After biting his lip in confusion, it dawned on Kole: the Souls probably rarely, if ever, took a human form. They wouldn't know one another that way. Not physically. But mentally...? *Worth a shot.* Instead, he noted their names, since Caradin seemed to respond to his own, along with the energies and auras the other Souls emitted during their time together. Russé's compassion, Issira's calming grace, and Obell's burning strength.

This piqued the stag's interest. A cloven hoof inched forward, and the animal leaned in. Not to attack, but to....

The nose wriggled. Probably assessing Kole's scent.

"That's it." He encouraged Caradin through their link while keeping his shoulders up and back in a powerful looking stance.

Caradin snorted. Trust resonated in the creature's thoughts, underlined with a small inclination of suspicion. Kole had predicted as much. His scent, he'd learned from their late Yamani friend, held a mix of human and god. Caradin must've picked up on the conglomerate fusion of his kin packaged in one small body. It must've been enough to sway the buck, because Caradin leaned away, muscles relaxed. Kole's pride hoped the submission had come from his own physical display, but he knew better.

Kole gave Caradin a moment to settle before probing his mind again. This time, that wall of dominance had gone, replaced with a docile energy.

It was clear to Kole that whatever intelligence Caradin had possessed before his imprisonment had long faded... regressed. The Soul had succumbed to the creature. Words meant nothing to the god. All hope of logic, lost. But it didn't doom communication. Eyes cast directly into the stag's, Kole thought about the end. Not the end of the day, or the end of his mission, but the *complete* end. The *after* Kole thought he would never live to see: a world rid of the Black Wall. He imagined the feeling of freedom—unburdened by the fate of Ohr so heavy on his shoulders. That lightness... that *hope* filled him. He cast that feeling to Caradin.

Something flashed in the buck's eyes. Longing? For a brief second, Caradin let his guard down and true awareness flickered, like glimpsing the stars through a thin patch of clouds. Then the elk did something unexpected: he lowered his crowned head, tucked one leg, and stretched back into a bow.

Now or never. Kole pulled his blade out and pricked his finger just like he'd done with Issira and Obell. The ballooning bubble of maroon invoked the stag's curious nose. The animal stiffened at Kole's approach but never faltered from its submissive position.

A simple touch. It didn't matter where. Kole just need to make contact with his blood exposed, and the ritual would commence.

Despite his assurance, worry flipped in his stomach like an overturned beetle. Kole would die briefly when the touch came. This bothered him less than he thought. He'd been through death three times prior; only now he had no one here to save him if things went awry. *Russé.* Maybe Kole was wrong. Maybe he needed him for this. Could he count on Russé — his compassion?

At the last second, with the warm fog of the stag's breath on his hand, Kole ripped through the barriers he'd erected to block his former mentor from his head and invited him in. A risk, for sure. What might Russé garner from their reconnection? Hopefully, his old friend would be too preoccupied to go wandering about his head. Russé had no knowledge of the deal anyway. He wouldn't *know* to look. And nothing meant more to Russé than Kole's wellbeing; Kole could bank on that. Once Kole was on the other side of the ritual, he would put his barrier back in place before any secrets slipped.

Kole let his eyes trail to Niko. "Don't worry. I'll be back soon."

Then he reached out to his mentor. *"Russé. I need your help."* Once he felt the Soul react to his call, Kole tapped his bloody finger to the star-shaped patch on the buck's forehead and greeted death once again.

CHAPTER 11

Piper stood at the edge of Lake Galen. The waves ran up and down the lakeside beach, approaching her feet like a timid animal, then receding before they could kiss the toes of her leather boots. Only when a prick of pain shot from her palm did she realize she'd been jamming her nail into her skin. She let out an irritated grunt and shook out her hands. But her thoughts, swirling with concern for Kole, pulled her focus, and she felt her nail push down on her palm once more. This time she left it; her human side's way of coping when things pulled from her control. A bad habit. She wondered if she'd gotten it from her mother.

Try as she may, most of her memories of Evangeline had yielded to the fog of time: still there, yet blurred. The only recollections Piper held of her now that stood crisp and vivid were filled with her sleeping face. A frail face with an equally depleting body. What a life her father had given Evangeline. An eternity together. That's what Aterus had wanted. But he never predicted the long-term consequences in thrusting immortality on a mortal. It had worked for a time, vibrant and happy. As time passed, her mother's nightly sleep would extend to days. Weeks. Months. Now it was rare to catch her awake. *What do you want, Mother? What is right?*

Unnatural life came at the cost of Ohr and thousands upon thousands of innocent people. And for what? The mere days or weeks every few years when Evangeline would wake? The last time her mother had come to.... She shook her head trying to remember. Six years. *Has it really been that long?*

Ah. She smiled. The ocean trip.

The smell of the lake water granted her that memory. She closed her eyes and took in a long, deep lungful, imagining a saltiness in her throat. And just like that, she was transported back to that distant moment.

"Piper, my love. What are you thinking?" her mother asked, sorrow in her voice.

Piper stayed silent, watching the waves crash into the base of the cliff below. She shifted, dangling her legs over the edge of the tall rockface. The warmth of her mother's body, side pressed gently into her own, gave her a shiver.

"Shall I leave you to your thoughts?"

"No," Piper snapped, her voice clipped and harsh. She found her mother's honey-colored eyes, which matched her own, and softened her tone. "I'm sorry. No, I want to talk. We don't have much time."

"Is that what's on your mind?"

Piper tilted her head. Her eyes ached, threatening tears. "Always. I can never escape it."

The fine lines running across Evangeline's face deepened as she frowned. "I keep forgetting how it is for you. No time passes between our moments together. For me I sleep, and when I wake, you are there. Always there. You and your father."

Piper leaned away at his mention. Surely her mother felt it because she retracted her arm and gave her some space.

"How long this time?"

The question sent a dagger into Piper's chest. Her breaths came fast as she answered, "Four years." It was all she could manage to say without choking on her guilt and worry. The lengthening sleeps had been gradual. A few days of unconsciousness at a time spiraled so far beyond what Piper or Aterus ever imagined. Now her mother barely woke. The pain of not knowing when she'd see her mother again—awake and responsive—plagued her every thought.

"Is that a long time?" Her mother asked. "For you, I mean?"

"Yes, Mother. I may not age like humans, but it still feels just as long."

Evangeline stayed silent for a moment. Too long.

Piper glanced over. The skin of her mother's arm turned a sickly gray, and her shoulders hunched forward, allowing her white and auburn mixed hair to lay like a curtain in front of her face. Her back raised abruptly every so often in her attempt to hide her quiet sobs.

Piper kicked her heel into the cliff. She'd done it again: let gloom get in the way of what should have been a happy, short-lived reunion. "Please don't be sad." That small gap between them diminished as Piper leaned in and wrapped her arms around her mother's small frame. "I'm glad to be here with you. Every moment is a blessing. I'll wait as long as the earth to see you again."

Soft sobs faded. Evangeline lifted her head and embraced Piper in an urgent hold. When she finally released her, her mother's eyes went to the waves.

They looked out on the ocean together. Piper thrust down the depression eating away at her heart and forced the bliss of this moment forward. *Another day, at least. All to myself.*

"It doesn't have to be like this," said Evangeline.

Piper peered over. "What?"

"It's painful for you and your father. I can see that." She dipped her head. "I don't want to be the source of it. I love you both too much to do this to you."

Piper opened her mouth to respond, closed it. She let the words sink in.

Before Piper had a chance to fully understand, her mother spoke again. "I would understand. You know that don't you, Pipes?"

The oceanic scene faded, replaced by the calm lake. Piper focused on that line her mother had said all those years ago. Although not the last conversation they'd shared, it stood bright in her mind ever since. *"I would understand."* Her mother's voice echoed every time Piper questioned the charge she'd appointed herself. *I hope you do.*

Piper was convinced. She'd undo her father's—Aterus'—past evils. No life, no matter how much she loved her mother, took precedence over another. She was destined to kill the only thing she truly loved.

A commotion shattered any peace the lake extended her. Piper spun at the anxious voices of the three gods down the beach.

Obell and Issira huddled around Russé, who sat on the sand, crumpled, as though he'd fallen. She hurried over just as his kin helped Russé back to his feet.

"What's going on?" Piper surveyed Russé for injury. He held a hand to his temple, eyes squeezed shut.

"I think it's Kole," Issira said in a warning vibrato.

"He's found him. He's—" Russé's eyes flashed open. Horror twisted his face, but a film lay over his eyes as if he wasn't fully anchored in reality. "No, Kole. Don't do it," he screamed and reached out to the empty space in front of him, as if to stop something happening far away.

"Someone tell me what the bloody hell is going on," Piper spat.

Issira and Obell locked eyes. Quick micro expressions came and went as they held a silent conversation.

Piper huffed and rolled her eyes at their secrecy. *You don't want to share? Fine. I'll do it myself.* She bypassed their arms when they registered what she was trying to do, too slow to stop her. Piper reached out and cupped her hand around Russé's cheek.

Vision swept to black.

In the vast darkness, a pinprick of light lay far off. Like a shooting star, it zoomed toward her, strengthening in brilliance as it neared. She fought off the instinct to recoil from it and was glad she did. Once the light came close enough, expanding, she recognized it as a portal rather than a sphere, like a giant mirror. But instead of her reflection staring back, Kole stood in the depths of the window.

"Please don't do this." Russé voice came loud in her ear. "I don't know if I can help from here."

Piper glanced around. Russé stood next to her, hunched over, obsessively watching the same image. His hands clasped the side of the portal so hard, thin veins swelled under his skin.

"What's happening?" Piper asked.

"The ritual. He's going to do it alone," said Russé as though barely aware of Piper's presence.

Her eyes went back to Kole in the mirror, who extended a blood-tipped finger to the head of some deer. She watched, cognizant of Russé's trembling body next to her, oozing anxiety, then gasped as an orange orb of light floated from Kole's mouth and absorbed into the animal. The sparkle of life snapped off in Kole's eyes, and he collapsed to the ground.

No. Not yet. Piper joined Russé in slamming her fists against the mirror. *I need you, Kole. You can't go yet.*

An orange glow stopped them both.

Within the portal, the stag rose from its bowed position, eyes vibrant and locked directly ahead. No. Directly at the *portal*.

Russé placed a hand over the image. "Please. Caradin. I beg you. Give him back. Let him live."

The stag moved his alien gaze down to the lifeless boy at his hooves. "Kole. Kole. Kole." Came a foreign voice. Caradin's. The animal nudged Kole with his nose, still repeating the name.

Kole didn't rouse.

"What is he doing?" Piper asked, alarmed at the breathlessness of her own voice.

"I think he's mourning." The wrinkles of Russé's face deepened with pain. "We were wrong before. Caradin was the one who'd lost his senses, not Braxus. Caradin's mind has become the animal. He won't see reason. He can't understand."

"You have to do something," Piper commanded. "Help him!"

"How?" Russé looked up at her from the bottom of the portal, where his body had sagged. "I'm not there. Kole's connection to Caradin was severed the moment he returned the Soul's piece to him. Without that piece within Kole, I cannot attempt to commune either. There is nothing linking us."

"But he can see us. Or sense us at least." Piper waved a hand at the mirror, hoping to draw the stag's attention back up. "Caradin looked at us a moment ago."

Something she said must've sparked a revelation, because Russé snapped up. "Kole's not dead."

Piper frowned. "Are you sure? He looks...." She hated being so far from where she was needed most. If only she had let the Souls deal with Savairo on the blasted volcano. Her own selfish fury had coerced her away. She never should've left Kole's side. He may not have known it yet, but she was his best hope in this whole mess.

"Kole isn't fully gone yet," Russé said, a trill of hope in his voice. "He still has the other Soul's pieces within him. He can be revived. It's how the ritual works. Only... I'm not sure how long his *body* can survive without that shard of his life source returned." His palm pushed against the portal to no avail. "If Caradin can truly sense us... but I don't understand how. I've never seen anything like this." He examined the mirror-like portal. "Kole pulled me here. He created it somehow."

"It doesn't matter what it is, just get Caradin's attention. Make him fulfill the ritual."

Russé climbed to his feet and centered himself before the portal. A dull green glow radiated from his skin.

Piper stood there, waiting for something to happen. *Useless Souls. Always relying on their powers for a solution.* If she were there, she'd take the beast by the antlers and force him into compliance.

As quickly as the aura had come, it faded away. Russé hunched over in defeat. "It must've been a coincidence. I can't reach him."

"Master." That alien voice came again. With a push of a hoof, Caradin rolled Kole to his back. "Master Kole. Live."

The mouth of the animal parted, and an orange globe glided back to Kole. It burst into mist as it touched Kole's paling face and disappeared up his nose.

Piper's lungs stopped as she watched, waiting.

All at once, Kole gasped, and his eyes flew open. Color came back to his burned skin.

"Thank Ohr!" Piper sighed.

"Kole," Russé called out.

Kole flinched at Russé's voice. Then his gaze locked onto the portal—onto Russé. His jaw flexed, expression clearly settling into resentment: a feeling she knew all too well. Something passed between the pair, then a hard line set on Kole's mouth, and he turned away.

Russé collapsed to his knees at the base of the portal, hands cupping his head. "I don't understand. Why?"

In the next instant, the portal shrunk, leaving Piper and Russé in complete darkness.

Piper pulled her mind from Russé's and opened her eyes to reality once more. Russé's blank face stared back at her. The lake lay calm over his shoulder, and Obell and Issira hovered beside them.

Piper let her hand slide from Russé's grieved face. She tightened her lips. The Soul's blue eyes conveyed his sense of betrayal, but she said it aloud anyway, "Kole is blocking you."

Russé kept her gaze, eyes searching her for an explanation, she thought at first. Then water brimmed his lower lashes, and she realized he wasn't looking for a way to fix it or rationalize it at all. He was hurt.

The raw emotion on the Soul's face sent a visceral reaction through her. An ache tugged on her heart. She was unprepared for such a human response from a Soul. That sadness trickled through her. Was she feeling sorry for Russé? *Stop this.* Unwilling to let the feeling develop further, she stumbled back and retreated to the lake, letting his kin deal with the aftermath.

Sorry for a Soul? They are the ones who made this mess. The reminder hardened her. She huffed, expelling all sympathy from her core. Levelheaded again, Piper faced their new truth.

Kole's trust had veered from the Souls. Had he pledged allegiance solely to himself? To Vienna and Felix, perhaps? Caradin. Caradin had called him master. Was there something more there she hadn't seen? Had Kole found a new ally?

Two things she could be sure of: Kole was on the run, and he didn't want to be found.

CHAPTER 12

Kole woke to a voice calling his name. The rush of sudden colors, smells, and sounds around him left him delirious. *That voice.* He knew that voice. With a stiff lip, he closed out Russé's plead. His bearings gradually returned after his brush with death, and he used every bit of this gathering strength to reassemble the walls around his head: a fortress to which Russé no longer held the key.

With his mind safe, Kole's attention moved to a figure barreling toward him. His first instinct told him that Caradin had finally decided to charge him, but the image focused as it neared.

Felix rushed to Kole's side, eyes urgent. "For the love of Souls, Blondie! I heard a thud, then came down ta see ya limp on the ground. Had ta chase the damned beast away. Are ya hurt?"

Kole blinked at him. He took a moment to flex his muscles and test for injury. Still tight and immobile as before. "I'm fine—well, normal. Where's...?" A snort came from the far side of the root-made cage. He glanced over, curious to see Caradin's new form, his natural form. When he'd released Issira, she'd appeared as a mesmerizing, flowing sculpture of water, and Obell a living flame before Russé had persuaded them into human form, but the same grand stag stood backed up to the roots, ears pinned on Kole.

"Caradin?" Kole lifted up, happily accepting Felix's assistance when he found his knees still wobbled, weak from the ritual.

The ears swiveled at the name.

"Did it work?" Kole asked, more to himself, but Felix offered a shrug.

Out of the corner of Kole's eyes, he caught Niko's ghost floating toward the beast. The animal moved one ear to Niko's location, as if tracking him. "Think he's like the Kayetan? He can see me?"

"Not exactly," Kole said. "I bet he can sense you, though. Strange."

"Uh." Felix peered over at Kole. "Blondie? You okay?"

Kole cursed himself. He'd done it again, answered Niko aloud. At least it hadn't been in front of Vienna this time. She seemed more intuitive to the odd behavior. "Yeah, fine. My head gets jumbled after the ritual. It's nothing. Just need some time to settle is all."

Felix tightened his grip around Kole's elbow, apparently interpreting the excuse as a hint for more assistance. It pleased Kole he had such a good friend. But the small smile on his mouth wilted when Kole's inner voice reminded him he actively lied to his companions.

Kole sent an apologetic frown to his ghostly friend, signaling their conversation could only be one sided for the moment.

Niko nodded, said, "I'll be around if you need me," then faded away.

With Felix's aid, Kole hobbled over to the stag. "Caradin." He held a hand to the beast.

The Soul stepped forward; tail tucked. *"Master."*

"Master?" Kole dropped his hand and pulled from Felix's grip. "What does he mean?"

"I dunno what yer talkin' 'bout, mate. I didn't hear anythin'."

Only then Kole noted the voice had come telepathically. And easily, too, the guardedness between them apparently knocked down after the ritual. It had worked... to some degree. "He called me master," Kole said.

"Well... that's good, eh? If yer callin' the shots, he won't use those antlers on us." Felix folded his arms over his chest and sized up the buck. "Now that he's not so hostile, he's kinda cute, ain't he?"

"I guess." The silver aura radiating from the animal remained. Regal rather than cute. Yet, as beautiful as Caradin's form looked, it was too conspicuous. Kole gently reached his thoughts to the Soul, bracing himself in case the current docile nature shifted in an instant. *"Lose the light. We need to keep you from drawing attention."*

"Master Kole," was all Caradin said. A confusion seeped from the stag. Through their connection, Kole heard the Orange Soul scrutinized the sounds of Kole's voice, its inflections, and replayed the words individually in his head as if studying them.

Kole sighed. It seemed the ritual hadn't fixed the language barrier. Yet Caradin had learned Kole's name and described him as master. Kole let himself hope this complication would be short-lived, like amnesia or something. In the meantime, he accepted that he would have to use images along with his words if he hoped to work with the god. He pictured a normal stag. Of course, "normal" to him meant the ones he'd grown up seeing in Solpate. Their appearance had been affected by the magic of the forest, and as such, they'd donned green mosses and vines in place of fur. Though beautiful, a green elk with wooden antlers and hooves would prove just as ostentatious as a glowing one. He tried to picture a creature with fur, plain and ordinary, and conveyed his wishes to Caradin.

"What the Souls?" Felix said in awe next to Kole.

Kole frowned at Caradin's shifting hide. The silver glow had died out, but the fur still held a strangeness. Kole blamed this on himself. How was he supposed to will the Soul to look like a normal stag if he had never seen one himself? The Soul's disguise, with white fur and sparkling ivory antlers, still looked too... grand. Despite his displeasure, he nodded to Caradin. *It'll have to do for now.*

The Soul's ochre-tinged ears suddenly tilted back, and he flicked his head up, nose twitching. A warning from the elk touched Kole's thoughts.

Suddenly, a horrible heaving echoed above them. Droplets of red splattered down on the roots.

"Vienna!" Kole and Felix said together.

"Stay here." Kole sent the command with an image of an unmoving stag, hoping it would be enough for the Soul to comprehend. He didn't hang around to ensure Caradin obeyed. Within two strides, he'd secured a root for himself and Felix. They grabbed hold and the rambler carried them aloft.

The roots placed Kole and Felix on the branch Vienna slumped over, the same place she'd slept — or, passed out cold — the last night.

After depleting the contents of her stomach, Vienna rolled over, her eyes unfocused, skin paler than the clouds.

"V?" Felix scooted down the bough to her.

"I'm fine," she slurred, but the subsequent wheezes called out her lie.

When Felix looked back at Kole, his eyes darkened with panic. "I've never seen anyone like this, and I've been 'round some nasty sickness back in Socren." He touched her forehead. "Hotter than a steamed dumplin'. It's getting' worse. We gotta do somethin'."

"Zeal is—"

"Do ya think she'll make it that long?"

Kole chewed his bottom lip. He had no experience with an illness like this. "I don't know."

"Can Caradin fix this?" Felix asked.

"Yes, I imagine so. It would deplete his pool, but...." *But what?* His thoughts battled against one another. He had to spare Vienna. No question about it. The one downside: saving her meant weakening his own chances at survival at the end of all this. He scolded the selfish thoughts — those self-preserving feelings — circulating through his head.

Vienna groaned.

They both snapped their attention back to her.

She mumbled something, too soft and scrambled to catch.

"What is it, Vienna?" Kole asked.

"No," she managed.

"No?" Felix asked. "No, what?"

"You will not use Caradin for me."

"Don't be ridiculous, V."

Her quivering hand lifted to grasp her brother's shoulder. "I won't take that from Kole. Take me to Zeal."

"But, V—"

"Take me to Zeal!" Her raised voice triggered a seizure.

Kole and Felix lunged for her, barely securing her before she rolled off the bough. They gently held her in place, letting the spasms ride out.

Panic left Kole breathless. *Could* they make it to Zeal before this escalated any further? Vienna was strong. If anyone could hold out, it would be her.

Felix's brows furrowed with fear as he held down his sister. His eyes glistened with building tears, and his jaw clenched. When Vienna finally went limp and passed out again, he sat back, but his expression remained.

"We'll figure this out," Kole promised.

Felix vacantly nodded. He leaned into Kole and silently cried.

Kole stiffened at the embrace at first, taken back at the abruptness, but he surrendered and wrapped an arm around Felix. The hushed sobs took Kole back to another time. A memory that seemed a lifetime ago. When Russé had once comforted him like this after Kole had learned his camp had perished and his scars would be permanent. Except this time, Kole took the role as the anchor... as the guardian. One long sigh, then Kole held Felix tighter. Any apprehension of closeness, of the anxiety brought on by people touching his scars, melted away.

Minutes passed. Felix's cries subsided and he awkwardly pulled from Kole. "Sorry, mate," he croaked.

Kole shook his head. "Don't be." He studied Vienna. Two times she had vomited blood now. *How do we stop it?* Worse, the continuous retching would make it hard for her to keep food and water down. That may be the only factor they could control, keeping her body as fueled as possible.

"Feed her. Make her drink," Kole said. "I'll get things ready for travel. We'll head out immediately."

Felix tended to Vienna without a word.

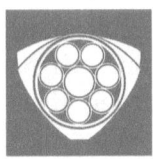

Kole rode atop Caradin. He very well would've ridden the rambler if not for his unfamiliarity with Caradin. Because the Soul had trouble understanding, Kole thought it better to keep a close eye on him. They raced against the icy wind. The cold bit at his skin. His ears, nose, and fingers had numbed hours ago. He tucked his face closer to Caradin's broad neck, lacing his fingers deep into the undercoat of the fair fur to find some relief. His skin warmed in an instant.

The Soul had shown no opposition when Kole mounted. Kole had simply pictured his desire to ride, and the stag obediently bowed for an easier climb. Their connection seemed simpler than Kole had anticipated. Words were unnecessary on most occasions, he found. Though the whole "master" thing made him uncomfortable, he'd take this way of communication over Russé's overbearingness.

The first signs of winter had arrived. Kole dreaded the cold. No chance of snow yet, thankfully. If the seasons of the west matched Solpate, it'd be several weeks before the temperature dropped low enough to freeze. *One less thing to worry about I suppose.* Snow meant another obstacle with the potential to slow his mission.

The rambler followed close behind Kole and Caradin. Felix curled up in the canopy alongside Vienna, tending to her every need. Before they set off, they had sacrificed every available layer, from extra clothes to some of the new-grown leaves of the rambler, and had lain them on Vienna. They couldn't let her become too cold. Her body no longer possessed the strength to fight off the chill.

Zeal by nightfall. Though a lofty goal, Kole felt determined, for Vienna's sake, to make it happen. Without meaning to, he pictured closing in on the city. Caradin must've picked up on his wishes, because the elk sped to such an unbelievable pace, the rambler struggled to keep up.

"Aye, Kole!" Felix's voice came quiet against the roaring wind whirring in Kole's ear.

Kole would've thought he'd imagined the voice if not for Caradin's own ears swiveling backward. He twisted in his seat just enough to catch sight of the rambler.

"There's houses ahead." Felix pointed north. "That way."

Caradin changed route for their new destination.

Stone houses, more solid and permanent counterparts of the small village they'd visited a day earlier, cleared on the horizon. He pushed Caradin as close as he dared, knowing the giant tree on their tail had sprung ill reactions from the last villagers. *Best to go on foot from here.*

Kole halted the Soul with a thought, then had him trot to the rambler, where Kole could send roots up for Felix and Vienna. He slipped off Caradin's back in preparation for Vienna to take his place. The moment his feet touched down, his legs gave out, and he crumpled in the grass. He sucked in a breath. The cold had numbed him so thoroughly, he hadn't realized the state of his body. His muscles throbbed, legs shook, but worse, the fragile skin of his inner thighs burned. While riding, he figured the warmth came from the animal's body heat. Not the case. Not solely, anyway. He'd been rubbed raw. The fabric clung to his skin, wet in places. Skin had broken. He gritted his teeth. Further inspection would have to wait.

A cold nose touched the back of his neck. It jolted Kole. Dark, concerned eyes set on him. Kole turned away from the stag, not bothering to explain.

Antlers lowered within reaching range. Kole grabbed either one. With one easy heave of his head, Caradin propped him back on his feet. He held on until his legs regained enough strength to stand on their own. Just in time, too.

The rambler held Vienna aloft over the stag and gently laid her down. Her eyes, though open, held a fog. She gazed at Kole, then weakly opened her mouth. "I'm fine," she said, but her voice came so soft, Kole was unsure if she spoke or mouthed it.

"We'll make sure of that," Kole said.

Felix hoisted two packs over his shoulders and the third across his belly as a counterbalance, refusing Kole when he offered to share the load. "Just lead the way, mate."

It only took a moment for the rambler to heed Kole's command and anchor itself. The roots drilled deep, and the trunk dropped snuggly into the grass. Even without the added height of its roots, the rambler towered unnaturally over any plant or tree in the whole landscape. Kole hoped no one looked too hard at the horizon between now and nightfall.

"Are we sure they'll have medicine?" Kole scrutinized the state of the houses as they approached the town. It felt odd leaving his rambler behind, like he left a piece of himself waiting out here. He ignored the hollow in his core and took in the small town.

Lush farmland surrounded them. Houses. Barns. A few other buildings he guessed were shops. Would a healer live here?

"I reckon no cure-all, but it's worth the chance even if it's somethin' for pain or what not." Felix stepped closer to Kole, shoulder to shoulder, and lowered his voice so his sister, hunched over Caradin's back, wouldn't hear. "She won't admit it, but another hour out here's gonna kill her. Her skin's ice. No rambler's gonna keep her warm once the sun goes down. Even with a fire. I say we find a room somewhere and hole up till mornin'."

Risk the cold or risk a whole night during which Vienna's condition could worsen? That's what they battled against. Though Kole would have preferred pushing through the night, Felix knew his sister's limits better. A night inside would do them all some good. Kole waddled alongside Caradin, a hand on the animal's neck for support. He managed to lean on him just enough to prevent further agitating his own wounds without drawing Felix's concern.

Kole pulled his hood low as they strode into town. The people bustling around gave them curious glances, more directed at the great buck and its cargo than the boys, yet no one stopped or questioned them. Their reaction, or lack thereof, meant the town received more visitors than the last they'd encountered. Kole hoped they could get through the night as invisibly as possible.

"There's an inn up ahead." Felix pointed out the small building. "Let's get her settled, then one of us — well," he glanced worriedly between Vienna and Kole hidden beneath his hood, "maybe it's best if I go searchin' for medicine. No offense there, Blondie, it's just — "

"For the best, I know." Kole had his own reasons for keeping a low profile. If Russé came this way, he wanted no trace left behind. Caradin drew a bit of attention, but he doubted Russé would expect the newly released Soul to keep his imprisoned form. As long as Kole kept his scars hidden, they had a chance at going ghost-like through the town.

Kole led Caradin to the side of the inn and reached out for Vienna. "Time to come down."

Vienna leaned into him. His strength gave out at her weight, and she slid too fast off the buck's back. Thankfully, Felix caught her before she and Kole both tumbled to the road.

"Nice 'n easy." Felix held up his sister with one arm, the other braced behind Kole's back, stabilizing him too. "Let's get her inside." Felix guided Vienna away.

Without his rambler, Kole was weak. He hated the helpless feeling, always relying on others. All the self-confidence he'd acquired over the last several days dissolved. It pained him more that he had allowed himself to feel that strength—that false hope. He couldn't even get Vienna off a mount. The rambler. The Souls. Without them, he was nothing, and he resented it.

As he went to follow the siblings, the clunk of hooves behind him made him sigh. He had given no thought to Caradin until then. An elk wouldn't be allowed in. Where would he stay? Surely not alone. No way he'd stick a Soul in a stable. Kole needed to keep eyes on him. As the siblings slipped inside the inn, Kole turned and pushed Caradin deeper down the alley. The Orange Soul had created animals and could clearly take on their shape. He let a curious thought float to the Souls mind.

"*Small,*" Kole urged in the Soul's thoughts.

"*Small,*" Caradin repeated, as if learning the word for the first time.

"A bird, a mouse, I don't know. An insect for Soul's sake! Anything." He cupped his hands and imagined Caradin fitting into them. "This small."

Caradin pushed his cold, wet muzzle into Kole's hands.

"No, not—" Kole released the stag's nose and ran an impatient hand through his hair. This whole communication barrier was tiring.

Just when he thought he'd have to stay on the outskirts tonight with Soul, Caradin stepped back, and his thick coat rippled. To Kole's surprise, the elk shrunk. He whipped his head up and down the alley looking for unwelcome witnesses. He should've been more specific. Made the Soul wait until he'd deemed the area clear. Too late now. The back way down the lane stood relative clear, so he stepped in front of the Soul as the stag morphed, praying his wide stance blocked the god from onlookers. When the warmth of the stag's massive form disappeared, Kole whirled around to find an empty space before him. A squeak came from his feet, and he looked down into the black, beady eyes of a white weasel. A runt of a thing.

Caradin jumped on Kole's pant leg and climbed up to his waist, where he jumped for Kole's hand. The shock of it all dulled Kole's reflexes. He barely caught the little thing.

The weasel curled up into Kole's cupped hands and sent a thought Kole's way, "*This small.*"

Kole snorted. "Yeah, this small." He couldn't hold back his smile. *"We have to go. Hide."* Kole pulled his collar open and let Caradin crawl in the dark space of his hood. The soft fur tickled his neck as Kole rushed into the inn, but he relished the warmth of the little body curled against him.

The door swung close behind him, and the small smile leftover from the alley dropped to a frown at the arguing voices, one of which belonged to Felix.

"We can't go back out there, she'll freeze." Felix had both arms around Vienna's waist, trying to keep her upright as she coughed sprays of blood onto the wooden table.

"I'm not risking infecting my patrons with whatever plague has befallen that girl." A tall, middle-aged woman held an accusing finger toward the siblings. "Get her out of here, or I'll have you removed."

Kole rushed to Felix's side, catching whispers from the tables as he passed.

"She's got the lung," Kole heard from one.

"Sure sounds like it," the other patron responded.

They paid no mind to Kole. All eyes lay on Vienna, half hunched in her brother's grip. "I'm so sorry," she mumbled. "I didn't mean to."

Once Kole reached them, he noticed her apology was directed at a surly man covered in specks of red. Vienna must've lost control. No wonder these folks were angry.

"She'll infect us all!" a cry came from a back corner.

"You okay?" Kole muttered low to Vienna.

Her face turned to him. Tears streaked down her cheeks. "I didn't mean to," she said apologetically.

"I know you didn't." Kole wiped a fresh tear from her face with his thumb. "C'mon, Felix, let's get out of here."

"Gladly. Cold-hearted lowlifes, the whole lot of ya." Felix rose his voice so no patron missed his insult.

Kole and Felix helped Vienna outside. The disturbance had reached the road, and a few passersby stopped and peered at Kole and his companions as they hurried away from the scene.

"What happened?" Kole sat Vienna on a stoop around the corner.

"I happened." Her shoulders slouched forward, but it seemed more from embarrassment than exhaustion.

"'S'not yer fault. Ya can't help it." Felix paced the road. "Next time, I'll go alone, and we'll sneak her in after."

Kole offered Vienna his water. She took a deep drink. "Next time?" Vienna croaked when she'd finished. "I don't think anyone will take us once word spreads."

Kole heard the trepidation in her voice. "She's right. They got a good look at all of us. We can try further up the road. Find a neighboring town maybe?"

Felix's gaze turned west. He frowned.

Despite the afternoon hour, the sun hung dangerously close to the horizon. Winter sapped the day away quicker than Kole expected. Even now, with the long shadows striping the town, the temperature had begun its nightly drop. By the time they made it back to the rambler and set off, they'd have maybe a half hour to search for shelter. And that "neighboring town" could sit anywhere between here and Zeal. Felix must've shared Kole's thoughts, because he shook his head, sending his curls bouncing.

"Caradin?" Felix asked. "Can he—hey, where is the bloody beast anyway?"

Kole lowered his eyes to his shoulder, giving the go ahead, and a strawberry-pink nose poked out of his hood.

Felix jumped back. "A rat?"

"Weasel," Kole corrected, then patted the small nose. The Soul sniffed in response.

"Whatever ya say, Blondie." His mouth pulled to one side. "Think he can help us out?"

"If you mean heal me, Felix, you know my answer." Vienna pushed the waterskin into Kole's hands, as if holding it was a sign of weakness. "It's needless."

"I wouldn't call tendin' ta someone sprayin' blood like a spittin' llama needless. You're sick, V."

"No." The force of her answer made her breaths come heavy, but she kept her back straight.

The weasel sent a feeling of worry to Kole. He responded with an image of Vienna weak and bloody. "*Sick.*" Caradin seemed to understand the word.

"Hey! You kids!"

Kole and Felix stiffened at the voice.

"Shit," Felix cursed. "Guess they sent for the town watch."

They both grabbed Vienna's arms and lifted her to her feet. She let them half-drag, half-carry her down the road, but they only managed a few yards before the voice called again.

"Wait up!" Whoever it was had gained, and a stout man rounded them to cut them off.

"We're on our way, sir, promise." Kole wished it'd be enough to defuse the situation before more people got involved. They'd already caused enough of a stir.

The man sported a bald spot and a thick beard. His rounded features softened at Kole's words. After a quick look around the road, he said just above a whisper, "No need for that. I saw what happened back at Jessa's place, and I can give you somewhere to stay for the night. Just follow me, will you?"

Kole and Felix locked eyes. His friend's expression almost made Kole laugh as they both held a face of heavy suspicion. A choking noise from Vienna erased both their concerns. Probably holding in another cough. She needed to get out of the cold.

At their nod, the man led them away from the noisy street. They avoided the crowded paths, whether for Kole and his companions' sake or the villagers', and eventually came upon a great field on the eastern outskirts. Cows and goats meandered in the blowing grass. A small house sat at the end of the worn footpath, but the man veered left and brought them to a large barn. He stopped them at the open door. The faint odor of manure and animal wafted from the interior.

"Feels like the first freeze is coming early this year. You shouldn't be out in it." He flicked his eyes to his house a little way off, then guiltily back to them.

"The barn?" Felix gave it a once over.

"I'm bringing the animals in so the place should be warm enough. You can sleep on the hay in the loft." When Vienna gave a weak cough, he took a step away, keeping his distance. "I wish I could offer more, but I can't risk...." His eyes stayed on Vienna, as if expecting a spray of blood like back at the inn. "She's got gray lung, I can tell. Hope it's no offense, but I can't have you staying in close quarters with me and my family. I can assure you no one else will take you in on this side of the Coroko. I can bring you food and water, but I'll need you out before dawn. Can't have anyone knowing I let you stay here. You understand?"

"We do," Kole said before Felix, who'd been fidgeting and passively huffing the whole time, had a chance to protest. "Thank you for your kindness. Mister...."

The man cleared his throat. "No names. Sure you understand that as well." He turned to leave and said over his shoulder. "The light'll come on at dusk, no need searching for lanterns. I'll put food out here by the door." Then he set off for the field.

Kole and Felix assisted Vienna up the ladder to the loft and settled her atop a pile of hay. Even with the cover of a blanket, the thick stalks poked and scratched Kole's skin. He set up his own spot while Felix cleaned the dried blood from Vienna's mouth and chin. Caradin jumped from Kole's shoulder and curled into a ball on the blanket. A draft whistled through the thin crack of the loft doors at the far end of the open room. Kole shivered against it.

"What's this?" Felix asked.

Kole turned to find Felix tugging the crystal pendant from the cover of Vienna's collar. She locked eyes with Kole instantly, then looked back to her brother, face flush. "It's a gift. Kole gave it to me."

Felix glanced to Kole for a moment, back to Vienna, then let the crystal flower drop gently back to her neck. "Where'd ya get somethin' fancy like that, Blondie?"

For some odd reason, Kole's voice refused to work. A mix of dread and embarrassment flooded him. His stomach flipped. "I, uh...."

"Grayfall. When he snuck out and had his little adventure without us," Vienna said, coming to his aid. She tucked the pendant beneath her shirt.

Kole flinched as Felix snapped up, hands on his hips, jaw set. He tapped his foot out of... impatience? Anger? Kole froze. He swore his heart skipped a few beats. Had he made Felix upset by giving his sister a gift? *Of course, how stupid.* Felix might think something more of the gesture. Then again, it had meant something more for Kole. He expected the worst when Felix opened his mouth.

"Hold on." Felix pointed a chastising finger toward Kole. "Ya mean ta tell me ya cheated me outta explorin' Grayfall, stole without me, *and* didn't bring back anythin' for me? Where's *my* souvenir, Kole?"

A gurgle came from Vienna. It took a moment for Kole to recognize it as a struggled laugh.

That small reaction cleared the nervous haze from Kole and allowed him to spot the signs he'd missed before; the slight half-smirk on Felix's mouth flinching every so often as if holding back his own laugh, the glint of humor growing stronger behind his green eyes as Kole's silence extended.

Kole cracked a smile of his own. "That color doesn't suit you."

Felix dropped his jaw dramatically, feigning offence. "How dare you."

Before Kole knew it, a waded blanket flew at his face. The soft thud did little more than bump his scars. The blanket had merely been a ruse, as the heft of a body tackled Kole into the hay. Caradin squealed and darted out of the way of Kole and Felix's wrestling match.

"Hey you two, be careful," Vienna said from the sideline. "I can't drag you out of here, you know. Best I can do is roll you down the ladder."

A few tumbles in the straw made Kole wince. His wounded legs had slipped his mind. Felix must've heard Kole's hiss because he jumped away.

"Ya all right, Blondie?"

"I told you to be careful," Vienna chided.

Kole prodded the sore spot. "Yeah, just... riding rash is all."

"It was from *before*," Felix snapped back at Vienna. He helped Kole to his blanket, then grabbed some clean cloth from their packs and tossed it over. "Wrap 'em. The pressure'll help with the pain."

Tapping hooves, snorts, and whines echoed below as the animals gathered inside. Kole peered through the wood-slatted floor and watched the man herd each animal to its appropriate stall. With the barn door leading to the pasture closed, a stuffy warmth permeated the loft. The man hurriedly put out fresh nets of hay for his livestock, then skittered out. The moment the door closed behind him, a faint light grew from the corners of the barn.

Kole looked overhead to the strange stone affixed to the roof's apex. He stood and squinted against the lights. That familiar glow... those faint lines in the white, radiant rock. "Moonstone? Out here?" He'd only ever seen it in the tunnels below Socren. The Liberation used the material to light their underground hideout.

"Huh," Felix followed Kole's finger to the stone. "Guess so."

"I'm not surprised." Vienna shifted to one side and pulled out the map. "The crystal trees aren't far from here. "We'll have to go straight through them to get to Zeal. They probably mine them out, but it is odd they'd be in a barn. They're an unrenewable resource. You'd think they'd use it sparingly."

"The trees don't grow back?" Kole wrapped his thighs, pulling tight enough that the pain subsided while leaving enough slack as to not agitate his scars. He remembered Piper, of all people, had been the one to inform him moonstone wasn't stone at all, but pieces of tree. Not wood per se, but somewhere between that and rock.

"They don't grow at all. They're petrified."

"But the lines...." Kole knew the trees had aged, for each ring meant another season of growth.

"They grew at one point when they were normal trees—alive. Since they petrified, it's like they're stuck in time," said Vienna.

Kole chewed his bottom lip. He knew the answer to his question before he asked it, but he needed to hear it to be sure. "When did they petrify?"

Vienna's eyes moved from Kole to the sleeping weasel. "When the Souls left Ohr. That's what Leo's research suggests. No one really knows, I suppose. It was a long time ago."

Just as he thought. The world turned upside-down when Aterus locked his kin away. He shivered again, this time from the sprouting guilt. Was he doing the right thing? Kole swallowed hard, pushing back the rising feeling. *There is no true right anymore.* "Shikar would know. She would've been alive then."

"That's right." Felix smiled fondly as if thinking of their old Yamani friend. "The whole, they don't die thing and all."

"Not naturally." Kole thought of her laying in the shallow grave he'd hastily made. She deserved better. He'd spotted Vienna's mark on the map flagging the location. One day, if he made it out of all of this, he'd return and give her a proper send off. "There's so much I wish I could've asked her."

"I hear ya, mate." Felix twisted a piece of straw between his fingers, but his jaw set hard.

Felix had the most to lose from her death. No one else on Ohr carried the knowledge of cohabitating with a Kayetan. In that loneliness, Kole felt a kinship. They shared more than that, though. They shared pain and scars, physical ones, life altering ones. Kole guessed that was another reason they got on so well.

"Maybe we can help." Kole finished securing the cloth on his other leg. "Have you tried merging with your shadow since the last time?"

Felix shrugged. "Hasn't really been a reason to."

"Merging? What are you talking about?" Vienna leaned forward, concern flickering in her gaze.

"I've been... playin' around with my Kayetan. Do things I don't think even Shikar knew 'bout." At her frown, Felix added, "Don't be upset. It only happened once, and I wanted ta keep it ta myself till I had a better handle on it. Don't even know what all it does really."

"We can find out now." Kole waved around the loft. "Not like we're going anywhere. Plus, if you wait for a reason to use it, you won't be prepared when you truly need it. It's all about practice." Kole surprised himself at his own wisdom. It seemed all those years training with Russé rubbed off on him more than he'd thought.

Felix peeked over at his sister sheepishly as if looking for permission.

"Might as well try while we're all together. What's the worst that could happen?"

"I dunno. It could take me over and kill us all," Felix mumbled.

Kole couldn't quite discern if Felix meant it or if it was a bout of sarcasm. "You know that's not true," Kole scolded. "You control it, remember? And if something does go wrong, we have Caradin."

Felix blew a raspberry. "Hear that, rat? Ya gotta job ta do."

The weasel only blinked up at him.

Felix stood then pulled up his sleeves, exposing the strange bracelets of shadow seeping from the scars on his wrists. Though Shikar could've offered wisdom and guidance to Felix about his shadow — communicating, co-existing — she hadn't possessed this. Kole reckoned these wisping shadows from Felix's wrists were an anomaly. Only Felix could figure out their mystery.

The Kayetan appeared at his master's call, emerging from the floorboards. The shadow remained still before Felix, as if awaiting command.

"Good so far," Kole said.

Felix's Adam's apple bobbed, then he held out both hands. The shadow mimicked his movements, and the moment darkness touched flesh, the green of Felix's eyes shrouded in a wave of black.

"How's it going?" Kole asked.

"Same as last time. I can see through both our eyes." The deepened voice must've alarmed Vienna because she flinched away and cast a wary glance at Kole.

"It's fine," he mouthed, then focused back on Felix.

"Think I'm gonna invite him in."

"You can do this," Kole encouraged. If coexisting with a Kayetan was anything like taming a rambler, Felix needed confidence more than anything. "Take it slow."

Immediately, the Kayetan slithered away, its entire body seeping into the dancing shadows at Felix's wrists.

"Any lights?" Kole asked. Last time Felix and his Kayetan had merged, they'd seen Niko, or at least his aura. But with Niko cast away at the moment, Kole felt confident his secret would remain just that.

"Not this time," Felix answered.

Kole sat back, a bit more relaxed at that answer. "What else do you feel? What's different?" The weasel curled up in his lap, and Kole absentmindedly stroked the length of his spine with two fingers.

"My body... it's—" Felix hunched forward, a snarl of pain ripping from his lips.

"Felix!" Vienna moved to touch him but stopped her hand when shadow pulsed from Felix's body. "What's happening? Kole?"

"I don't know. He has to do it on his own."

She glared at Kole but snapped her mouth shut and dropped her hand, allowing the experimentation to continue.

"It wants... more of me," Felix said through his teeth, resisting.

"Stay in control. Only go as far as you feel...." Shadowed claws sprouted from Felix's knuckles. "Comfortable," Kole finished. He swept Caradin off his lap and climbed to his feet.

Felix lifted his hands, his black eyes widening at the sight of the ghostly claws. "No!" he screamed. He rattled his hands, as if trying to shake them off. When Felix moved, his body blurred—delving further into a shadow-like state. Felix must've noticed it too, because his whole demeanor changed. Pure panic took him. He doubled over and screamed, "Get out!"

The Kayetan funneled out from Felix's body through his wrists. The shadow reformed and lingered in the corner while Felix collapsed into the pile of hay. "I can't do it. I can't. I'm sorry."

Vienna hushed him and stroked his arm. "You did good, Felix. That's enough for one night."

In that moment, at the sight of those ethereal claws extending from his friend's hands, Kole realized Felix's potential—what powers he possessed beyond anything Shikar had at her call. Shadow and flesh separated had its own advantages, but this... coming back together as one....

Felix could be more than human. More than Kayetan. Something Ohr had never seen. The possibility excited him. But that feeling fled faster than it came as he watched Felix curled up in the straw. His friend's trauma proved too much. Kole could only imagine what it must be like to ally with the creature that killed not only your parents but tormented your whole city for years.

Vienna was right: it was enough for tonight.

CHAPTER 13

The heavy breaths of the farm animals below along with the rasp of Vienna's desperate gasps of sleep and the bright glow of the moonstone kept Kole awake. Felix had retrieved the food from the door, where the man had promised to drop it off. They'd eaten their fill and saved what they could for morning. Felix's Kayetan had been sent to patrol the barn. The animals had shuffled uneasily at the streak of shadow when it exited the building but had since settled.

"Niko?" Kole whispered.

He appeared immediately. "Yes, shepherd? Is it safe to come out now?" Niko teased.

"Sorry. I just can't risk getting caught talking to you. They'd get suspicious if they knew you were here."

"I get it. No need to explain. They don't understand your decision." Niko sunk down so his ghostly form lay next to Kole, mimicking the same position with his elbow propped up.

"I don't think they ever will."

Niko's mouth twisted to a half frown. Then his gaze fell to the white weasel curled up next to Kole's stomach. "Is that him? The mighty Caradin? I think the stag form was more regal."

"It's also more noticeable."

"The form doesn't matter, I suppose. At least you have another ally, right?"

"Right...." Kole sighed. "About that."

Niko lifted his brows expectantly. "The ritual worked. I saw you do it."

"The ritual worked, but the deal is... not exactly made." Kole filled Niko in on Caradin's limited language.

"So, you never actually made the deal?" Anger flashed behind Niko's eyes. The crease in his forehead deepened the way it always had when he disagreed with Kole.

"He doesn't understand it. How can I?"

"But he calls you master?"

"I think that's an aftereffect of the imprisonment. He was far more gone from reality than Issira or Obell. He acts like an animal. But I think he's learning. He seems to understand some words. I can teach him and make the deal when he's regained himself."

Niko sat up. "That's not the issue, Kole. You've lost your bargaining chip. Why would he agree now? He's already free."

Kole ground his teeth as he thought. Maybe Niko was right. Did he really have nothing? He huffed. What luck? The first Soul he had released on his own for his cause and he'd already wrecked it. Would Aterus know? "I hadn't thought of that. I just thought I'd make him when it came down to it."

"You need to do it soon. He has to agree before he learns too much. Convince him. Tell him your story—all that you know—from the very beginning. He might understand."

"Sure hope so. Or it's all for nothing." Kole shook the matter away. He'd save the worry for another day. "I called you to be a look out."

Niko folded his arms. "For what?"

"I'm going to reach out to the next Soul."

"So soon? Don't you need rest or something? I mean you did just die. Guess I don't know how this all works."

A rough laugh escaped Kole. "Neither do I. Better to get things done fast since Russé... well, he knows something's up. Nothing about the deal, I know that much, but I bet he's more anxious than ever to find me. I have to release the rest of them before he gets to me."

Niko nodded.

"Just tell me if they wake." He waved a hand at the siblings. "Or if I get too loud."

"Sure thing, Shepherd Kole."

Kole smirked and shook his head. That title brought back a sense of his naive self, when the greatest danger had been the ramblers. Looking back now, things had been so easy and peaceful. He let the thought fade and nudged Caradin awake.

The weasel yawned. Heavy lidded eyes trained on Kole.

"Protect Master," Kole sent the thought along with an image. Only when Caradin perked up, seemingly understanding, did Kole begin his delve into his mind.

Focused, calm breaths just the way Russé had trained him. He stilled his body until his heartbeat grew louder, deafening within his ears. He swore he could hear blood pulsing through his veins. Silence. Control. Each time seemed easier than the last.

There was a chance, Kole feared, that when he opened himself up to the next Soul, it'd leave him susceptible for Russé to connect again and learn his whereabouts, maybe more.

"Keep Russé out," Kole instructed Caradin, whose presence swelled in response.

Kole quickly found the state of a waking dream as he'd been taught before. A moment later, he met the stronghold around his private thoughts that separated him from the other Souls. Behind this invisible barrier lay seven doors, like pathways or portals, which served as connections to each god. A thicker wall stood before Russé's, Issira's, and Obell's door. He couldn't have them finding him. Caradin's lay open, free to roam Kole's head as he pleased. The others, the Souls that had yet to be released, possessed no barriers, but they remained locked. One drew Kole's attention.

A longing—no, something much stronger—a ravenous urge thrummed from the opposite side. The next Soul in line.

Kole's body shook with a deep-rooted shudder, then he thrust his mind from the safety of his own consciousness and barreled into the ominous door.

It burst open and....

... quiet.

Pure nothingness.

Kole lingered in the doorway. *"Hello?"* His greeting echoed in the void beyond the portal.

No response. Not even a feeling... as if it lay empty. Was that even possible? Every Soul he'd opened up to had given him something. If not words, then a feeling of some sort. And he had felt an urge *before* he'd opened the path not a second ago. Where had that gone?

While Kole waited for something—anything—Caradin issued a warning. A building pressure poked against the bubble of Kole's mind. An intruder.

Russé.

Kole cut his connection with the new Soul short, then retreated to his own head, fortifying the barrier as he passed through. With Caradin's and Kole's strength combined, Russé had no chance of breaking through. Pressure built here and there along the edges of Kole's mind where Russé prodded for a weak spot. After a short while, his old mentor's presence faded away.

Kole pulled from himself and opened his eyes.

"Finally back?" Niko floated before him. "I thought you'd fallen asleep."

"How long was I out?"

"Almost an hour."

Strange. The whole thing had felt no longer than a minute in Kole's head.

"What did you get?"

Kole plopped back onto the blanket. Pieces of straw shot free and zipped over the floorboards as he sighed. "Just when I think I've got a handle on things."

"Not good, then?"

"I didn't get anything." Kole scanned the area for Caradin, who he found nestling up next to his hip. "Russé tried to get in while I was distracted." He patted the weasel on the head with a finger. "Good thing I have you, I guess."

"You'll get it next time," Niko said.

Kole propped up on his elbows. "I don't know if I will. This was different. When I connected... it was like the Soul was gone. Missing." He let his head fall back and stared at the rafters. "Why is it always so complicated?"

"Vara."

"What?" Kole asked.

Niko shook his head. "I didn't say anything."

"But I heard—" Kole paused. The name had been a thought sent from Caradin. Their connection was growing so fluid, sound and thought registered the same. He glanced down to the weasel.

"Vara." Caradin nuzzled his nose under Kole's hand and crawled under, using it as a blanket.

"How do you know it's her?" Kole probed. "Tell Master."

"Feel Vara."

"Where do you feel her?"

The animal held a sense of confusion that then morphed to irritation, probably unable to find the proper words. Caradin slipped from Kole's hand and wandered a few steps toward the doors of the loft. *"There."*

"Vara is here?" Kole said aloud.

Caradin pointed his nose again. *"There."*

"What's he saying?" Niko leaned in.

"Vara is there?" Kole pointed a finger in the same direction as Caradin's wriggling strawberry nose. To the corner of the loft. No way a

Soul would be held in some random, mundane barn. Then it dawned on him. "In that direction?"

The weasel squeaked a confirmation.

"The weasel is a compass now?" Niko asked.

"Better than what *I* got." Kole opened his hand and let Caradin curl up around his wrist and palm. "*That direction* could mean anywhere between this barn and the Black Wall. How are we supposed to find her? Time isn't really a luxury."

"Triangulation," said a hoarse voice.

Kole snapped his head to the noise and tensed. Vienna had sat up, but Felix slept, out cold, next to her.

She stared at him. A blankness washed her features as if a deep sleep still weighed on her. "Who are you talking to?"

He fought the urge to glance at Niko. "Caradin," he said steadily, hoping her grogginess would aid his lie. "I reached out to the next Soul. Vara."

"I heard." Vienna's gaze swung to where Niko's ghost hovered. She blinked a few times, analyzing the spot, then returned her attention to Kole and the weasel. "We could try triangulation."

The muscles in Kole's neck eased. "What's that?"

"Something Leo taught me. You plot a location based off two points or directions. I'll show you." She waved him over.

Kole scooped up Caradin and crawled over, careful to keep his inner thighs from touching as to not loosen his wraps. By the stiffness and occasional sharp pain, he could tell they had already started scabbing. He settled in beside her.

Vienna had her map out, and she smoothed the curling edges. She placed a finger on their position. "You said you know which way, right? Like a compass?"

Kole nodded. He risked a glance at the ghostly form of his friend, who swirled behind Vienna and peeked over her shoulder.

"Don't worry, she can't see or hear me, remember?" Niko said. "Just pretend I'm not here."

Kole rolled his eyes and let out an involuntary huff that drew Vienna's attention. The sides of her mouth pursed, but she ignored him and grabbed a piece of straw.

"From this point, if you lay down a line like this," Vienna placed the straw down in the direction Kole had indicated, "you have a million different places the Soul could be hidden along this line." A second twig of hay graced the map. "But if you add one more location along with the direction, then at some point the paths will cross." The two pieces of straw crossed over each other like an X. She poised her finger above the location. "The intersection—where the two lines meet—would be your target. The Soul."

"Where did you find this girl? I like her." Niko stared at the map in awe, and Kole couldn't help but smile. This sort of thing—mapping, logging, tracking, measuring—was Niko's specialty. Back in the forest, he'd had a raggedy old journal he'd never be without and was always scribbling away in there. About the ramblers mostly. Niko had been fascinated by them. Probably hoped collecting enough data on them would finally reveal the secret to their abnormal size and nature. The truth behind the trees had been grander than either of them had expected.

"Seems simple enough," Kole said. "We just need a second location, then, right?"

Vienna merely stared at the map. Chunks of hair, fallen free of her mangled braid, curtained her face. A drop of maroon tapped down on the parchment.

Blood. Not again.

"Vienna?" Kole leaned in, trying to catch a glimpse of her face through the mask of hair.

She lifted up, body swaying slightly side to side like the inebriated drunkards Kole had seen back in Socren; her eyes solid green, the pupils so small they resembled black pinpricks. But it was the streak of red down her cheek that frightened him the most. A tear of blood.

"I don't... feel so well." Vienna fell back.

Kole dove in and caught her. He screamed for Felix when more blood-like tears slipped from the corners of her rolled-back eyes. Once Felix jumped up and took Vienna from him, Kole raced for their supplies and sent Caradin scurrying down the ladder, where the Soul transformed into his previous elk form on Kole's commanded thought.

"C'mon, V. Fight it." Felix held his sister's head upright so the blood pooling in her mouth and nose would drain out instead of collecting in her throat and choking her. Breathing already proved laborious. They needed to ensure she kept an open airway.

"Get her down the ladder," Kole said as he slugged a heavy pack over each shoulder. The weight nearly crippled him, especially with his wounded legs, but he gritted his teeth and pushed on.

"Down... Kole? What?" Felix's eyes trailed up from Vienna's limp body to Kole. Panic had set in at the sight of his sister's deteriorating condition. No longer cool and collected. He merely sat there, dumbstruck.

Kole clenched his jaw. An overwhelmed Felix meant he'd have to take the lead on this one. "Get her down the ladder and onto Caradin's back," he said more sternly. "We are going to Zeal."

For a moment, Kole wondered if Felix would comply or if he had strayed too far into panic mode to register a thing Kole had said. Then Felix began dragging Vienna toward the ladder.

Kole dropped their bags over the ledge, where they landed with a hard thump. The barn animals jumped at the noise and skittered around the stalls, some squealing in fright. He helped lift Vienna over Felix's shoulder then followed down the ladder.

Kole and Felix slumped her over the stag's back, but her body rolled to one side in her unconscious state and nearly fell off the other side. One of them needed to accompany her. Kole worried if Felix could handle it after his reaction in the loft. No. Felix was the best option. He *had* to be ready for this. "Get on," he tapped Felix's back encouragingly.

His friend, dazed, followed the command without question. With the support of Felix's arms, Vienna lay securely on the elk, pinned to the back of the animals' neck. Once settled, Felix reached out to help Kole up.

"Run to Zeal," said Kole, stepping away from the open hand. When Felix's face finally registered the words, he opened his mouth to protest, but Kole cut in, "I will catch up. Just go. Keep her safe."

Something between concern and understanding passed over Felix's expression as his mouth twisted in a frown.

"Lead him there. Caradin won't know the way." Kole shoved the map into Felix's hand. One last look at Vienna's bluing face, then he ran to the barn doors and shoved them open. "Run," he shouted aloud and into Caradin's thoughts. That word the Soul knew, for the mighty stag sprang forward and within the span of Kole's long exhale, disappeared into the night.

"Kole?" Niko's voice came beside him.

He'd forgotten about Niko in the madness. "A part of me wants to follow them."

"You're going to, aren't you?" Niko asked.

If Kole had gone in Felix's place, he would've had a more difficult time convincing anyone for help, what with his notable scars and Vienna's sickness. They barely attained assistance here. "They don't need me."

Niko stayed quiet at that.

"The other part of me wants to search for Vara alone." Something sat odd within him. Had Vienna's need not been dire, would he have called the rambler instead? Sent the siblings on their way with the tree and kept Caradin to begin their search? Abandoned them?

The joyful memories of the earlier hours crept into his mind; wrestling with Felix, the siblings' teasing. How quickly it had soured.

"They don't need me, but I need Caradin." Kole smiled at the ghost. "Keep me company on the rambler?"

"Always."

CHAPTER 14

The journey back to the rambler with both packs took longer than Kole anticipated with his limping stride. Blankets of frost settled over the grass, silver tipped in the early-morning hour. The first freeze of the year, as the villager had predicted. Though the chill nipped Kole's ears, nose, and fingertips, the cool temperature kept his body from overheating. That alone kept him moving.

The rambler stirred when he neared. By the time the gear had been loaded and the tree took off east, Kole had surrendered to exhaustion. He fell back against the trunk and let the rambler take over navigation after he declared their course.

Only when he opened his eyes did he realize he'd fallen asleep. A root slid under his chin and pointed his gaze to an ethereal glow in the distance. An ocean of radiant light. The hue reminded Kole of the aura Caradin had held before he'd been released. They neared, and the distinct shape of trees emerged. The forest he'd long heard of right before his eyes.

The Crystal Trees.

He'd made it. Not far to Zeal now, which, according to Vienna's map, lay just beyond the forest.

The trees here looked like bone, not just from the whitish color but the way the leafless branches poised themselves. No smooth or curving lines reaching for the sky. Instead, they compared to skeletons. Each shift in direction of growth in the branches held a bulbous quality, like a joint in a leg or arm.

"I think I prefer these over ramblers." Niko hovered beside Kole. "Less likely to get killed by them."

"No arguing with that," Kole admitted.

The rambler shared in Kole's sense of awe, even finding more speed to close in quicker. On the edge of the forest line, they slowed pace. The divine-like trees crowded too closely for Kole's rambler to barrel through without desecrating them, an important thing to avoid, since Vienna told him the crystal trees had stopped growing long ago. Kole smirked as his rambler lifted its roots and arced them over the trees, which stood at a normal height to anyone else but appeared dwarfed in the presence of a rambler. The walking tree continued in a sort of tiptoe through the delicate forest.

Vienna and Felix would have passed through already. Surely Caradin had an easier time maneuvering through the terrain. Any distance Kole and his rambler had gained in the open fields had certainly been lost now.

He let the beauty of the place dull his senses for a time. They passed too closely to a shining crystal arm reaching out its frozen fingers. His rambler chipped off a twig or two. They shattered like glass and glittered down to the forest floor. Kole longed to hold one, inspect it. The rambler must've sensed his curiosity because without command, his tree retrieved a piece and presented the rock-like shard to Kole. He flinched as it dropped into his palm. Cool on his skin. He had expected it to hold a warmth, though he couldn't say why. No wonder it had been named moonstone. Everything about it reminded him of the half-obscured orb poised overhead.

"What're you doing?" Niko asked.

"I want to try something." Closing his hand, Kole let his connection with the rambler move to the fragment of crystal in his clutched fist. The presence of the stone differed from his rambler. Older. Ancient. But he still felt a sense of life, however faint. Vienna had claimed them petrified, yet he could clearly tell that wasn't the case. The feeling coming off the jewel-like wood felt more like... hibernation?

When Kole opened his eyes again, he found Niko's keen gaze on him. "It's alive to some extent. A living fossil."

Something about his words made Niko laugh. "Like me, I suppose."

Kole laughed too. He pocketed the fragment and glanced around at the wavering light of the trees. The brightness waned like dying coals of a fire. Night was coming to an end.

Before long, all was gray. Not the dreary gray of the Ashland Plains but blue tinged. The quiet moment just before dawn. Memories of the early mornings of his childhood played in his thoughts. The time when the walking trees of Solpate Forest would wind down from their nightly romp and root back into the soil like normal trees. Twilight marked the end of the dangerous times for him and his fellow refugees. That was back when Kole had feared the ramblers; feared their size and strength, feared being trampled by the gargantuan beasts who barely acknowledged the insect-like existence of the refugees. So far he had come, now in control over those distant fears, leading a rambler of his own.

And being here with Niko like this—the two of them riding atop a tamed rambler together—was something Kole had dreamt about doing since he could remember. Except he never imagined this as their fates. Kole glanced over at Niko's ghost then at his own mutilated skin. *Bittersweet.*

Here in the dawn, he felt at peace with himself—of what had become of that naïve and ignorant boy. Innocence had dissolved along with his skin when he passed through the Black Wall. That had marked the end of his childhood.

Colors grew vivid as the sun pulled the tip of its crown over the land, gilding the tops of the darkening crystal trees. The forest thinned, and in the distance towered a sight that sparked a new marvel within Kole. He caught a root to the canopy and climbed to the peak of the rambler.

Niko followed, flying easily beside him.

To call this place a city seemed like an affront to the grandeur—the sheer size. Kole looked left and right. Structures as far as his eyes could see, even with his vantage point. How far did it extend? No mere city. Zeal was its own world.

An assortment of buildings decorated the landscape. Some tall and pointed like massive stalagmites, others rounded domes, and scattered here and there, structures art-like in design. Not simply squared or rounded but pointed in star shapes and curved swirls Kole never thought gravity would allow.

"Wow." Kole caught a metallic reflection off one of the taller buildings embracing the first light of day. "Metal? All the way up there?"

Niko followed Kole's pointed finger to the building. "Not just up there, the whole thing. Look around."

His friend was right. More brilliant flashes gleamed about the city as the sun bounced off the sides of buildings. Brick and wood, it seemed, were predominately used in the smaller, more quaint counterparts, yet none could be called plain. Subtle flairs like flipped-up edging on the roofs or grand mosaic chimneys decorated the houses. It pained Kole to think he'd never seen Zeal before—never knew of its splendor.

"We should go on foot from here," Kole said as he anchored the rambler a half mile after departing the Crystal Trees. He'd only ridden this far because he felt confident no one would notice the giant tree in the background of a city like this. "See if you can spot Caradin's tracks while I grab our things."

Niko nodded and flew off.

Three packs. Easy enough to get them down with the roots, but how on Ohr would he haul them alone? At least the trek to the city offered open, level land. He even spotted a well-maintained road a little ways north. The harder part would come when he got to the city. The last thing he wanted was to wander about alone, blindly searching for his friends. Maybe by then he'd be close enough to tune into Caradin's thoughts. If not through words, the Soul may still reveal their position with a detailed enough image.

Kole placed a hand on the rambler's root and encouraged it to anchor. "Rest well. This might take some time."

Like a child stretching before settling down, the great tree rose to its full height, wood groaning, then burrowed its roots until the base of its trunk plunked on the grass. One root brushed playfully along Kole's waist before drilling down with the others.

"I'll miss you, too," Kole murmured to the goliath.

The rambler groaned, then fell into a deep, still sleep.

Kole slung the packs over his shoulder one by one and began his shaky hike toward Zeal.

Niko had discovered deer tracks, but the trail ended on the paved road a quarter mile from the city. Kole followed the prints to their end, regardless. Tracing their steps led to smooth ground, which was what Kole needed at the moment, and there was a chance he'd run into someone who might have seen where the trio had gone.

Just Kole's luck, he encountered no one until the post on the edge of Zeal. Kole made a point to keep his mask down, hanging loose at his neck, but pulled his hood over his brow, casting a shadow on most of his face.

"Stop there, boy." The guard wore a uniform instead of armor. No leather hide or metal chest piece, just a collared shirt tucked into navy slacks and a slim-fitted, matching vest. An array of metal buttons and pins lay proudly fastened over his breast.

Kole stopped before the guard, eyeing his comrade, who casually leaned against the post.

Niko positioned himself between Kole and the guard. "If he gives you any trouble, I'll blow in his ear while you make a run for it."

Kole rolled his eyes in the safety of the shadow his hood provided. Any more than that and the guards may think Kole deranged, talking to himself.

"Where are you coming from?"

"The town on the other side of the Crystal Trees." Kole made a point to slump his shoulders and look smaller. His already petite figure aided in this feat. Farmhand. Some sort of apprentice. He'd be grateful to pass for either.

"Folks don't usually return to Zeal, even for trade."

Maybe this would prove trickier than he'd thought. Getting caught in a lie wouldn't help his cause, so he tried for the truth. Sparingly. "My friends came through here earlier. One of them is sick."

That was all it took. The guard stepped back, putting a healthy space between him and Kole. "The girl with the gray lung?"

"That's them. Do you know where they've gone? We're supposed to meet up." Kole shrugged, bringing attention to his packs. "I have their stuff."

"Yeah, we sent them to the central temple." The guard turned and pointed to a shimmering gold spire that seemed to prick up from the opposite side of Zeal. "Can't miss it." He moved aside, allowing Kole to pass.

Kole dipped his head in thanks and passed him.

"You need help with those?" The guard called after him. "I could...," he cleared his throat and stepped back, "find someone to...."

"I've got it, thanks." Truth was he *did* need help. The straps dug so deeply into Kole's shoulders, it felt as if his bones themselves had bruised. But accepting help meant prolonging this encounter, and he wanted to stay as inconspicuous as possible. Not to mention, the guard seemed to backtrack on his offer. Probably afraid of getting too close to someone who'd been exposed to gray lung.

"Stick to the city limits," the guard called after him "No traveling west of the walls, kid."

After a deep breath, he braced his belly and trudged on, eyes fixed to his destination, the gold needle of a building.

"I'd help you if I could." Niko swiped his hand through the strap as if checking on his spectral status.

"I know. Just scout ahead for me."

Past the wall, the bustle of morning activity hit Kole's ears. Dozens of animal-drawn carts and people crowded the street. It was the widest road Kole had seen, yet he barely managed to squeeze through to the marginally calmer foot traffic on the north side. There were so many people, he seemed to blend right into the crowd. *Invisible*. He smiled at the thought.

In windows to his right, a store owner flipped a sign, and the crowd that had piled up by the door rushed in. Kole gave them a wide berth as he passed. His stomach practically roared at the tantalizing scent of sweet bread streaming out from the bakery. Cinnamon. He knew that smell. Kole had a sudden urge to explore the town with Felix. Last time they'd been in Socren, Kole had frowned upon Felix swiping food. But Kole's stomach had known nothing but fish, stale bread, and wild game for the last few weeks. He craved something with the kind of sweetness that would ache the back of his jaw. And something fresh. He'd kill for fruit!

Kole shook the images of plump berries from his head. No distractions. The temple. That's where he needed to be.

The gold needle peeked over the line of shops. He turned right at the corner then staggered back as a shout rose above the steady babble of the city. A few paused, too, glancing in the direction of the noise but soon returned to their tasks and conversations. Kole spotted a blur rushing into the road. Horses and mules whinnied and reared as the person swerved dangerously close to the animals. Carts collided. Logs tumbled onto the road. Two guards, dressed in the same suit-like uniforms as at the city entrance, pursued and tackled the instigator.

"The fire will cleanse! Receive it and be enlightened!" The man pinned to ground struggled against the guards.

Kole stared at the man spewing more and more of these odd lines, not because of the words, but because of his face. Red. Corded. *Burned*. The skin held a thick sheen as if oozing, and dark patches flecked his face and neck. It was how Kole's skin had looked right after Russé had pulled him from the flames of the Black Wall. Before he'd healed. This man's wounds were fresh. Maybe hours... a day at most.

Kole wanted to run to him. *And do what? Draw more attention to myself?* He huffed. Not much he could do in an unfamiliar city with three packs weighing him down. Still, as the guards escorted the burned man away and the road resumed its flow, his thoughts stayed on those burns. What did it mean? His paranoia was taking over. *I'm reading too much into it. Anyone can be burned.*

"Kole, this way," Niko called from up the street.

Kole made sure to keep his head down as he lumbered to the temple. The sun reflected so brightly off the metal roof, he had to shield his eyes from the brilliance. Finally, he found escape under the overhang of the plated roof of the spire. He let his hand fall from his eyes and stopped before two giant hammered metal doors embossed with an intricate design, which depicted an arm bringing down a forge hammer on an anvil. Seven circles encased the carving. He'd know that imagery anywhere.

"They really go all out here, don't they?" Niko nodded to the ornate door.

The cold metal nipped Kole's skin as he shoved his shoulder into the broad side. They opened easy and smooth.

Niko hesitated by the door.

"What's wrong?"

"Nothing. It's just... your friends are in there, and I tend to get in the way."

"You don't get in the way, Niko. Never say that."

Niko smiled. "Thanks, but I guess what I mean is, I distract you. Let's not give them more reason to think you're losing it."

"They *have* been noticing," Kole confessed.

"Go on without me. I'll be around."

Kole nodded then slipped into the grand temple.

He reveled in the warm air. The décor inside, however, contrasted with the cozy feeling. Stark, rigid metal pews lined the hall-shaped room. The ceiling towered overhead. Stained-glass portraits of forges and fire glittered the gloomy gray interior with splashes of orange, red, and yellow. Large banners hung from the crossbeams. Seven. Each held the same illustration as the door but in different colors—colors that represented the Souls. Kole turned his eyes from the green one and continued down the aisle to the pulpit.

"You must be Kole." A slight woman draped in long earth-toned robes, well-made, yet plain, stood under an archway off to the side. Her silver hair smoothed back into a tight bun and her face, though gaunt and thin-skinned, held fewer wrinkles than Kole expected given her frail appearance. How could one look so old and youthful at the same time? The sparkle of stone lay on her chest. The Seven Souls symbol. Kole had an identical one tucked away under his shirt yet smaller—no bigger than a coin. The one that sat atop the woman's simple garbs compared to two fists in size. He wondered how her neck bore such a piece.

"I am," Kole answered. He pulled the tip of his hood further down his face out of habit.

"Welcome to Zeal." Her clasped hands, bandaged in thin cloth from her fingertips to mid-forearm, opened to the empty room. The extra ribbons of fabric dangled like willow branches from the knots at her wrists. "I am Orla. Your friends will be glad to see you have arrived. Set your things down. They must be quite cumbersome. I will send someone to gather them for you."

He scanned the massive temple, clutching the packs.

Orla gave an encouraging smile and said, "They're set up in one of our rooms for now." She turned and waved, signaling him to follow, then disappeared into the side hallway.

Kole released his tight muscles and dropped the packs to the floor. A roll of his shoulders sent a shockwave of soreness over his body. The warmth of the temple made the raw patches of skin between his thighs flare up, but he hurried after the priestess. Free of his burden, he felt as lithe as the siblings.

The corridors lay quiet and empty like the main hall. Kole followed close behind the short train of Orla's robes, careful not to step on it. They turned a corner and stopped at a door.

Orla knocked then stepped away as a familiar voice called from within.

"Come in," Felix said.

The priestess nodded to Kole. "I'll give you some privacy. The councilwoman will be coming to visit you all today. I expect her a little before noon."

"Councilwoman?" Kole asked.

"It's not often Zeal sees the gray lung. Or any sickness for that matter. Councilwoman Tena herself will examine your Vienna before we move on with treatment." Something about her voice soothed him despite the curious words.

"No sickness? How is that—"

"You'll find Zeal has many advancements." Orla dipped her head. "I must go. The congregation will be arriving shortly, and I must prepare. You are welcome to sit in if you like. If you do decide to wander the city, stay within the walls." With that, she rounded the corner and left.

CHAPTER 15

The door swung open, and a wave of medicinal air burned up Kole's nose.

"Blondie!" Felix lunged for Kole and wrapped him in a bear hug. The impact slid Kole's hood off. "By Souls, I'm glad ta see ya made it. And in one piece, too. Gotta tell ya, I got a little nervous when I woke up and ya weren't here yet." Felix released him then showed him inside. "Pretty great, eh? Best night's sleep I got in my entire life."

The simplicity in design matched the rest of the temple's interior. Hard to believe this was what lay beneath the glittering golden spire. Sculpted metal rods curved around each of the four beds in the corners of the rooms, framing the stuffed mattresses like mundane jewels. Vienna lay in the one nearest the door.

"How is she?" Kole spun, taking in the empty room. "Where is Caradin?"

At the name, a tiny head lifted from behind Vienna's side. The Soul, who had reverted to weasel form, snuggled her. His ears perked toward Kole.

Felix crossed the room to Vienna's bed. He scratched behind Caradin's ear. "He changed once we made it ta the main road. Had ta carry V while this guy tickled the back of my neck the whole way through town. Ain't that right, little guy?" Caradin rubbed his cheek against the petting hand.

Kole found his mouth had fallen open. It was amusing, to say the least, to see a god cuddling and begging for scratches. Worse, Felix enabled the behavior—like he'd found a stray dog and decided to keep it. "Looks like you've bonded." Kole nodded to the weasel.

The joy of seeing Kole dissipated from Felix's face. He tugged his hand away, leaving Caradin with longing wide eyes. "Oh, I dunno—well, sure, I guess. Maybe a little. Helps when he's all cute and small." A shrug. "I'm an animal person." Then he scooted away.

Caradin rested his head between his paws on Vienna's stomach, casting those beady eyes Kole's way.

Kole leaned against the bedpost and peered down at Vienna. Her face looked whiter than the bed sheets, a shocking contrast with her dark freckles. The sound of her forced, shallow breaths filled the momentary quiet. Sweat beaded across her forehead. A good sign. The fever had broken. For now.

"Orla got her ta sleep. Made her drink somethin'. Smelled foul. V could hardly get it down, but it did the trick."

"When I talked to her, she made it seem like the people of Zeal rarely get sick." Kole spotted the chipped flower necklace peeking from the hem of the sheet. He hid his smile. "What do you know about Zeal? I've never seen anything like it."

"I had a feelin' you were gonna ask that. Tell ya the truth, not much. Vienna is the one ya wanna ask, but I doubt it's much more than what Leo's got in his books."

"These buildings. They don't seem real."

"It's even better at night, Blondie. The whole place is lit up with moonstone. You saw the crystal trees. Imagine that glow on every corner of every building. Thought I was racin' toward the stars last night." Felix gave that roguish grin. "They got gold on their roofs. Ya know they gotta have some good stuff here."

No amount of imagination could conjure up how much trouble Felix could get into in a place like Zeal. A massive city with hundreds of buildings as cover and swarms of people to conceal himself. Kole longed for the carefree rush of kicking up a bit of trouble. *Those cinnamon buns in the bakery.* He clenched his jaw and shut out the fantasy. They had a job: Vienna. The Souls. None could wait for a night of fun, unfortunately.

"Wait until Vienna is on the mend," Kole said, letting his tone hold a promise he didn't intend to keep, for he'd already decided once her health improved, he'd take Caradin and his rambler in search of the next Soul alone. This whole thing, despite their oath back in Grayfall, clearly proved too dangerous for anyone other than Kole. He'd protect them by leaving them—what Russé had wanted from the beginning.

Kole's answer caused one side of Felix's mouth to rise. "Deal."

"So what *do* you know about Zeal?"

Felix had absentmindedly gone back to stroking Cardin's cheek. "Leo said they had stuff here that put his inventions ta shame. Never thought he'd be right 'bout that." He paused for a moment, thinking.

"They don't send word ta Socren often. Kinda run their own things here. The city sent shipments of moonstone ta Leo years back. Sometimes he gets materials for spells from here."

"How do they communicate? Fiona?" Kole wished Leo's messenger hawk were here now. No matter how versatile his ghostly friend and Felix's Kayetan had been for scouting, nothing beat an aerial messenger.

He shook his head. "Zeal's got their own way of communicatin'. Somethin' they created. Has ta do with the moonstone. Leo's got a special rock he uses in his lab."

"It seems like everything has to do with the moonstone around here."

"Orla might know. I've been too worried ta really ask her much."

Kole wandered around the room. He opened a drawer. Fresh linens for the beds. He moved to the window at the back, letting in the morning sun. The pane still held the icy chill of night. "Orla said she's bringing the councilwoman here for Vienna. Think we can trust her? Any of them?" Outside, he gazed at the growing traffic. More and more people filtered out to the walkways along the roads.

"What's not ta trust, mate? Not like we can do much 'bout it anyway. The state we're in."

"I guess so." A deep thrum vibrated the temple as a bell tolled high above. A stream of people hurried across the street toward the temple entrance at the sound. The congregation Orla had rushed off to, he supposed.

"Ya gotta be tired. I'll watch the door if it makes ya feel better."

"Sleep can wait." Kole crossed to the door and peeked out to the empty hall. "I want to see what's going on."

Felix jumped up from the bed. "I'm comin' with ya."

"What about Vienna?"

He shrugged. "Caradin can watch her. I mean, he *is* a god. Who better?"

A Soul on babysitting duty. *If Russé ever finds out....* "All right, fine. Let's go." He sent his wishes to the weasel, and the animal hopped on Vienna's chest and curled up. "This all looks a bit ridiculous." Kole shook his head then stepped into the corridor, Felix close behind.

They retraced their steps to the nave, but Felix stuck close to the walls and checked the corners before progressing as if in the middle of a heist.

"What are you doing?" Kole asked. "She invited us."

"Right." Felix slowly lifted from his low stance, then shrugged. "Habit."

They reached the arch, and beyond, the empty pews were filled to capacity with patrons. Something about their faces made him pause. Each held a similar expression—blank—but he couldn't pinpoint the root of it. Not quite sadness, not quite fear. Somewhere in the middle.

Kole found himself pressing against the wall the same way he'd teased Felix for, yet his friend made no comment and followed suit. They took a spot on either side of the arch.

"Welcome, my friends." Orla's voice echoed high up into the spire. "I am glad to see so many of you here this morning. For those of us who have left this world, let us raise our palms to the Souls in their honor."

Hands rose throughout the room, waiting.

"May the lost find their way," Orla prompted.

The congregation repeated her words. The strength of their combined voices thrummed through the walls as had the bell. A sob or two broke the succeeding silence.

Death. On a grand scale, it seemed. Something had happened in Zeal. And recently. *They're grieving.* Kole's heart urged him to leave. Listening in and watching seemed wrong. Intrusive. What sort of disaster could take a city where sickness was rare and buildings nearly touched the clouds?

The man in the street flashed in his mind. Those fresh burns... they had to be related to the lost Orla spoke of.

"We are a mighty city with gifts from the Souls." Orla cradled her hands around the pendant resting on her chest. "It is bound these gifts will fail from time to time, as they were made by human hands. But the Seven did not abandon us. They were here, watching, protecting. The flames retreated with *their* help. The Black Wall will never take Zeal."

Kole's blood turned to ice at the name. Something snapped in him. He pushed from the arch and hurried back to their room as fast as he could without opening his scabbed-over wounds. Felix followed, his footsteps pounding behind.

"Oi, wait up, mate."

Once Kole had gone far enough that Orla's voice faded, he finally slowed.

"What's goin' on?"

Kole settled his breaths, but his words came shaky. "The Black Wall. It's here."

"Whoa, hold up. What are ya goin' on about?"

"You heard her. The deaths. Those people's faces. It was the Black Wall. It's here."

"No way. That thing is massive. We'd have seen it comin' inta town. Wouldn't we?" Felix ran his fingers through his curls, eyebrows low and concerned. "Guess I've never seen it ta know. But you have. It can't pop up out of nowhere."

Kole thought back to the destruction of Socren. The refugees had lived so near to the wall for years. It never moved. Yet that one night....

He remembered it so vividly, escorting the refugees through the forest while escaping a Kayetan. The Black Wall had been miles away at the time, and somehow those flames had surged forward in an instant, annihilating everything in sight. Kole had been swept up in those winds and pulled into the fire. After he woke from his brush with death, the Black Wall had gone, snapped back to its original post like the cord of his slingshot.

"No. It can't pop up out of nowhere. But it moves fast. Ebbs in and out around the boundary of Ohr as it pleases. Or as whoever controls it pleases."

Aterus. *Is this his doing? Why would he toy with Zeal?* His focus was on Kole and releasing the Souls. Surely Aterus knew Kole's whereabouts—would focus on keeping the flames at bay especially when his asset stood so near.

"Kole?"

"What?" Kole snapped.

Felix filched at his harsh tone. His face had darkened with worry. "You're shakin', mate."

Kole swallowed and looked at his hands. Tremors shook his arms. Even his jaw quivered. Not from cold, but fear. The mere mention of the Black Wall had him on edge. "I'm fine," he dismissed, then slipped the corner and barged into their room.

A blur of white sped by his feet. Caradin climbed his pant leg and took a spot on Kole's shoulder before he could enter. Concern radiated from the Soul's mind. He must've sensed Kole's distress. All this worry over him. He had no desire to explain it to either of them.

"I need to be alone for a little while." Kole turned from the door and blindly wandered farther down the hall, leaving Felix behind.

With no end in mind, he walked, following through the halls of the temple. At this point, if he turned around, he'd have a hard time finding his way back. Still, he walked with the warmth of Caradin's body draped around the back of his neck. He came to a dead end.

A stained-glass window filled the alcove. This one held more detail than the ones in the grand hall. It depicted a variation of the Seven

Souls symbol. The window's perimeter split into seven sections, each the color of a corresponding Soul. Rather than simple stones like the necklace Kole was so familiar with, the glass took on the elements of the Souls. The green portion, Russé's, held twisting vines wrapped around a grand, flowering tree. Kole searched for the blue one. Aqua to cerulean waves thrashed under rainfall. Fire and molten rock for Obell, and a subtle geometric pattern of feathers and claws sat behind a pair of orange feline eyes for Caradin. He followed the pictures around the edge until he returned to the first. The morning sun backlit the window, giving it an aura-like quality. As if the piece lived — breathed.

Save for the middle.

The center circle lay empty. No pictures. Dull. Merely black dye on glass. His face reflected in it. Even with the cover of his hood, his sagging left eye showed over a drooping, scarred mouth. The texture of his marred skin, mirrored on the clean glass, made him look away.

A warm nose nudged Kole's ear as he sat, back to the window. Caradin crawled from his spot and nestled in Kole's hands.

"I don't want to stay here. If the Black Wall is as close as —" A lump formed in his throat at the thought. He swallowed and took a deep breath. "I can't stay here. Let's get our second point and find Vara."

Though Kole had tried to forget the colorful glass behind him, the sun cast the image on the floor before him. He stared into it. *Better this way — without my face there.* He used the image to help him calm his mind, then narrowed in on the violet patch belonging to Vara.

Kole retraced his steps back to Vara's door. Opened it. The same empty void confronted him. Caradin shifted in his hands.

"Do you feel her?" Kole asked.

"*Vara.*" The weasel hopped down and scurried around Kole. His tiny claws scratched at the base of the stained glass.

"*Southwest... you're sure?*"

The beady black eyes held a confidence in them when they turned back to Kole.

"Good. That wasn't so hard." Kole held out a hand, which Caradin climbed all the way to Kole's shoulder. "Let's get Vienna's map and figure this —"

A horn blew long and deafening outside. Kole covered his ears. Somehow, no matter the thick walls of the building, the sound cut straight to Kole's bones — chilled him. The note rolled up and down the octaves continuously, unnatural. Whatever it announced, Kole guessed nothing good to come from it.

CHAPTER 16

Kole felt the small body of the weasel tremble against his neck. He tried to reach out to Caradin, but the horn even overpowered his thoughts, which meant words were just as futile. Kole stumbled back down the hall. The long corridor seemed like a maze. Which way had he come from? If only he could concentrate.

He ran. If he was to fumble around the temple, he'd at least do it with as much speed as possible. He'd find his way sooner or later. Minutes passed. A figure dashed from the far end of the hall he'd just turned down.

Felix!

The fear in his friend's eyes evaporated slightly. Felix's mouth moved, but only the horn carried between them. He waved Kole toward him, a panic in his rigid movements. The moment Kole got close, Felix grabbed Kole's arm and pulled him faster down the path.

Kole lumbered along, struggling to force his burned legs into a longer stride. Without his rambler, he was slow, weak—a burden. Pain shocked through him with every step as the fragile scars on the back of his legs threatened to tear.

Felix pulled Kole through the bedroom door, dropped his grip, and rushed to his sister's bedside, where she writhed in pain, hands clasped over her ears. Felix dragged her from the bed and onto her feet. Her arm wrapped around his neck, and she took a few weary steps before her legs buckled.

Movement out the window caught Kole's attention. Masses of people darted down the streets. *Running from something.* Kole didn't know what, but his instincts told him to do the same. They needed to get Vienna out of here.

Kole caught Caradin by the furry waist and pulled him from his hood. "Change. Take her," he pleaded aloud and in his thoughts, hoping the Soul would understand one of them through the chaos.

The petite body within Kole's hands thickened. He dropped the animal. By the time gravity sent the creature toward the ground, hooves touched down on the wood floor.

Kole and Felix lifted Vienna onto Caradin's back, then leapt up themselves. The giant elk squeezed through the door, taking off chunks of the frame as they passed.

Out in the main chamber, the pews sat empty. Sunlight poured in from the propped open double doors. A wide-eyed Orla stood in the doorway, eyes snapping to the stag and its riders as they jumped over the benches. She pointed a finger out the door. Kole patted the Soul's neck in affirmation, then the animal galloped to the priestess.

Despite the deafening sound, Kole made out the words by reading Orla's lips.

"Follow them," she said, then scooted them out the golden doors and shut herself inside.

Then, as suddenly as the horn had started, it tapered off.

Kole squeezed his heels into Caradin's side, and the Soul sprinted up the street, following the crowd.

His ears rang. As the buzzing faded, the chorus of screams that had been masked by the blaring alarm rose like a cheering crowd. Kole looked to the people of Zeal. He expected a chaos that matched their cries, but they all moved with a purpose in the same direction. Organized. A planned response. But to what?

Suddenly, a child darted from the stream of people and into Caradin's path. Kole caught sight before the Soul did. "*Stop!*" he yelled inside the stag's head, then pulled the animal's neck left, away from the running youth.

Caradin flexed his legs and slid to a halt. With Kole leaning to swerve their course, the sudden change in speed hurled him from the animals' back.

He landed hard on his hip, sprawled out on the road. His side ached from the rough landing.

"Kole!" Felix called from the stag.

Kole grabbed Felix's offered hand and wrenched to his feet. Though, he wished his eyes had looked upon anything but the sight before him. The thing that had put Zeal in a frenzy.

Between the towering spires to the west, the sky had darkened. At first, he thought it an oncoming storm, but the clouds, although far off, took on unnatural shapes. They moved too fast, and instead of sweeping horizontal storm clouds, the darkness lifted straight up from the earth. A vertical wall of —

A breeze picked up, bringing the smell of bitter ash with it.

No. Please, no.

The Black Wall.

Kole jerked back, ripping his hand from Felix's. A deep shudder made him shake to his bones. Felix said something, but the words fell on deaf ears. The shriek in his gut took control of his body. Kole's heart pumped frantically within his chest. All he could see was black. The sight, the smell, the gradually strengthening wind lashing at his clothes... it took him back to that dreaded moment: the day he burned.

Then something caught his eye. A figure running down the road. Toward the flames in the distance. Kole snapped his head around in a frantic search for the child.

In that split second, all thought—all reason—abandoned him. He left his friends behind and chased after the kid, who ran west, closer and closer to the oncoming flames.

Despite the fleeting moment Kole had taken to gather himself after falling from Caradin's back, the child had put a rather large distance between them. Even as Kole pumped his legs to the limit, he still found himself losing ground. With every step, his head begged him to turn around. But the massacre of his camp had sprung up from the depths of his repressed memories. All those children had burned. The Black Wall had taken them all by surprise then, but here—*now*—Kole knew what lay in store for that toddler, and he refused to let another suffer like that.

The wind whipped up. A gust slipped under the lip of Kole's hood and yanked it back. The city darkened around him as the wall of flames rose and eclipsed the sun.

Suddenly, the child came to a dead stop in the street. Kole finally gained and closed in. He opened his arms, preparing to snatch the kid up and take him back to Caradin for a quick escape. Yet as he neared, a signal going off in his brain told him something was amiss. The child... too large, too tall.

A brown robe draped the figure. *A man.* Kole had been following a man this whole time, not the kid he'd seen fleeing from the line.

Kole stopped. "What are you doing out here?"

The man turned. Kole had seen that face before—one so similar to his own. *The man from the street.* His burned face held a sheen in the diminishing light.

Those eyes, surrounded by drooping red skin, brightened as he gazed upon Kole's exposed face. "The burned savior comes to unleash destruction. The fire will cleanse me. I will be enlightened and worthy of you, holy one."

"The fire will cleanse? What are you talking about? You mean the Black Wall?"

"The flame calls me."

At that moment, a high-pitched buzz sounded from the top of the city wall. Kole shielded his eyes at the white flood of light shooting out from a nearby post. The ground shook as the ray connected with the black flames. The Black Wall roared in response. Another beam came from the next tower and the next. All along the city wall, as far as Kole could see, dozens of these white lights shot into the dark flames.

The Black Wall halted.

Then, it retreated.

Kole gasped. He blinked, unsure of what he was seeing. Those lights. They were... fighting off the flames?

"No!" The cloaked man fell to his knees. "Don't hurt it."

Kole grabbed the man and lugged him to his feet. "Come on. We have to get out of here."

An explosion cut through the roar of the black flames as one of the white beams flickered. The light waned until it completely shut off. The Black Wall moved through that small gap in the defenses. A column of fire surged toward them.

Kole's body froze. His fear planted him like a statue, unable to run or breathe. The fire reached Zeal's wall and consumed it like the stone was nothing more than dry underbrush. Dark ash polluted the sky.

"Into the flame. I will be enlightened. I am worthy."

The words shocked Kole back to reality. He could move again. The man in his grip wriggled. Manic desperation flared in the stranger's eyes and a sense of glee. He ripped from Kole's grasp and sprinted away toward the oncoming flames.

Kole watched, too stunned to move. Why would anyone run straight for the wall? *No one in their right mind....*

That was it. The man wasn't of sound mind. The earlier incident in the street with the guards clearly proved that. But insanity didn't deserve death. Kole wished to help him. Save him. His heart wanted the impossible. If Kole followed....

Unaware of his feet slowly backing away, his eyes never left the stranger's back as he ran toward his demise. The dark flames lashed out as the burned man neared. A scream found Kole's ears. Not of fear but one of euphoria. The sound cut off, and the man vanished into the flames, disintegrated in an instant.

Burned alive.

The Black Wall continued toward Kole, faster than he could run. There was no escape.

Something about the sight of the oncoming fire lured him. No matter how hard he tried to rip his gaze from those flames, he found them glued in place. It came for him now—surged as if sensing Kole had escaped its grasp once before and wished to claim him once and for all.

"*Kole,*" a woman whispered.

That voice. Was it Issira? No. It lacked the serene timbre the Blue Soul possessed. Maybe it was the afterlife calling to him, trying to soothe his spirit as the end neared.

Then it came again, a desperate edge in the tone. "*Kole. I'm here. Save me, please. The pain... it's unbearable.*"

Something squirmed in the back of Kole's mind, and he knew. "*Vara? Is that you?*"

Of all the times to reach out to him, she had to pick now. Despite the spiking heat and raging wind, he closed his eyes and concentrated on her energy. For some reason, the space behind the door that led to their connection—the one that had been empty—now held a great essence.

"*I feel you, Vara. Tell me where you are,*" Kole directed through the portal.

Vara sent a clear image, but the scene was unlike any Kole had witnessed. A chunk of floating earth suspended in the air. Multicolored veins encapsulated the floating island. In the distance, strange black holes pulsed in a gray-and-black swirled sky.

"*I don't know what I'm looking at. Where are you, Vara?*"

"*Beyond the flame.*"

Kole's eyes snapped open at her words, and he forced her away—back through her doorway, where he slammed it shut and locked her out.

CHAPTER 17

All this time and they'd only managed to reach the marsh. Piper gazed down at her boots, disgusted by the thick coat of mud and grime incasing them. The thick leather had done little to block out the cold wet of the soggy landscape. Even her trousers had soaked through. Her shivers penetrated her bones, and her toes hardly moved at her command, but she kept pace. With the winter temperatures cloaking Ohr, more frigid by the day, it surprised her the mud hadn't frozen over yet.

Though no one voiced it, Piper and her companions all knew they'd fallen ridiculously behind. Russé had promised to wake any tree they passed to use as a mount and gain ground, but that required them to come across said trees. The thorned bushes and crawling vines of the marsh did nothing for them. Piper had grown excited after spotting the dried trunk of a long-dead tree a couple days ago. Unfortunately, the stunted size, no taller than Piper herself, had a hard time handling the weight of a single person. Russé had seemed to forget that the trees outside his precious Solpate forest grew a reasonable size, unlike the freakish mammoth ramblers. Until they found a suitable way of travel, they'd continue to fall behind.

A deep ache burst in the depths of Piper's marrow. The feeling froze her body and she gasped, heart stopping as dread gripped her every muscle. She knew this feeling, for she'd had it many times before. The noises of the Souls around her ceased just as suddenly. *They must feel it too.*

"What's happening?" Issira's normally musical voice fell flat.

Piper forced herself forward. The joints of her body ached and ground, resisting. "The wall is moving."

"Kole," Russé gasped.

"No use worrying all the way out here. It's out of our hands," Piper answered the Soul's anxious tone. "Think of it as good news."

All three cast horror-filled faces at Piper. The air's temperature around her spiked as Obell's anger bubbled. She made a note to get under his skin the next time she grew tired of braving the cold.

"Things happen around Kole, if you haven't noticed. He either causes them or draws them to him like blood in the water." A glow in the distance caught Piper's eye. "Kole is near the Black Wall. I don't need to bet on that. Now we know where to look. And he's not dead." After pushing mud-crusted hair from her face, she gave them all a hard look. "Every living being in Ohr would feel that—the hope sucked out of them. They wouldn't know what it was or why, but they'd feel the end heavy in their bones."

A wolf howled in the distance as she made for that glow.

Closer now, Piper found the source of illumination. A puddle of silver light streaked and swirled with the sludge of the marsh. She crouched down for a closer look. Liquid silver. After all her centuries with Aterus and her short time journeying with the blood sorcerer Savairo, she knew that metallic scent well. Blood. And not just any blood.

Piper reached for the empty vial at her belt. "Kole was here. Caradin, too. And...." The deep prints in the mud unveiled a clear trail. "We have something to track."

Russé examined the prints. "It's the rambler. And these...." He knelt next to another set of indents. "Deer?"

"Caradin. Like we saw in Kole's mind-link," said Piper. Certain of the blood's source, she uncorked the vial and dragged it through the silver liquid, filling it to the brim, a mixture of mire and blood. When she noticed Russé staring, brows raised, she straightened and tucked the bottle away. "Don't be so shocked. I know you've done worse."

Issira and Obell, by the way they looked down on her, had watched her stash away the god's blood as well.

"You've all done worse," Piper insisted.

A beat passed, none saying anything further on the matter.

Russé tucked his staff under his arm. "Kole has decided to do this alone, but we won't abandon him. I know him. He thinks he's helping by going ahead."

"You keep saying that." Piper opened her arms. "That you know him. If it's true, then why did he push you out? No, I think Kole knows exactly what he's doing. It's only his motive I need to figure out."

The truth must've sank into the Soul a little, for his eyes dulled after her words. "What happened with Caradin...." Russé's scraggly gray hair jounced as he shook his head. "A lucky fluke. Whether he likes it or not, Kole needs our help. We must reach him before he gets to the next Soul."

At least that's one thing we agree on. She sighed and pushed into a run, a chorus of more slapping feet on her heels. The cold temperature proved a blessing as it preserved the rambler's tracks. *We'll find you soon enough.*

CHAPTER 18

Kole opened his eyes to a void. Darkness enveloped him. He felt his limbs yet had no sight of them. When he spoke, the sound never registered, as if the surrounding shadow sucked up the words. Something nipped at his ears. A small pinch of pain at first, then the feeling shifted. Burned. He felt the skin bubble and burst, searing like cooking meat. The skin of his fingers and toes joined in. The heat slithered up his limbs and consumed his face.

Licks of flame danced before his eyes. Kole opened his mouth to scream. No sound. Only the agonizing pain of being burned alive. Black fire dove down his open throat and scorched his insides. He screamed for it to end — for it to end *him*. He could bear no more.

He was flame. He was fire. His body disintegrated, and he scattered among the Black Wall, becoming one with it.

"Save me, Kole," Vara's voice echoed through the fire.

But who will save me?

CHAPTER 19

Kole woke up screaming. His throat burned raw from overuse. A pressure wrapped over his chest and legs. He kicked and fought against the restraints, still screaming from the memory of pain in his nightmare.

"Calm down, Blondie. Ugh, yer stronger than I thought."

Upon recognizing the voice, Kole stilled. He clamped his mouth shut, but his yearning lungs made him heave for air. "Where am I? What's happened?" Light streamed in from the window, which held little clue as to how long he'd been asleep. The same day? A week? Maybe no time had passed at all, and he'd found his way to the afterlife.

"We're back at the temple." Felix kept his weight on Kole for a moment as if testing, then leaned off. "Don't ya remember?"

Kole thought back. The dream lay fresh in his head. Once he pushed past that awful scene, he did remember... a bit. He'd run from the wall—from Vara—the Black Wall fast on his trail. Blurs of people and voices. No matter how hard he tried to connect the pieces, they eluded him. The last clear thing he remembered was his body overheating. Something had picked him up and carried him, then he'd promptly passed out.

"Had ta carry ya all the way here," said Felix.

"But the Black Wall... it was right behind me. How did I...?"

"Ya didn't outrun it if that's what yer askin'. The city guards wheeled out this weird cannon lookin' thing." Felix stretched his arms out to illustrate the size. "Used it ta stop the fire from spreadin' right after ya started runnin'. I was already on my way back ta find ya, so I saw the whole thing. Tried ta wave ya down—call ya back, but ya ran right past me. I followed ya until ya collapsed."

"I'm sorry, Felix." The mere thought of being so close to the Black Wall again made his stomach sour. And Vara? Kole chugged the glass of water by his bed, then wiped his mouth clean.

Felix shrugged. "All ended well, at least."

"Vienna. Is she...?"

Felix leaned to the side, revealing Vienna, who sat upright on the bed in the corner with Caradin, in his weasel form, curled around her neck.

"I was worried sick," Vienna said hoarsely. She swallowed and winced. "I couldn't even go after you. What were you thinking going off like that? Alone!" She coughed from the rise of her voice.

"I just...." He thought back to the man he'd seen in the road, burned like him. The things he'd said. "I wasn't thinking. I really am sorry."

"We know." Felix patted Kole's shoulder. "Just give us a head's up next time ya wanna go runnin' for the Black Wall. It'll give me a chance ta knock ya out first." He winked.

Kole felt their stares on him, probably waiting for his explanation. "I heard Vara."

Felix repositioned himself with an invested plop and rested his chin in his hands, eyes eager for the details.

"She found me." Kole's skin itched as he recalled his fiery dream and her words. "But it's bad news. I think she's a lost cause. We should leave Zeal and move on to the next Soul."

"Why? What did she say?" Vienna asked.

"She's not in Ohr." Every time Kole blinked he saw the Black Wall looming over him. The vision made him shudder, and he pulled the blanket tighter around his trembling frame.

"Spit it out already, mate. All this doom talk is makin' my belly ache."

"Vara is beyond the Black Wall," Kole said evenly. His skin prickled at the mention of the flames.

Both Felix and Vienna stared at him, mouths ajar. The line in Vienna's forehead grew more prominent by the second.

"Wasn't expectin' that," Felix whispered. "Guess he's right, then, eh?" He looked to his sister. "Don't suppose Leo mentioned anythin' ta ya 'bout... slippin' past it?"

Vienna shook her head, expression firmly stuck between shock and fright. "Only that it's impossible."

"Ya can't just go ta the next one, can ya, mate?" Felix asked. "Skip a Soul in the line up?"

Kole fell back against the headboard. "If we can't we're stuck."

Felix perked up with a shrug. "Maybe Russé'll know what ta do."

"We should wait for him before moving on," Vienna agreed. "And if not Russé, Issira or Obell may know. I can send word to Leo, as well. We can figure this out together. We have hope, Kole."

"So, we just sit around tapping our feet until they get here? That could take—" Kole held his tongue before he said too much. All this time, he'd been racing ahead to keep away from his old mentor, and now the only thing that could potentially solve this mess was Russé. There had to be a way around it. Something Kole had yet to think of. Maybe he could force Vara back in the line. Save her for last. By then, he'd surely figure out a way to get to her. If Zeal had developed a way to fight off the Black Wall—something Kole thought impossible—then *he* could manage *this*.

The thought triggered an idea. Zeal, the most advanced city in Ohr, held the knowledge to combat the Black Wall. Kole had seen it with his own eyes. Felix had seen the actual contraption. The answer to get through those flames might lay here in the city.

"Did you tell her about the beams?" Kole asked Felix, whose curls bobbed as he nodded.

"Told her 'bout 'em. But we don't really know *what* they are."

"We can find out." Kole glanced out the window at the golden rays of sunshine. "If we go poking around, we should wait until nightfall when we have your Kayetan, Felix."

Felix smiled at that. "Sounds like fun."

A knock came from the door. "I have brought company, my dears." Orla opened the door. She held a tray full of sandwiches. "Also thought you might be hungry after this morning. It is a shame you had to visit during this commotion."

A tall, slender woman followed Orla in. Gray-streaked brown hair fell in a neat braid over the stranger's shoulder. She wore pants and a vest, similar to the guards of Zeal, but this outfit, unblemished by stains or wrinkles, seemed suited for a higher status. Her stiff and commanding posture made Kole straighten in the bed. The air about her reminded Kole of Leo, only her jaw set more sternly.

"This is Council Leader Tena." Orla placed a plate by Vienna's bedside table and gave her a warm smile. "She's here to inspect your condition, dear girl. Don't you fret now. We'll have you feeling better quite soon."

Councilwoman Tena dipped her head at the introduction. The metal pins affixed to her breast pocket jingled. Kole quickly counted at least a dozen more than the guards at the gate. "You may call me Tena in this casual meeting." She scanned the room, eyes stopping longer on Kole, like all who first met their group.

Kole kept her gaze, very aware of his hood laying loose at the back his neck, putting his scars on full display. Her eyes revealed no pause or horror toward him, but when she glanced at Felix next, Kole could tell by the subtle downward shift in her stare, she noted his Kayetan scars.

"Our patient?" Tena rounded to Vienna and swiftly took a knee. "Gray lung, you say?"

Unsure if the question was meant for them or Orla, Kole stayed silent.

"Seems that way. They came from the Ashland plains. Tea?" Orla said as she poured a cup of steaming liquid and handed it to Vienna, who took it graciously with hands Kole could see quivering clear across the room.

"What business would three children have in the Ashland plains?" Tena allowed Vienna a sip of tea then ordered her to open her mouth to inspect her throat.

Felix and Kole checked each other while the women were distracted.

Felix shrugged as if to say, "What do we tell them?"

"And more curious," Tena tilted her head toward the boys, "how the toxic air affected her alone."

"I dunno. We were all wearin' masks," Felix offered.

Tena lifted a graying brow at them, then pulled a strange contraption from under her vest. Two pieces went into her ears while the other end, fixed with a coin-shaped metal piece, she placed on Vienna's chest. "Cough."

The forced cough triggered a violent bout. Tena slipped a handkerchief from her pocket and covered Vienna's mouth. Bright-red speckles soaked through the fabric.

"I'm afraid it is as you guessed, Orla. Gray lung...." She tutted and gave the tissue to Vienna, then braced her shoulders. "You are in for a rough recovery."

"She's strong," Kole said. He caught Vienna's gaze, fearful and unsure.

"She will have to be. Your friend will live, but that's the only guarantee we can grant her." Tena stood from the bedside and tipped Vienna's cup, encouraging her to drink. "You will have lasting effects. The poison has gone too long unchecked for a full recovery."

If Vienna could have paled anymore, she'd have been as stark as the moon.

"What's that mean?" Felix asked.

"Worst case, bedrest...." Tena frowned. "Indefinitely."

Kole jumped to his feet. "What?"

His reaction startled Orla, who dropped a plate. It shattered and cast a few berries rolling over the floorboards.

"Medicine, even in Zeal, can only do so much. I imagine only an act of the gods could cure gray lung entirely." Tena's eyes bore into Kole. "Pray tell, boy, you never mentioned your name."

His mouth clamped shut in defiance. Then again, Orla already knew his name. Not exactly a well-kept secret. "Kole." He swore he saw the councilwoman's jaw twitch.

"Kole, Vienna, Felix." Tena addressed each one with a nod. "Orla has taken great care of you thus far, but with today's events, she will have more work to tend to. I will relocate you three to our personal quarters in City Hall, where I and my assistants will care for you."

Orla had just finished collecting the broken ceramic and runaway berries. "It's really okay, councilwoman. I don't mind —"

"Orla." A dip of Tena's head made the priestess go silent. "Bring the transportation, please."

Orla set the debris on the side table and hurried from the room.

"An interesting pet you have there," Tena said, eying Caradin, who poked his head from the pile of blankets. "We don't have these creatures around Zeal. Native to Socren?"

"Yes, ma'am." Vienna scooped him up and set him loose on the floor to go to Kole.

"I'm not a fan of rats." Tena watched the weasel run into Kole's arms. "But it will be welcome in your rooms as long as it doesn't... multiply."

"Here we are." Orla wheeled a chair through the door and saddled it up alongside Vienna's bed.

Bronze-colored metal and polished wood made up the framework. The two materials intertwined like braided vines. The detail and curvature made the contraption look like a grand throne. Two large carriage wheels flanked the cushioned seat, allowing the contraption mobility. Kole had never seen anything like it. He reckoned Zeal had a solution to every problem.

Orla tapped Vienna's shoulder. "In we go."

Kole and Felix rushed to Vienna's side when the priestess attempted to load up Vienna herself. With Vienna settled in, Felix gathered their bags, and they all exited the temple.

"Call on me should you need, Council Leader Tena." The dangling cloth around her wrapped hands swayed like ribbons in the wind as Orla waved them off.

The streets lay completely empty. Wisps of ash played in the breeze: remnants of the Black Wall's destruction. Hazy sunlight touched down on Zeal. The black flames had gotten some parts of the city. A giant chunk of stone wall had been consumed where the breach had occurred, and razed plots buried in ash flanked either side. Yet with all of this destruction, Kole's thoughts stayed on that man in the street. He'd watched him run into flame. How many more had perished like him, willing or not?

"Felix and Vienna, members of Socren's Liberation. Leo's associates." Tena pushed Vienna's chair at the head, leaving her face concealed from Kole. "And Kole, a guest of utmost importance, and to be treated as such as requested by Leo himself. Won't you tell me what all this is about?"

"How do you know—" Kole started.

"Every city in Ohr knows of you. Your names at least. Leo has contacted all the leaders informing them of a potential arrival. He stated that he knows not where your mission will lead you but to prepare for an appearance nonetheless."

"Guess that explains Azmali." Felix shrugged to Kole.

Kole nodded. The last major city they'd visited, Cresthaven, led by the hardened woman Azmali, had mentioned a favor to Leo. She'd only extended help to Kole and his group upon learning their names. It seemed the Liberation still managed to help them on their journey from miles away. As for the details, Kole thought it best to keep as many of their secrets close unless necessary to proceed.

"It is a shame about the evacuation. And on the heels of the victory of the rebellion, no less! Were you there for the battle?"

"Sure were." Talk of overthrowing the warden's reign seemed to pep Felix up. "Sent him fleein' with his tail tucked."

"What evacuation?" Vienna wheezed.

"I received a letter two days prior. Leo has reason to believe the Black Wall is heading their way. I offered our weapons of course, but he refused. All of Socren is relocating to the coast. Rush, I believe. He's calling for reinforcements from every city, claiming a war is to come."

At the news, Vienna pulled on her fingers.

Moving Socren? Reinforcements? A war? Kole felt this mission would come to a head, but so soon? Did Aterus know of Leo's plans? The war would be unnecessary if Kole could make good on his deal. Ohr would unite under Aterus. All would be safe.

"Should we be talking about this now?" Kole asked, surveying the streets.

"Zeal will stay in lockdown until the horn sounds again. We keep everyone off the streets until the city guard has cleared the destruction." Tena sighed. "Which might take a while. The wall has shifted dozens of times on us over the years, but it hasn't nicked the city in decades. But, yes. I do believe we should save the rest for a more private location."

Nicked? A whole block of builds gone, and she calls it a nick? "We saw the beams," Kole said. As they walked west toward the city gates, where the Black Wall had loomed hours ago, he tried to spot the source of the lights that saved Zeal. "What are they?"

"Cannons, for lack of a better word. They are Zeal's greatest creation. We've designed a machine that can counter the doom of the gods." Tena's chin lifted in pride.

"How do they work?" Kole asked.

"My knowledge of them doesn't go far beyond the basics. I can arrange a tour with the engineer if that suits you."

"Very much." To say the cannons intrigued Kole would be an understatement. He wanted to know everything about them. Their mere existence meant Ohr wasn't as helpless as he once thought. A hint of anger laced his curiosity. If Zeal had such a weapon, why did they keep it to themselves?

Tena turned them north, down the next vacant intersection. A grand, towering white building with eight peaks sat at the end. The roofs of each conical spire took on a color of the Seven Souls. *A theme around here, it seems.* So much of Zeal decorated in their names and colors, yet the way Tena had talked of her cannons... "counter the doom of the gods." Kole had a hard time pinning the councilwoman's allegiance.

That same insignia, welded in metal on the temple doors with the anvil and hammer, graced the front of what Kole presumed was their destination: City Hall.

"Now, back to my questions, please. I was told your party would be bigger." Tena cast a stern eye over the three. "Where are the others? I was expecting a master shepherd."

"We got separated in the Ashland Plains," Kole said. His heart fluttered at the twisted truth.

"Do they know where you are?"

"We've been in communication," Kole said. Not *exactly* a lie. "He should be heading this way, though he doesn't know we arrived in Zeal."

"I will send scouts out to find them. Which way are they coming from? Southeast?" Tena asked.

"Guess so," Felix said. "That's the way we came."

"No," Kole blurted. "They went a little off track. Too far north up the river. You should look northeast."

Felix cast Kole a scrutinizing side eye.

"I'll explain later," Kole mouthed at his friend's frown. Thankfully, Felix decided to play along and let the conversation die.

"Very well."

The rest of the trip remained fairly silent. Tena commented on the décor inside the building, which consisted of stonework and metal beams. Any wood merely served for stylistic purposes. The Seven Souls symbol lay everywhere Kole sent his eyes: gem-encrusted doorknobs, accents on the grand pillars, embroidered tapestries. A massive stairway sat in the middle of the building, but they turned down the hallway to a lift similar to one the Liberation had used to get to their underground hideout back in Socren, except this one gleamed like a jewel, with a golden metal frame and glass panes.

"Council Leader Tena." A man dressed in a fine suit jacket dipped his head as they approached the lift. He reached out to Vienna's chair. "May I?"

"Unnecessary." Tena waved him off. "I will accompany them myself, thank you."

The man smiled and returned to his stoic stance.

Tena motioned Kole and Felix onto the platform. This design had a more advanced touch, with sleek, metal lattice and a decorative cage that surrounded its occupants. Once Tena rolled Vienna's chair over the platform, she secured the door then produced a key from her pocket. The councilwoman inserted it into an opening below a panel of buttons. At the click, the panel lit up. She entered a combination Kole lost track of after the fourth button, then stood back.

If not for the rotating gears, Kole would've never guessed their ride had begun. The platform's ascension made no noise, and the sturdy floor never jolted or swung. As they rose, the view stole Kole's breath.

Beyond the ground floor, a vertical glass tunnel encased the gold-caged lift. The city revealed its entirety the higher they rose. They soared above the surrounding rooftops, which continued to shrink until they resembled toys. The forest of crystal trees at the eastern edge of

Zeal put the entire city to shame; an ocean of diamonds sparkling beneath the cresting sun. Kole never wanted to look away.

A soft chime marked their destination. Tena pulled back the gate and wheeled Vienna onto the floor. The highest level of City Hall. Rich navy tiles lined the hallway in distinct contrast to the white walls. Gold archways rounded the doors lining either side of the corridor.

Tena gestured to the ornately welded doorframes. "These rooms are occupied by our council, though it seems we never spend much time in them."

Tena led them to a dome room at the middle of the building, where a lavish scene of the Souls graced the ceiling. From this central room, halls splayed out in every direction like a sunburst. When a signet above the hall caught Kole's eyes, he realized the layout of the floor had been inspired by a compass. Eight corridors named for the cardinal and ordinal directions. Tena took them down the southwest path. He put to memory the lift's location, then hurried after Felix.

"This place is unreal. Ya sure this ain't a dream?" Felix gently nudged Kole in the ribs with his elbow. "Maybe the Black Wall swallowed us whole back there after all, eh Blondie?"

Kole gave a half-hearted smile. The mere mention of the wall sent a cold shiver under his skin.

"I'm glad Zeal impresses you." Tena stopped Vienna by the last door of the hall and unlocked it. "The beauty alone is enough to stay."

Kole thumbed the intricate vine-like patterned doorframe. "Stay?"

Tena's lips thinned at Kole's question. She opened the door, and the most extravagant room lay beyond.

Every bit of furniture was its own piece of art. Deep-blue velvet couches embroidered with gold specks, like the night sky, filled out the middle of the space. Orbs of polished moonstone sat atop gold, floor-length rods at either side of the sofa arms, which Kole guessed acted as light sources at night. Glass tables and cabinets peppered the room. Even more impressive, an entire glass wall looked out over the cityscape, bookended with inky curtains. Even the floor shined, glossy like wet ice. The white-and-black mosaic pattern swirled under Kole's steps.

"There are four rooms to choose from, each with its own bed and bath." Tena gestured to the closed doors around the room after she parked Vienna by the extravagant glass wall. "You will need rest, dear. Shall I bring you to a bed?"

"I don't want to be cooped up in a room." Vienna pushed forward and stood on shaking legs. "Here is fine."

Kole and Felix settled Vienna into the couch, which proved as soft as it looked—softer even than Caradin's coat currently warming Kole's neck.

"I will send my personal medical staff to treat you. We'll get you the first dose before nightfall. In the meantime," Tena opened her arms to the room, "relax and rest. All of you. This floor is exclusively for the council, so no one will bother you here. Wander the halls as you please, just know the rooms are locked and access to the lift requires a councilmember's assistance. I will assign someone to stand outside your door. Should you need anything, ask him. Food, drink, whatever you desire."

"Thank you, Council Leader Tena. We appreciate your hospitality. It's been a long time since we've slept indoors," Kole said.

"The barn was technically indoors," Felix corrected. "But hay's got nothin' on a cushion."

Tena gave a tight, obligated smile. "Stay as long as you like. You are in Zeal's care now." Another stiff bow and she moved for the door but paused in the frame. "Oh, the council will want to meet with you all. I will have someone fetch you when I've gathered them."

The door gently clicked behind her, and Kole and his friends finally found themselves alone. For some reason, a great weight lifted from Kole's shoulders at the privacy.

"I'm going to get some fresh air," Kole said, excusing himself from the room while Felix threw himself on the couch next to Vienna, sending an explosion of beaded pillows tumbling to the floor.

The glass door swung shut behind Kole. Up this high, the singed scent of ash had diluted. Clear skies above. Empty streets below.

Caradin, who squirmed around Kole's neck, nibbled at his ear.

With a thought, Kole summoned his ghostly friend.

"I can't believe it's this close," Niko said as he appeared. His phantom form leaned against the half wall encasing the balcony, eyes focused west.

Kole followed his gaze. A shiver passed through him. The Black Wall stood miles off, dark and haunting. He looked away. The space should've relaxed Kole—the wall had retreated—but he'd be a fool to shed all caution. An instant of instability and the flames could charge at Zeal's doors once more.

"What a view. It's sort of beautiful in an odd way." Niko turned to Kole. "Guess that's a bit morbid to say about the thing that killed me."

Kole shrugged it off and set his back firmly toward the window before he answered. "You see what you see."

A frown overtook Niko's face. "What do *you* see?"

"I...." Kole set his sights back on the distant blaze. Deep-rooted pain clenched his insides. A simple look from such a great distance spiked his anxiety. Yet he forced his eyes on the Black Wall even while his hands grew clammy. That coldness moved over him. The longer he looked, the more severe the reaction. Now he shook—his *bones* shook. The memories of that night... nearly swallowed whole by flame.... And Niko. Kole had desperately clung to his friend in the raging winds. That precise moment when Niko's hands slipped through his own... that last time Kole had seen his friend alive... it haunted him every time he closed his eyes.

"Danger, Master." The thought came from the weasel, who intently peered west.

"Yes, Caradin. Danger. This is what we are trying to stop," Kole responded. "You will help me, won't you? Destroy it?"

"Destroy what hurts Master."

Kole could no longer take it. He ripped his eyes away and bottled the agonizing past.

"What do you see?" Niko pressed again.

Kole swallowed against his dry throat. "When I look at the Black Wall—speak or think of it—I see your death over and over again. Relive it."

"It wasn't your fault."

"Don't say that."

"Kole." Niko set a ghostly hand on Kole's shoulder. The shadow under his cheek bones darkened. "It's the truth. You have to know that. I don't blame you for anything."

Heat flooded Kole's eyes. "It never should have happened. You could have been saved. If I only had better shepherds' skills back then like I do now...." Unwanted tears streamed down his cheeks. "I could have saved you. I could have saved so many."

"Not even the gods can change the past." Niko cradled Kole's face in his hands, though the touch was as non-existent as Niko himself. His friend wiped at the tears with his thumbs. "But you, my shepherd, can shape the future."

"We shape the future," Caradin repeated in Kole's head. *"For good of Ohr."*

Kole sniffed back the tears and half-smiled. Reason and language were returning to the Orange Soul. Soon, Kole would bind Caradin to his and Aterus' cause.

CHAPTER 20

Four rooms. And yet, Kole and the siblings ended up sleeping in the same one. At first, they had split up, but Felix insisted Vienna needed company with her illness, so he bunked with her. After Kole settled into his massive bed, alone, Felix had appeared in the doorway and towed Kole over to the shared room. They all slept in the bed, which could comfortably fit at least two more. Silky soft sheets, chill against Kole's skin, had lured him to sleep.

A few restful hours later, he lay awake, staring at the gilded ceiling while Felix and Vienna breathed softly next to him. The last time Kole had slept so soundly had been in his fur-lined hammock back in Solpate. The strain of his eyes had vanished. Still groggy with the weight of sleep, his body and mind felt revived.

Every now and then, Vienna would make choking sounds in her sleep, involuntary coughing fits, but since Tena's medical personnel had visited shortly after the councilwoman's departure and administered the first dose of her treatment, her fits had greatly diminished. Her recovery seemed hopeful.

Kole wished this serenity could last forever. With the three of them holed up in their own quarters, he felt like the doom of the world beyond the thin layer of glass could never get to them. A foolish thought. But he entertained it for a time, nonetheless. *No cares, no problems....*

The bed shifted. "Hey, Blondie, you awake?" Felix whispered.

Kole grunted, unwilling to let his newfound sense of peace slip away so soon.

Felix propped himself on an elbow. "'Bout that thing ya told Tena—Russé and the others comin' from the north. Ya gonna tell me what that's all about?"

Kole hoped the pale light of morning stayed dim enough to hide his frown. How to explain? Another lie to hide the first? He wished Niko were around to help him out, but Kole had sent him away to avoid any more growing suspicion. The siblings were smart. They knew something was off with him. Kole could tell by their frequent curious gazes—keeping watch—yet they could never imagine what truly went on.

"Not much to explain." Kole kept his voice low as to not disturb Vienna. She needed all the rest she could get. "I got in contact with Russé. Apparently, they tracked us to the river and thought we'd followed it." Kole feigned a yawn, hoping Felix would let him go back to sleep.

Felix's mouth pulled to the side. "Why didn't ya tell us before?"

"Didn't think about it. With Vienna's thing last night and the wall this morning... well, you know." Kole waited a moment for Felix to roll back over and end the conversation. When he didn't, Kole squared off to him. "We should keep quiet about things."

"Whaddya mean?"

"We can't be sure how much Tena knows about us, the Souls... our mission. It's best for everyone if we keep our business to ourselves. Think about it. If Leo wanted Tena or the council to know what we are doing, he would've written it in the letter—the one we haven't seen, nor has she offered to show us, which leads me to believe he didn't go into detail."

"We follow Leo's lead, then. Do this under wraps." Even in the darkness, Felix's eyes glinted. "Under wraps's my specialty."

Polite knocking came from the door. Kole sighed in relief. Felix's open mouth made it seem like he wanted more answers, but Kole rolled away. He slipped his legs from beneath the warm covers and braved the icy tiled floors. The slap of his bare feet echoed in the chambers.

Kole opened the door to a smiling face. Daveen, the assistant Tena had assigned to them. Kole and the siblings already met him once before, when the medicine man had stopped by with Vienna's treatment.

"Rise and shine, Kole." Daveen, with his glossy brown hair tied at the nape of his neck, held up a tray of food with the mouthwatering scent of sausage. "I brought breakfast. Also, Council Leader Tena has arranged the council to meet in an hour. They'd like you all to join them. Well, given the young lass is up to it, of course. If she'd prefer to stay in bed, I can keep her company."

Kole moved to the side as Daveen sauntered through. The tray tapped down on the glass table, then Daveen drew back the curtains

Kole had shut to block out any view of the Black Wall. Gold morning light attacked Kole's eyes. He recoiled as Felix's peppy voice chimed like a bell in the room.

"'Mornin', Daveen." Felix smiled to their doorman. Whatever concern he'd held a moment before had diminished.

"Sir," Deveen gave a slight bow.

"Nothin' like wakin' up ta the smell of food, eh Blondie?" Felix winked at Kole, then loaded up a plate of sausage, toast, and fruit. A final pastry topped his mountainous pile, teetering and threatening to slide off with every movement of Felix's arm.

"Felix?" Vienna called from the bed.

"Oh, right. Ya need the wheely chair?"

"No, just some assistance, please."

"Right, uh...." Felix looked between his heaping plate and the room, apparently torn between filling his belly and tending to his sister. The compromise he made was stuffing a whole sausage in each cheek and chewing it while he clomped back to the bedroom.

Kole sandwiched a sausage inside a steaming biscuit and savored his first bite. Warm food always gave him a surge of joy. This, though, was something else. Fresh bread sent straight from the ovens to their room. No stale crust to gnaw on or mold to pick off. Between bites, he took handfuls of fresh berries. Their red juice stained his fingertips, which he remedied by licking them clean.

Daveen set out two glasses and proceeded to pour milk to the brim. The glass fogged from the chill.

Kole took the offered drink and gulped it down. That first swallow hurt. He was unprepared for the frigid temperature, which numbed his belly as it filled.

"Slow down, mate." Felix held Vienna up and walked her to the couch. "What's yer rush?"

"I'm not the one who downed an entire sausage in a matter of seconds," Kole teased.

Felix made a face at that. "Fair. And it was two."

While his stomach recovered, Kole made a plate for Vienna, who ate just as ravenously as the boys. She reached for a glass of milk, but Daveen stopped her.

"Oh no, miss. I was told the warm one is for you." He tipped the contents of a kettle into a mug and handed it over. "It will help the throat."

Vienna sipped on it.

Daveen stood back. The look he gave the group stood somewhere between awe and concern at their ravenous appetite. "If there's nothing else, I will leave you to eat and fetch your clothes."

"Clothes?" Half-chewed pastry dough fell from Felix's mouth.

"Well, yes. You will need to change for the meeting with the council."

"What's wrong with these?" Felix opened his arms and presented his dirt-crusted tunic. The trousers he wore had frayed at the hem, and a hole in either leg exposed his knees. Kole didn't look much better.

"No offense, young man, but you all smell of marsh and animal droppings."

Felix sniffed the length of his arm, then shrugged. "Fair."

"We did sleep in a barn," Kole muttered. He took in the new holes on his own tunic and the frayed, mud-stained hem of his trousers. Their journey had really done a number on him. His companions looked just as ragged. How had he not noticed the state of them all? Maybe they only looked dirtier because of the pristine room they sat in. Felix still had dirt on his chin, and a twig stuck out of Vienna's curls.

"I'll be back to fetch the dishes." Daveen leaned and peeked into the bedroom. "And the blankets...." His voice had lowered as if dreading the damage done during the night. "When I return, I expect all of you washed."

Once the door shut behind their doorman, they all laughed.

"Guess it's good we stayed together last night," Vienna said. "Contain the mess to one room."

"Who's goin' first?" Felix asked, shoving his thumb over his shoulder toward the hall with the bath. "Vienna?"

"That depends. Is there going to be food left when I'm done?" She stabbed her fork at Felix's hand grabbing his third portion.

"Oi!"

"We'll save you some," Kole promised.

"You, I trust." Vienna gave a look of venom to her brother. "It's him I'm worried about."

"Oh, come on, V." He nursed his hand, thumbing the indents the fork had made on his skin. "Just one more sausage and I'll be done."

Vienna scoffed. "Fine." Another sip of her steamed milk, then she stood. Her hand went to the armrest when she wobbled. "I might need an escort."

Kole leapt up and wrapped an arm around her waist before she fell under buckled knees. "I'll get you there."

"Hey, V? Ya ain't gonna need like...." Felix raised his eyebrows, trying to convey something he'd shied away from saying. His mouth drooped in an uncomfortable line. "Ya know... like help or anythin'?"

A surge of warmth radiated off Vienna. Kole caught her face reddening bright as the diminished bowl of berries on the table. Something obviously embarrassed her, but he had no idea why. His hand. Where had he placed it? He checked, and it still lay around her waist. Was that a bad spot? *Felix holds her here.* Maybe he held her too tightly? Kole adjusted, but that small movement made her unsteady, so he regripped her.

"No," she snapped at Felix. "Just *to* the bath."

Felix's shoulders fell forward, the stress on his expression vanishing. "Thank the Souls," he muttered, but the quiet of the room let his words ring out.

Then it dawned on Kole. The awkward exchange... Felix's relief at her dismissal for assistance.... Kole felt his own of face warm. He kept his eyes on the floor while he helped Vienna limp around the table, hoping somehow if he stared hard enough, the cold floor would grant him its chill. Ridiculous, he knew.

They walked to the bath in silence. After sitting her on a cushioned bench by the door, he fetched her a towel and filled the tub. With everything set and ready, he moved to leave.

"Wait," Vienna said weakly. She turned away from him and pulled her blonde waves over her shoulder, exposing the back of her neck. "Will you take it off? I'm too weak to fiddle with the clasp."

Kole stepped forward. Last time he'd tried to work the clasp, he'd found his scarred fingers useless. The sooner he could remove the necklace, the sooner he could leave and give his racing heart a moment to relax. He fumbled, as he knew he would. *Damn fingers.* But Vienna waited patiently. Kole used the side of his nubby fingernail to level the fastener, and it came loose. With the chain undone, his eyes trailed to her neck and hair. He had never noticed the state of her during their journey. She's always looked like... well, Vienna to him. Besides the sickly color of her skin from the gray lung, traces of dirt settled over her neck. Large mats of her golden hair hung frizzy at the base of her neck, knotted so tight, the roots pulled on her scalp and left angry red skin.

As Vienna pulled the chain from her neck and coiled it in her hand, Kole touched one of the tangles. "Does this hurt?"

She flinched. "Not too bad."

"Wait here." Kole wandered back to the cupboards and found a brush. "Do you mind?"

She nodded weakly. "I don't think it'll do much good."

Kole started gently at the tangled mass of hair that had pulled free from her braid. The bristles tore at the strands and snapped them no matter how softly he combed. *Stubborn things.*

"It's fine, Kole, really. I have half a mind to chop it all off anyway. The braid isn't working as I thought it would." Her fingers pulled the tie from her hair, and she unraveled her tresses. "There has to scissors around here."

Kole remembered seeing a pair alongside the brush in the cabinet. "There is but... are you really going to cut it off?"

"No... you are."

"What?" He froze.

Vienna pulled the brush from his grip and set it aside. "It's not hard. I'll walk you through it."

Kole blinked, wondering if she was serious or pulling a prank like her brother. Her silence told him she'd meant it, so he did as she asked and retrieved the shears.

When Kole returned, Vienna had pulled her hair back in her hand, clumping her tresses within her fist. "Cut below my hand."

But he hesitated, the razor-like jaws poised over her waves.

"It's fine. Really," she encouraged.

Kole clamped down on the scissors, which proved duller than he'd anticipated. The simple, sweeping cut he envisioned turned into a sawing battle—metal versus twisted mats. Chunk by chunk, gold threads piled over his feet, tickling his skin. Vienna had him cut out the larger tangles pulling at the nape of her neck. Some nested so close to her scalp, no length could be salvaged. He hoped the longer pieces would cover his butchered job in the end.

With the final cut done, her hair just skimmed her shoulders. Vienna sighed.

"Do you want to see it?" Kole set the shears down, readying to assist her to the mirror.

"I'd rather not," Vienna whispered. The drain in her tone made him recoil. "That's all the help I needed."

"Right." Kole lingered there for a moment. He knew he should say something—anything—to reassure her. To comfort her. But any words he'd thought of in his head got caught in his throat. Kole spun on his heel and hurried for the door, desperate to put distance between them. Standing there in silence only made the tension deepen.

"Kole?"

Her voice stopped him. Kole took a breath, then turned.

Vienna still held her back to him, shoulders slumped. "Thank you."

Words of gratitude, yet Kole felt as if he'd committed some horrid deed. With his voice still refusing to pass his tongue, his "you're welcome" came out as a grunt. Kole left her there alone in the bathroom.

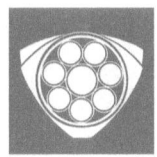

The stiff fabric of the vest felt as if Kole had buttoned a cage around his torso. Every move from his arms to his legs pulled the seams of these borrowed clothes. Kole was unsure if Daveen had given him the wrong size or if fancy clothes had always been made to plague the wearer with discomfort. Kole had never owned anything of such fine quality to know.

Sleek emerald material made up the vest he currently tugged on in hopes of stretching it out. Gold buttons fastened the front together, engraved with the hammer-and-anvil symbol that seemed to grace every knickknack in Zeal. A darker green made up his new trousers and matching long-sleeve tunic. More pieces lay in the box Daveen had given him—something white and frilly with a strap around it, socks with ruffle around the ankle, and a pair of elegant baubles. Kole had no idea how to wear them and neither did he have the will to try and figure it out, so he left them to rattle around in the box. *No more. I feel like an overgrown dolly.* The ruffled socks looked as though they'd itch and scratch the tender scars on his ankles, so he settled with going barefoot in the fresh black leather boots Daveen had provided. They squeaked as he laced them up.

Bathing had been the best thing out of all this. A *real* bath with *real* soap and hot water. His body had soaked up the heat. The tension in his muscles had fled, and his skin felt supple as ever after a good rubbing of scented oil. Kole got a whiff of himself. He smelled like a literal flower, crushingly so.

"Hey, yer not wearin' yer mascot," Felix accused.

"My what?" Kole turned to an impressively dressed Felix: the same basic outfit in a charcoal gray trimmed in silver, with an addition of a frill of fabric puffing from the top of his vest.

"Yer mascot." Felix pointed to the odd thing. "Ya got one, didn't ya?"

Kole frowned at the lone piece he'd left in the box. "I guess."

"It's called an *ascot*, Felix." Vienna stood in the door of the bedroom. She'd hidden from them since she'd finished cleaning up, keeping a towel wrapped around her head to hide her hair. She stood before them, both arms grasped on the doorframe for support. The towel gone now, her straw hair poofed around her face like an aggravated storm cloud. She wore a burgundy dress of satin that cascaded in folds to her feet. The bodice fit snugly around her waist, detailed with embroidery in an even darker shade of wine. Slight puffed sleeves and a high collared neck finished the silhouette.

Despite the grand dress, something about Vienna had disappeared. Kole couldn't quite pinpoint exactly what, but the clues screamed at him. Her green eyes, which never rose to Kole or Felix's gaze, had lost their light. The line of her relaxed mouth deepened at the ends, like she held a permanent half-frown. Everything about her sunken posture betrayed the Vienna Kole had known over the last few months. And it was at that moment Kole wondered if the change had come from losing most of her hair, or if it had been there all along—Vienna gradually fading before his eyes—and in the chaos of the events around them, he'd missed it. Maybe refused to see it. The pride of the Liberation now a meek mouse. The realization pierced Kole straight in the heart.

"Whoa, what happened ta you?" Felix said, mouth ajar. After Kole elbowed his stomach, Felix cleared his throat. "I mean... ya look nice, Sis."

Vienna hobbled to her rolling chair and sat. The extra fabric of the dress twisted around her ankles, entangling her, though she paid no mind to it and simply stared out the massive window, eyes lost.

"She's...." But Kole stopped himself, unable to pinpoint the problem.

"Copin'," Felix finished for him. "She'll get better." His mouth scrunched to the side as he looked at Kole. "*We* did. And she's stronger than both of us together."

That Kole could agree on. Vienna was the backbone of everything she'd been a part of, from the Liberation to their small journeying group. *It's just the sickness.* The reminder eased him slightly. Better yet, Vienna had yet to succumb to a coughing fit all morning. Zeal had been the right choice.

A knock came at the door. Daveen let himself in. "Looks like everything fit," he said after a quick assessment of the three of them. "Right, let's get going, or we'll be late." Daveen took charge of rolling Vienna out the door.

Kole beckoned Caradin from the couch, where he'd been snoozing in a beam of sunlight. *He's more animal than Soul.* Kole rolled his eyes at the thought. The weasel's claws tapped the tile floor as he scurried over and climbed Kole's pant leg to his usual spot half curled around Kole's neck.

The east wing housed the meeting room, which held a plain round table surrounded by chairs. Tena rose from her seat at the far end as Kole and his friends entered. Her stiff posture commanded the room.

Four others settled at the table; none rose, and Kole was surprised to find a familiar face among them: Orla, the priestess from the temple. She wore her same ensemble, with those strange hand wrappings, and a warm smile lit up her face as they entered. Concern faltered her grin when her eyes found Vienna.

The other three council members, one other woman and two men, donned more elaborate clothing, sleek and tailored like the garments Daveen had styled Kole and his companions in. Each one bowed their heads in welcome and waited as Kole and Felix took a seat where Tena instructed. Daveen slid Vienna in on the far end of Felix, then bowed and took his leave.

"You all look well rested," Tena said after the door shut. "I hope the accommodations were to your liking."

"Yes, thank you," Kole said. Up until now, he'd fought to keep his eyes on Tena because he knew how strangers looked at him, and in these clothes, all lay exposed. But now he let his gaze roam, taking in the new faces. They stared as expected, though not in horror. Instead, curiosity. As if he were some puzzle to work out. *That* Kole could handle. No doubt the furry friend on his shoulder added to the interest. Still, when Kole found their gazes too much, he moved back to Tena or Orla for escape.

"As I mentioned, this is Kole, Felix, and Vienna." Tena gestured to each one, leaving a pause between names so the council could take them in. "They come to us from Socren on an errand for Leonardo. They've already met Councilwoman Orla, as she graciously took them in upon arrival."

Councilwoman? Kole studied Orla, wondering why the priestess never mentioned her status before. Though, in all honesty, he had no idea what the title meant.

"I'll let the rest of you introduce yourselves." With that Tena sat and tilted her head to the woman on her left, who sported short black hair, nearly a buzz.

"I am Jax, head of the Hasic here in Zeal." She paused at Tena's waving hand. "Oh, pardon me. The Hasic are the branch of military I train to work my moonstone cannons. My job is to keep Zeal defended from the Black Wall specifically."

As Jax spoke, Kole took in the extra accessories on her person: a timepiece on her wrist as well as a compass hanging from a gold chain anchored in her breast pocket. She wore a pair of gold-rimmed glasses with horned tips, and while she spoke, she spun one of the many rings on her fingers in what looked to be an unconscious habit. Kole's ears perked at the mention of the cannons. *Hers. She called them hers.* If Jax created them, she'd be the one to question about the Black Wall.

"Jax and Orla are our council appointed members," said Tena. "Our other two, Aljander and Solt, were picked by the people," Tena said.

"I represent the businesses of Zeal," said Aljander. His clothes of brilliant red made Kole's eyes ache, and he found the shape of the man's long, curled moustache, which bounced as he spoke, a bit distracting. Felix, however, poorly suppressed a giggle. Normally, Vienna would scold such behavior, but she slumped in her chair, eyes glazed.

Solt wore less ostentatious colors. Muted earth tones matched his warm skin. "And I was voted into the council for the interest of the people."

"Now that we are all introduced, let's set some things straight." Tena clasped her hands on the table. "These three will stay with us as esteemed guests of the city for however long they deem necessary. Their presence here is to remain as hushed as possible—a *must know* basis. Even then, it will run past the council in a majority vote before anyone outside our circle is permitted to interact with them."

"What about their arrival?" Solt asked. "The guards already speak of the girl with the gray lung. Rumors are sure to spread to the people."

"Since the issues of the people fall into your realm, I will direct you, Solt, to the task of silencing the rumors." Tena tapped her nails on the great table. "Nothing grandiose. A girl from the abandoners sought treatment after wandering too close to the plains. It's not far from the truth and will keep fears at bay."

Kole's ears perked at the odd name. "Abandoners?"

The council shifted their shoulders toward Kole. Some held a note of sadness in their eyes at the change of subject. But Aljander's posture stiffened, a cold aura growing around him while Tena's demeanor stood solid, unyielding to her inner thoughts.

Solt answered, "There are some who have chosen to leave Zeal in light of the... more frequent occurrences of the Black Wall."

"Bunch of cowards," Aljander seethed under his breath. Only Orla gave him a disciplining look.

"Those villages you passed on the far side of the Crystal Trees are former citizens of Zeal." Tena's fingers stopped their tapping.

"They are still our people," Orla corrected, a bandaged hand on the Seven Souls pendant at her chest.

Tena dipped her head at the priestess. "Yes, of course they are, they just... no longer hold our views and wish to distance themselves. Not from Zeal per se, but the wall."

"It's those damn rundown cannons," Aljander snapped.

"I beg your pardon?" Jax huffed, which sent the chain of her compass rattling.

Aljander squeezed the edge of the table so tightly his knuckles blanched. "Morale dropped when they started falling apart, letting the Black Wall creep closer."

Falling apart? Kole thought back to the moment in the street when the cannon fighting off the flames exploded, and the wall surged forward. Things like that must have happened before and frequently by the way Aljander fumed. A static-like energy sprouted in Kole's marrow. Though his heart spiked at the swelling worry that the Black Wall could surge past Zeal's defenses, he forced air coolly through his nose, unwilling to break with an audience. *The alarm. I'd hear that evacuation siren if it moved on us.*

"They aren't falling apart!" Jax slammed a fist on the table. "It's sabotage."

"We are not getting into this right now." Tena massaged her temples.

"Shifting the blame," Aljander sneered. "Putting it on some made-up cult."

"Enough!" Tena sprang from her seat, the chair screeching from the sudden thrust. "Additional queries can be discussed at a later time. I will hear none of it before our guests."

Aljander leaned back in his chair with a defiant scowl. Jax, though, fiddled with her timepiece, clicking the rotating face, refusing to let her eyes drift to her accuser.

Kole scanned the table as an uncomfortable silence suffocated the room. Even Orla had closed in on herself, shoulders sagged low and fingers rubbing anxiously on her wrapped hands as if in quiet prayer. Aljander's allegations had set everyone on edge, including Felix and Vienna, who sat on Kole's left. Felix peeked wide-eyed over to Kole with a tension in his lips. He wanted to ask more, Kole realized. Normally Vienna acted as diplomat of the three of them, but with her sickness and daze of fatigue, Felix seemed willing to step in. Kole narrowed his eyes in warning. Felix shrugged back, apparently letting whatever lay at the tip of his tongue go.

"In Zeal we pride ourselves in mastery." Tena stepped from her chair and walked slowly around the table. "What we set our minds to we not only seek to understand, learn, and innovate, but to conquer. The Black Wall is no exception. Jax and her team have learned to master the wall. When it surges, we drive it back like a whimpering, injured beast." She slowed at Vienna's side and took in the three of them, hands clasped over the buttons of her vest. "Forgive us for our tempers. Rarely do our adversaries best us. I assure you Zeal is safe for you." Her gaze lingered on Kole. No, not Kole, his neck where Caradin rested. Kole saw Caradin yawn out of the corner of his vision.

"Now." Tena's voice returned softer. She finished her turn around the room and poised her fingers on the table but kept standing. "Jax. Kole and his companions require a tour of your workshop. Answer whatever questions they have regarding the cannons and the wall. When can you be ready?"

Jax nodded. "If it's to be a private tour, I will need until noon."

"That would be best, I think. We will have someone escort them over." Tena's attention turned to Solt. "As I was saying before about our guests?"

"I will handle it," said Solt. "No doubt the... excitement of last night will have them preoccupied anyway."

"Very good."

"I suppose you want goods prepared in case of another wave?" Disdain dripped from Aljander's words. By the way he said it, Kole knew the businessman spoke of the abandoners. More people would leave after the lockdown ended — go to the villages beyond the forest of crystalline trees and put as much distance between them and the Black Wall as possible. Kole would, too. Even now, despite Tena's confidence, his entire being urged him to leave this city and never return. Duty — his deal with Aterus — outweighed the horrors plaguing him. For now, at least.

"That would be excellent. Thank you, Aljander."

A jet of blood spouted from Vienna's mouth and splattered the polished table. Everyone gasped and shoved back in their chairs save for Orla, who leapt from her chair and dove for Vienna as she slumped forward in her wheelchair. Orla caught her before her head slammed down on the table.

"What in Soul's name!" One of the council members yelled.

"V?" Felix draped an arm over her back.

No answer. Vienna had passed out. Her cheeks sunk in, and her skin held a gray hue.

"What's happenin'?" Felix cried.

"A reaction to the treatment." Orla carefully leaned Vienna back in her seat, where her head rolled to the side and her tongue hung out, dripping blood onto her dress. "We need to get her back in bed."

Kole shook his head in disbelief. She had looked so well this morning. Not recovered, *far* from normal, but better. Were the symptoms supposed to get worse before improving? Kole hoped so, because the alternative was too horrible to entertain.

"Leave us." Tena instructed the council. They all scrambled out of the room, eager to distance themselves. A couple sent horrified glances to Kole and his companions. Jax's brow set firm, troubled, and she gave a quick nod in farewell as she passed by Kole.

"Orla." Tena's voice held an edge in the emptied-out room. "What does this mean?"

The priestess tore her eyes from her patient. She shook her head saying, "Her body is rejecting the medicine. I fear she was exposed too long to the plains."

"Whaddya sayin'?" Felix croaked.

Orla placed her hand on Felix's shoulder. "Zeal cannot help her."

CHAPTER 21

Kole waited on the balcony of their quarters, Caradin on his shoulder, while Felix and Orla settled Vienna into the bedroom. He stared at the distant shadow of the Black Wall and found the fear he'd held for it slightly numbed in the wake of a greater threat: Vienna's waning mortality.

As far as Kole could tell, what little Tena and Orla had whispered to each other in the halls on the way back to the room had been grim. Kole refused to believe there was no hope left. Not when he had the cure sniffing in his ear.

"You could heal her," he relayed in his mind. *"She said she doesn't want it, but I don't think she has another option. You could save her right now."*

Caradin crawled down Kole's outstretched arm and faced him head on. *"Does Master wish it?"*

Kole clenched his teeth so hard his jaw popped. Yes. The answer was an astounding yes. But that meant another chance for him and his survival gone. The Souls, in their fragmented state, only had so much power in their reservoir once released from their prison. Russé and Issira had already depleted most of their strength saving Kole from the Black Wall and Felix from succumbing to his wounds after being turned into a Kayetan. If Kole wished to survive the process when Aterus extracted the Soul fragments from Kole's head, they'd need every ounce of divine energy. *A life for a life.* The goal of all of this — releasing the Souls, his deal with Aterus — came down to saving Ohr and the people in it. If Vienna died and he held the power to cure her... he'd never forgive himself for keeping it from her.

There was one course he had yet to try. Using it would leave him vulnerable, but he had few options left.

"Be on guard." Kole commanded Caradin. Before the Soul could respond, Kole dove deep within his mind and rapped on Aterus' door.

He hoped Caradin could pull him back out of the link if anything went awry.

No shifting of scenery this time when he found Aterus, and the balcony remained empty. Only the Soul's voice answered the call.

"*Kole,*" was all Aterus said.

"*I need your help.*"

"*Haven't I given enough gifts to you?*" The Soul said with a clipped tone.

"*Vienna is dying of the gray lung. Help her, please.*"

"*She is not part of our deal.*"

"*I need her alive... for the mission. If you can't help, I'll have Caradin heal her.*"

A beat of silence.

"*It will drain his pool of magic. I know, I've seen the others do it,*" Kole added. "*He won't be as strong when I hand him over. It's your choice.*"

"*My kin have used up their power....*" A shiver of excitement came from Aterus. "*A useful point, Kole. It seems things may be easier than I thought.*"

Kole stiffened. So, he'd let it slip. What of it? Not like they shared the same side anymore. "*So you'll do it? You'll help her?*"

"*You have the tools to do it yourself: Caradin's blood. But you'll need a blood sorcerer to administer it. You are in Zeal. That task should be easy.*"

"*A blood sorcerer? But I can't use —*"

"*You ask for a favor then balk when I give it?*" Aterus' voice bellowed in his head. The sound made Kole's limbs shake. "*You test my patience. Take it or let her die.*"

With that, Aterus slammed their connection shut and threw Kole back to reality. He opened his eyes, then cradled Caradin in his hands.

"There's no way she'd let a blood sorcerer near her."

Caradin's beady eyes almost drooped as if mirroring Kole's sadness. "*Caradin will give.*"

"I know you would. But even if we can talk her into going along with this, we'd need to find a sorcerer. And not just any old one."

"*Kole?*"

He whipped around. The glass door stood open. Tena stood in the frame with an unreadable expression and a mass of deep-green fabric balled up in her hands. A smear of blood stained her immaculate vest, yet she stood tall, calm as ever.

"Jax is here to take you to the cannons."

"I thought she said noon."

Her eyes narrowed, and she tilted her head. "She did."

As if on cue, a bell tolled in the city marking midday. The sun beat straight down on him. How long had he stood there? No one had come for him.

"Would you like to postpo—"

"No, I'll go." He stalked through the door to the foyer.

Jax waited by the entrance, offering him a smile when she noticed him. "Ready, lad?"

The bedroom door was shut. Quiet. Vienna must've fallen asleep, and Felix probably stuck like sap to her side. He'd go alone. Kole nodded to Jax.

"Kole." Tena offered him the green material. "Wear this. And keep your hood up until you return to this floor."

A cloak. The stiff, hardy fabric felt surprisingly soft on the scars of his hands. Without a thought, he swirled it on and flipped up the large hood. Caradin wiggled beneath the added garment until finally settling.

"Keep the boy out of sight," Tena warned.

"You have my word, Council Leader." Jax opened the door wider, inviting Kole through. "I'll have you back in no time."

Kole followed Jax to the heart of the city. The streets, for the most part, lay empty. They passed a few guards here and there, who seemed to be scouting the roads, and a group of workers cleaning up lamp posts and other large debris the Black Wall's wind had toppled. It seemed clearing the roads stood as the main priority.

While they walked, Kole noticed fresh stains on Jax's vest and sleeves. Even her hands had darkened with black smudges. Her posture, too, had weakened since he last saw her at the council meeting.

"How often does the wall move?" Kole asked.

"Depends." Jax glanced over her should at him. "The thing isn't on a schedule—doesn't have a yearly quota. Be easier if it did. It's the unpredictability that gets us." She shrugged. "A couple times a year. Usually, the wall doesn't move like what we saw yesterday. It has flare ups, and we keep those contained with the cannons. Yesterday... the entire wall... well, I've heard stories of it moving like that, coming in like an ocean tide. Of course, those were the times it has wiped-out entire cities. Modern Zeal hasn't seen something like this. Not in my lifetime."

"I've seen it." Kole pulled his hood further down his face so only the road before him lay visible. "It happened in Solpate a couple months back."

Jax's pace slowed next to him. "Then it may be a trend."

"A trend?"

"Once is considered an anomaly—a freak accident. Once you have two incidents of the same nature, it could mean something has changed. The Black Wall could very well be shifting."

Kole considered her words for a moment, then shook them aside. The incidents may have looked similar, but Kole knew the true motive for the wall moving on Solpate. Savairo's prized Kayetan had set it on the refugees as an act of intimidation. But the Kayetan was dead. Kole had killed the shadow himself. No way these two events could be linked. Not in the way Jax thought.

But something sat sour with him. "When the wall claimed my camp, it moved miles at a time. A lot like what happened here."

His tone must've conveyed his confusion, because she gave him a curious look. "Sounds like it, yes."

"I always thought the Black Wall moved as one. All the borders shrinking at once. But if Zeal never had that same swell when my home was taken, then...."

Her mouth pursed, then she nodded. "There is a lot we don't know about the wall. It is true there are times when it moves in a singular location as well as a whole. The local movements I call flare ups. Those are movements where the border ebbs and flows, mostly returning to its original position after a short time. These only affect that singular location. When the fire shrinks on Ohr and claims a permanent new border, *that's* when the rest of the ring will follow suit and close in everywhere along the continent."

"What causes a flare up versus a full move?"

"*That* is the question isn't it?" Despite the grim topic, her eyes glinted with excitement. "Can you imagine what we could do with that information? We could save so many."

One thing Kole knew for certain: the Souls had something to do with it. Aterus specifically.

They came up to a building of white stone. Jax pushed open the door and ushered Kole through. "This is where we work on the moonstone cannons."

The scent of metal and oil assaulted Kole's nose. The temperature in here was at least twenty degrees warmer than the cool winter day trying to whisper in through the door as it swung shut behind him.

The building lay open, one giant room, with iron staircases along the walls leading to second, third, and fourth levels of metal lattice floors, which looked more like floating bridges to Kole. The slats in the lattice allowed him to see all the way to the glass roof above.

"This way." Jax climbed up the nearest spiral stair to the second floor, where a dozen or so cannons lined the path in various states of assembly or repair. Tools lay strewn across the platform as if discarded in a hurry. It seemed Jax had stopped work rather abruptly for this tour.

"These are the current cannons we have in development. They are exact copies of the ones on the walls and outposts protecting the city — well, the ones that *were* on the outposts. All our western posts were destroyed yesterday. We are working to replace them as fast as we can." She held a handout to the cannon before her. "Take a look."

The empty quiet gave Kole enough courage to take down his hood. Jax had already seen the state of his face. No reason to keep hidden. He approached the back, eyes free to see past the encumberment borders where his hood had blocked. *No more blinders for this horse.*

The shape of the cannon reminded him of a telescope, except on a grand scale, and if that telescope rolled on two massive spoke wheels. The whole outer casing was a deep-colored metal. "It doesn't look like moonstone," he said, grazing a finger over the cold material.

"The name comes from the power source." Jax pulled on the handle at the back of the contraption. Metal scraped like the sound of swiping swords as she pulled a long capsule from the cannon. Though the arm-sized piece appeared heavy, Jax had no trouble handling it on her own. She set one side down, leaning it against her leg for stability, and opened a small box. A thumb-sized shard of stone sat propped up within a metal setting, like a great jewel.

"That's moonstone?" Kole asked.

"Sure is." She plucked it with delicate fingers and passed it to Kole.

In the light, the faint grains of the crystal wood stood clear. "This one piece powers a whole cannon? How does it all work?"

Jax took back the moonstone and reset it inside the box. "We concentrate the power with a series of glass pieces. Come, I'll show you." After locking the capsule back into the heart of the cannon, Jax rounded to the front of the weapon. "Here." She smoothed her hand over the thick, round glass at the tip.

"Like a spyglass?" Kole inspected the lens.

"In a way, I suppose. The glass magnifies the power of the stone." She tapped a boot on a tank wedged between the wheels. A hollow sound resounded. "And this is how we make the beam constant. Distilled alcohol. Concentrated to the point it burns long and slow. Without it, the cannon would shoot a single flash of energy and need reloading. Not much good against the Black Wall. With the longer running beam, we can have fewer people on duty when it's time to use them. My people run along the wall and power them on."

"How long can the beam last?" Kole asked.

"As long as the fuel holds. Never had to use it for more than a few minutes at a time, but I suppose they could go for nearly half an hour if need be. It's the moonstone that's the problem." Jax fiddled with her timepiece. "The stone only works for one shot, however long it lasts. They need to be replaced after every use."

"It's good you have a whole forest at your disposal, then," Kole said.

"Not exactly. Any piece of crystal won't work. It's the heart of the tree. The center core that holds the most energy. We can salvage maybe three from a large tree, one from most. *That* with the unfortunate reality that the moonstone only works once has made things difficult." Jax folded her arms. "The crystal trees don't grow back. They are a finite resource. The forest may look large to you, but the size is minuscule to what it once was. We will raze the land if I can't find an alternative source."

"Is that what you're working on now?"

"It's what I *should* be working on." Deep shadows bloomed under her eyes. "There's been more pressing problems calling me away recently. Malfunctions."

Kole remembered back to the exploding cannon that let the wall breach the city. "I saw what happened. The explosion."

"Yes, well, things don't explode on their own, though Aljander sure thinks so."

"You think someone made it explode?" Sabotage, she had called it back in the council meeting. "But messing with the cannon only puts Zeal in danger. Who would want to do that?"

Jax gazed at Kole for a moment, then turned her back. "No one in their right mind."

Those words struck Kole like a static shock. That man he'd seen in the street. The one who ran to his death—into the Black Wall. But how could he have caused the explosion from the street? And so far away?

"Tena told me you might have questions about the cannon?" She straightened her vest with a tug.

Her tone made it clear there would be no further discussion on the matter, so he tucked away his curiosity for another time, perhaps. In the grand scheme of things, the city's problems lay outside his responsibilities.

"How does the beam interact with the flames? How does it drive it back? How far can it be pushed back?"

Her mouth opened at the questions. One side lifted into a smile. "Let's go one at a time." Fresh excitement laced her voice as if such interest came as a rarity. "I'm sure you know the flames of the wall aren't actually fire, otherwise we'd be pumping water at it instead."

"I know that much."

"It's a burning darkness. For whatever reason, moonstone—the properties in the magic we harness from it—lays on the opposite side of the spectrum. Not powerful enough to destroy but enough to block. The goal with the cannons was never to eradicate the wall, that is outside my skills. I am an engineer, not a sorcerer. Instead, I control. The cannons allow us to push the flames back to its original stable position."

"Can you push it back further if you wanted to? Ever tried to take back the land it consumed?"

She laced her fingers, face turned solemn. "A long while ago. But the lands behind those flames are gone. There is nothing to return to Ohr."

"But is it possible?"

"What are you asking, Kole?"

"I need to find something that lies outside the border."

Jax straightened, one hand fidgeting on her timepiece. Her eyes brightened, almost eager at the thought, but her jaw flexed in contrast at his forbidden venture. "Why?"

Kole deflected the question with his own. "Will you help me?"

Her dark eyes narrowed at the redirection. Jax folded her arms and tapped her fingers on her biceps. "How far from the wall is this something that you seek?"

The real question. One Kole still needed the answer for. "I'm not entirely sure."

"Pushing the wall beyond its stable point could lead to things I can't even imagine. A few meters maybe, but if you think leagues... even if it were possible, it brings danger to Ohr. The sheer variables we'd be working with. Shifting one side of the Black Wall that far could pull the entire ring west."

Kole chewed his lip when he finally grasped her meaning. The balance of it all. "Which means risking anyone who lives on the eastern side of the continent."

"Precisely."

A risk Kole would never take. There had to be another way to get to Vara.

Jax clasped her hands behind her back and paced the grated path, head down and mouth moving as if talking to herself. A minute passed before she paused. "Your goal is to get to the lands beyond, no matter what greets you on the other side?"

"Yes." Kole hadn't given much thought to what he'd face if he made it that far. A realm of black fire? Desolate lands void of life? City ruins? Corpses? Maybe hell itself. Still he'd go. His life depended on it. His and Niko's.

"Then we should forget brute strength and change our thinking to something more cunning." Bright teeth shown through her grin. Kole flinched as she darted to a nearby workstation and grabbed parchment and a pen. Jax furiously dragged her ink up and down the page, sketching something out.

Kole peered around her arm. The drawing looked similar to the cannons perched on the platforms, but she'd added to the model: a larger lens, and more of them, and instead of the large opening at the tip of the weapon, she'd narrowed it significantly to the point where it resembled a beak.

"This could work. In theory, at least," she mumbled, but her words came in a slur as if she only meant it for herself.

"What?"

Jax slapped the pen down. Ink splattered the side of the paper. She tapped her finger on the end of her drawing, where she'd minimized the tip. "A more concentrated force. I can make a beam that can pierce the fire. Create a portal."

"A window to the other side," Kole said, realization dawning. His head spun, thinking it over. *Pass* through *the Black Wall*. If what Jax said were possible, he could go freely without causing destruction or instability in the flames. His rambler could carry him through, speeding his travels. "How big can you get it?"

"No telling. I imagine just big enough for you. I'm afraid anything else would take a great deal more energy. A power source we haven't got."

That meant the rambler was out. He'd go alone with Caradin.

"Time is our problem. The beam would last as long as the fuel does." Jax signaled to the tank of the nearby cannon. "I'll have to build a bigger canister. How long do you need?"

"As long as you can get me." Whatever Jax could offer, he'd take — make it work. Caradin, in his elk form, could carry him far and fast. He only needed the location now. Another talk with Vara may give him more hints. "How long will something like this take to make?"

"A month or more."

"*A month*?" Kole ran a hand over the fuzz of his hair. Russé would catch up by then no matter how much Kole deterred him. "I don't have that kind of time. A few days. A week at most."

"I'd need to make the prototype, test it, leave time for a possible redesign — not to mention the extensive testing on the Black Wall itself."

Kole only noticed his tapping foot when she glanced to it. He stopped and turned his frustrations inward. "There has to be something to speed things up."

"I...." Jax studied her sketch, then strode to the cannon they had been inspecting earlier. "I could make the adjustments on one of my current models instead. More of a headache really, but that would shave off time."

"And the testing?" Though Kole had stopped his tapping foot, the bones seemed to rattle in protest. It took all his energy to keep his voice calm. "One successful test is all we need."

Her jaw dropped. "That is quite dangerous. I don't advise —"

"I'll take the risk."

The building harbored a thick silence. Kole swore he could hear the wind outside caressing the glass ceiling.

Jax's expression, frozen, finally melted into a forlorn grimace. Not from the proposed work, it seemed, but her eyes took in Kole as if he rushed to meet death. Or maybe it was all in Kole's head — reading too much into a simple frown.

"If that is what you wish, I will make it happen." She bent at the waist in a deep bow, her eyes refusing to meet his again.

CHAPTER 22

Kole threw off his cloak, and Caradin leapt from his neck and scurried over the tiles to Vienna's room, those claws tapping the whole way.

Jax had led Kole back to City Hall without so much as a word. She'd put him on the elevator then abruptly left, leaving him to ride alone. Daveen had been waiting at the elevator door for him. The council took careful precaution with him, as Tena had instructed. What was probably meant to make him feel safe did the opposite. He felt trapped. Especially now when he had a mission to do but no privacy to start it.

As Kole lay back on the sofa in the foyer, a knock came from the door. Daveen announced Council Leader Tena, then stepped back and let her through.

"I heard you were back from your tour with Jax." Tena dipped her head to the doorman, who left them to their privacy. "She said she has quite a task ahead of her. She didn't even have the time to explain it all to me. I'm assuming things went well?"

"I guess." If things went *well*, he'd have his contraption by tomorrow, but he knew from Jax's flustered state when he left her, that would prove an impossible feat. "Have you found Russé yet?" Kole was eager for the answer. He needed to keep tabs on his mentor and make sure he stayed ahead of him.

"No word yet, but my scouts are searching." Tena strode to the glass door. "How about we talk in private?"

More of a command than a question. Despite Kole's sore feet from the trek through Zeal, he lifted from the couch and followed Tena outside.

She leaned against the half wall and stared off at the scenery. "I've always loved this view." At first Kole thought she meant the city, but her sights had turned west. "It's beautiful, isn't it?"

Kole shifted. That sense of panic returned to him. The fear for those flames would never leave him.

When he didn't answer, she faced him. "I've lived my whole life here. I've seen the flames move on the city, witnessed the death and pain it caused. But there is a beauty to it. The raw power."

Kole had moved his gaze to the crystal trees. The key to getting to Vara.

"Did you know that the burns from the black flame are different than ones from true fire? The scarring is different. And the wounds... they never fully heal. The skin forgets how to repair itself, and every injury after is permanent." The sounds of her footsteps came up behind Kole. "But yours have repaired." Her shadow loomed over Kole, and she held out her hand. "May I?"

The intent was clear. Tender skin pulled as he rolled back his sleeve and offered his arm for inspection.

Tena smoothed her hand over the scars of his forearm. "It's healed over, but the pattern of the burns are telling. After all I've seen, it's easy to differentiate. You've walked to the Black Wall and back."

"Something like that." The interest in her eyes made him uncomfortable. He pulled his arm back.

"No one survives something like this. A full body wound." Tena's intent gaze made him shift. "You've had help."

Kole pulled his sleeves over the burns of his hands. "What do you want?"

Her mouth drew into a firm line. "Leo's letter said you are an important piece in returning Ohr to its former glory."

Wary of revealing any more than she already knew, Kole waited quietly.

"Good. Very good. I'm glad you know what's at stake." She gave a sigh of relief, her head tilting back with a content smile. "I will be forthright with you, Kole. I know what you are, what company you keep, and what drives you through the Black Wall."

"How—"

Tena put a finger to her mouth. "I will speak, you will listen." She turned her head over her shoulder for a moment, as if checking for unwanted company, then said, "You cannot confirm anything I say. It will only make me more of a target and in turn, you."

"What are you...?" Her harsh look shut him up. *Right. Listen.*

"I expect you *not* to confirm a thing I say. I beg you to listen." The strange look Kole cast her way pushed her to explain. "It's tricky being lead of the council. I take precautions, of course, but I'm an all-too-easy, one-source target when it comes to mind-links."

A sigh pushed through Kole's lungs. He thought he'd seen the last of mind-links after crossing half the continent. If Tena worried about them, it meant sorcerers had roots in Zeal, too, and not just the good kinds like Leo.

"There are those with powers in the city who could read my mind. Ones who would use this knowledge for destruction. Everyone has their inklings of what you are and what you came to do, but none have confirmation. That is what they desperately seek right now. And *that* is what I need you to keep secret. Tell no one. Answer no questions. Not even mine, when it comes to the specifics of your mission."

So she knows, or has at least guessed. That relieved Kole, if only slightly. It meant fewer questions, less scrutiny over his requests. One thing she said, though, stuck out like a flash fire. "You said 'they.'"

Tena's eyes slid down to him with a dark glint. "Zeal's shame." Her hands smoothed the front of her uniform as she walked to the far edge of the balcony. After a brief moment to compose herself, she acknowledged Kole's question. "You heard Jax and Aljander argue in the meeting. The sabotage of our cannons."

Kole nodded.

"Those are the *they* I speak of. It's more than just a few people. We have a cult in Zeal. One that wants to see the whole city burn. They're called The Dark Hand."

Her words brought forth the image of the scarred man he'd met in the street. "I saw a man, burned like me, out in the open when the wall moved on the city. He... he said some strange things before he ran into the flames." Kole searched his thoughts for the exact wording. "'The fire will cleanse?'"

Tena nodded. "From what we have gathered, we believe the cult thinks the Black Wall will grant them power if they prove their worth. They sacrifice their bodies to the flames. Those who survive are regarded as higher beings." She leaned against the half wall and massaged her temples. Head still down, she said, "I know there is a leader, but identifying them has been a nightmare. Even the few cultists we have captured refused to speak. We let them sit in cells hoping the isolation would break them." She looked up, face sullen. "They all end up dead—taking their own lives or... with help."

"They've infiltrated your ranks?" Kole guessed.

"Yes. More the reason you should keep every truth from me. I could be passing these cult members every day." Her fingers gripped the glass wall as she forced a grunted laugh. "*Could.* I say it as if there's hope against the thought. No, they are here. In this very building." After a final huff, she straightened. "These are burdens for Zeal, Kole. I will handle The Dark Hand. *You* focus on your mission. Anything Zeal can offer is yours."

An alarm blared in the city. Kole's blood ran icy. He snapped to the Black Wall straight away but found it in the same position as a moment earlier.

"Not to worry. That sound marks the end of lockdown," Tena yelled over the siren, which ceased a long moment later.

A flood of people exited the buildings below. One group, three dozen at least, had a large escort of guards surrounding them. Kole pointed down to them. "What's going on?"

"More have decided to abandon the city."

The defeated tone of her voice gave Kole a clearer picture of Zeal. Grand as it would have seemed to an outsider, they had their own set of problems. He wondered if the strength the city put off was merely a proud façade.

"I must go." Tena dipped her head in farewell and moved to the sliding glass door.

"Wait." Kole gritted his teeth. He couldn't believe he was actually exploring this route. The Kole two months ago would've cursed him. But things had changed, and he was desperate. "You said you have sorcerers here. I need one trained in the blood arts."

Tena's upper lip lifted into a sort of snarl. "You speak of dark things, Kole. Blood magic is prohibited in Zeal."

Blood magic. The same source of power Savairo, the previous warden of Socren, had used to kill hundreds of people and turn them into his Kayetan servants. Savairo had done the same to Felix. Abhorrent magic fueled by hate and pain. Of course it would turn to this. He should've guessed the moment Aterus said it. The miracle he sought would come with a hefty price. It had been Piper who'd told him the price of such magic. The energy came from grief and pain. The more agony, the stronger the spell. What sort of cost would bring Vienna back to health?

Tena's jaw twitched as if she ground her teeth. "Every sorcerer in Zeal is registered. No one casts without proper authorization. We prohibit any materials affiliated with the darker magics from entering the city. There are wards in place that censor the language for outlawed spells. If the forbidden words are attempted, there are tracking components within those wards to identify the place they were spoken. There is no way to use blood magic without the council's knowledge."

"And if, as you said, nefarious people have infiltrated your ranks...."

Tena folded her arms over her chest, medals clinking together. "The chance of something slipping through is slim, if any." She took him in for a moment. All the while, Kole kept his expression as solid stone. "If you seek such magic, I can't help you. My aid would hinder you, anyway. The people you seek would flee the second they learned of my involvement. Pursue this at your own risk, but I will not hear of it, and I can't send an escort with you." Her hands dropped to her side. "Please don't give up hope for your friend. I have my best alchemists, medical staff, and sorcerers working on remedies for Vienna's disease. Give it time. We will find something."

Kole answered with a nod. Time. Everything came down to time: the moonbeam cannon, Vienna's cure. It was the only thing he couldn't afford.

"Do me a favor." Tena jerked her chin toward the foyer. "Wear the cloak I gave you wherever you go outside the room. Even onto the balcony. I fear The Dark Hand may find you...," she paused, searching for the right word, "interesting. And I need you safe."

Another nod.

The council leader left Kole in the chill winter air, where he sagged over the balcony wall and stared after the group of citizens below, who'd left their homes — their entire lives — behind. Their numbers eluded Kole from this high up. Maybe three dozen. Not much in the grand populace, but if groups like this left after every breach of the Black Wall for years... it added up quickly. How many buildings and homes sat empty below?

Such a vast metropolis. No way the council could keep track of everything within the walls. Secrets hid in the streets and abandoned buildings. Kole only needed to know where to look.

"How'd it go?" Felix asked as Kole walked back in and grabbed his cloak.

"Fine." He draped the cloth over him and pulled the hood on.

"Ya saw the cannons, then?" Felix pressed.

"Jax is building a new model. She thinks she can make an opening in the Black Wall, but it will take some time to build."

Felix let out a low whistle. "These Zeal people sure are advanced. Leo'd be giddy ta see it all." He held a bowl of pink water and a blood-splotched rag.

"How's Vienna?" Kole asked timidly. He felt a bit guilty leaving them both here while he figured out the cannon situation.

"Asleep." Whatever enthusiasm he held for Kole's news vanished at the new topic. He motioned for Kole to follow him to the bathroom. "I dunno what we're gonna do," he said as he dumped the dirty water down the sink. A pink tint stained the porcelain bowl.

"There might be a way to help. But Vienna won't like it—you won't either."

Felix wrung out the sullied washcloth. "Might surprise ya. Lay it on me."

"Blood sorcerer."

The cloth fumbled in Felix's hands and dropped into the empty basin. "What?"

"Hear me out. We can use Caradin's blood, but we need a sorcerer to administer it. Cast some spell on it or something—honestly, I don't know how it all works, but I know that it does. That's what Piper used on me back in Grayfall after the cursed attacked me." Kole studied Felix, trying to get a read on his thoughts, but Felix stood quiet as an ice-covered pond. Water dripped from his friend's fingers into the sink. Still, he didn't move.

"That blood healed me. It can do the same for Vienna," Kole added.

The lines creased in Felix's forehead. "It did more than heal ya, mate. That's the thing that got ya caught up in a mind-link with Aterus."

"It won't be Aterus' blood. She'll be safe. Caradin listens to me. He wouldn't hurt her." As if on cue, the weasel poked his nose out of the hem of Kole's shirt and squeaked.

"How do ya know all this?"

"I...." Kole grasped the first thing that came to his mind. The first thing Felix would never think to question. "I spoke with Russé before I went with Jax."

"He told ya ta use a blood sorcerer?" Felix's mouth scrunched to one side in a skeptical grimace.

"He said it's an option if things are bad."

Felix turned to the mirror, both hands gripping the stone counter. His shoulders sagged forward as if a great pressure weighed down on him. His voice came in a whisper. "Things *are* bad, Blondie. But how are we gonna trust a blood sorcerer?"

"It's a risk. But if it can bring Vienna back...." All these lies kept piling up. What hurt most was that Kole had always been a poor liar, so the only reason Felix bought any of his words now stood solely on the trust built between them. Kole wanted so badly to tell his friend everything. But not even the most eloquent of words could get Felix to understand Kole's predicament. When he'd tried to come clean before back in that barn, the looks the siblings had given him had crushed him.

"So how do we find a blood sorcerer?"

A familiar voice echoed in the room. "Tena's right, you know." Orla stood in the hallway, a load of fresh towels in her arms. "You should stay scarce, Kole." The priestess walked to the tub and set the stack on the bench.

Kole and Felix shared a look. A similar panic reflected in his friend's eyes, which told Kole the same question posed in their both their heads. *How much has she heard?*

"I'll keep that in mind, thanks," Kole said, trying to seem as relaxed as possible. The shake of his hands gave his nerves away, so he clutched them tightly behind his back.

"As priestess of the Soul's temple, I meet many people. They come to listen, to pray, to confess... no one is turned away." Orla must've noticed Kole and Felix's rigidness, because the corner of her mouth lifted in a warm smile. "What I'm saying is, I can find what you're looking for." She flicked a look between the two of them. "Just promise you won't leave the safety of your room. Vienna needs close watch right now."

Neither Kole nor Felix uttered a word as the priestess exited into the hall. Only when Daveen's farewell and the click of the door marked Orla's departure did Kole release his held breath.

"Well, shit, mate. We're makin' a criminal outta a priestess."

CHAPTER 23

Piper's stomach growled. Her throat rubbed together with each swallow, choked her as if she'd gulped down a lump full of sand. The good thing about traveling without humans meant they had no need for rest stops. Piper and her divine companions hadn't eaten, drunk, or slept for two days. Sure, she felt the drain accumulating in her muscles, but her body proved more resilient than any human. The gods, though, would outlast her half-blood lineage. Where she could likely go without sustenance for a week at most, they could probably double that in their human forms if needed. Which is why she hated to be the one to pause their trek.

"I need time." Piper dropped her pack and settled on a drier patch of grass in the marshland.

Russé stopped without a word, set his things down, and began rummaging through his pack. Issira responded similarly—silent—yet she remained standing, an anxious eye on the horizon. The annoyed grunt came from Obell, as Piper had expected. The Red Soul paced back and forth as Russé handed Piper a scrap of bread.

"Why not be useful, dear brother," Issira directed to Obell. "The girl must be cold."

"She is no girl," he snapped back.

"And you are no man." Piper tore into the stale bread, her stomach growling loud as an earthquake, but she took her time to eat. Though she may be a demigod, some human annoyances plagued her body, such as reintroducing food too fast in such a hungered state. The bread went down with a struggle, catching on her dry throat. Her eyes teared up as the crust cut its way deeper.

It was true, though. Her body looked young. Not exactly as young as Kole. Perhaps a handful of years older. Late teens, early twenties. But she had been alive far longer than that. The older she got, the longer it took to see any changes in her body or face. It came from the Soul's blood in her veins. Though what it meant for her in the long run, she'd only know as she experienced it. No other demigod existed.

A heavy wind built. Thick clouds darkened the sky, sounding off rolls of thunder. The soft plops of rain surrounded Piper, yet no water pricked her skin. Without looking up from her bread, she knew Issira was at work.

The small storm chilled her. Her body shivered. Though the cold held no actual threat to her, the dropping temperature still annoyed her. Piper tried her best to shrug it off like she had her growing hunger and thirst. To her surprise, as she chewed, the air around her warmed. Obell had stopped his pacing and stood a couple meters away, though he refused to look at her, as if warming her up had been more a happenstance than an intentional decision. Piper let herself smile before sinking her teeth in the dry bread.

"Russé, your waterskin." Issira held out an expectant hand. Once Russé passed it over, Issira circled a finger toward the downpour. A blue aura glowed from her fingers. The rain siphoned together at her beckon, merging into a thin string of water, then trailed its way through the mouth of the waterskin. "Drink all you please. I can get more." Issira handed the fresh water to Piper.

The ice-cold liquid ran down the back of her throat. That sand-like feeling dispersed on contact, and her belly constricted with joy when the water reached her stomach.

While Piper ate, the Souls waited, eyes cast to the surrounding habitat. She'd need rest. A couple hours would do. Just enough to rid her body of the oncoming aches. If Obell stayed by her side while she slept, his presence fighting off the bitter cold that settled around them, she'd recover faster.

The sun hung heavy, closing in on the horizon through the cover of storm clouds. The shortening days of early winter had made their pursuit of Kole more difficult. Piper could barely see her hand in front of her face once night came, let alone any signs of Kole and his companions, even blaring ones. All she could hope for now was that Russé succeeded in breaking through Kole's barrier and stealing away their location.

Once the last of the bread dwelled in her stomach, Piper leaned against her pack and stretched out her legs, allowing the muscles a well-deserved stretch. Piper studied Russé, who held his hand over a clump of crab grass. The weed lifted its stocks up, the end of the blades tickling the skin of his hands. She knew the Soul was itching to use his powers, but the foliage around here proved no more than weeds and bushes. Nothing substantial enough for use. Piper wondered if Russé would grow so desperate as to uproot hundreds of weeds and tangle them together to form some sort of abomination for quicker transport.

"You're worried." Piper kept her gaze on him. Out of all the Souls, Russé acted the most human. Whether a learned trait from living with the refugees for so long or that he'd actually developed these deeper emotions remained unseen. "As you should be. But of what, exactly?"

Russé removed his hand from the weed and folded his arms. The others shifted their heads to listen but made no motion to engage.

"Same as you, I suppose," answered Russé.

"Not likely." Piper's sole purpose, the reason she endured this quest, came back to her mother. She doubted Russé would care for Evangeline. The opposite. The Souls saw Evangeline as the catalyst of their problems.

"When we find him, will you chain him to yourself so he doesn't disobey again?"

At that, Russé's brows sunk, an appalled expression contorting his wrinkled face. "Never. He has his own will. His own freedom. Always."

"Until it doesn't suit you anymore," Piper quipped. Aterus had done the exact thing with her: a doting parent until her views veered from his. Why did the Souls think they could muscle their will on humans? On all creatures. "You know why he blocks you. He's chosen to do this alone. And yet here you are following him in hopes to get Kole back under your thumb."

"As opposed to what you're doing?" Obell asked. He'd turned toward them now, fully invested in the conversation.

"I seek to help Kole. Guide him. I will respect whatever path he chooses." Piper rubbed the tops of her stiffening legs.

Obell scoffed at her.

"Then we are one and the same," said Russé. He'd gone from fiddling with the plant life to twisting his hands around his wooden staff. His eyes, though on Piper, seemed distant, as if his mind were stuck on something else.

Piper sat up and crisscrossed her legs. "How can you say that when your only goal is to release your kin? The very thing that will kill Kole. You know that."

"We are searching for another way." Russé's voice had dropped to a whisper.

"Are you?" Piper placed her elbow on her knees and rested her head in her palms. "And what have you discovered?"

Silence.

Russé lowered his eyes to the ground. Even Issira shifted uncomfortably.

Just as she'd thought. Well intentioned but nothing to show for it.

"*Is* there another way?" Piper pressed further. "Or do you tell that to Kole so he feels better."

"I will *not* let him die." The adamancy in Russé's voice made Piper want to believe him. The Soul's knuckles paled as his fists tightened on his staff.

Piper pursed her lips and abandoned the line of conversation. Apparently, she'd hit a sensitive spot in Russé.

"It's already happened once," Russé said after a time. "The true death, not what happens when he released Issira or Obell, and now, I imagine, Caradin. In those, he still clings to a string that connects him to Ohr — to *us*." Russé waved to him and his kin. "All I do is tug him back. But the first time, when he released me...."

Piper leaned in, ears perked for the story.

Russé dug his nails into his staff, leaving tiny, crescent-shaped gouges. "Goren used Kole as a blood sacrifice. I'd always wondered how that old man had done it. He refused to tell even me about the specifics."

"Wait. Goren?" Piper had heard that name before. No, not heard. Read it somewhere. But where? Then it came to her. That name had been in the book of escapes Leo kept to record all of the outgoing refugees transferring from the city to the forest. "He was the first refugee Leo sent to Solpate."

Russé nodded. "Whatever ritual he used did the job. I remember that moment so clearly." A glaze fell over his eyes as he stared ahead, lost in thought. "The imprisonment had droned on. I couldn't tell days from years or voices from the wind. There was a point when I forgot who I was — what I was. I thought I was nothing more than the tree I sat trapped within."

"Then I felt a tug. Something pulled my attention. It caught me off guard. A crack appeared. An opening. I inspected it. When I realized it led to the outside world, beyond my confinement, I charged through without a second thought. No concerns of consequences. I look back on that creature I had become. No more a god, but a creature driven by instinct. Selfish."

Obell and Issira dipped their heads. They both held similar grim expressions as they looked on Russé. Perhaps they'd had comparable reactions to their own prisons.

When it seemed like Russé wouldn't speak further, Issira gracefully lowered next to him and placed a hand on his shoulder.

For a moment, Piper thought a stroke of rain had landed on Russé's cheek, but the drizzle had long passed, cast away by Issira. *A tear? What on Ohr could make a Soul cry?*

"When I stepped out of that tree, I saw what had happened—what I'd done. Kole had been a child. No taller than my hip. And I'd killed him. Taken hold of his life source and used that energy to break free and return to Ohr."

"You didn't know at the time," Issira offered. Her soft, melodic voice seemed to soothe the entire area. Even Piper's muscles relaxed as the Soul spoke.

Russé shook his head. He frowned. Those deepening wrinkles portrayed something worse than grief: shame.

"It wasn't like what happened when Kole released Issira and Obell," he repeated. "I had taken it. The exchange complete. I had devoured his life source. That boy, whoever he was... was gone. I realized my mistake immediately. I shook him, trying to wake him, though I knew it was far too late."

"Kole died." Piper shrugged. "We all know this. Even Kole."

"No, that boy was not Kole. He was some innocent child. Murdered by a selfish god." Russé held his head in his hands and sobbed.

The marsh quieted as if the land itself listened intently, waiting for the end of the story.

Issira flicked a hand Russé's way. Tears lifted from his cheeks where they'd streamed down his neck, then floated away.

"But Kole isn't dead." Obell's rough voice grated against the silence. "You revived him. You paid for your mistake."

"I paid for it by giving him a false life." Russé swallowed. "Reviving him isn't the same as bringing him back. I used a piece of my own soul to resurrect him."

"To do to one is to do to all," Piper whispered under her breath. The story ignited a flaming new truth she had never guessed before. "*You're* the one who split the Souls. Not Goren and his ritual—not Kole. *You*."

"Yes." Russé straightened, staff still tight in his knuckles. "The spirit of that little boy is gone forever and instead replaced with a mixture of the six of us. Kole has no memories of his life before that moment because there is nothing to remember. Everything had been wiped clean."

"Kole only lives because you allow him to," said Piper.

"Not allow. I owe it to him."

Something bothered Piper. She mulled the source around in her head before asking, "Did you know? Before you gave Kole a piece of you, did you know what that meant for his fate?"

Russé's shoulders slumped forward. The shame rolled off him in waves, so much so, Piper swore the air thickened with a metallic tang. "No. And if I had, I would've left him there, dead in the grass."

What horrible luck you've been dealt. Kole had been killed and gifted a life with an expiration date. "Does *he* know?"

"Yes. Aterus told him he's living on borrowed time."

"No, not about that." Piper straightened. "Does he know you saved him... without knowing what would become of him."

Russé shook his head. "At this point, I'm afraid he won't believe me anyway. So why bother?"

"*Why?*" Piper nearly choked on the words. "Because it's important for him to know. You keep telling him half-truths and you're right, he won't forgive. The first thing to earning his trust back is including him in everything. All your dark secrets." She cast an accusing stare at the Souls surrounding her. "Every last one of them. Only then can he decide what to do with the curse looming over him."

Kole's situation held parallels to her own mother, lying comatose in a bed leagues away. When Evangeline had gotten sick, Aterus had ensured he and Piper kept the state of Ohr and the Black Wall out of conversation. That lasted for a while. But soon, her mother began to notice things—question Piper why they never visited the cities anymore, and why they'd moved to such an isolated place. Piper could only lie so much before the guilt gnawed on her. Why shouldn't her mother know? The day Piper mentioned the Black Wall, Aterus raged at her. From then on, Piper and her mother never had a moment alone. Her father watched over their times together, monitoring every word. How angry Evangeline would've become if she'd known of the deceit. *Just as angry as Kole.*

"Are you willing to do that?" Piper asked the Souls.

"I am," said Russé, stamping his staff in the mire.

The temperature around Piper surged as if she sat next to a fire. She took that as a yes from Obell. And finally, Issira nodded.

"It's a start." Piper readjusted her pack into a makeshift pillow. Before she laid back to rest, she asked. "Is there truly a way to do it without killing Kole? Or is it a hope that you're clinging to?"

Russé stood and jammed the butt of his staff into the spongelike grass. "I will make a way."

He has no clue. She lay back and tucked her chin to her chest, eyes closed, welcoming the swiftly approaching sleep. It baffled her that with all their power, the Souls needed so much help from mortals—or demigods in her case. There was *one* way of bringing down Aterus that she knew of. But that plan might spark more destruction than Ohr had ever known. She hoped Russé could figure out an alternative.

CHAPTER 24

"You ready to try this again?" Kole sighed and let his head fall into his hands, a lazy gaze on Caradin. "Do you know how ridiculous this is? Me talking to a rodent?" The weasel's black, beady eyes blinked.

Maybe it was a bad time to do this, but Kole needed the distraction. After Orla had walked in on his and Felix's conversation yesterday, his every thought knotted with anxiety. How much had Orla heard? How much did the priestess understand? And more importantly, how could Kole have been so stupid as to talk freely without ensuring they were alone?

Felix had brushed off the encounter. In his opinion, Orla knew Zeal better than either of them, and if the priestess wanted to help secure them a blood sorcerer, he'd let her.

It just unnerved Kole how Tena had been so adamant about keeping the details away from everyone and now Orla had been exposed to nearly everything. It also put that poor priestess in danger. What if a cultist found out what Olra had overheard? He hoped nothing bad would befall her. What sort of shady corner of Zeal would that old woman need to traverse to find a blood sorcerer?

"Ugh, enough." Kole shook his head, hoping to shake free the worries, then focused on the task at hand.

The map of Ohr, which Kole had pulled from Vienna's things, lay open on the short table before him, smoothed out and held in place with a couple of heavy knickknacks Kole had collected from around the room. A line graced the western portion, the one Vienna had previously drawn back in the barn loft: the first hint Kole had to finding Vara. Last time, he'd reached out in the temple, the Black Wall had interrupted before Kole could mark the second line that would narrow in on the Soul's whereabouts.

"Southwest from the Seven Souls temple," Kole mumbled. Unfortunately, the map held minimal details of the city, with an outline of its borders but void of buildings or landmarks. The temple lay south of City Hall. That he knew. From the southern portion of the city, he drew his line, then leaned back and studied where it intersected the previous one. He drew a circle around the cross point. *Seems simple enough.* He had a destination now. On the map the area looked precise, but he knew better. The scale of the map versus the actual land was massively skewed. That small space could have been miles wide.

"We need more," Kole said to the animal on his lap. Vara had shown him images during their last contact, but they served no purpose. Floating chunks of earth? Bizarre dark voids dotting the sky? Figments of a dream. "We need something distinct so we'll recognize the prison when we see it—make our search as short as possible."

Caradin answered in Kole's head. *"More specific."*

He smiled at the Soul's growing vocabulary. Each time they spoke, the Orange Soul seemed less and less motivated by instinct, by the feral nature. Maybe he'd have a better chance at binding the Soul to him now. *Vara first.*

"All right, let's find her."

The connection came effortlessly—the way Caradin's mind melded with his. As a unit, they sank down to Vara's door, hiding at the back of Kole's mind. Even before Kole began to ease the barrier open, Caradin had swelled at the entrance, ready to protect against Russé if he should show. Kole shoved his way through. To his disappointment, an empty void lay beyond the threshold.

"*Vara,*" he called into the abyss. He'd heard her voice once before, so he knew she was there somewhere.

Kole waited.

And waited.

Nothing.

Why wouldn't she speak with him? Vara had begged for freedom. Wouldn't she want to answer Kole's questions? Help him end her agony?

A bang sounded.

Kole snapped his eyes open, the noise ripping him from the connection too fast for him to secure the barrier between him and Vara's link.

Orla stood in the doorway, panting, a small bottle clutched in her hand. "I came as fast as I could."

A whirlwind of voices and people ran to and from Vienna's bedroom.

"What's going on?" Kole jumped up from the couch, Caradin clawing his way up to Kole's shoulder.

Orla's fervent gaze pierced Kole with scrutiny. She shrugged off the question and rushed to Vienna's bedroom.

"We got her breathing again." An unfamiliar voice came from the bedroom.

"Come on, V. Ya gotta hold on." Kole knew that voice clear as fresh ice: Felix.

Kole followed the noise to the doorway and peered in just as Orla commanded, "Everyone out. Now!"

He stumbled back, clearing the path for three aproned people covered in splattered blood. When had they arrived? Why hadn't he heard them before? Once they exited their quarters, Kole turned the corner and faced a horrific scene.

Fresh blood stained the bed, floor, and walls, and even a few speckles glistened on the ceiling like some animal had been mauled. Vienna lay at the center of it all, soaked in that horrible bright color. A manic Felix, tears streaking down his freckled cheeks, held his sister's hand.

Kole's jaw dropped open. "What happened?" Vienna had been fine enough a moment ago. How had she gotten so bad so quickly? Her skin appeared stark as a corpse.

Felix flashed him a terror-filled, resentful glance, then turned his back to Kole. "Please help her."

After a sweeping gaze around the room, Orla pointed a finger to Kole. "Get in here. And shut that door."

Kole obeyed.

Orla unscrewed the bottle she'd brought with her, then lifted it toward Kole. "I'll need him now."

"Need what?" The quickness of everything left his head swirling. "Someone tell me what's going on."

"There's no time. Just give her Caradin." Felix snapped. "Ya said he'd help."

The casual mention of the Soul's name in front of Orla made Kole pause, but the pain on his friend's face and Vienna's unmoving body on the bed forced him to concede. The weasel stared at him from Kole's shoulder. After giving the Soul a nod, Caradin scurried down Kole's leg and hopped onto the bed.

The priestess lowered the bottle to the weasel. "A drop or two is all she needs."

Caradin dragged a claw over the pad of his paw, then held it over the mouth of the bottle. A sphere of silver grew from the wound. It swelled until the weight dropped it down into the glass, turning the red liquid pink. When Orla seemed satisfied, she swirled the contents.

"This is the last thing I can think to save her. Pray the Souls it works." The priestess wiped the slick of blood from Vienna's face, unconcerned by the aftermath that marked her sullied white hand wraps.

A dream. This was all a dream. It had to be. Nothing else could explain it. Kole watched the scene play out in a daze. Had Vara conjured this? Was she trying to tell him something? *Show* him something? *What is she playing at with this sort of torment?* Vienna, it seemed, on her death bed.

"Help me, dear boy. I need to lift her." Orla reached for one of Vienna's shoulders while Felix hurried for the other. "Keep her up. Keep her steady."

"Kole," Felix called in desperation. "Will you help now?"

Kole blinked, unsure of what Felix meant, but he rushed to the bedside and relieved Orla of Vienna's shoulder.

The priestess poised the open vial at Vienna's mouth. "Keep her steady. She *will* fight."

Kole and Felix hardened their grips, prepared.

That blood-soiled hand clamped over Vienna's mouth, and Orla shoved the bottle under her patient's nose. Pink liquid sloshed against the glass under a heavy, gaseous layer, which crept up, flirting with the banded lip of the vial.

Vienna's eyelids popped open. She screamed into Orla's hand.

"She's suffocatin'! Let her breathe."

"Don't you dare let go," Orla snapped at Kole and Felix. "Breathe it in, dear girl. Don't resist."

Kole locked eyes with Felix and saw his own fear in his friend's face. Together, they gritted their teeth and leaned into a thrashing Vienna.

After a tense moment that felt like an eternity of cries of distress, Vienna ran out of breath, her face so red Kole feared it could spontaneously burst into flame. Then she gasped. A desperate attempt for air, forced through her nose because of Orla's iron grip over her mouth.

The concoction shot up her nose in one seamless motion. Vienna's eyes widened before rolling back into her skull. Any trace of strength left her, and her body went limp in Kole's hands. She landed softly on the pillow, unconscious.

"Orla?" Kole turned his concern to the priestess.

"Give it a moment," she answered, her eyes equally intent on Vienna's still body.

Felix's hands flexed against the crumpled blankets of the bed. "She's not *breathin'*."

"The body can last a couple minutes without air." Orla pulled a small watch from the pocket of her garb. "Give the medicine a chance to find the lungs. I can resuscitate her if need be."

"How long?" Dread filled Kole's stomach. Already, Vienna's reddened face cooled — paled by the second.

"Two minutes."

The ticking clock in Orla's hand grew loud and echoed in Kole's mind — each one sounding more like the toll of a grand bell tower. He counted them. With every passing click, pressure in his body built....

And built....

And built. By the first minute, he doubted his skin could hold back the panic much longer.

Felix sat equally pained two feet away, hovering over his sister with his eyes moving from her face to her stagnant chest. But it was Felix's face that made Kole lose count; the emptiness behind it. And that hollowness grew more apparent with every click of that damn clock.

"Wake her up, Orla." Kole couldn't do it — watch Vienna suffer a slow death right before them. Not only for his own sake but for Felix's.

"It's not yet —"

"Wake her up!" Kole's throat trembled from the force of his command.

The priestess flinched, then returned the clock to her pocket. "As you wish." Orla waved the boys off the bed.

Kole went straight to Felix's side, and his friend sagged against him. "It'll be all right. We'll find a way, " he said, rubbing his friend's shoulder.

Felix made no motion acknowledging Kole's words, only stared ahead.

When Orla gripped her fingers around Vienna's mouth and pried it open, she said a quick prayer in a language unfamiliar to Kole. All he caught in the phrase came at the end. Something about the Souls. A deep inhale. Orla meant to fill Vienna's lungs with her own breath. But as her head lowered, Vienna's eyes opened.

Orla lunged for her shoulders. "Lift her up. Hurry."

The boys obeyed.

Once Vienna sat up, she coughed, hacked, and wheezed. Kole looked on in horror, his arm tight around her shoulders. Veins in her face began to burst; one by her mouth, one in her neck, and another in the white of her eye. The convulsions came so violently, Kole feared she may break a rib.

Finally, a dribble of black ooze seeped from the corner of her mouth.

"It's working. The medicine reached the lungs!" Orla caressed her patient's face. "Go on, dear girl. Keep strong. Fight."

The dawn of the purge. Over the course of the next ten minutes, Vienna coughed up more and more of that stuff. Then it thinned and she breathed—a full-bodied breath, easy and smooth. Sweat-drenched, she lifted her quivering head unsteadily as if it took every last morsel of her energy. "What happened?"

Orla hushed her. "Save your strength. Rest. The gray lung has left you."

"She's gonna make it?" The question weighed tight in Kole's chest.

"Yes, I think she will." The priestess put a gentle hand behind Vienna's head and lowered her back onto the pillow.

Kole sank against the headboard, his own body drained from the event.

"Ya hear that, V?" Tears broke from Felix's eyes. "Not rid of me yet."

The sides of her mouth twitched as if she were trying to smile.

With the tension in the room released, Kole picked up the discarded empty bottle Orla had used on Vienna. "What was this stuff?"

"What you asked for." Orla hung her head as if ashamed. "Straight from a blood sorcerer."

"You found one?"

She nodded.

"What was it? A healing medicine?" Kole peered at the pearlescent residue glazing the bottle. The liquid swirled in small clusters. The way it moved reminded Kole of a swarm of earthworms blindly wiggling to find soil.

"Blood sorcery doesn't heal. It only takes," Orla answered. "The concoction is meant to absorb the poison, but without Caradin's blood to heal her, she would've succumbed."

"How did you do it?"

"I...." Orla looked down and fiddled with the ribbons of her cloth covered hands. "I made a deal. One that I am ashamed to collect on." Her hand reached for the bottle, and Kole returned it. She hid it away in her robes.

"And Caradin? How did you know about him? Did Felix tell you?"

Felix shot a glare over his shoulder to Kole. "I'd never. She already knew."

"I heard your conversation. But I knew about the Soul well before that."

"How?" Kole racked his brain. No way he'd slipped up.

"When I saw you riding out of the temple on an elk that never came in," Orla said plainly. "The rest I pieced together from your conversation." The priestess pressed a hand to Kole's cheek. The soft fabric dotted with Vienna's blood felt warm on his skin. "Don't worry. The truth will not go beyond me. The blood sorcerer who enchanted the liquid doesn't know who I helped—just that I promised them the poison." She dropped her hand from his face. "You are safe here."

"But what about the poison? It's danger—"

"Now," Orla snapped, " Get her out of here while I clean up. Even a fleck of gray lung can pose a threat." She tugged off one corner of the bedding, then looked back to the pair of boys when they hesitated. "Go on!"

Kole and Felix caught eyes then slipped their hands under Vienna, heaved her up, then shuffled through the doorway.

They stayed with her in the foyer while Orla stripped the bed. The priestess insisted on disposing of the poison alone. And by disposal, did Orla mean to pass it on to the blood sorcerer as payment? What sort of awful things could that substance do in the wrong hands?

Caradin twirled around Kole's feet as he lugged Vienna's legs to the couch. "Stop that," he scolded the weasel. "You're going to make me trip."

But Caradin continued to circle his feet, speeding up when Kole ignored his dancing.

By the time Kole and Felix set Vienna on the couch, her sweat leaving his own skin clammy, he'd had enough. "What do you want?" he snapped at the Soul.

"Vara reaches out."

It wasn't Caradin's words that made a chill creep up Kole's spine but rather the return of the god-awful siren blaring through the walls of the tower. *Not again.*

Felix clamped his hands over his ears. "What the bloody Souls is goin' on?"

"The Black Wall moves?" Orla's face paled, her retreating steps betraying her fear. "It's only been a day."

Kole rushed to the glass door and swung it open. A mistake. It had to be a mistake. A false alarm. But the wind picked up, angry and harsh on his skin. The curtains whipped behind him as he stepped past the threshold, eyes glued to the dark shadow slowly crawling across the barren land toward Zeal—toward the ash drifts, where the fortified wall of the city had crumbled in the last encounter. No false alarm. The Black Wall moved again.

"*Vara calls.*" Caradin perched on Kole's shoulder, nose sniffing into the wind.

That did it. Finally, everything clicked. "It's Vara," Kole said, his voice drowned out in the roaring gale assaulting the tower.

When Tena had spoken of the Black Wall before, she'd said it moved a couple times a year. Twice in two days' span? Kole knew better than to peg this on coincidence. Too many times he'd seen strange things during this doomed journey. They all happened because of him or the Souls. This proved no different.

"Away from the window, Kole." Orla pulled him inside and pushed on the door. "We have to get it closed or it will shatter."

Kole and Felix aided her. They pushed, battling the tempest. No more than a hand's width from the latch, a snap filled Kole's ears, and the pane cracked. Tiny fissures lengthened across the door. With one last shove, the three of them secured the door. Kole looked back at the disheveled foyer, panting. The pictures had fallen from the walls and décor lay in pieces on the tile floor.

"Crazy winds. Glass walls. Not the best buildin' strategy, I reckon," said Felix. "Don't think closin' that thing will help any."

Orla waved a hand at him. "There is a ward over the buildings for the high winds as long as the exterior is secured." Breathless, she changed focus and rushed the wheeled chair to the couch. "Quickly, get her in. We must make it to the basement."

Felix kept glancing over his shoulder while he helped Kole lift Vienna into the chair.

The wheels screeched as Orla pushed Vienna to the door where Daveen stood, waving them on with a frantic hand.

"If we're safe up here, why are we going to the basement?" Kole asked.

The priestess paused. Darkness swirled behind her gaze. "There's more than the wall to worry about."

Though the wards protected the tower from toppling in the churning winds, they did nothing against the roaring sound. If Kole had closed his eyes, he might have thought a pride of wildcats prowled the building. And the tremors. The floor shook at the ferocity. Even the elevator swayed to and fro while they rode it down to the bottom level. Orla remained calm. Her composed aura seemed to relax Daveen, too, though the bead of sweat clinging to his neck betrayed his fear. The priestess' façade influenced even Felix a bit. The tension in his posture had softened — or maybe that had more to do with the new reality that his siter would live.

The close quarters in the glass tube made Kole's skin crawl. He felt trapped, and the easy view of the creeping black fire baring down on Zeal only perpetuated the feeling. Tearing his eyes away from the flames still a few miles off, he spotted movement from below. He blinked, unsure of what his eyes had just seen. Only a flash, but he almost thought he'd seen a figure climbing up the metal lattice of the tower. Nonsense. His fears were conjuring ghosts — tricks. The people in the streets scrambled for their safe shelters. No reason to scale a building.

Though Kole's nerves swirled, souring his stomach, the weight of the weasel curled around his neck kept him together.

The elevator chimed as it arrived at the bottom level. Orla took the lead, towing a groggy Vienna into the vaulted hallway. "Down the main stairs. It's not far." They veered left and crossed over the massive emblem of the Souls embedded in the tilework. All the while that blaring siren wrecked Kole's eardrums.

They had to turn Vienna's chair around and bring her down backward to traverse the stairs.

Kole had taken his first stride down the marble step when a bright blast of orange light illuminated the eastern portion of City Hall. Through the cacophony of noise — the wind, siren, and rattling tower — the explosion made a mere thump.

"What was that?" Kole clutched the banister and squinted through the swiftly clearing smoke, carried away in a blink by the gale.

"It's not our concern. Leave it be," said Orla, who helped Felix rock Vienna's chair side to side, maneuvering one wheel, then the other down the steps.

Kole took another stride down the staircase, eyes preoccupied to the east. Then he saw it; the empty space where a moonstone cannon had once perched. *Sabotage.* The Dark Hand Tena had mentioned. They were here, outside City Hall. He *had* seen right in the elevator. That figure had been a cultist heading for the cannon.

A cloaked figure ran past the window of the entrance and leapt onto the ledge to scale the building. Another cannon sat above the double doors of the building. The cultist was going for another—the only protection City Hall had against the oncoming fire if the wall made it this far into the city.

"Stop!" Kole sprinted for the doorway. The scars of his legs ached at his long stride, and he quickly reigned in his speed to avoid injury. Still, he covered ground faster than the cultist could climb.

"Where ya goin'?" Felix called behind him.

Kole pulled his slingshot from his belt loop and prepped a pellet. He shoved his shoulder against the door and heaved it open. The first push proved difficult, but once the wind curled its fingers around the lip, the gust slammed it open, nearly ripping it from the hinges. Kole pressed his back against the metal archway and dared not go further. One shift more would surrender his body to the mercy of the razing winds. Small pinches flared between his neck and shoulder where Caradin latched on tighter.

With all the chaos, the cultist, who climbed the building a dozen feet above the entrance, hadn't noticed his presence. Strange equipment covered the cultist's hands and feet, keeping them attached to the glass, and a red handprint graced the back of the cultist's flapping cloak.

Kole aimed as best he could. His arm swayed from the ebb and flow of wind. With a swift pull, he let a pellet fly. The current carried the bullet far from its target. At his next attempt, Kole veered his aim drastically into the stream. *Quantity over quality.* He reloaded before seeing if his hit landed and shot another and another. Only when the cultist faltered did Kole realize he'd hit him.

A second pellet hit his target—the cultist's hand this time. The shot made the figure lose grip. After a half dozen more attempts, Kole finally hit a knee, and the cultist fell at Kole's feet. A disfigured face stared up at him. Feminine. Her eyes opened wide at the shock of the fall. The burned tissue at the left side of her cheek held an eye of milky white. Whatever fire had lashed her had left her half blind.

"Why are you destroying the cannons?" Kole called, standing over her.

The cultist narrowed on Kole, whose own hood had long since been pulled down by the wind. In one swift motion, she pushed to her knees and grabbed Kole's collar, pulling his face so close to hers the warmth of her skin tickled his nose. "The burned savior has come to unleash destruction upon us." She smiled. "We are worthy, holy one."

"Holy one? Savior? What are you talking about?" He'd heard the same words from the last cultist before he ran to his death.

"I will take you there." Her grip around his collar tightened, then she jumped to her feet and pulled him from the doorway toward the road.

The deafening gale pushed Kole off his feet, but the woman dragged him on, whatever device attached to her feet giving her the strength to power through the force.

"Let go." Kole pounded his fists against her hold. When that failed, he tried prying her fingers open.

"Do not fight." Kole heard her passing words. "The dark flames will welcome you. It will reward me for delivering you. You will—" She cut off in a yelp as Caradin bit down on the meat of her hand.

Kole scrambled back in the time it took her to recompose. She came for him again, stalking him while he retreated to the safety of City Hall. In his panic, he fell through the threshold. Cold stone slapped his face. The sting registered for a split second before he shrugged it off. He flipped over from his stomach, facing her.

As she bent down, reaching for his boot, a hole appeared on her forehead. An immediate lift of her brows in surprise, then her face fell vacant, blood dripping from the circular wound, and she collapsed at his feet, dead.

Kole slowly drew his head around. Orla stood several paces away, a strange smoking weapon clutched in her hands. Her arm shook, making the long-nosed metal barrel rattle. He never imagined someone so frail could wield a weapon of such power. "Get to the basement." Her words came harsh, but her dilated eyes stayed on the cultist's body slumped at Kole's feet.

CHAPTER 25

"What the bloody Souls were ya thinkin'?" Felix sat on the arm of Vienna's chair. Though she lacked the strength to join in the scolding, her downturned brows matched her brother's tone.

"She was going to destroy the cannons. Those things are the only defense the city has against the wall." Kole couldn't stop thinking about Orla's weapon. She'd promptly stashed it away after the incident, so Kole only got a brief opportunity to see the thing. Like a small cannon, the barrel had arched from the base, which anchored in her fist. The pellet must've compared to the metal rounds he used for his slingshot, for the wound it left in the woman's forehead appeared no bigger than his thumbnail. Except Orla's hand cannon pierced deep—past the skull.

"Ya believe what Jax said 'bout people sabotagin' the cannons?"

The cultist's blank face stayed in Kole's mind, unshakable. "I saw her do it. But I believed her before that, yeah."

"Why would the people here want ta destroy their defenses?"

The siren had long since stopped, giving his ears relief. Kole scanned the open room. Anyone within or around City Hall when the alarm raised had come here to wait out the lockdown.

The basement stood as a large, singular room set up with chairs, couches, and tables. Dried goods and jars of water lined the shelves on the far wall, sustenance in case the lockdown dragged on.

The mood around the room varied from face to face. Some appeared worried and held their families close, while others wore masks of exacerbation and annoyance as if the approach of the Black Wall had been an inconvenience in their day—desensitized to it. How sure of their technology they'd have to be to forget to fear the entity that had destroyed the majority of Ohr. *Must be nice.*

Orla, who had made Kole promise to keep his hood low, had promptly left him and the siblings once in the safety of the basement to tend to any injured, but Daveen settled close to them, apparently assigned to their group.

Sure no one stood in earshot, Kole leaned in to answer Felix's question. "Tena told me of a cult residing in Zeal called the Dark Hand. That woman scaling the building? She was one of them. I saw the symbol on her back, a red hand. She was after the cannons."

"A cult, eh?"

Even Vienna frowned.

Kole filled them in on the knowledge Tena had shared with him and his brief encounters with the cultists. All the while, Felix's and Vienna's faces grew more horrified.

"That's messed up," Felix said as Kole finished. "Ya think they were talkin' 'bout you? The burned savior?"

Kole shrugged. "I don't really know. It could be what they say to anyone they try to recruit. It is a cult after all."

Vienna reached for Kole's hand. Her warm fingers brushed his palm. It pleased him to know her strength was returning. Her mouth moved, but her voice came too low to hear, so he bent down, drawing closer.

"Stay in the tower like Tena said," Vienna wheezed. Tremors shook her arm as she tugged Kole's hood lower, deepening the shadow over his features. "Keep your face covered. She has reason to take precaution even if she hasn't revealed it yet. We can't risk you drawing attention to yourself." A flash of Vienna's old self returned—that scrunched nose she always made when something displeased her.

"That I can handle." Kole rubbed his temples as the revelation he had an hour earlier gnawed at him. "If that were the only problem on our hands...."

"What could be worse than a cult comin' after yer ass?"

Kole looked hard at Felix. "I think I'm responsible for the heightened activity with the Black Wall."

"Don't put that on yerself, Blondie. Bad luck is all."

"Bad luck that both times I reached out to Vara the wall moved?" Kole shook his head. "I don't think so."

"You heard her again?" Vienna piped up. At her voice, Caradin crawled down Kole's arm and jumped into her lap. He wiggled his head under her hand, begging for scratches, which she obliged with a smile.

"That's what Caradin and I were doing when... when you were... you know."

Felix's mouth sagged in a sheepish frown. "Guess that explains why I couldn't wake ya up. Vienna started havin' a fit. Found ya in a sorta trance on the couch. When I couldn't snap ya outta it, I had Daveen call for help."

That explained Felix's angered glares before. "If I had known what was happening with Vienna, I would've helped. I didn't hear anything." Kole squeezed Felix's shoulder. "I'm sorry."

"S'not yer fault. I was just panicked."

"Well, it all turned out fine in the end, didn't it?" Vienna swept her thumb gently along the weasel's whiskers. "What did Vara say?"

"Nothing this time. We broke connection too soon, I think. That may be why the attack wasn't as aggressive this time. But it makes this whole thing more difficult. I have the location set." Kole pulled out the map and showed them the cross point. "I just don't know if it'll be enough."

"If ya really think contactin' her is movin' the wall around here, ya can't do it again."

"I know." That cultist Kole had met in the street on that first day here, running willingly into the flames to his death. Kole had felt a sense of responsibility for it, thinking he could've done more. Even more so now, knowing he was the one who'd enabled the wall to move by reaching out to Vara.

Vienna rolled her head back. Though her color returned little by little, it seemed the lengthened conversation drained her. "Does the Black Wall only move at the spot you're near? We could try contacting her somewhere outside the city."

A good point. Had the entire wall moved or just a portion of it? If the latter, Vienna's idea held promise. Kole shrugged. "I don't know. It'd take some testing out." And time Kole couldn't afford to waste with Russé' on his tail, though he refused to admit that to Felix and Vienna.

"No way. We're not gonna go out ta some deserted area and egg on the Black Wall. Whadda we got ta stop it if it moves on us? Not puttin' my chances on outrunnin' it, even if we get our rambler back."

Felix was right. The only thing with enough power to fend off the wall lay here in Zeal. Leaving would be a mistake.

"I guess we stick to the plan, then," Kole said. "Hope Jax can make the modification on the cannon work... and I go in blind."

"*We*," Felix corrected. "We go in blind." He held his hand between them the two of them, palm down like when they had made the first pact back in Grayfall.

Kole and Vienna added their own atop his.

Before Felix pulled his hand away, he said, "Just tell me you'll work on the whole throwin'-yerself-in-danger's-way thing. Let us help."

Kole straightened and folded his arms. "You sound like Russé."

"Well, he is a Soul. I take it as a compliment." Felix propped his hands on his hips. "Ya gotta trust us. That's what we're here for."

"Sure." Kole gave a forced smile. Usually when someone said something like that, it was meant to comfort. The sentiment did the opposite for Kole.

Trust. Everyone kept using that word. *Trust me. Trust us.* Russé had said it. Leo had said it. Aterus expected it. Always trust. And always asked of *him.* When would someone give Kole the same? Trust him to know what he was doing in all of this. That his deal with Aterus remained viable—a way they could all end up happy. End up with their lives....

Only Niko understood. And soon, so would Caradin. The Soul had already proven he'd fight for Kole, follow his word. Now Kole only needed the Orange Soul to pledge his allegiance and enter Aterus' deal with him.

Daveen approached asking if they needed water or food and telling them the lockdown would last a bit longer than expected. Kole took the distraction to coax Caradin from Vienna's lap onto his arm, then left the siblings for an isolated spot in the corner. The animal settled in Kole's palms and stood on his hind legs. The tiny nose wiggled as the Soul sniffed Kole's face. The progression of Caradin's language—his understanding—had finally come to a head.

"I know you're ready. All I need from you is trust."

"Caradin trusts Master."

"And Aterus?" Kole posed.

The weasel's fur stood on end at the name. *"Captor."*

"He sent me to free you."

The beady eyes searched Kole's. *"What cost?"*

"I want to reverse what's happened on Ohr. Save it. The people in it, and me. Aterus promised this. But he needs the power of the Souls to do it. After I free the rest of your kin, we can bring peace with an exchange in power." Kole sent the image of Caradin's essence transferring to Aterus.

The weasel cocked its head. *"Pass on my power?"*

"Ascend like the Souls intended all along."

"Ascension, yes." Caradin settled on his rump, his tiny front paws resting on the bulge of his soft tummy. *"I remember now—speaking with my kin. We wanted ascension."*

"And that's what you'll have if you help me. If you trust me." Kole sucked in a long breath. *"Join in my deal. Help me free the others, then give your powers to Aterus so he can look after Ohr without you. You can be at peace, then."*

"My other kin?"

"They don't know about it yet. I'm probably going to need your help to convince them."

"Is that why we block Russé?"

Kole nodded. *"Russé can't see the whole picture, yet."*

Caradin's little claws scratched his chin. *"No deal with Aterus. Only deal with Kole."*

"What do you mean?"

"I trust Master, not Aterus. Follow Master's command."

An odd stipulation, but Kole saw no reason to deny it. As long as the result remained the same, his deal with Aterus should hold. The slight tweak in the plan, though, may displease the Gray Soul. Kole decided to keep it to himself if they spoke again.

"I accept." Kole held out his hand at first, then outstretched a pinky. *"Shake on it?"*

The weasel placed both paws on Kole's finger, solidifying the pact. *"Follow Master Kole."*

Hours passed, stuck in the stuffy basement. Finally, Orla returned. She approached Vienna and Felix. After a quick word, she glanced Kole's way and waved him over, so he lugged himself up after opening the side of the hood for Caradin to hide away.

"The lockdown will end soon," Orla said as Kole neared. "Tena has been informed of our little encounter and wants you three to meet with the council immediately. We'll slip out before the rest of the civilians are cleared to leave."

Back at the main entrance, all traces of the cultist had been scrubbed clean. No body lay in the doorway. No blood. Any of Kole's slingshot pellets, strewn across the floor from his assault, had been collected or blown away by the wind. Kole might've thought the whole thing a dream if not for the warped and melted platform where the explosion had occurred. Any broken pieces of the cannon had been dragged away, but the platform stood as a beacon to Kole. No matter how Zeal tried to hide the Dark Hand's existence — shelter its people from them — they were very real. Maybe more dangerous than the Black Wall at this point. A force they knew little about: the leader obscure as well as their true purpose. Not to mention they targeted the only tools Zeal possessed to ward off the Black Wall. How many other cannons had fallen during the lockdown? To think the cultist Kole encountered had been the only one dispatched for such a mission was foolish.

Orla led them back to the lift. On the way, Kole snuck glances as they passed the large glass windows. Guards hurried about the street, driving wagons of debris away; anything from crumbled stone dislodged from the buildings by the wind to piles of ash they'd swept up. Kole set his sights to the city limit. From here, at least, he found no further damage from this last surge. The Hasic seemed to have driven the flames back quicker this time despite their dwindled cannons.

The council met in the same room as before. Tena stood behind her chair, knuckles braced and pale on the wooden back. In his respective place sat Aljander, who tapped his fingers impatiently on the table, and Solt, back straight and still as a trunk. All turned to the door upon Orla's entrance.

"Thank the Souls you're all safe. When I heard word of the cultist...." Tena rounded the table and put a hand on Kole's shoulder. "If I had known they'd be so bold... I apologize. I will assign more guards around the building to ensure your safety."

"And where are you getting these guards from, Tena?" Aljander spat. "Going to pull from the cannon operators? Not doing their jobs as it is."

Tena threw her daggered eyes across the room. "That's a valid point, Aljander. Maybe I should start assigning my council members."

He grumbled something unintelligible under his breath.

"They were after the cannons, not me," Kole offered, trying to calm the tension. When Felix raised his brow, Kole quickly added. "Well, not at first."

"That lady tried ta kidnap him," Felix added.

Tena led them to their seats. Her gaze trained on Orla, she said, "I was informed of the encounter." Her clipped tone gave Kole the feeling she wanted no further discussion on the matter.

Once Kole and his friends had settled in, Jax burst through the door covered nearly head to boot in dirt and grime. The potent smell of smoke and oil followed her in, and her short hair stood on end, wild and disheveled as if she'd run hand after hand through it. "Sorry I'm late. Twelve cannons destroyed. If I can't replace them, we won't survive another onslaught. I'm sure you all understand." After a quick bow to the table, she leaned against the wall, probably too wound up to sit.

Tena only nodded at her arrival, then returned to the far end of the circular table. "It is as we feared. The cult is targeting our cannons. Kole witnessed it himself—here of all places, at City Hall." She tilted her head his way. "Tell us what you *saw*."

Saw. She'd emphasized the one word. Unsure of Tena's game plan, Kole attempted to play along and did just that: recounted the incident without the extra details.

"We were able to recover the body of the assailant thanks to Orla." Tena pursed her lips. "Unfortunately, because of the state of the scarring on her face, we were unable to identify her. No personal effects in her possession that would give us a lead, either. Only the usual markings of the Dark Hand: the brand on the center of the back, burns across the body in varied states of recovery. Odd contraptions on her, though. Things that allowed her to climb glass."

"That means they have access to not only supplies, but creative minds—inventors," Jax added. "I had a chance to look them over. It's a material we use in our cannons."

Solt leaned in. "So you're saying the cult could be in the Hasic?"

"I'm saying we shouldn't rule it out." Jax wiped at her eye, but the dirt on her hand only sullied her cheek more. "We *have* been missing parts recently. Either they have an inside man, or they break in or—"

"Sounds like a security problem." Aljander's mouth set in an accusing scowl. "Can't keep tabs on your own faction or your own equipment."

Jax pushed from the wall. "Very likely, *my dear councilman*," she mocked. "Maybe I should switch up my priorities. Focus on inventory like a businessman rather than keeping the city from burning to the ground."

Tena snapped her fingers. "Let's not veer."

They both looked away, fumed.

"What did she call you, Kole?" Tena asked.

Kole studied the faces in the room before continuing. "Holy one. The burned savior."

"Sounds of religious significance." Orla clutched at the Seven Souls pendant hanging at her neck.

"Prophetic, almost," said Solt. "You think they've developed that far? Created their own rules of worship? It would take a while to grow to that extent. Makes me wonder how long they've been around and why they've only emerged these past few months."

Months? News to Kole. When exactly the cult formed seemed unknown, but only showing themselves, according to Solt at least, in the last few months sent an alarm through Kole. The timing lined up with the tragedy in Solpate. The refugees' demise. The start of Kole's journey for the Souls. What could it mean?

"A good point, Solt." Tena pulled her gray-and-brown braid over her shoulder and stroked it while she took a turn around the room, silent in thought. When she passed behind Kole, her footsteps stopped. "We have an opportunity to learn more here."

Orla perked up next to Vienna. "You have a plan?"

"The Dark Hand has shown a great interest in our new guest. The connection is there. The burns. That's what interests them." Kole felt Tena walk up behind him and hover there. "We could use that to our advantage."

"Use Blondie?" Felix asked. "I'm all for takin' some risks, but whaddya got in mind?"

"Use Kole as bait. Put him on grand display." Her hands gripped the sides of his chair. "Maybe we can lure out the cultists. They certainly want him for whatever reason."

Want him they did. But how could they use him without making it obvious? Kole was open to this only if it left his current plans with Jax unhindered.

Orla's head snapped up, eyes bright with an idea. "We hold a celebration."

"Celebrate at a time like this? When the Black Wall has moved twice in days?" Jax huffed. "No one would buy it."

"A party to honor the Hasic's success at keeping Zeal safe," Orla clarified. "You have done that, after all."

"That may work," Tena said.

Jax shifted off the wall. Her face contorted in disgust. "You want me dancing, drinking, and stuffing my face while cannons need fixing?"

Tena held out her hands in a way that demanded calm. "Only for a short time. Make an appearance, give a quick speech, and you can leave."

Jax's eyes moved around the room before landing on Kole. "I have quite a lot to do." Kole caught on to her pointed look and the edge in her voice. She spoke of their special project on the cannon. "But I could spare an hour if it means stopping those cultists from destroying my equipment."

Tena nodded, satisfied. "And what of our Liberation, hmm?"

Kole, Felix, and Vienna glanced to one another. The sly upturn of one side of Felix's mouth conveyed his stance, but Kole had already predicted his friend would be up for such a plan. However, Vienna pursed her lips. Kole and Felix both knew she had the final word on the matter.

"I'll leave it up to you, Kole." Vienna's voice came full on, smooth even, now that the poison had left her lungs. Kole hadn't heard her voice that clear since their time back on the volcano. The potion Orla had acquired from the blood sorcerer worked fast.

The cultists' destruction only caused more work for Jax, and any time spent fixing the city's cannons meant a delay in his own project. Even if this party put him in danger, getting to Vara was more important and time sensitive. Every passing day gave Russé a chance to catch up. Kole turned in his seat to face Tena. "I'll do it."

CHAPTER 26

The ball was set for the following night. Kole feared he'd be stuck in their guest quarters twiddling his thumbs all night and day until Daveen delivered news that Jax was calling on him. She must've made progress on the modified cannon, or so Kole hoped. Still, that left an hour with nothing to do.

"A ball," Vienna said as she came out of the bedroom, back in her tunic and pants. "That's their answer to all of this?"

Felix sprawled out on the couch, feet propped up on the glass table, while Caradin stretched out over Felix's stomach, enjoying scratches to his tummy. "We're not goin' for the dancin' 'n stuff. We'll be undercover just like old times, eh V?"

When they had returned to their room, they found Daveen had tidied up from the wind that had rattled and destroyed some of the fine trinkets. Not only had he removed all traces of shattered glass and dust, but anything broken had been replaced with new art pieces.

"Except we will be expected to dress for the occasion." Vienna huffed and rolled her eyes. "Another dress."

Kole grabbed the marble knickknack from the table, some abstract indiscernible shape, then sat in the armchair across from Felix. His fingers moved over the cold surface. Anything to keep himself busy.

"What's wrong with dresses? I think ya looked nice. Kole did too, didn't ya, mate?"

"Uh, yeah." Kole gulped when her focus turned to him. Those eyes that had been so dull a day ago had reignited with that old spark. Vienna walked and talked on her own again. The recovery was astoundingly quick. Even the dark circles under her eyes had lifted a bit. But her skin still held some thinness, and she could only move so much before she needed a short break. "You looked... the dress...." What could he say? Despite her sickness, she had been the most beautiful thing he'd laid eyes on? Absolutely not. But his hesitation had them both looking at him, their gazes more curious by the second. He shifted on the cushion. "It showed off the necklace well."

She shrugged off the comment and sat by her brother. "Yes, I'm sure we were all very handsome, but unlike you two in your stuffy suits, a dress is heavy and a hindrance to my mobility. I won't be much use if something should go wrong."

"Who says you'll have enough energy ta fight, anyway?" To Caradin's delight, Felix smoothed down the weasel's whiskers. "You were on yer deathbed this mornin'. Shoulda seen yerself."

"I'm feeling a lot better, really." She folded her arms over her chest as if to disguise her heavy breaths. "Another day and I might be back in fighting condition."

The last light of sun dipped below the Black Wall far beyond the window of their quarters. The crystal forest lit up the horizon with a cold white glow. Kole stared at it until a shadow streaked by in the corner of his vision. Felix's Kayetan. Since the shadow would leave in a moment, off to patrol on Felix's command as it did every night, Kole ignored the creature.

The squeak of a cushion filled the room. "I wanna try again." Felix had sat up from his spot.

"Felix... " Vienna said as a low warning.

"I have ta try."

Vienna grabbed his arm when he stepped toward the waiting shadow. "You don't *have* to do anything."

Instead of pulling away, Felix placed a hand atop hers. "Ya showed yer strength today. It's time I grow inta mine." After that, her hand fell away.

Caradin hopped off the couch and settled in Kole's lap. The weasel cast a jealous glance at Kole's hands, busy on the marble piece. Giving in with a sigh, Kole replaced the trinket on the table and stroked the soft fur of the animal's back as he watched Felix approach his shadow.

"It's strange how this city can go on existin'. It shouldn't, bein' so close to the Black Wall." Felix's voice sounded disconnected, as if he spoke his string of thoughts as they came. "Folks should be runnin' away screamin' like the rest of 'em. But most choose ta stay even though they've seen the destruction." Felix lifted his hands to his Kayetan, then looked back at his sister. "That's what I gotta do. For Ma and Pa. Brave like you and Kole and the people of Zeal."

When he turned back to his Kayetan, Felix spoke so low, Kole barely caught it. "I ain't gonna be afraid."

The moment Felix and his shadow connected, the Kayetan's body siphoned into Felix through the dark wisps of his wrists. Felix doubled over, grimacing, and a whimper of pain escaped him.

"Felix!" Vienna cried.

Kole crossed the room, placing himself between her and her brother. "Don't interfere." Her wide eyes, filled with worry, made him add, "He can do this. Give him a chance."

She obeyed but perched on the edge of the couch, ready to pounce.

Quiet growls came from Felix as he battled the Kayetan inside him. His face reddened. Sweat beaded across his forehead and dripped down past his ears. Then his neck discolored in streaks as the veins beneath turned black. The lines led all the way up to Felix's eyes, which he'd clenched shut.

Kole's head told him to trust Felix—trust that he knew his limitations and not to push too far—but Kole's heart willed to interfere as much as Vienna. Even the Orange Soul, squirming on Kole's lap, whined at the sight.

Then, Felix went limp. The strain had gone. No more resistance. He hunched over, gasping. When he straightened, black eyes landed on them.

"You okay?" Kole tested, taking a small step toward him.

Those dark, unfamiliar eyes narrowed on Kole within the flick of a second. The veins still held that purplish black color under his skin.

"I'm fine." The voice came from Felix's mouth, but it sounded off, like it had before when he'd let his Kayetan in: a mix of his own voice with a deeper sound, almost harmonizing. "I feel... strange... but good." Felix flexed his hands. "Great, actually." As his fingers stretched, shadows extended from them. Longs claws. *Shadowed* claws like a Kayetan's.

Kole tensed. His fingers braced on the sofa cushion tightened. "What's happening?"

The claws must've surprised Felix, too, because he jumped back at the sight. But when he did, his body flashed away in a cloud of smoke and reappeared a dozen feet away in the corner, quicker than Kole could blink.

"What the bloody Souls!" Felix cried. The sudden burst of panic led to another doubled-over struggle. Whatever pain Felix had overcome a moment ago had returned.

"Keep your mind calm!"

This time, though, as Felix struggled with his Kayetan, the skin around those black veins darkened, the color spreading. Kole had no clue what would happen if the shadow continued to advance, but a damning feeling in his gut told him he needed to get Felix back under control.

"Fighting against it makes you unstable. You have to relax."

The fast breaths coming from the corner slowed, little by little until they became steady and calm. The discoloration on his skin retreated. "You're right, Blondie. Gotta stay calm," came the bizarre, echoed voice.

This time, Felix brought his hands up to inspect them. The fingers remained, yet shadows encased them and jutted out an extra six inches or so before they curved into sharp points.

Vienna stood and slowly circled her brother. "They're Kayetan claws."

"Did you see the way he moved?" Kole asked.

Vienna nodded. "He's something between shadow and human."

"Do you think the claws work the same? Cut through anything?" Kole eyed the strange new appendages, whereas Caradin shifted side to side, uneasy.

Felix dropped his hands to his sides. "Stop talkin' 'bout me like I'm some experiment."

Kole and Vienna shared a glance, then returned their attention to Felix.

"All right, all right, I get it. I kinda am." Felix moved to the curtains draped next to the glass door. With his hand drawn back, poised for a strike, he paused, took a deep breath, then swiped.

The fabric fell in ribbons to the tile.

All three stared at the tattered fabric on the floor.

Caradin nibbled on Kole's ear. "Stop that." Kole swatted him away, but when the weasel came right back to his ear, Kole lifted the animal from his lap and placed him on the couch.

"That'll be useful." Felix turned back to them.

"How did you move like that before?" Vienna asked.

"I dunno." Felix jumped back again, but he landed like normal. "Somethin' I'll need ta play with, I guess."

"Your eyes, Felix," Vienna pointed to the mirror hung on the wall. "And your skin."

Felix wandered over. When he spotted his reflection, his body disappeared again and reformed by the bedroom door, streams of smoke trailing around him.

Kole and Vienna turned to him.

"I look like one 'a them." The shadow pulsed from Felix's veins as his control faltered.

"Shh." Vienna crossed the room to him, but she stopped short. "Only a little. But that doesn't matter."

"How do you feel?" Kole followed her over. A tug on his ankle told him Caradin had jumped on his pant leg. Why was the Soul being so clingy? They'd treated him too much like a pet rather than a god. Spoiled him.

"*Kole.*" Caradin's voice rang in his head.

"*Not now. Can't you see this is important?*" Kole responded, then closed off his connection to the Soul as best as he could.

"Don't feel as different as I look, that's for sure." Felix tucked his hands behind his back as they closed in. "Just in case." He winked. "Actually, feel a little more like me. The whispers are gone, at least."

"What does that mean?" Kole asked. He wished he had more answers, but the Souls wouldn't even know about such things. Leo maybe. Or Shikar. But one was hundreds of miles away and the other dead. All this the three of them would have to figure out on their own.

"Maybe it's because he's whole again... sort of." Vienna took in their confused gazes, then added. "Think about it. A shadow is a piece of us — one that we don't really acknowledge, but it's still there. Maybe the whispers were the Kayetan calling to you, wanting to be reconnected again. And now that it is the shadow is content."

"That's a bit of a leap, Sis, but I'll take it for now." Felix frowned as he slowly slipped one hand from behind him. "Is this permanent? What happens when mornin' comes? I'm not gonna vanish like a Kayetan, am I?"

"You invited the shadow in, so maybe you can make it leave, too," Kole suggested.

"Ya, all right. I'll try it." Felix set his shoulders back as if readying himself, then he peeked up at them. "Maybe give a guy some room, eh? Just in case."

Kole and Vienna retreated to the sofa and squatted behind it for cover. Meanwhile, Caradin had made it back up to Kole's shoulder and clawed at his neck.

"Will you knock it off?" Kole lifted the animal by the scruff and held him firmly in his hands.

Meanwhile, Felix held his wrists out before him, that smoke still dancing from his scars like ethereal manacles. "Go on, then. Get outta here." The muscles in Felix's body tensed and twitched as a swirl of smoke and shadow seeped from his wrists. Black fog filled the space, building into a humanoid shape. The Kayetan stood before him, and with that departure, the discoloration in Felix's veins and eyes faded. Perfectly separate once more. "That wasn't so bad."

Vienna stood from her spot with a gleaming smile. "You're learning fast. Shikar would be proud."

"As long as I can control this thing...." Felix eyed his shadow up and down. The Kayetan mimicked his every move. "Yeah, maybe it's not so bad."

Just as Kole opened his mouth to congratulate his friend, a sharp pain bore into the fleshy part of his hand. He cried out. Caradin had clamped his fangs deep into the muscle and hung on despite Kole's attempt to shake him off.

"Caradin!" Vienna scolded.

At his name, the Soul released his hold on Kole then lifted to his hind legs.

"What in Soul's name?" Blood beaded and dripped from the puncture wound. "Why'd you do that?"

"Russé reaches out."

"Then block him!" Kole snapped at the weasel. "You didn't have to bite me." The throbbing intensified as the full shock of the event subsided. He cradled his hand to his chest and closed his eyes. When he opened them again, Vienna and Felix stared at him, faces pale, mouths slightly ajar.

"Kole, what's goin' on?" Felix asked, accusation crisp on his tongue.

Vienna's brows shifted low over her eyes. "What do you mean 'block him'?"

Kole stared at them for a moment, his face matching their confusion. "How did you—" His mouth snapped shut as he replayed the last moment in his head. They'd heard his conversation with Caradin? They'd *heard* it?

"It is done." The familiar voice of the Orange Soul rang out. But not in Kole's head. It came to his ears. The Soul had finally found his voice, and their brief spat had been heard.

After taking a step back, Vienna asked, "You're blocking Russé? Why would you do that?"

"Ya told Tena ta take her scouts north," said Felix. "Are they really north, or is that a fat lie?"

"No, they're not north," Kole conceded. No sense denying it now that they heard it straight from Caradin's mouth.

"How long has he been trying to find us?" Vienna touched her temple as she shook her head.

"It's not what you think." Despite his words, Kole knew better. It was exactly what they thought.

"*Then what is it?*" The inflection in Vienna's voice shattered Kole's heart. Felix had come to her side, letting her lean against him for support.

This was it. He'd been found out. *Might as well get it out there quick and clean.* Kole took in a long, slow breath, then said, "I've made a deal with Aterus. We—"

"You've *what*?" Vienna crumpled against her brother, who caught her. With his help, she rested on the couch.

Felix stayed on his feet behind her, his Kayetan alert at his side.

"He's offered me my body back. To keep me alive. And Niko," he added. "He can bring him back, too. I already have his spirit with me. I can show—"

"What are ya thinkin'? What 'bout Russé? Issira and Obell? All the other Souls? What 'bout Ohr? Yer just switchin' sides?"

"I'm not switching sides. We want the same thing: keep Ohr safe. Aterus wants that, too."

"Bullshit," Felix cursed.

"Keep us safe? How can you say that after all that he's done?" Vienna held her stomach as she coughed. She swallowed then added, "He's killed thousands."

"He didn't...." Kole stopped himself before he sank as low as to defend Aterus. A great sigh passed his lips. "I know. He promised to stop. It's part of the deal. No one else has to die. Including *me*."

"Is this about what Russé revealed to you back in Grayfall?" Vienna reached out and grabbed Kole's hands. "We promised to find a way, Kole. Felix and you and me. Did that mean nothing?"

Kole remembered that pact distinctly. Complete trust and honesty between them. But when he had tried to bring his deal to light, they'd shown little tolerance. "I tried to tell you, but you barely listened. How could you possibly understand? I'm the one who's going to die in the end unless someone finds it important enough to save me. How much time is there until that happens? Who has done anything about it except me? Aterus isn't just going to save me, he's going to heal me and give back the only person I've ever loved. *Along* with Ohr's safety. Russé and the others...." Kole pulled his hand from hers. "They've never offered that."

"Maybe 'cause it's impossible ta bring back the dead. It ain't right, mate." When Felix poised his hands on his hips, his shadow did the same. Twice the reprimand. "Knowin' Russé, he won't tell ya a way ta save ya unless he's sure. Fear of false hope and all."

"You're wrong." Kole flinched at the feel of the weasel's fur nuzzled against his neck. Caradin had taken his place there again, but instead of the usual relaxed nature of the animal, the Soul gave off a protective aura. "Russé would lie until the end."

Silence thickened the room. The air stuck in Kole's throat like molasses.

"You must break it off," Vienna said so quietly, Kole thought he'd imagined it, but her eyes weighed heavy on him. "Please."

He stared at her until his heart could no longer bear the disappointment on her face. Felix bit the side of his lip, anticipating Kole's answer.

The siblings—his only true allies. Would Kole lose them if he refused? But what could they do for him? What could any of them do against gods, the Black Wall, a dying planet? Nothing. Not even Kole held the power to save any of it. That promise he'd made with Felix and Vienna back in Grayfall had been a mistake. Naive and foolish.

"Ya haven't done anythin' yet, right? It's not too late ta call it off," Felix whispered.

"It'll leave my survival to chance," Kole snapped back.

"V and I would both choose death if it meant savin' Ohr."

That Kole knew. The greatest good. The mass survival. That's what the siblings believed. What Russé and his comrades believed. But it was not *his* belief. *One life is enough. One life is worth saving. My life is worth something more than sacrifice.*

And so Kole looked them both straight in the eyes one last time before the bond between them would sever forever. His heart grew quiet as he said, "I won't go back on my deal."

"Then yer a traitor." The Kayetan swelled behind Felix as his temper rose, but when Vienna held up a hand, he calmed.

"It's his choice, whether we like it or not." Vienna had slumped forward, any strength left in her long faded. The lively spark she'd regained since her sickness had reverted to that distant gaze. "Our mission doesn't change."

"Ya can't be serious," Felix moaned.

"Entirely," she said as she held out her hands to her brother. "Help me to bed. I need to rest."

Kole sat on the balcony in the winter night. His body had grown so cold and for so long, the temperature no longer bothered him. Numb. Both body and mind. Caradin, curled around his neck, snored, perfectly content.

No sign of Felix and Vienna. They stayed in the confines of the bedroom, door shut. Kole wondered if their anger would ever thaw or if he *had* lost them forever. Time would tell. For now, they needed space, and Kole would give that.

But the thought of losing them....

Kole tried to shake the thought away. It clung to him.

Here he was in an unfamiliar city on the cusp of the Black Wall completely alone. No allies.

"Why did you have to speak?" he said softly into the continually dropping temperature. The thickening clouds overhead promised snow soon. "Why couldn't we have kept our secret until the end?"

Caradin kept in a peaceful sleep.

Alone. But not truly. He still had Aterus' gift.

"Niko?" Kole summoned his friend, who appeared in an instant. Seeing his friend's face lifted his spirits, if only slightly.

Niko leaned against the half wall of the balcony.

"I told them. Not everything — they didn't listen that far. I think it'd make them angrier if they knew the details."

"You knew they wouldn't understand. It shouldn't be a shock."

"Still hurts. They don't trust me."

"'Course they don't. Their lives aren't hanging in the balance of Ohr's survival." Niko placed a hand on Kole's shoulder.

He tried to feel it. Imagine the warmth radiating from his ghostly friend's hand. Pretended he was *actually* there. Real.

"If they care about you, they'll come around."

"I'm not so sure."

Niko sighed and dropped his hand. "You've always had this... hmm, *instinct*, I guess. Not smarts like me." He pushed an ethereal elbow at Kole's ribs.

A smile tugged at Kole's mouth.

"It's something indescribable." Niko shifted and leaned his back on the wall, propped there as though trying to appear more corporeal when they both knew he could phase right through it. "It's what makes you throw yourself into danger. That thing that made you know the way home no matter how lost we got in Solpate." His tone turned low and serious. "Kole. You know what to do. Trust your gut. It may lead you to trouble, but it's always kept you safe."

"I guess so." The particular quirk Niko spoke of was precisely what Russé had tried to steer Kole away from: impulsiveness, recklessness. Maybe he could embrace both sides.

"I think we can agree that you need to stop reaching out to Vara, though. It's putting everyone in Zeal at risk, including you."

Kole nodded. "I'll have to go on what I already know." The image of those floating chunks of land he'd seen during his last connection came rushing back. *However strange those clues may be.*

"Someone's at the door," said Niko, before swirling away.

With a bit of weight lifted from his spirit, Kole turned hoping to see Vienna and Felix there waiting to talk with him.

Jax stood in the foyer, a proud smile on her unusually clean face. She beckoned him to follow.

Time to see what she'd done with her cannon.

Chapter 27

Puffs of fog trailed from Kole's nose and mouth with each breath. The temperature had plummeted since sundown and pierced straight through Kole's thin cloak. After following Jax a block down the road, the Hasic leader turned a corner and opened the door of a strange, three-wheeled contraption.

An oval, glass capsule sat between the front two wheels, tilted back like a tipped-over egg. Some sort of carriage, if he had to guess. But where were the horses?

"What is that?"

"Our ride. Unless you want to walk the whole way, that is?"

Kole ducked under the roof and sat back in the cushioned, molded seat in the center. *Any excuse to escape the cold.*

Jax followed in after him. "Not there, that's my spot." She shooed him to the small space behind the legless chair, where chests of open toolboxes littered the floor. "It'll be a tight squeeze. The back is usually meant for storage."

Kole found a small toolbox to rest his hip on and leaned against the side of the glass wall to steady himself. *It's no rambler, but it'll do.*

Once Jax settled in, she pulled a glowing stone from her vest— moonstone, Kole recognized—and shoved it into a compartment next to the command seat. Suddenly, the carriage pulled forward. Kole braced himself, expecting a bumpy ride, but the wheels glided smoothly over the road. Without the city passing by outside, Kole never would've known they were on the move. Jax seemed to control the vehicle through a stick protruding from the center console. Wherever she leaned it, the carriage followed suit, like reins on a horse.

The interior warmed a bit with their two bodies inside, but Kole pulled his cloak tight across his frame, thankful for what little heat Caradin gave off curled about his neck.

Jax drove them west. A jeweled city. That's what Zeal looked like in the night, glittering with the aura of the moonstone lanterns. The glow of the buildings rivaled the crystal forest itself. Perhaps more enchanting, Kole dared admit, as the metal and glass of the curved buildings reflected that white glow back out into the darkness. A city so bright, he wondered if the stars mistook them for one of their own.

Kole had been so entranced by the beauty of Zeal, he only now noticed they had come up to the wall marking the city limits. "I thought you were going to show me the cannon?"

"I am."

"Then why are we leaving the city?" The carriage passed the outer wall and drove into the desolate wasteland. A small sense of panic flipped like a switch inside him. "Where are we going?"

"To the flames," Jax said. "How else would I show you what I've done?"

"Oh." Kole should've guessed that, but the pit inside his stomach grew. "Is it safe to go so close with everything going on?"

"Nothing about the Black Wall is safe." Her tone darkened. Jax turned in her seat and looked at Kole before focusing back on the path ahead. "I apologize I didn't mention it earlier. I didn't mean to alarm you. Only, with the Dark Hand and everything that's happened recently—not knowing if there's a mole in our ranks—I couldn't risk telling you. It's best we go alone. Not even Tena knows where we are."

Neither did Felix or Vienna. They only knew Jax had called on him. That fact sent a shiver down Kole's spine. If anything should happen.... He acknowledged that initial fear, then let it subside. Jax was right. No one knew who acted as an informant to the Dark Hand. Best to keep their mission—the tweaked cannon—a secret. If anything *should* go wrong, Kole had the help of the snoozing weasel. He latched onto that fact, for without it, he'd be clawing at the glass of the carriage to escape and run back to Zeal on foot.

In the dark of night, the Black Wall remained indiscernible from the surrounding landscape. Only the dull roar of flames told them they closed in. Kole shut his eyes and focused on his breathing, grasping at any sense of calm.

Jax stopped the glass contraption. "Here it is." She opened the door and climbed out, then offered Kole her hand, which he took with hesitance.

Though his body had begun to cramp in the small, cold space, a wave of warm air slapped his exposed skin, inviting him out. Caradin stirred awake. *"About time. You'll need to see what's going to get us through the flames,"* Kole said through their connection.

The difference in temperature between the city and here was astounding. If Kole closed his eyes, he could imagine a scorching summer day.

The area lit up as Jax pulled out the moonstone shard she'd used to power the carriage. "Here it is. Take a look."

He jumped at the chance of a distraction—anything to keep his eyes from those flames.

From the back, the cannon seemed fairly similar to its counterparts in Jax's workshop. Only the fuel container had been enlarged. Kole rounded the cannon, where bulging lines of metal striped the shaft like scars. Welding marks. He traced a finger over one of them.

"Didn't have time to make it pretty, but the added lenses do their job. It's the cap stone that was a bitch." Jax led Kole to the tip of the modified weapon, where a smooth glass orb fit into the mouth. Except it glowed.

"After a preliminary test, I realized I needed more power. Made the lens straight from the stone. The sphere shape focuses the power to a direct point rather than the flood shape we use for the wall."

Kole lifted to his tiptoes to get a better look. Not one imperfection on the surface. "Does it work?"

"We'll see here soon." Jax put the moonstone shard between her teeth as she moved to the fuel compartment. "Just have to get her lit," she said through clenched teeth as she rummaged with the back. A hum came from the cannon. "Stand back." She'd removed the shard from her mouth and gestured him over. "The wall is a quarter mile out. I figure the closer this beauty is," she patted the cannon, "the better she'll work."

Kole tried to ignore that fresh tidbit of information. A quarter mile was nothing. If the wall grew unstable there'd be no chance of an escape, even with Jax's odd carriage. Despite the warmth, his body chilled with a mighty shake. If he could have sweat, a sheen would've cast over him by now.

And there it went: his worries getting the best of him. He had to remind himself he stood beside the only weapon capable of fending off those flames. If he was unable to muster the courage now, how would he possibly go through the Black Wall when the time came?

"Ready?" Jax asked, hand on the lever.

Kole set his jaw. "Do it."

A swift pull had the cannon bursting with energy. One narrow stream of white light erupted from the barrel. Though the wall lay a distance away, Kole witnessed the impact clear as if he stood next to it. Black flames extinguished on contact in a gray haze. Within a few seconds, the Black Wall roared louder, and the temperature in the deadland spiked.

"Is this normal?" Kole shouted over the noise.

"Don't worry. I've got everything under control." She pulled a pair of odd specs from her pocket and put them to her eyes. "Well I'll be damned. It works. Here, take a look."

Kole took the specs and lifted them to his eyes like she had. His vision hopped forward as if he stood within an arm's reach of the flames. The fire had recoiled from the cannon's beam, leaving a clear portal through the Black Wall. The specs made it difficult to tell the scale of everything, but he'd guess the opening stood large enough for him to walk through. He smiled. Finally, something had gone right. If all went well, maybe he could leave after the ball. He'd need to if Felix and Vienna told Tena where to *actually* send her scouts in search of Russé.

When Kole pulled the specs away, the cannon sputtered, and the beam died down. The absence of the brilliance left his eyes blind until they could adjust.

"What in the...?" Sounds of Jax fiddling with metal parts found Kole's ears. "Well, that's not good."

"What happened?" Something moved to the west. A lick of flame? He prayed he was wrong. It moved quickly, though, across the plain like a dart.

"The thing ran the fuel dry." The moonstone shard was back between her teeth as she examined the tank.

That extra bit of light allowed Kole to spot her hunched over the back of the cannon. A peek west confirmed whatever he'd seen had gone. Surely the flames in the distance, but that only fished out his fears. A quarter mile from the dark fire without fuel to power their only defense. "Can you add more?"

"Not as simple as it sounds." All the while, the crystal bounced at the side of her mouth. "Breaking the seal while the cannon runs would cause the whole thing to explode—and whoever opens it is as good as dead. I've made the biggest tank I could in the time allotted. So yes, after the fact, I could add more fuel, but that'd leave us with the beam down for a time."

"What are you saying?"

"How long did that last, you think?" She moved the stone from her mouth and hovered it over her timepiece. "Thirty seconds, perhaps? You'd need to be a lot closer to make it through, but that doesn't solve our problem." Jax folded her arms over her vest.

Kole immediately latched on to her meaning. "If you turned it on and I got through, the thing might go off while I'm in there. I'd be stranded on the other side." A sense of nervousness came from Caradin, who'd watched the ordeal from the cover of Kole's hood. Neither of them knew what lay beyond the Black Wall—if a person could even survive in a place like that—and they were going to risk not only crossing to it but staying there until... until....

Not five minutes later, Jax and Kole had returned the carriage and made their way back to Zeal in silence. Every second drifting farther away from the Black Wall settled his nerves. He set his sights on the bejeweled city.

This whole idea was a mess. Kole thought he could do this on his own, but he hadn't even managed to secure a real way through the fire yet. Not to mention, whatever confidence he'd built staring at the flames from the balcony—ready to tackle it head on—had fled the moment he neared it. *How am I going to pull this off?*

While Jax steered, she sent a quick glance over her shoulder to him crammed into the back of the carriage. Eyes again on the road, she said, "If you make it through, I will get you a way back out. It's the timing that's tricky."

Kole furrowed his brows. *If that were the only tricky thing....* "What are you thinking?"

"We have a way to portal through the flames, if only for a moment. I can refuel the cannon while you're in there and give you safe passage back out when you are ready to return. How long do you need?"

He thought back to the location he'd narrowed in on with Vienna's triangulation method. A few miles out, time to locate and release Vara, then the return travel. If all went as planned.... "A couple hours. Four at most to be safe."

"I can make that happen on my end. All you'd need to do is remember the location." Jax slowed the contraption as they entered the city. "If you're in the wrong spot when the hours are up, you'll miss your chance."

Kole had always been keen on navigation. He had no doubts about finding his way back. One thing bothered him, though. "There's no way to make it bigger?" He'd feel more comfortable with the rambler at his side.

"I imagine I could create a grander cannon with bigger, customized lenses and a scaled fuel tank. In theory, it would work, but that sort of creation would take months of around-the-hour labor. As I understood it," Jaz parked the carriage at the steps of the City Hall, "this wouldn't work with your time frame."

"No." Kole had hoped never to be parted from his rambler, for the separation only reminded him more of his scars. His limits. Biding time in Zeal was one thing. Going into the unknown without his crutch stood as a completely different feat. Caradin would be his only tool—his only aid should he find trouble. If nothing else, he felt comfort in the Orange Soul's confirmed alliance. And once he released Vara, he'd have two Souls to help him get back to Ohr. "When can you be ready?"

Jax climbed out then assisted Kole from the carriage. "I will have a few of my team retrieve the cannon tonight so I can make last-minute adjustments. It should only take a few hours, but we both need to attend the ball, too." She surveyed the empty streets before continuing in a whisper, "Keep up *appearances*."

"As soon as your duty is done, then?" Kole followed her up the steps and through the grand doors, where a pair of guards acknowledged the councilwoman as she passed.

Jax nodded to them. "I will retrieve you from your room as I did tonight." Now in full cast of light, the fresh smears of grime from working on the cannon stood out on the Hasic leader's face. One across her forehead and another running down her cheek.

Once they made it to the elevator, Jax bowed then shut the cage doors. "I hope you find rest tonight, Kole. Until tomorrow."

The lift began its slow ascent, leaving Kole alone. *"Think we can do this?"*

Caradin poked his head out and crawled down to Kole's waiting hands. *"No harm will come to Master Kole."*

"I'm glad you're so sure about it." Kole's eyes wandered beyond the glass tube as he ascended. He stared out at his own shadowed reflection in the pane. Only, something seemed off about it. The pose was all wrong, with open arms and extended feet as if he were mid-jump. An icy shot of panic surged through him when Kole realized it wasn't his reflection in the window but a Kayetan flying up alongside the lift. Kole stumbled back and braced himself against the panel of buttons. The silhouette displayed bushy hair, and a stature similar to his own. *Felix*. But the eyes. Kayetans had none, and yet this one held a prominent pair of pure onyx. Despite being discovered, Felix's Kayetan kept pace with the elevator until it chimed and stopped at the top floor.

Kole ripped open the gates and stomped down the hallway back to his quarters.

"Master Kole, are you well?" Daveen opened the door for him, then quietly let it close after Kole gave a curt nod.

He barged into the foyer. "You sent your Kayetan after me!" But Kole found himself yelling into an empty room.

Vienna appeared in the bedroom doorway. "He didn't send his Kayetan. He sent himself."

"Don't try to twist—" Kole paused, wondering if he'd misheard her words. "What did you say?"

She walked over to the glass door to the balcony and slid it open.

Over the terrace wall rose the same Kayetan that had stalked the lift. The creature flew over the lip of the railing and touched down on the balcony. Smoke billowed out from the shadow's feet in a small puff on the landing, then it glided in through the open door beside Vienna.

"I said, he sent himself." Vienna shut the cold out.

"Felix?" Kole mumbled. The face. *That* was the thing that caught him. Where Kayetans alone held blank faces, this one had Felix's eyes and bone structure poking through the shadow. The two merged together seamlessly, unlike what he'd seen Felix attempt before. Even more alarming.... "You can fly?"

A brightness sparked in Felix's gaze the way it did when excitement got the better of him. Not a second later, it dulled again as if Felix had caught himself, and he turned stoic again. "It's kinda a new thing." Felix shifted. The tone of his voice told Kole he wanted so badly to show off his new ability. "And useful," he added. "We need eyes on the enemy, now don't we?"

Felix extended his arms. His head tilted back, a wince on Felix's face as the darkness streamed out of his wrists, and his Kayetan detached. The shadow drifted to the corner, where it swayed, watching and waiting his master's command.

"Enemy?" Kole asked. "Is that what I am now?" Even though the shadow had removed itself from Felix, his friend still held a darkness around his eyes. Not bags from sleep deprivation, but the vibrant green in them had changed color. Deepened.

"Aterus surely is. And yer workin' with him." Felix plopped onto the couch and propped his feet on the table. "I'd say that makes ya the same."

"This is ridiculous, Felix."

"Ridiculous?" He swiveled and let his feet fall to the floor as he leaned in. "Almost as ridiculous as dealin' with the devil, Blondie?"

"You should be using your Kayetan for protecting us from the Dark Hand. Not following me around in the middle of the night." Kole let down his hood to free Caradin. The rodent climbed down and ran into Vienna's arms, who made no sign of stepping in.

"How 'bout I take one from yer book and do as I please?" With a huff, Felix shoved back the curls that had plagued his eyes. "'Sides, I can't trust ya ta tell us anythin' 'bout those cannons, so I decided ta find out myself. Were ya even gonna tell us 'bout tomorrow night?"

"You haven't given me the chance, yet," Kole said through clenched teeth. Felix had a point, though. He never planned on telling them when things would go down. Kole had already decided against extra company. He'd do it alone. For their sake. But *that* held a bit of falsehood as well. Now that they knew Kole's true purpose, the siblings might try to stop him if they crossed the flames with him. Kole sighed. "Well, you know now, anyhow. Will you keep off me?"

Felix stared at him. His eyes softened for a fraction of a second, then hardened. "'Fraid I can't do that, mate. Not till Russé gets here ta knock some sense inta ya. I've told Tena ta reroute her scouts. Should find them soon."

Felix's words hit Kole hard in the stomach.

"You what?" By that time tomorrow, Kole would have either crossed the flames with only Caradin, or been detained by the gods he'd been avoiding. If Russé got to him first, he'd never live up to Aterus' deal. His body and Niko forfeit....

"You can't do that," Kole growled.

"It's for the best. V thinks so, too."

Kole let his eyes drift her way to find she'd been staring at him. Whereas her brother held clear anger, she exuded a deep sadness. Still, she said nothing.

"Then I'll have to get you two to see differently." Kole stomped toward the ajar door. A streak of shadow flashed before him, and the door slammed shut. Felix's Kayetan stood guard.

"It's best if ya take a different room tonight." At Felix's words, the Kayetan swelled in a defensive stance.

"You can't be serious."

"Serious as a leakin' dumplin'." When even Vienna gave him the eye, Felix's mouth twisted to the side and added, "Ya know what I mean. Very serious."

Kole's mouth had fallen open. In a matter of hours, his friends had judged and condemned him—turned into something unrecognizable. The only thing lying behind Felix eyes? Suspicion. "Maybe you're right." A night alone would do them all some good. Time for things to settle. A chance to rethink.

Felix rubbed the back of his neck. "I put yer stuff in the far room." The slightest hint of remorse shaded his tone.

Though he tried to keep his expression neutral, he gritted his teeth. Clearly, Felix and Vienna had discussed this while he had been out with Jax. Whatever the conversation, the result ended in isolating themselves from Kole. Heat prickled in Kole's eyes. He turned and sulked toward the room before they could see him cry.

Hiding proved impossible now that the Kayetan patrolled his every movement. Despite closing the door, the shadow swept under the threshold and positioned itself inside. Felix would know if he attempted to leave. At this point, he couldn't even call upon Niko without his friend using the shadow to listen in.

Just as Felix had said, Kole's stuff lay in a pile on the bench at the foot of the bed. His pack with his waterskin and his sunstone dagger inside, along with his old change of clothes and the fabric he'd tied together to use as a makeshift balaclava to cover his face. His slingshot and pouch of ammunition were absent. Kole rifled through his things, checking if it hid somewhere in his wadded-up clothes. After dumping the contents from his bag, he came to the truth. Felix had taken it back. The only weapon Kole could reasonably use with his burns.

He took in a sharp breath. The pain in his chest... it felt like a stab straight to his heart. Of course, the slingshot had been Felix's to begin with. Vienna had given it to Kole when Felix had been ill from the Kayetan ritual and only kept it when Felix gave his blessing.

Weaponless. Ramblerless. Friendless.

He'd hadn't felt this alone since the night the Black Wall razed the forest.

Anger brewed within him. It took complete control, trembling his fingers and shaking his legs. He closed his fist to contain it, but like a drop of water against a forest fire, it did little. Kole shoved his things off the bed in a fit of rage.

To keep from destroying anything, he opened the window and let the winter in. The chill sunk through to his bones. Some of the anger waned. Enough to get control of himself and steady the growing emotion.

Kole climbed under the covers, but warmth eluded him. The cold he could bear, but the loneliness....

As far back as he remembered, he'd never been alone. Back in Solpate, their anchored ramblers housed dozens of orphans, all hanging in their hammocks with their steady breaths as the swelling bass in the night's orchestra of crickets and owls. Even when he'd left the forest, he'd had Russé, and then the siblings at his side after.

No sound penetrated the stone and metal of City Hall. Alone. Deathly quiet. Even Caradin had left him, chosen to stay in the siblings' room.

Sleep came, restless and patchy. Every time he woke, his heart jumped at the sight of the Kayetan still guarding the door. He rolled over and kept his back toward the shadow for the remainder of the drawn-out night.

CHAPTER 28

Piper tapped her foot anxiously, though her body had become so cold over the last two days, she could only feel the vibration of her foot touching down on the iced-over marsh in her bones. Not long before, the sun rose and chased away the chill.

Her companions stood in silence while Russé attempted, yet again, to connect with Kole. Useless. She rolled her eyes. Kole had shown he wanted nothing to do with them. Though it did surprise her that he possessed the strength to block Russé. Either he'd grown stronger, or he had help. Perhaps Caradin aided him, but the idea seemed outlandish—a Soul working against their own kind. Maybe not unheard of with Aterus and all, but the others wanted the same thing: freedom.

Though Piper would like to blame the purpose for their short stop on Russé, it had been *she* who needed rest. Days searching and running with hardly any food or sleep had taken a toll on her body. The human side of her kept her from pushing on. *So frail and needy.*

Russé had snared a rabbit for her within the vines of a crawling ivy, and Obell had used his fire to cook it. Issira had used her powers to filter the marsh water into something drinkable. All together, they composed Ohr's best survival team. Piper grunted a laugh at the thought. With her belly full and body hydrated, she still needed a bit more time off her feet or her fragile body would give out soon. Sleep. She needed that more than ever. A full night's rest would rejuvenate her completely. They'd also lose precious hours in the search for Kole.

Finally, Russé opened his eyes. He stared at his feet, either unable or unwilling to look his kin in the eyes.

"We will find him," Issira said in her sing-song voice. Days of scrounging through the marsh left the hems of her blue silk dress muddy to her knees, but her skin and silky black hair remained pristine, untouched by the grim around them.

Obell crossed his arms. Every time he moved, a wave of welcome heat carried through the air. "You keep saying that."

"If we do not, we are all doomed. Would you rather I say that?"

"It's the truth, is it not?" Obell barked back.

Those two mixed as well as water and oil. Piper had watched all three Souls interact over the course of their travel. Their dynamic was interesting to say the least. At first, Piper assumed Issira and Obell's clear indifference of each other came from their prolonged imprisonments. Time apart had changed them and made them strangers. Maybe they needed time to warm up just as humans did. And yet, Russé and Issira, though only together maybe a week longer, had such a fluid understanding of each other. They worked together seamlessly and showed signs of kinship. Witnessing the difference in the relationship between Issira and Russé versus with Obell tickled an odd idea in Piper's head.

Maybe the Souls integrated best with those who complemented their true nature. Water feeds nature. And oh, how Issira doted on Russé. Fire, though, the outcast in that little duo. All of it was a mere hunch. Piper would need to interact with more Souls to test her hypothesis.

A rumble through the ground caught Piper's attention. Tempoed. Familiar.

"Horses." Piper stood and pointed north, though the night ruined any chance of seeing them herself. The impossible odds of a herd moving that fast before dawn confirmed her hunch. "They have riders."

"Maybe they've seen Kole." Russé reached his staff toward Obell, who lit the tip with a touch. Russé raised the flaming staff in hopes of waving down the band of horsemen. "Hard to miss a rambler out here."

"Or maybe we can take their mounts," Piper suggested as she waved them down.

The pair of riders, one older with a gray beard, the other not much older than Piper appeared, closed in and slowed. They wore mud-stained clothing with darker patches of rust-colored stains accumulated on the sleeves. Dried blood, Piper assumed by the fawn tied down over one of the horse's rumps.

"You bunch are an odd sight to see 'round here." The older man looked the Souls up and down. His eyes lingered cautiously on Obell. Even his horse stammered back nervously.

When Russé opened his mouth to speak, Piper placed a hand on his shoulder and pulled him back. "My companions and I are lost, I'm afraid." She put on her sweetest smile, hoping to draw back whatever wall the traveler had put up at the sight of Obell's intensity. "Can't seem to find our way out of the marsh."

"Not many can." The rider squinted his eyes at Piper as if not quite convinced.

"Excuse my grandpa," said the younger rider. He pulled his horse around toward Piper. "People around here know the dangers of the marsh. That's why it's a bit odd to see folks out here." The younger rider seemed to fall for her act.

"We wouldn't be here if not for...." Piper gave a deep sigh and looked up at the young man through her lashes. "We're trying to find our friends. They came through here a few days ago, but it seems our search has gotten us all turned around." As she spoke, she carefully walked toward the young man, stopping just short of arm's reach."

"Maybe you've seen them?" Russé asked. "Two boys and a girl. They would've been riding a —"

"Let's not worry these two with our problems," Piper said through her teeth.

"Oh, it's no trouble at all, miss." The young man smiled, but his grandpa shifted in his saddle. "We were just heading back from a hunting trip. We haven't run into anyone except you, unfortunately, but we can show you the way out."

Piper sighed, annoyed at having to play this whole thing up. If she'd been alone, things would've gone so much smoother. Russé and Issira never would've gone for her plan, which is why she avoided mentioning it, but Obell might help. She cast a dark look to the fire god and dipped her head. He must've understood because a surge of warmth encased the area.

With one graceful sweep of her hand, she pulled the knife from her belt then launched herself at the man. Her shoulder collided with his stomach, and he tumbled to the side, arms and legs grasping at the saddle to keep from falling to the mud.

The other horse reared, knocking the older man off along with their kill. Piper struggled with the young man. She managed to pull herself halfway atop the horse, but the boy grabbed at her, screaming when he spotted his grandpa knocked out in the mud.

"What are you doing?" he yelled at her.

The horse stamped and bucked, but still they both held strong. She sighed. *Give it up already.* Instead of waiting for the man's strength to fail, Piper grabbed onto the horse's thrashing mane then slid her knife under the saddle strap and cut it free. The man landed beside his grandpa with a thud. It only took a second for him to find his feet and lurch back for the horse.

Piper threw herself over the horse's bare back and pressed her heels into the tender spot behind the animal's ribs. The beast burst into a gallop.

She only needed one horse. The Souls could do as they pleased with the other and the humans. The plan had been to steal the horses, but the freedom of speed evoked something in her. The Souls bogged her down, and they were of no use currently. Only Kole mattered. She needed to get to him no matter the cost.

The horse continued, and she never tugged on the reins. Her eyes remained straight ahead.

By now the Souls had surely realized her intentions. Thunder rumbled overhead, confirming Issira's rage. They'd never catch up to her. Not with one horse.

Kole is mine.

CHAPTER 29

"What *is* this?" Kole held up his arms before the mirror, gawking at his reflection. When Tena had mentioned getting him a special outfit for the ball, Kole had expected something like the traditional garments they'd provided earlier. Maybe another ascot, or a billowing shirt with a jacket. He'd definitely prefer those.

Caradin sat up on his back paws and cocked his head at Kole from the armchair in the corner.

The black sleeveless tunic stretched tight over his chest and tucked into equally form-fitting trousers. The thick material, however fine, aggravated his scars. The neckline stood as an entirely different affront. It dropped low in a deep V-shape, showing the corded scar tissue of his upper torso and neck, where his Seven Souls pendent lay perfectly framed. He felt exposed and uncomfortable despite the outer piece layered over the ensemble, which draped down from his shoulders and looped low at his waist. The tails of the fabric continued freely down his back like a pair of dangling wings. All completely black. All completely unlike him.

"Where am I possibly going to hide you now?" Kole tugged at the clothing, hoping to find a suitable spot for the weasel when a knock came from the door. He knew better than to think it one of the siblings. "Come in, Daveen."

The dark-haired man cracked the door open. "Have you got it on?"

"I think so." With open arms, he turned for inspection.

At that, the door swung open and Daveen came in, eyeing the garment. "Wonderful. Just wrap this around your waist." He held out an embroidered gold belt.

Kole reluctantly took it. As he buckled the belt in place, he noticed the symbol of Zeal woven into the leather. The mark of the Seven Souls, as well, with glass beads acting as the stones. Beautiful, but not for him. Not *on* him.

Kole had grown accustomed to tattered tunics and unfinished hems. The pants he'd worn back in Solpate had slowly been torn away until they had turned into shorts. Back in the forest, clothes only changed for their weekly washing. New outfits only came when he'd severely outgrown his old ones. Kole never minded living in the dirt. His appearance always seemed insignificant compared to the struggles of life as a refugee. Yet now, as he peeked over his shoulder at his image in the mirror, concerns about just that dominated his head—ever since he'd gotten his scars really.

"Why does it have to be so...," Kole rubbed his arms, "open?"

"Councilwoman Tena wants your scars on full display. They make you easily identifiable. The Dark Hand will know you at a glance."

"Isn't my face enough?" He longed for a billowing cloak to wrap himself in.

Daveen fiddled with the draped cloth at Kole's shoulders. "Nothing to chance tonight, dear boy. Besides, it is quite striking on you."

Kole tucked his chin to hide his rolling eyes. "Will you be attending?" Anything to draw the attention away from himself.

"I will be there." Daveen smiled. "In the wings in case you or your companions need me."

"Are they ready?" The hallway had been rather quiet the last few minutes. He wondered if Vienna and Felix had retreated to the balcony, trying to put as much distance between them and "the traitor" as possible.

"They've already been escorted down to the grand hall. They wished to go early."

More like they didn't want me with them. Kole sighed. The night alone had done nothing to change their minds. Would they ever see his side?

"Is there a satchel I can wear to hold my pet?" Kole asked as he gestured to the armchair.

Daveen eyed the animal. Then lifted his brows. "You wish to bring your creature to the ball?"

"Can't leave him up here all alone, can I?"

"I could assign someone to the room to watch over—"

"I'm bringing him." Kole walked to the chair and gathered Caradin up. *He's the only true friend I have right now.* The weasel curled up in his hands. "Do you have something I can hide him in?"

The frown on Daveen's face clearly relayed his reluctance, but not ten minutes later, Kole, Daveen, and Caradin, tucked safely away in a cross-body satchel at Kole's hip, rode down the gold-and-glass elevator to the ground floor. The pink light of sunset beamed through the glass tube. Lines of guests crowded the roads outside City Hall, waiting to get inside.

The elevator chimed and Daveen pulled open the cage, an arm gesturing for Kole to exit first.

His boots clicked on the polished tiled floor. The hall gleamed. Either someone had thoroughly cleaned the space or the sunlight pouring in through the windows did a grand number on the place. Everything from the sconces to the grout between the tiles held an opulent, gilded glow. Echoes of conversation and laughter filled the vaulted hall, so much so, Kole barely noted the warm whine of stringed instruments under the cacophony.

Only a few steps out of the elevator, and he stopped. He'd never seen so many people gathered in one place. The very air in the building held a twinge of electricity, a feeling Kole recoiled against. A hand on his back encouraged his feet forward.

"There's a private section for you inside," Daveen assured.

Kole followed along but slipped his hand inside the satchel to the familiar warmth of weasel fur. Whiskers nuzzled his fingers.

As they passed, the citizens stopped and stared at Kole. A hush accumulated. Once Daveen brought Kole to the grand archway leading to the great room of City Hall and onto the first step, the orchestra halted their music. Several hundred eyes drifted to Kole, his scars on full display. He cringed back at their stares.

Daveen dropped his hand from Kole's back. "You go alone from here. My duty is by the door."

Before Kole could protest, the man had gone. He turned back to the full room. Glittering gowns and shining suits stood still. He recognized some of the navy vests of the city guard uniforms, as well as the tailored silhouettes of the members of the Hasic, similar to what Jax wore, but the faces... all strangers. Every one of them.

Some faces held curiosity. Others raised their brows, no doubt casting quick judgments on him. Maybe they suspected him as one of the Dark Hand with his burns. Maybe they took pity on him. Or maybe, they thought his attire as ridiculous as Kole did.

His stomach clenched as he took that first step down the short staircase. Every pair of eyes trained on him like hunters tracking prey. Surrounded by hundreds, yet utterly on his own, he yearned for Felix and Vienna at his side. A tough tongue lapped at Kole's fingers, which he still held tucked inside the satchel, reminding him that one friend remained.

That last step down to the tiled ballroom floor acted as the end of whatever trance had come over the attendees. The orchestra struck back up, and the room returned to private conversations. He wanted nothing more than to run to a dark a corner and spend the rest of the night hidden. The reason for tonight's festivities would never succeed if he gave into such whims.

"Kole."

He turned, clinging to the familiar voice.

Tena stood before him, a smile on her face. A simple silver gown replaced her usual uniform. "How are you?"

"I feel... seen," he admitted. "I'm not used to all of this."

The councilwoman dipped her head. "Understandable." She wrapped her arm around his and pulled him close. "It's only for a short while. I have a space you can use for yourself."

Guests parted as Tena escorted Kole across the floor to the far end of the room, where a banister encased a small space. A handful of cushioned chairs decorated the space, but the woman in green, who'd taken one as her own, caught his eye.

His feet refused to move once the face registered. *Vienna.*

The satin gown shifted from bright emerald to a deep viridian in the shimmer of the chandeliers. That color brought back images of Solpate forest in late summer, when the leaves turned so vibrant from months of abundant sun, their thirst quenched from the seasonal thunderstorms. The deep hue beautifully complemented her skin. Her hair, which Kole had been used to seeing drawn back in a braid, coiled like twisting vines around her face and grazed her shoulders. The initial freshness of the haircut had passed. The new length suited her.

In the long day since he'd seen her, she looked fully recovered from her illness. Fresh light shone beneath her skin. Even her eyes had bounced back from their sunken state. Vienna's gaze set passive on something in the distance. Her lashes stood out—darker, perhaps—and a glow of red touched her cheeks. At her neck sat the broken-flower pendent Kole had gifted her.

He gulped. Seeing it there made him hope that forgiveness was possible.

A tug on Kole's arm snapped him out of his brief trance.

"Here we are." Tena led Kole to an empty chair.

Vienna's head turned at the sound of the councilwoman's voice. She peered at Kole, but the moment he returned it, she stood and walked out to the main floor, disappearing into the crowd.

"Thank you," Kole said, trying to keep his voice light despite the sinking feeling in his heart.

Tena took the seat next to him, then leaned in and whispered, "I have my guards watching you. If anything should happen, you will be safe."

As she spoke, Kole scanned the walls. Nearly two dozen uniformed men and women stood along the perimeter, their faces straight ahead to the middle of the floor, but their eyes flicked to Kole and back again every so often.

"Felix helped set up the security. He's very protective of you."

"Felix is here?" Despite another quick sweep of the guests, his sly friend eluded him.

"Somewhere. Probably telling one of my guards how to do their job," she chuckled. "You are lucky to have friends who care so deeply for you."

Kole snorted. Sure, they wanted him safe, but for reasons of their own. *They just want to hand me back over to Russé.*

"I only need you for a short while once the festivities have commenced. Until then, you are free to do with the night as you please. Should you leave this area," she gestured to the surrounding banister, "I have assigned guards to accompany you, so do not be alarmed to have a few people on your heels." At that, Tena rose, bowed her head to Kole, then left.

Kole folded his arms, attempting to cover as much of his bare chest as possible. Ten minutes passed by and still he sat like that, eyeing every new attendee as they walked in, wondering if *they* were one of the Dark Hand. So many extravagant outfits, yet no scars in sight. Surely the Dark Hand would cover them. He wondered why he even bothered watching.

"Not your thing?" Jax leaned into the banister. Unlike the rest of Zeal, she wore her same vest and pants getup, but the lack of oil smears and dirt showed she'd put in a bit of effort. The medals pinned on her chest gleamed as well, freshly polished. Kole wished she'd been the one who'd dressed him.

"Not yours either," Kole countered.

The side of her mouth lifted, revealing a dimple. "How could you possibly guess that?"

Kole matched her smirk.

"I have good news." Jax glanced back and forth before stepping closer, her voice low. "I made the adjustments that we talked about on the cannon. The test this afternoon went well."

"You tested it already?"

"When else could I do it? Had to get this done before the *ball*," Jax said the last word dramatically. "I would've called on you, but I thought it might look suspicious bringing you out of the city with me in broad daylight. Just know that it works. Better than I anticipated. You have a longer window to walk through the portal now."

"That's amazing." Kole smiled.

"Don't get too excited. Seconds longer, nothing substantial." Her gaze swept over the folks gathered nearby, and she lowered her voice a bit. "At the end of the night, I'll come find you. The ride will take a bit longer tonight. I have the cannon secured outside my workshop. Didn't want to leave it in the wasteland in case the wall moved again. We'll have to tow it out ourselves. Do you have all that you need for the journey?"

Kole gently patted the satchel at his side, from which Caradin poked his nose out. "We're ready."

"One more thing." Jax fumbled with her wrist. After unbuckling her watch, she held it out to Kole. "Take this."

"What? Why?"

"You'll need it to track the time." When Kole made no move to grab it, she took his hand and laid the face on his wrist. "Don't be so stubborn. We don't know what it's like on the other side."

"I don't know how to read it," Kole admitted. The sun and moon had been the only tools he'd used for telling time. Vague, sure, but he'd never needed to be so specific before.

"See this needle here?" Jax tapped the glass. "You only need to watch for that one. It's the hours. From the moment you cross, it needs to pass three of these marks along the face. *That's* when I'll open the portal again."

"How will *you* know the time?"

Jax pulled out her pocket watch. It swayed on the chain. "They are perfectly synched." After tucking it away, she finished clasping the wristwatch to Kole. "The strap will stay in place. No fear in losing it. I've thought of everything, Kole. I have a pack of food and water set up for you by the cannon. We'll make this work." She pulled back and scanned Kole's face. "I apologize for sounding excited. I know this journey is dangerous. It's just... the possibility of everything. The discoveries. No one has been past the flames. There's so much to learn. I may be eager to get you through, but know that I am just as eager to get you back."

That Kole believed. Sure, she worried for his safety; she was the leader of the Hasic after all. Protecting people was her job. More than that, though, she yearned for knowledge. The ultimate mystery of Ohr: the Black Wall. What had become of the earth behind it? Jax would never know unless Kole made a safe return. If he could count on nothing else, he believed her in that.

"Thank you." Kole twisted his forearm to better examine his new wrist piece.

A pat came on his shoulder along with Jax's farewell "With that, I leave you. Good luck tonight." Jax turned to leave. Before passing the banister, she looked back with a wicked smile. "If you're anything like me, the dancing terrifies you more than the Dark Hand."

His throat tightened. "Dancing?"

Too late. She'd already gone. But her laughter trailed to his ears.

Maybe it had been a joke. A cruel one. Kole knew nothing about dancing. Tena already intended to flaunt him around in this ridiculous outfit. Did she really expect him to dance, too? He would bumble around the floor looking more like a floundering fish than the Dark Hand's burned savior. Maybe that alone would make them lose interest in him. Kole snorted. He could only hope.

The anxiety bubbling in his core must've sparked Caradin's attention because a cold nose poked out and pressed into Kole's elbow. After a quick, reassuring pat to the weasel's head, Kole sighed, wondering how many ticks the watch needle would have to pass until this whole thing ended.

CHAPTER 30

Piper dug her heels into the stolen horse's ribs, urging the beast faster. With the marsh well behind her now, she galloped past a few small villages. No sight of the rambler meant no Kole, so she continued, following the towns peppered over the landscape to the west. *They would've followed civilization. For comforts or directions.* But she had yet to spot any rambler tracks or abandoned camp sites. Her frustration came out in a groan. How hard could it be to track a giant tree?

Late afternoon had turned into the first hour of evening. The sky glowed a brilliant orange as the sun prepared its final descent toward the horizon. A fire-like luminescence drew her attention to the forest ahead. Crystal trees.

Piper tugged the reins. The horse snorted and skidded to a stop in the small stretch of land between the forest and the bordering town. With no tracks to follow, she'd come to an impasse: stay and look in the village, or cross into the Crystal Trees. The wrong choice could lose her head start on the Souls. She needed to get to Kole first at any cost. Though her mind had been made up, she dreaded the next step.

Still atop the sweating, shuffling horse, Piper closed her eyes and centered her focus. She held no connection to Kole—no *direct* connection— but she knew of a way into his mind. A loophole. One that she herself had forced upon Kole when she'd fed him Aterus' blood. With her father's blood inside Kole, it allowed them to mind-link. If Piper could use that road for herself, she'd be able to speak with Kole, too. But that meant going through Aterus' head—sneaking through *his* mind to get to Kole. Her body shuddered at the thought, but she withdrew into herself anyway, letting her mind sink back through her bloodline, back to her father.

If she were caught... if Aterus so much as felt her presence sneaking through him... Piper's fate would be in his complete control. Her father could take over her body—move her like a puppet. He could lock her mind from her body indefinitely.

Last time she had linked with her father, she'd been fueled by Souls' blood. That blood had been the only reason she'd been able to overpower him before. This time, she would be on her own.

Piper's hands shook on the reins as her exhale quivered in her throat. *You are a demigod. Daughter of Souls. You have more power than you know.* The pep talk did little to settle her nerves, but it gave her the last bit of courage she needed to forge ahead.

The terrain felt so familiar. She'd know her father's mind anywhere. When she snuck through that barrier, Piper remained still at the cusp. Should Aterus sense her immediately, she had a better chance at escaping her father's grasp the closer she stayed to the exit. To her surprise, a calm demeanor claimed his head. Rarely was he calm. Unfortunately, it might make her task more difficult.

She wished for a distraction. If he could focus on something, her presence could traverse a bit more freely. Instead of barreling through, Piper waited, watched, tried to sense what he was doing.

Slowly, the picture of her mother's face entered the space. Aterus' hand caressed Evangeline's cheek, stroking her wrinkled skin with his thumb.

"Soon, my love. We will be like before." Aterus' voice echoed all around Piper, who still pressed her consciousness as close to the door as possible.

Too risky. She needed a distraction. Waiting for one wouldn't do. She would have to create one herself.

Piper retreated from Aterus' head, abandoning it for another route, another door. One she always left open.

She moved freely through the cusp to the empty void of her mother's mind. A vast space of darkness met Piper. It had been years since any sort of thought had resonated there. The coma had taken even her dreams by now.

"Mother, hear me, please. I need you." Piper let the words swell in the emptiness. The moment came and went with no response. *You really are beyond saving, aren't you?* She stifled her grief. As much as she hated to do what came next, she pushed on. Evangeline would have forgiven her.

Piper let her presence grow and envelope her mother's mind, every crevasse and void. Once in place, she took control of Evangeline's body and made her mother open her eyes. There, she saw through borrowed eyes and looked upon her father's face.

"My dear," Piper made her mother say.

Aterus snapped up, eyes meeting Piper's. "Evangeline? You're awake?"

"How long has it been? Where's Pipes?" Those were the first things Evangeline always said when she roused from her comas. Piper flexed the muscles around her mother's mouth and pulled them into a soft smile, held there, then pulled away from Evangeline's head.

Piper only had a short time before Aterus would suspect something. Things needed to go quickly. No mistakes. It only took a second for her to slip back into her own mind and return to the door that linked to Aterus' head.

With his full, elated attention on his wife, Piper entered and slid along the border of the Soul's mind until she found the door to Kole. She built up her energy and slammed into it. What she had expected to be barred shut from the other side gave way at the gentlest of touches. It meant... well she could only guess at the truth, but it did tell her Kole had no barriers against her father. That discovery made her gut shrivel with worry.

What in Soul's name have you done, Kole?

CHAPTER 31

The dance floor swirled with colorful dresses and suit tails. Kole slumped in his chair, his chin propped up on his fist, watching all the happy couples glide by. Neither Felix nor Vienna had come to see him. Though Kole had spotted both patrolling the room several times, they refused to make eye contact with him.

The swell of music died to the end of the song, and instead of picking up in another lively beat, the musicians set down their instruments. Tena, with the other council members falling into formation behind her, took the stage.

The ballroom silenced.

"Welcome, citizens of Zeal," Tena began, her arms stretched out in greeting, "I hope you have all been enjoying the celebrations so far. I pause a moment here to recognize the reason for our gathering, our great Hasic."

The crowd clapped and cheered.

A couple dozen people garbed in matching uniforms had gathered in impeccable lines off to the side of the stage, Jax at the head.

Tena waved them forward. "Please join me."

Kole clapped with the crowd from his seat as the Hasic joined Tena on stage.

"The increased movements of the Black Wall have troubled us this week. Our one defense, the Hasic, continue to show their skill and dedication to Zeal's safety. Our city stands because of these women and men." The small silver train of her dress followed Tena as she retrieved a stack of medals from a table at the back of the stage. She, Solt, and Aljander took a handful each and bestowed the medals on the Hasic members.

Once done, Tena returned to the middle of the floor. "We give these medals for their courage, bravery, and for their duty to us and to Zeal, the mightiest city on Ohr."

Another round of applause.

Kole hadn't noticed Orla break from the group until she stood at the banister and reached out to him, saying, "Come, Kole. Tena would like you up there."

He pulled in a deep breath and stood. Orla took his arm and wrapped it around her own. While everyone else had dressed for the occasion, the priestess still wore her usual robe-like garbs, hands and wrists wrapped in the same ribbons. But her Seven Souls pendant sparkled in the chandelier light. Probably suitable for a priestess to dress humbly no matter the occasion.

Orla escorted him up the steps of the stage, where Felix and Vienna had gathered, too, then the priestess left his side. Standing there with the siblings made Kole feel a little less vulnerable, when the weight of every attendant shifted to him in his revealing outfit. Felix's wild curls had been slicked back with some kind of oil, leaving the tattoo of the Seven Souls symbol on his earlobe exposed for all to see. He wore a dark-green suit, which matched his sister's in color, and held an aloof posture.

"We have honored guests visiting from Socren." Tena gestured a hand to Kole. "One who has lived through the touch of the black flame."

Hushed whispers spread throughout the ballroom. Kole met looks of awe and horror alike.

"They have seen the true power of our peoples," Tena continued. "Watched us battle the fiercest enemy our world has ever seen. We give hope to Ohr that one day we will tame the Black Wall entirely, and make it bow to us as we have been made to do for centuries."

The crowd whooped and hollered.

"Now," she said, waiting for the room to die back down, "may none of our Hasic or guests be without a dance partner or a drink in their hands this evening." Another round of applause. "With that, we will begin the formal open of the festivities."

Tena turned and nodded to Kole. "Time to show you off."

It looked like Tena would be his dance partner. He hoped she'd be understanding when he inadvertently stepped on her feet. But as he moved toward the councilwoman, she turned away. Vienna stood behind her, staring at him expectantly.

"Shall we?" Those were the first words Vienna had said to him all day.

His heart pounded. The green of her dress made her eyes pop like fireflies in the dead of night.

"Sure," Kole croaked as he took her offered hand.

Vienna led him to the center of the floor, then turned him to her, arms out and ready for his to link into. When he hesitated, her eyes, cold until now, soften slightly. "Don't worry, I'll show you."

Kole's entire body warmed as she guided his arm to her waist. The slick of her satin dress barely registered on his fingertips. Instead, his senses latched on to the soft curve of her body beneath his palm. The distraction hid the moment her fingers locked with his other hand. She lifted him into the dance frame. Unsure where to look, he kept his stare straight ahead, but their height difference left him looking at her lips. They stood in that frozen stance until the draw of a single violin sent the room spinning around them.

"We'll go slow, for both our sakes." Vienna stepped to the side, pulling him along with her.

Kole quickly moved his gaze from her lips to the floor.

"Uh, uh. Look up," she instructed.

"I might step on your feet," Kole warned.

Her eyes caught his, then looked away. "I've known much greater pain than that lately. Stomp all over them if you like."

The way she said it... no doubt she spoke about more than the gray lung she'd endured. Kole had caused her pain. He'd never forgive himself for such a thing. But it had to be this way.

And he did step on her feet a few times, when Vienna spun them along with the other couples around the ballroom. Lines formed around her mouth as she clearly fought back her winces.

They danced with a building silence between them. Compared to Vienna's gracefulness, Kole felt like a bumbling statue come to life, rigid and stomping. They danced so close, Kole could feel the heat from her skin pressing into his own. The perfume of her hair filled his nose and sent a fresh wave of goosebumps down his limbs.

Yet he'd never felt so distant before. Her eyes no longer registered him. She kept her attention to the surrounding crowd. After another swooping turn of their dance, Kole spotted Felix slinking along the wall at the far end of the grand hall. Only for a moment, though. When Kole blinked, his friend had disappeared into the crowd again.

Surveillance. Kole peered over the blonde curls cascading to Vienna's shoulder. Others joined Felix in his promenade around the perimeter — people in fine yet plain clothing. Undercover members of the Hasic, Kole guessed, by the way they looked from the crowd then back to Jax, who, like Kole, had been obligated to join the dance. Jax's partner seemed oblivious to the operation and happily twirled and laughed to the crecsendoing bridge, the train of her dress whirling with every step.

Halfway through the song, Vienna finally spoke. "Why did you lie?"

The question made Kole misstep and stomp Vienna's foot. He muttered his apology, then looked her in the eye.

Suddenly, the room emptied — the crowd forgotten. Only Kole and Vienna existed, dancing over the polished marble floor, drenched in the warm light of the chandeliers, whose crystals casted spectrums on the surrounding walls.

"I hoped I wouldn't have to," Kole said, unwilling to look away in fear of breaking their connection. "But when I tried to tell you before, your and Felix's reactions made it very clear I had to."

She continued to stare for a moment. Not even a blink gave away a hint at her thoughts.

"Aterus can return my body. I don't have to be lesser anymore."

Vienna's hand tightened around his. "You are not lesser, Kole. No matter what you look like or what you think you can't do."

"Is that what you thought about yourself when you were on the brink of death a day ago?" Kole cocked his head. "I saw the fear in your eyes. It grew the weaker you got. Either you feared death or becoming a burden. I know because I've felt the very same things since I burned."

Her eyes searched his. In that brief moment, she let her guard down and Kole noted a glimmer of understanding.

"It's more than just my body. Aterus will bring back Niko. He already has, to some extent. I can see his spirit — call on him as I please and talk with him again."

Vienna squinted curiously. "Is that who you've been talking to? You said it was Caradin, but sometimes I wondered."

Kole nodded, unable to keep his smile away. "It's like no time has passed." At this very moment, he wanted nothing more than to summon his ghostly friend and finally introduce the two of them. "What would you do to have your parents back?"

She frowned and her expression turned distant, as if old memories preoccupied her thoughts. Then, her jaw set firm. "I won't deny I've dreamt it. I miss them so badly it makes my heart ache. But resurrection? It's not right, Kole."

"You don't understand."

"I do. I really do," she said with such fervency, Kole almost believed her. "But this is not the way to go about it."

Kole's head began to pound. Either the droning of the stringed instruments or the spins of the dance left him with a sense of vertigo. Though his feet dragged against the tempo the music had set, Vienna held him firm. She must've detected his dizziness, because she slowed before Kole could voice his discomfort. Instead, they swayed side to side at the center of the floor like the sun, the other couples planets locked in the pull of their gravity.

Despite the relaxed pace, Kole's head pained him. Each pulse of his heart sent a hammering throb through his brain.

"I've angered you," Vienna said.

Kole shook his head. "It's not that, I just... my head hurts."

"Do you need to sit? I can get us out of here." Vienna swung her head side to side, either searching for a way through the other dancers or to spot her brother.

"No, it's fine. I can hold out until it's over." Kole wanted to last through the song. Stay here with her while he could, for only he knew what the rest of the night truly entailed: a departure. In a few hours, he'd leave them behind in Zeal, not just while he searched for Vara, but until he'd lived up to his side of Aterus' deal, however long that would take. Would she even want to see him at the end of it all?

Another stab of pain sent him reeling. He broke from her embrace and clutched his head.

"Kole? What is it? What's wrong?"

Kole had been so distracted, he hadn't noticed the signs. Someone was trying to mind-link with him. An unfamiliar presence. "Mind-link," was all he could sputter between breaths.

"Is it Russé?" Vienna put her hands on his shoulders, steadying him. "Kole, let him in. Please. Let him in."

Not Russé. He'd been around him long enough to know what he felt like. Issira and Obell, too. He would recognize them as easily as a familiar face. Aterus, then? Doubtful. He'd come to know him, too. This force, whoever it was, hit him like an avalanche.

"*Caradin. Help me!*" But the plea came too late. Just as Caradin poked his head out from the satchel, Kole succumbed to the stranger.

CHAPTER 32

Pain exploded through Kole's mind. It felt like a hundred knives poised over his brain, slowly driving their blades through his flesh. He cried out and stumbled forward. The feel of Vienna's arms around him, keeping him from falling to the floor, barely registered.

"*Kole?*" A voice resounded inside him. Familiar. But the pain fogged everything. He couldn't place it.

"*Stop fighting me. You're only making it worse for yourself.*"

Kole opened his eyes. Vienna held her face close to his, concern thick in her expression. Though her mouth moved, her words were lost on his ears. The stranger in his head held all his attention.

"Get out!" Kole meant to yell it in his head, but by Vienna's flinch, he'd screamed it in her face too. Her grip only tightened around his shoulders.

"*No, Kole. Not until we talk. Let me in and the pain will pass.*"

Finally, the voice registered. Flashes of fiery red hair. A hand forcing a vial of blood down his throat, back in the ashen streets of Grayfall.

Piper.

Kole had no idea how she'd found her way to his mind, but the questions would have to wait until he got a grip on himself. Heeding her instruction, Kole pulled back his defenses. The pain worsened before it fell away. He gripped his fingers tightly around Vienna's arms, who still stared at him, the look in her eyes morphing from worry to terror. He closed his eyes, blocking her and the noise of the ballroom out. Slowly, he controlled his breath and allowed Piper inside.

When the pain subsided, leaving his head quiet again, Kole finally acknowledged her. "*What are you doing here? How did you get in my head?*"

"*Does that really matter right now? I need to find you. Where are you?*"

"*I don't want to be found.*"

"*Don't be such a child. Tell me where you are. Things are dire.*"

Kole felt her anger and impatience swell within him. He matched it with his own. "*Don't you think I know that? I'm tired of being a puppet for the Souls. I'm doing this on my own. Now get out."* With all his energy, Kole pressed against her presence, forcing her back, but she retaliated.

"If you won't freely give me what I need, I'll take it myself."

Suddenly, a cold encumbered him, and Kole's body filled with an icy numbness. Piper's presence expanded within him, dominating him. He knew what came next because he had lived through it before. Issira had done the same to him weeks ago, controlling his body and forcing her will on him. Kole never thought it would happen again. Or that Piper, of all people, would have the power to do it.

Before he could react, she had gained complete control. He stood in the back of his own mind, watching as Piper opened his eyes to see Vienna standing there, still holding him upright.

"Vienna." Kole heard his voice say, but it was Piper who acted.

"Kole? What's going on?" Vienna put her hands on Kole's cheeks, forcing him to look at her.

"Kole is fine. I need you to tell me where you are."

A moment passed where confusion swept over Vienna. Mouth open, she stared at Kole as if mulling over the words. A spark then, behind her green eyes. "Russé? Is it you?"

"Close. It's Piper," she made Kole say, then added, "but I'm with Russé." *Was. Is. What's the difference? Just give me what I need.* The words came in a string of thoughts. Piper's mind swirled and intertwined with Kole's so thoroughly, he could sense and read every shift of her emotion and train of thought as if they were his own. "Kole is in danger; we need to get to him."

It was enough. Vienna nodded and took Kole's hands in her own. "More danger than you know. And he's made a deal with Aterus. He plans to release the Souls and hand them over."

Even Piper flinched. *So that's why the portal between you two is so thin.* Piper turned her questions back to Vienna. "You've released Caradin. Any more?"

Vienna shook her head. "Vara is next, but she's somewhere behind the Black Wall. Kole has plans to pass through, though I don't know when. You have to get to him before then."

Could you really be so foolish? Going through the wall... even if it were possible, why would you do it alone? Kole felt Piper's irritation rumble through him, but he couldn't respond. "Where are you?" Piper growled.

"Zeal. City Hall. Please hurry. Kole has enemies here, too."

"Enemies in Zeal? What am I walking into?"

"Kole knows more than I do. Search his head if you must. I wouldn't be surprised if he's hiding more."

All the while Kole watched their interaction from the back spaces of his mind. Trapped. The puppet once again. He wanted Piper out—everyone out.

But Piper went deeper. She dove into his memories and sifted through his thoughts without remorse; quiet moments shared with Niko in the treehouse, training sessions with Russé, who scolded him about his reckless handling of ramblers. Kole recoiled when she swept through the moment when he first laid eyes on his newly burned face. That vulnerable moment meant for him alone, tainted by unwanted eyes. All in search of what? Things Vienna had already told her. When Piper forced herself through a more recent memory, the instant Kole gifted Vienna the crystal necklace, and shared in the heart-racing lightheadedness he felt in that moment—sensations he himself tried to suppress—Kole'd had enough.

His anger boiled over, and an idea came back to him. He'd chased a Soul from his mind once before. Demigod or not, he could do the same to Piper.

Kole dove into a past memory: one that he had promised to shut away forever. But his rage forced him to reopen it. He surrounded himself with that fateful day. The day he burned. He felt the heat of the Black Wall as those winds pulled him in. Searing, bubbling flesh. His eyes sealing shut from the heat. He recalled the scent of his own burning flesh. Complete and utter agony. He held onto it. Immersed himself. Mastered it.

Then, he set it on Piper. Chased her down.

Piper recoiled and let out a gasp through Kole's mouth.

"Piper?" Vienna shook Kole's shoulders. "What's happening?"

"Keep Kole... in your sights," Piper said through gritted teeth. A cry ripped from her, and she released control over Kole's body.

That failed to satisfy him. Kole sought to torment her. Make her think twice about entering his mind again. He pursued her, casting the dark flames on her until she'd retreated to the edge of his mind. Cornered, he pressed further. No way he'd let her dwell here in the shadows. He refused to stop until she'd gone.

One last press and she fled through one of the portals in his head: the door that led to Aterus. *Strange.* He never thought another could use one of the Souls' links to get to him. The fact that she'd used Aterus' door gave him more insight. Their relation, their shared blood, must have made it possible. Another thing to worry about. Who else had a free road to his head?

Once her presence had gone, Kole let the memory of the flames fade. *Finally, alone again.*

Little by little he felt the tingle of his limbs once more. He flexed his muscles and twitched his fingers. When he regained his vision, he found himself crumpled on the ballroom floor, Vienna crouched over him.

"Piper?" Vienna asked quietly. "Is it still you?"

Kole looked up at her and croaked, "Would you be disappointed if it wasn't?"

The ballroom had gone silent. Every attendant stared at the pair slumped on the floor. Their eyes: some concerned, some scared, but one, he spotted through the crowd, held a glint of interest. Before Kole could get a better look at the face, the person had disappeared behind the mass of people. It appeared Tena had gotten what she wanted, if through different means. Kole definitely stood out now. Any Dark Hand in attendance knew who he was. Vienna and Piper had practically screamed the Souls' names during their conversation.

Felix and Jax pushed through the stalled dancers, trying to get to where Kole and Vienna sat. Before they could reach them, Kole cast his anger on Vienna. "You set her on me," Kole whispered. "Had her probe my memories. Do you have any idea what that's like?" He ignored Caradin peeking out of the satchel.

She leaned back, eyed their audience, then said, "I'm sorry, Kole."

"I don't think you are."

Her face stretched into an expression of shock and confusion.

"You wanted something from me. And like the Souls you did whatever you needed to get it. Even if it meant hurting someone you supposedly care about."

"That's not what—"

"Save it," he snapped. "I don't want to hear it."

"You're not yourself." Vienna stroked his arm.

"I'm exactly myself." Kole jerked his arm from her touch. "And you're finally showing me who you are." Once the words had left his lips, he instantly regretted them. The pain in her eyes pulled on his heart, but he clambered to his feet and nudged through the crowd, away from Felix and Jax.

As he moved through the ballroom, hushed whispers grew to mutters. He heard his name on their lips. Still, he kept his head down and shoved his way to the exit. He'd done his job well enough, garnered attention. Now he wanted out—to wait in his room until Jax called him to cross the Black Wall.

That was when a scream pierced the ballroom.

CHAPTER 33

All Piper remembered was searing heat. Not only within her head but down to the bones in her own body, where she'd left it standing outside the crystal trees. Yet as she fled from Kole's mind and raced back to herself, a force caught her, like teeth catching the neck of an escaping rabbit.

The familiar voice of her father filled her. *"Sneaking through my mind, are you?"* The force closed around her, encasing her in a prison. *"A risky move after what you've done to your mother. Killing Savairo. Betraying me."* The last words rippled in a growl.

"I didn't betray you," Piper tried, though she knew her chances of deceiving him were near impossible. *"Savairo was crazed. He fell from your orders."*

"You fell from orders!" Aterus raged. *"Left me to handle things myself when my powers are already thin. Look at your mother!"* He forced her mind into his and linked their vision. Through his eyes she witnessed her mother's face, thin skinned and yellowed as if disease had taken her. *"Her light barely flickers."*

"As it should. She shouldn't even be alive. You've tainted her body — her soul. Let her be free." Her answer raised a fresh ripple of anger, which tore through the both of them. Though her mind still lay disconnected from her body, Piper swore a stroke of terror struck her spine, like a bolt of lightning.

"You've betrayed this family too many times. Abandoned me and your mother for what? Your humans?"

"They're your creations! Mother's people. They live and breathe and love. Have you no respect for them? The form you've taken? The woman you claim to love?"

"Everything I do is to keep you and Evangeline safe. But it seems my faith in you is best spent elsewhere. If you are not here to save your mother, you are against me." His wrath built with each word. The tension around Piper's mind tightened to the extreme. She feared if he pushed any harder, he'd

annihilate her. *"The pain of losing you, daughter, breaks my heart. Let me show you what it feels like."*

In a swirl of light and color, her head spun. Round and round the colors whirled, until finally slowing. An image settled in her mind. Crystal clear, as if she looked on it with her own eyes, yet she knew the vision as an implant from Aterus.

The city of Socren stood before her. She looked down at it from the sky. The streets seemed quiet and empty in the last moments of twilight. Red sunlight shaded the buildings a deep blood-like color. Why was he showing her this?

"I made a promise to you that I intend to keep." Aterus' tone had turned soft—almost sweet. *"So watch it burn."*

A rumble shook the air.

"No." Piper glanced north toward the Poleer Mountains. The towering peaks seemed to shake in fear. *"Don't do this, please."*

"You forced my hand, my darling."

"Stop it. Please, you must!"

But her protests gained no mercy from her father as the licking black flames crested the mountain range and stormed straight for the city nestled at the base. She cried out in warning, though she knew only Aterus could hear.

The Black Wall swallowed the city gate. Then the prison, the housing district, and the shops. She tried to look away, put another picture in her head, but Aterus forced her attention to the destruction. Held it there so that she could watch it burn. Within seconds, the entirety of Socren had gone: the wall of death standing where the farmlands ended. Gray ash billowed around the scene, like a dense fog.

Piper's mind went blank. Numb. She knew this fate had been coming. That Socren stood in a dangerous position since she'd killed Savairo. But to witness it.... To see Aterus intentionally massacre an entire city.... *"What have you done?"* Was all she could think to say.

"What you intended to do to my Evangeline." A pause, then his voice lay thick with something Piper never thought she'd hear from him: sorrow. *"And what I intend to do with you."*

The grip around her mind immediately snapped back into place. Piper knew in that moment, Aterus would never let her go. She'd stay trapped in his mind forever... or he'd kill her here and now.

"Kole is mine," Aterus said as he sent another ripple of pain through her. *"The Souls are mine. Ohr is mine. I will not let you get in my way any longer, daughter or not."*

The force around her made her thoughts jumble. Memories of the past swelled and fell back to the depths like ocean waves over the sand. Her mother's face burned into her. Those golden, honey-colored eyes that radiated warmth and love so thick, it seemed to caress her skin. Never to see that face again. Never to know what happened to Evangeline and her endless suffering. No one else would fight for her mother. Only Piper, and she couldn't fade away like this.

"She will hate you forever if you kill me." With that, she fought. Not only for her life, but for Evangeline. For Kole and everyone on Ohr. All the strength that being a demigod granted, she cast at Aterus. Yet all that strength did nothing to gain ground—only prevented him from crushing her further into oblivion.

How long could she hold out? Already she felt the walls of her defenses tremble under his grip. Aterus squeezed her like a bug in his hand. Even if she could hang on indefinitely, time in the outside world ticked by. The world that needed her now more than ever. *Kole* needed her. If only she could reach out to him. The door linking Aterus to Kole's head stood open. He could come and go as he pleased. Kole might be the only person other than Evangeline that Aterus would never harm. If only she could move. If only she could do something.

The pressure never let up. Piper searched for a weak point in his hold. Even the smallest crack would have given her the opportunity to send a message out, a single thought. None existed. All the poking and prodding only expended more energy. So she holed up and braced, hoping Aterus grew bored or had a change of heart.

It can't end this way. Please. She kept the thought tucked away inside herself. The last thing she wanted was for her father to hear her begging for her own life. Her weakness. It'd only encourage his onslaught. *Help.*

Then.

An answer.

From the last place she expected.

A familiar twinge of warmth ignited within Piper's head. Small. Like a freshly birthed flame on the tip of a matchstick. Yet it grew. Raged to the might of a wildfire.

"My darling," came Evangeline's voice. *"Run when I say."*

"Mother?" Piper clung to the presence. Where it had come from... how it was possible... she hadn't a clue.

"There's no time for a reunion, Pipes. I have no strength. Just, please, run when you have the chance."

The presence started to pull away from Piper's core and everything grew colder. *"No, don't go yet."*

"I love you, Pipes."

That was the last thing Piper heard of her mother. She lashed out. Pounded her mind against the cage her father had set around her.

The wall around her held firm. Until the fifth blow.

Suddenly, her consciousness expanded in the void of Aterus' head — her father nowhere around, pulled back, it seemed. But why?

Whatever the reason, this stood as Piper's only chance at escape. Like Evangeline had told her, she fled to the cusp of the Soul's head to the portal that led her back to her body. Before she passed through, a singular thought consumed every expanse of her father's mind. One that halted her and urged her to stay despite the danger.

"Evangeline is awake."

Piper longed for her mother. A chance to see her — speak with her. Hold her. Even if it was secondhand through her father's senses. She wavered at the portal, heart torn in two.

Then she dove through.

Her mind slammed back into her body. She lay face down on the ground, the crystal trees glowing orange in the sunset. The scent of damp earth engulfed her nostrils. Sounds of a stamping horse came from nearby.

Hands closed around her arms and lifted her to her feet.

For a moment she suspected her freedom some sort of trick. Did she still lay in Aterus' mind, pinned under his power? Her father feeding her memories and visions? Was she truly back in the safety of her own body?

She fought against her captor. Tore her arms free.

"Steady, child."

She knew that voice. Piper turned. Russé stood before her, hands up with open palms toward her, as if he were calming a wild animal.

"How did you—" She stopped herself upon noticing the other Souls standing around her as well. The heat radiating off Obell's skin came as a pleasant relief against the bite of cold.

"Catch up?" Issira finished Piper's train of thought. Mud stained the blue silk of her dress all the way to her knees, but the Blue Soul still looked as radiant as ever. Those almond eyes bore into her. "It's not hard when the one you're chasing decides to stop. You must've been unconscious for the better part of an hour."

"Did the beast buck you off?" Obell chuckled. "Serves you right for leaving us behind like some unwanted company. We are Souls, for Ohr's sake.

Piper shook the settling dust from her head. Before her encounter with Aterus, she'd spoken to Kole. "He's going after Vara. Soon."

"Kole?" Russé stepped closer. The weight of his body leaning against his staff made the bottom sink into the soil.

"Yes, we have to stop him. Vara rests on the other side of the Black Wall. He intends to cross it."

"It's impossible." Issira's voice shook, giving away her concern.

"How do you know all of this?" Russé insisted.

"I went into his mind."

"But—how? His defenses are too—"

"His defenses are meant for you and the other Souls. Not for Aterus. He's made a deal with him." Confusion struck all their faces. But Russé... his eyes held a deep pain behind them, as if Piper had stabbed a dagger straight through his back. "There's no time to explain what or how, but I got to Kole," Piper continued. "He's in Zeal. And he may be in danger."

Russé's bottom lib stiffened. "Then we go with haste."

"One more thing." Piper cast her eyes down. "My father knows of my betrayal. He's gone mad. Madder than I could've imagined. He's... he's moved the Black Wall over Socren. The city is dust."

"Leo." Russé looked to his kin. "We should split up. Look for survivors. Kole would want that."

"No need. He forced me to watch it happen. There's nothing left. No one could've survived that." Piper remembered the note she'd sent to the Liberation leader a week ago, before she'd killed Savairo. "Aterus knows I'm going after Kole, now. We will all need to stick together if we hope to keep Kole out of his hands."

"Ride ahead." Russé nodded to the stolen horse. "We will be right behind you. I fear if Kole knows we are near, he might flee. But you... he won't run from you."

I wouldn't be so sure about that. Piper realized she never gave the full details of her interaction with Kole. No doubt he'd run if he spotted her, but she wasn't about to give up the chance to get to Kole first. "Very well."

Piper climbed atop the horse and pushed her heels into the animal's sides. A glance back showed her the Souls pursued, slowly falling behind as her horse increased in speed and swerved in and out through the crystal trees toward the city that lay beyond.

All the while, Piper found her thoughts far away from herself. On Leo. On the Liberation. The people of Socren. She only hoped Leo had received her warning. And heeded it.

CHAPTER 34

A loud bang followed the scream, and the ballroom erupted in chaos. Kole turned toward the noise, but shoulders clipped him, throwing him off his feet as the grand celebration turned into a stampede. He hit the stone floor. Boots kicked and tripped over him as he struggled to lift himself back up. One foot of a fleeing attendee caught his stomach. The air forced from his lungs. Kole clutched his core, waiting for the pain to pass.

Another bang followed the first, giving the already panicked crowd another fresh dose of fear. Yet all that lay within Kole's sight were dozens of scrambling legs and skirts.

Something gripped his shoulder. Kole snapped around. He came face to face with a pair of horror-filled brown eyes.

"They've come for you," Orla said, breathless. The fear plastered over her normally calm face made Kole's heart constrict.

The Dark Hand.

"Come! Quickly!" With surprising strength, the priestess hoisted Kole to his feet with a forceful yank.

"What's going on? What was that noise?"

The bangs he'd heard before popped off one after another from the edges of the ballroom. Red splattered the walls. At first he thought it was spilt wine, but it was too thick, clinging to the paint like honey. A whiff of metal and he knew the scene had become more dire.

"Tena has been shot. They're coming for you." Orla confirmed his fears.

"Shot?" Kole whipped his head about as she tugged him through the clamoring crowd. "*Stay hidden,*" he urged Caradin, still tucked away in his satchel.

In one corner, a Hasic guard hunkered down behind a table. No, not a guard, *Jax.* When she peeked up, Kole spotted the weapon tight in her grip: a hand cannon like the one Orla had used the day before. Jax pulled the trigger. That same bang exploded through the air. Smoke seeped from the end of the barrel. She ducked under the table once more, fiddling with her weapon. As she did, a hooded man rushed the corner. At first, Kole thought him another member of the Hasic, but the mark on his back—that red handprint—forced a warning from Kole's lungs.

"Jax," he screamed, though Kole doubted his voice rose above the crowd. He tried to run to her aid. To distract the man, who so clearly homed in on his target. "We have to help."

But Orla tugged him away. "We *are* helping," she snapped. "Tena wanted to lure them out, now let them fight."

A spray of dust rained from the ceiling. Kole and Orla's progression slowed once caught behind the masses trying to push themselves up the stairs leading to the main exit.

A quick glance over the drove, and he shivered. Another man locked eyes with him, calm and intent. The moment he saw Kole, he ran toward him.

"We've got one." Kole pointed the cultist out.

The priestess jerked him the opposite direction so hard Kole's shoulder popped. He gritted his teeth and rolled it back into place.

They hurried back across the ballroom. His boots slipped on something wet, and he knew it was blood. A slew of bodies crumpled around the frantic room. Some curled up on the polished floor, others slouched against walls or draped over banisters. Another rush of panic set in his skeleton. Where were Felix and Vienna?

His feet stopped. "Wait. My friends. I need to find them." A hasty look around the room gave him nothing. No sign of either sibling. They couldn't have gone far. Vienna had been right next to him when the fighting broke out.

He stumbled as Orla dragged him on, but he yanked his hand from her hold.

The priestess spun around to grab him again, but her eyes flared wide. The silhouette of a looming form reflected in her eyes for a split second before a hand clamped around Kole's mouth from behind.

The cultist on their tail had caught up. The smell of smoke laced his captor, so pungent, the scent smothered Kole's nose and made his eyes water. Kole tugged at the hand on his mouth. The iron vice held firm and dragged him backward, away from Orla, who fumbled her hands in her robes.

Kole pulled his knees to his chest then stomped his boots on the cultist's feet and bit down on the fleshy palm until blood filled his mouth. A roar deep from the cultist's chest, and Kole fell freely to the floor. Before the cultist could recover, Kole spat the assailant's blood from his mouth then pushed off into a sprint toward Orla.

"This way," she said, one hand outstretched to him, the other concealing a hand cannon beneath her robes.

Though his heart wanted him to stay until he had Felix and Vienna at his side, he knew how capable they were. This is what they were trained for as Liberation members: combat. They could take care of themselves. Without a rambler or his slingshot, Kole was out of his element. He'd only muddle the situation if he kept himself in the heat of battle. His friends would have grown distracted, keeping him safe rather than nullifying the enemy. Besides, Kole had his own mission, securing the Soul stowed away in his satchel.

Orla pulled Kole to a small archway. A hall led away from the event room, empty. A few paces in and a third pair of footsteps echoed in the chamber behind them. Kole glanced over his shoulder and met a furious glare set firmly on him. Blood dripped from the man's hand. Kole's attack had offered them only a small opening at escape. They'd need a better plan to shed the cultist.

"Orla," Kole warned.

She never looked over her shoulder. Instead, she pulled him right, through another corridor. This one dark, void of windows or lanterns. The glow from the ballroom faded behind them, and before Kole knew it, he was jogging near blind with only his hand in the priestess' to know where to go. The slap of boots told Kole the cultist kept true on their tail.

"Follow my lead," Orla whispered over her shoulder. "I have a plan."

Kole squeezed her hand in response when he remembered she couldn't see him nod. For an old woman, the priestess proved quick and lithe. Kole's legs had a hard time matching her pace. If not for her constant tug, he'd have fallen behind and at the mercy of their assailant. Kole prayed Orla acted soon. His body warmed with every stride. If he held out much longer, he feared he'd pass out.

Without a word, she answered his prayers and slowed. A door tore open. The bright light of sunset struck his eyes. Kole shielded his eyes with his free arm, but Orla threw him to the cobbled road at her feet. He landed roughly in the side alley of City Hall. Orla's skirts brushed his cheek as she twirled around. He peeked up. The priestess leveled the hand cannon, barrel pointed into the darkness they'd emerged from a second earlier.

A deafening boom. Then another. Kole plugged his ears. They rang from the sound and sent his head spinning. A silhouette formed in the shadows of the hallway. One last pull of the trigger, and Orla brought down the cultist.

Kole scrambled back as the man stumbled out the door and fell face first on the road beside him. The crack of bone on impact shifted the man's lower jaw into an unnatural, lopsided position. Blood trickled from the man's gut and pooled into the grouted veins of the bricked stone road. Kole sat there, stunned, watching as the cultist's back continued to rise and fall.

The eyes of their assailant drifted up and locked on Kole. A smile pulled on the man's lips, but the broken jaw made the expression look like something out of a nightmare. The cultist stretched a hand to Kole. Red scar tissue encompassed his palm and fingers — burned like the others.

"Come." Orla fiddled with her weapon, reloading it.

Kole lifted to his feet, his eyes still fixed on the dying man, whose mouth moved as if he were trying to speak, but the words came out as a gurgle of blood. A nibble at Kole's hand pulled his attention away from the brutal scene. Caradin had poked his head out, those curious weasel eyes on Kole. *"It's fine. Stay inside."*

With that, the god burrowed back down in the deep pouch.

Kole had no weapon. No hope of protecting himself. His dagger, his slingshot — everything, he'd left in his room on the top floor of City Hall. Caradin was his only tool, but risking exposing the Soul here would cause more trouble. He needed to be careful. Stay with those who could protect him. And right now, Orla, despite her old, frail appearance, fit the role, so when the priestess moved for the back roads, Kole followed.

They moved slower than before. At first Kole thought she'd changed pace for him, but here and there stood lone men and women posted on corners and up on balconies. No bloody print marked their clothing, but their slow-turning heads and watchful eyes raised suspicions of his own. The city wouldn't be so quick to take posts. Not with the mass chaos back at City Hall. No. These people were at the ready. As if they'd known.... The Dark Hand had risen.

All this for me? No. Something more than kidnapping. Their presence around the city — the exposure of their numbers, which proved vaster than Kole had guessed — meant they had more in mind for tonight than infiltrating City Hall and capturing Kole. They intended something darker. They intended to claim Zeal.

Orla stopped him at the corner of a building. Her breaths came as heavy as Kole's as she braced herself on the wall. The old woman looked as tired as Kole felt.

"We need to find a place to hole up. Rest for a moment." Kole leaned out, eyeing a cultist who'd taken position next to a streetlamp at a crossroad, one of those hand cannons hanging at his hip.

"The temple. That's where we're headed," Orla wheezed. "Just one moment to catch my breath."

"We'll be safe there?"

"There's a bunker of sorts dug beneath." Orla had closed her eyes. "An old project long abandoned. No one will find us there."

Not a minute later, her ragged pants had smoothed. Standing in the cold night air helped Kole cool his internal temperature as well, despite his thumping heart that refused to calm.

"It's a straight shot from here." Orla pointed out the spire a block away. It shone like a needle of molten gold in the sunset. "Ready?"

Kole nodded. When he peeked out from the corner to where the cultist stood, he cocked his head. "He's gone."

A hopeful smiled bloomed on the priestess's face. "The Souls are with us." She touched the bejeweled symbol heavy on her neck, whispered a soft prayer, then grabbed Kole's hand and led him into the street.

From that point on, the two ran freely. No sign of the Dark Hand, only the hope of that gilded building. Safety. When all of this ended, he'd come out and reunite with Felix and Vienna, then leave to find Vara. He just needed to hunker down until everything blew over and the Hasic ran the cult out of Zeal.

Kole ran behind Orla up to the decorative door of the Soul's temple. One shove of her body and the double doors swung open. When Kole passed the threshold, an explosion wrecked the city. The rumble made him lose his feet. He gripped the archway, keeping steady, but an invisible force thrust him into the metal door. His head hit hard, then he crumpled to the floor.

The blast deafened him, save for a shrill ringing in his inner ear. A shake to his head helped little.

A sound that loud... no mere hand cannon. A weapon much bigger.

Something inside him begged him not to turn around, but he forced himself to lay eyes upon the source.

Heat pricked Kole's eyes. Water welled up, blurring the horrific scene in the distance. He shook to his core, right down to the marrow deep within his bones. *No.*

Stone and metal catapulted into the air and fell back to the earth like burning stars, boring holes and destruction wherever they landed on nearby buildings and streets. Shimmers of shattered glass glittered sky-high.

It took but a second to register the origin—to notice the empty space where a grand building had once stood, but its tower had vanished from the cityscape.

City Hall... collapsed.

Billows of dust darkened the streets and expanded toward the clouds, hazing the scene.

Felix... Vienna....

Suddenly, something slammed into the side of his head. The pain shocked him for a flicker of a second before his eyes rolled back and he fell unconscious.

CHAPTER 35

The crystal trees rushed past Piper. Another time, she might've paused to admire their beauty. It had been so long since she'd visited the sight—last with her mother. But that sound. That distant boom not one minute ago made her skin crawl. Something horrific had happened in Zeal. Piper couldn't shake the feeling it had something to do with Kole. Trouble always had a way of finding him.

She pushed her stolen horse into the ground. Hooves clipped up soft mud, flinging it into the air behind the galloping animal. Despite the cooling air of sunset, she and her horse held a shimmer of sweat over their skin.

Up ahead, Piper spotted buildings beyond the thinning trees. Finally, she'd made it through the blasted forest. Once out in the open fields surrounding Zeal's city wall, Piper spotted a towering tree rooted a short way south of where she'd exited the forest. A rambler. Seeing the mighty tree without its rider only worried Piper more. Kole was at his strongest with his tree—formidable, even. Without his greatest weapon... well, he'd need the extra allies.

When she set eyes on the glittering towers, a billowing cloud grabbed her attention. It rose toward the sky and expanded outward, engulfing the neighboring buildings one by one as it spread. She hoped it a displaced cloud of fog, but the time of day shot down the thought. Fog burned off by midmorning. And the color, a mixture of brown and gray like dust. Something was terribly off.

A chorus of screams plagued the air as Piper clattered down the main road to the gate. The sounds must've frightened her horse because it skidded to a full stop. Piper squeezed her heels into the horse's side, urging it on. Muscles flexed under her legs, and the horse reared in protest with a whinny. Piper flung herself from the animal's back. She fell hard on her rump on the cobbled path. The hit knocked the wind from her, but in one swift motion, she'd jumped to her feet and set in a dead sprint toward the gate. She should've known better than to bring a farm horse to a scene like this. Still, she cursed the loss of speed.

Streams of people fled the city, making a break for the crystal trees. In the chaos, no one manned the entry gates. She charged straight through, unchecked, to the streets of Zeal.

Crowds of people stood in her path, some running while others gawked at the growing cloud Piper had spotted on the way in. She needed to get closer to the site.

Road signs meant nothing, for the cloud of dust stood as her beacon. She twisted down alleys and corners, whichever led straight for her target. At the heart of the chaos, that's where Kole would be. She felt it.

More cries and screams of panic. Soon, she met hordes of people head on, stampeding in the opposite direction like spooked cattle.

When a fallen man, struggling with a leg wound it seemed, appeared through the crowd, laying in the middle of the road, Piper changed course. She shouldered through the passersby, who never registered her presence, and ran to the man's aid.

"What happened?" Piper asked, while she studied the damage to his body. A broken leg all right. The shin bone poked straight through his skin.

He looked up at her, wide-eyed, like an angel had flown down to save him. "I was trampled."

"No, not to your leg. The city. What happened? What did you see?" Piper crouched down, her fierce stare set on the man. His skin held a layer of dust and dirt so thick, Piper couldn't tell his true hair color.

"City Hall. It collapsed."

City Hall? The conversation with Vienna replayed in her head. *Shit.* That was where Kole and his whole gang had been when Piper had linked with him. The building may have fallen, but Kole had not. No. Piper would've felt that. The *world* would've felt that. He was alive to some extent. She needed to find him before that could change.

Just as she stood and pushed her heel into the street for a quick sprint, the man grabbed her hand.

"Wait. My leg. Help me."

Piper looked back to him. What did he expect her to do, walk him to a healer? But his eyes and his cheeks, stained with streams of muck where tears had passed, made her sigh. She wrapped her hand around his wrist and pulled him along the street.

He groaned in agony.

"This is the best I can do." Piper sat him up against a building whose windows had been shattered. "If you can crawl, go as far to the city's edge as possible. But stay out of the road." Then she pried her hand away and left. The man might survive yet if he heeded her words. Piper heard him calling after her, but she blocked him out.

City Hall. Her only goal. No other pleas would slow her. She only stopped to assess when dust hit her face and she'd found that she'd enter the demolition zone.

Small pieces of rock and metal littered the streets here and there, remnants of the building that had flown furthest during the collapse. As she moved through the obstacles, climbing over larger chunks of stone and bent metal frames of some sort, she noticed other things among the wreckage. Dust-laden forms. *Bodies.* Crumpled and broken. Some strewn motionless across the ground and others pinned beneath heavy loads — their arms and legs peeking out.

The party Vienna had spoken of... so many people gathered in City Hall at the time of the collapse must mean the body count now stood in the hundreds. Buildings never fell on their own. A poorly fixed shack in high winds, maybe, but nothing of this scale. Not structures of Zeal's quality. Piper expected something sinister had claimed City Hall.

The area here stood quiet. The city people had either fled or perished.

Piper's throat tickled. Half from the accumulating dust caught in her mouth, half from wanting to call out for Kole. *Foolish.* Vienna had said there were those here who posed a threat to Kole. Calling for him would only draw attention.

A quick succession of pops sounded somewhere deeper in the dusty haze. Shouts followed. Voices of command. Aggression. Piper pulled out her knife, then bounced back into her stride. She veered for the noise. They were sounds of a fight rather than cries from survivors.

With each breath, more muck laced her nose and mouth. The fog of drifting dirt on the wind made her eyes blurry, but she caught sight of a figure moving on her left. Piper dove behind what looked like a piece of decorative pillar, fallen on its side. The ground here, though littered with rubble, felt smooth underfoot. She pushed aside the dirt, revealing a chipped piece of polished tile. The presence of such a fine floor meant she had made her way into the footprint of a former building. Possibly City Hall. That building, as she remembered when she'd visited with her mother, had towered over the others. Surely the remnants of such a tall structure would leave behind a mountainous pile.

It took but seconds to calm herself and capture her bearings. Piper lifted her eyes over the ribbed pillar and scanned the scene.

The figure she'd seen stood atop a cracked stair. Short in stature. Thin. Male, if she had to guess. Beige dust muddied every inch of the man, covering up any distinguishable features.

She needed a closer look.

Another pop sounded. Close, too. A small explosion of rock and dust sprayed up at the feet of the stranger on the steps, who dove out of sight at the shot.

Time to make her move. Piper launched from the pillar and raced for the stranger. Rocks slid under her feet, threatening to ground her, but her quick feet kept her in a graceful gait. As she ran, those pops chased her. Small objects whistled past her head and arms. More dust spit up from the rubble around her.

Finally, near the stair, she rolled for cover behind the broken banister, cursing her attacker. The firing ceased, but she kept her guard up. Piper crouched low, keeping hidden from the long-ranged weapon, and stalked around the steps until she caught sight of a cowering form. From the looks of it, his back turned to her, he had yet to notice her presence. A few more calculated steps, then she tackled him.

Piper easily overpowered the man, who proved scrawnier than she'd expected. The hair, the build, more boyish than full-grown man. Still, she left no risk of escape by pinning her knees hard on the back of the boy's thighs, then roughly slamming his wrists down with her hands, allowing the full weight of her body to aid her.

The boy huffed in surprise, then groaned. His body convulsed beneath her, wiggling for freedom, but she refused to let up. A little pain and fear would make him talk.

"What's going on here? Tell me what happened to the city hall," she demanded.

"I dunno. Ain't you the ones who blew it up?"

Piper growled. Up until now she'd been holding back, monitoring how much strength she used as to avoid killing the boy outright. At his reluctance, she tapped into the strength her demigod blood gave her and squeezed her fingers deeper into the boy's wrists. "You'll tell me what you know or risk never using your hands again."

Quick, seething breaths came from her victim's teeth as if holding back a cry. "Ain't tellin' the Dark Hand nothin'. Do what ya want with me. You'll never get ta him."

In her building rage, a lick of clarity made her relax. The slang. The voice. *The attitude.* Piper rolled her eyes. "You've got to be kidding me." She climbed off her mark. "Felix?"

Felix clambered to his knees, hands up and ready when he turned to get a look at her. "Pipes?" His jaw fell open like a gaping trout. "What the hell ya doin' out here?" He winced and rubbed the darkening marks around his wrists, where each of Piper's fingers had left a clear mark.

Though the nickname irked her, she shrugged it off under the circumstances. "Where is Kole?"

At that, Felix's shoulders collapsed forward, and his dirty forehead creased. "Dunno. We were on his tail when the Dark Hand attacked. When the explosion happened... lost sight of him and V." His voice deepened. "They could both be dead for all I know."

"The Dark Hand. They destroyed the tower?"

Felix nodded. "They're after Kole — the cult. I dunno all the details, but they think he's some messiah. 'Burned savior.' That's what they're callin' him. They've been attackin' the city. Knockin' out the cannons that keep back the Black Wall. They got these pain-in-the-ass little weapons, too." He clenched his fists. "Once night falls, I'll show 'em."

Felix alluded to his Kayetan. She had to admit, the whole 'only appearing at dusk' thing was a proper agitation about now. She doubted this cult or whoever Felix mentioned were armed with sunstone, meaning they stood defenseless against a Kayetan. Felix's singular shadow could take out every enemy in the area in a matter of minutes.

"You'll get your chance, Felix. Right now, I need you to tell me where you last saw Kole." Shuffling near the stairs piqued her attention. Whoever had been shooting at her and Felix had mustered the courage to track them down. *That courage will cost you your life.*

"Wish I could. Can't even tell which way is up in this mess."

Piper hushed him, then crept to the edge of the stair. Sounds of scuffling on her tail told her Felix had decided to follow. Usually, she'd classify him as a good fighter, but without a weapon and unsure what sort of condition the explosion had left him in, she decided to act on her own. "Wait here," she mouthed.

Felix's pout displayed his clear disappointment, though he did stay hunched against the steps while she moved closer to the incoming enemy. No doubt Kole would show Piper his full rage if she had anything to do with injuring Felix. She already felt a stroke of responsibility for Felix's transformation into a Kayetan. Piper had been there, hidden, when Savairo had performed the ritual that cut the shadow from his body. Though she helped Felix escape after the fact, unbeknownst to anyone, Kole — and Vienna for that matter — would be hard pressed to forgive her if they knew.

Heavy breaths came from around the stone stair, followed by the rattle of metal. Once the sound of a boot touching down on the bottom step reached her ears, Piper lurched for the pair of legs. She wrapped her arms around them and forced the cultist to the floor.

The man grunted on impact. Before he could make more noise, Piper crawled up and clamped her hand over his mouth. She crouched over him, studying his face. If she had looked too quickly, she would've thought she'd found Kole. The cultist wore similar burns on his face, but the scars ended at the neck. She expected a fearful gaze from her prey. Instead, she got one of anger. *I can change that.*

Strewn on the cracked tile beside him lay an odd hand weapon. She kicked it away, in Felix's direction, then called over her shoulder. "Take it."

As Piper inspected the cultist, she noted the red handprint embossing the front of the cultist's shirt. *Well isn't that a bit obvious?* Palm still smothering the man's mouth, she said, "I'm going to pull away. When I do, you are going to tell me where the burned savior is and what you want from him. If you scream or try to fight back, you'll find it a mistake."

Fury practically beamed from his eyes, straight into her. She knew as she loosened her grip, this would take a bit longer than expected.

Immediately upon release, the cultist reached for her. Piper grabbed him by the collar. She lifted him up and slammed him back into the tiles, extracting a guttural groan from him. She allowed one side of her mouth to curl into a smile as the anger in her enemy transformed to alarm, then slowly settled to terror. His whole body shuddered.

"A mistake," she soothed. "Now, answer my questions."

The cultist's silence kindled a rage in her belly. One she knew all too well. A false step—the faintest twitch of her hand—and she'd snap her victim's neck. That rage had cursed her since her youth. A trait she'd inherited from her father. If she hoped to get the cultist to talk, she'd need to reign it in. Piper inhaled through her teeth, though her jaw remained tense.

"Answer me," she said with as much composure as she could muster.

No reply.

"Answer me!"

CHAPTER 36

"Master?"

Kole's eyes rolled in his head. Try as he might, they refused to open. Sounds came in and out. A ringing. Clanks of metal. His head spun, swaying between sleep and reality. A thick scent assaulted his nose. Fragrant wood. Burning spices. Yet all he could taste was blood. He drowned in it.

"Master?"

Caradin. Where was Caradin? Kole heard him in his head, but his state prevented him from answering. He could hardly concentrate enough to get control over his eyelids.

The air wrapped him like a warm blanket. Something icy, though, bit at his wrists. Second by second, his sense returned to him. The more he drifted away from sleep, the more he noticed. More sounds. Nearby. Mumbles. A single voice chanting. The words eluded him. Maybe the fog over his mind had something to do with it.

Finally, the muscles in his face twitched at his command and brought on a wave of fresh pain. The right side of his face felt stiff and puffy. His cheek and ear throbbed with a deep-seated ache, as if the bone itself had bruised. Kole remembered something flying at his face before he passed out.

A slit of light came through as he forced his heavy lids open.

Warm firelight greeted him. Torches set on the walls around the shadowed room. His throat tickled. Kole swallowed. Thick, half-congealed blood rolled down his throat. He choked on it and coughed it up. When he moved to wipe it from his lips, his hands stuck in position.

That clang of metal. The bite around his wrists. *Shackles.* Kole struggled against his restraints as the lump of blood slid down his chin to his neck.

The chanting ceased. Through the darkness, he spotted a form hunched in the middle of the floor.

The Dark Hand. They'd gotten him. And Orla. Where was she? If they discovered she'd shot one of their members.... Kole shivered thinking about it. *Please be alive,* he prayed.

"You're finally awake." He knew that voice.

"Orla?" Kole squinted to make sure. The soft outline of her robes. A long braid draped over her shoulder. "Where are we?"

"You were hit pretty hard. I was afraid something terrible had become of you." She hunched a bit as if she too nursed an injury, but nothing bound her wrists. Without her fancy weapon, Orla posed no real threat to anyone. At least their captor hadn't let the poor priestess unconscious on the side of the road while the Dark Hand ran rampant.

Kole struggled against his cuffs. Though his hands stuck firm, he found the shackles only kept his hands together. Nothing attached him to the wall or kept him from rolling to his knees and standing.

"I wouldn't do that just yet, Kole," Orla warned.

Kole immediately knew why. His head spun as he reached his feet. Black spots formed in his vision, and vertigo took him. The spinning left him reeling. He stumbled into a nearby wall, letting the stone keep him from falling to the floor. To him, sitting back down was a step backward in his progress so he stubbornly waited for the feeling to pass rather than returning to the floor.

"You need to rest."

Rest. Yes, that sounded good. But something in his mind told him not to. He fought through the drowsiness that followed because... because something had happened. Something terrible. Something he could not quite remember, but it played at the edge of his mind, teasing Kole, while remaining ever elusive of his grasp. Kole shook her words away. He needed to figure out where they were and how to get out.

"Do you know where they've taken us?"

"Underground." Orla cast her gaze around the room.

Just as his head settled, his eyes adjusted to the dim light of the torches in the chamber. A large space for underground. Floor and ceiling, the room stood fortified with stone walls. One door, probably locked, set into the stone at the far end. The center of the chamber, near where Orla knelt, held an odd-shaped table. Though rectangular, the top fell inward like a bowl, smooth and polished. The symbol of the Seven Souls sprawled on the floor in front of it. Except, the emblem had been drawn incorrectly. The black stone at the center had been changed to gray, and the colorful surrounding stones stood black. The entire thing had even been inverted. What did it mean?

"The Dark Hand's lair?"

"Seems so." Orla lifted to her feet and strode over to Kole. "Don't worry. I'll keep you safe."

As she approached, Kole noticed blood spots and dirt on her once pristine white robes. How much had they roughed her up? She seemed to walk normally, no limp or wince on her face to portray an injury. At least the Dark Hand had taken mercy on an old priestess. Close to Kole's face now, she frowned at the wound.

"Is it bad?" He flexed the muscles in his cheek to test it, and a shot of pain greeted him.

"It'll get worse the longer it festers." Orla grazed a light finger over his cheek. He sucked in a breath at the fiery burst of agony. "It's good you can talk. That means your jaw is intact." She pulled her hand away. Fresh blood soaked into the cloth of her hands. "Unfortunately, they've taken my things. I have nothing to help you."

It wasn't the lack of healing ointments that sent a fear through him or the fact it meant they had no weapon. Kole assumed any competent enemy would remove those. But the empty space at his side sent his heart into a sprint. His pack. They'd taken it. Where was Caradin? He'd heard him calling his name when he woke.

Kole stepped from the wall. "Where did they take our things?"

"I don't know." Orla caught him as he lumbered forward. The priestess tried to push him back to the wall, but he rolled from her grip and scanned the room.

No sign of his satchel.

He kept his ears open for tiny paws slapping against the stone or scurrying shadows in the corners.

Nothing.

"*Caradin.*" Kole found the lingering presence of vertigo made it more difficult to reach out. Still, he tried and hoped. He thought he'd heard Caradin calling him moments before. Had he dreamt it?

"*Master.*" The voice came clear as spring water, and just like bathing in a river of it, cool relief calmed Kole's heart.

"*Where are you? Are you hurt?*"

"*I am on Master's shoulder.*"

A cautious glance left Kole staring at a small insect on his shoulder. A beetle no bigger than his fingernail. Its black shell flipped from green to blue in the light of the torches. Two antennas circled and flicked at Kole.

"*You've changed forms.*"

"I had to stay with Master. I changed and flew from the bag when they took it off you."

"Good thinking." Maybe even great thinking. Caradin's new size might help them escape. Kole moved across the chamber to the door.

"I've already tried it," Orla called behind him. "They've locked us in."

Still, Kole approached the door. With a gentle finger, he scooped Caradin from his shoulder and placed the beetle at the base of the door. "See if you can find us a way out. A key or something. Last resort, we'll break it down." The easy solution would command the Soul into a bulky animal with the strength to ram the door down, but that would announce their escape. If they barreled out of the room, he had no way of knowing who waited on the other side and which direction the exit lay.

Caradin waved his antenna at Kole before crawling beneath the door.

"We have to find a way out before they come back," Kole said.

"They may be gone for a very long while." Orla's lips scrunched to the side. "The city is under attack."

That was all it took for Kole's last moments to rush back. The explosion. City Hall crumbling and falling into the towers next to it. Felix and Vienna... they had been in there. His throat tightened at the onset panic. "My friends. We have to search for them."

"Kole, you may not want to hear this, but —"

"You're right, I don't," he snapped. How dare she even think it. He refused to give it weight. Not until he found them himself — saw for himself. "They're good at what they do. They escaped. Probably looking for us right now."

"Even if they survived the explosion, they won't get far. I've put targets on their backs."

Kole's fingers gripped the door behind him. Even the crackling torches seemed to go silent as he echoed her words in his head. He'd heard her wrong. "What did you say?"

"They'll be dead soon if they survived." Orla stepped onto the inverted symbol, facing Kole. Something about the flickering firelight playing across her face made him shudder. Her eyes, once soft and friendly, stuck on him like a predator watching its prey. Hunger. Need.

"Orla?"

The priestess tugged the knot free from one of her wrapped hands and began unraveling the ribbon. "I felt your presence enter this world ten years ago. The moment you arrived, I felt a pull in my blood.

Something left me that day, and my powers have been weak ever since. You stole that from me. Today, you will give it back." Beneath the ribbon lay scarred skin that shone red in the low light. Burns and cuts festered on her wrists, palm, and fingers. Angry flesh.

"You're—no, you can't be." Kole denied the clarity shrieking in his head. Orla was just an old woman. A priestess of the Soul's temple. Member of Zeal's city council.

City council. A position like that gave her access to inside information. Every plan Tena and the others made to eradicate the Dark Hand, Orla knew about. Their mole.

"You can't be," Kole whispered again, as if saying it would make it real.

Her deep laughter echoed around the chamber. "But I am."

"Why are you helping them?"

"Helping? Oh, no, child." She held her palm toward him, discolored to a deep burgundy from scarring. "I *am* the Dark Hand."

CHAPTER 37

Piper squeezed the cultist's shoulder until she felt the bone snap beneath the skin.

The cultist cried out.

"Eh, Pipes, lay off a bit," Felix said behind her.

"It's only a broken arm. He'll live." Piper kept her hard gaze on the cultist. "I could make it a pair if you'd like. Or maybe a leg?"

When her hand moved down the cultist's body, then hovered over his femur, the cultist shrieked, "Wait. Please. The Dark Leader has him." The words came out shaky. "She is going to use him to cleanse Zeal."

"Cleanse how?"

"The Burned Savior's blood will give the Dark Hand complete control over the Black Wall. Only the survivors will be worthy to live in the utopia we create after the cleansing. The daughter of Aterus will lead us to prosperity."

Piper lifted her brows at that. "Daughter of Aterus?"

"He talkin' 'bout you?" Felix piped up as he rounded into her vision, fondling the weapon they'd commandeered from the cultist.

"There is only one daughter of Aterus." She pressed firmly into the cultist. "Who claims this title?"

"Sure ya ain't gotta long-lost twin?"

Piper's pointed glare shut Felix up. Her rage turned back to her prey.

The cultist shuddered, mouth pressed so firmly closed, the skin of his lips turned pale.

She snarled. "You fear the wrong person." With one hand clasped around his throat, Piper lifted the man from the ground so high his feet dangled helplessly in the air, as if searching for the rubble below. He gurgled, face reddening and eyes bulging at her tightening grip. Though the cultist pawed at her hand, it did nothing against her.

"I'd talk if I were you." Felix rested his hands on his hips. The thick layer of dust and dirt made him look like some kind of statue come to life. "I mean, ya already told us yer plan. What's one name, eh? 'Sides, Pipes is more ruthless than anyone yer gonna meet. I bet if ya tell her what she wants, she'll let ya run outta here alive."

"Maybe." Piper stared down the man in her grip, who shifted his sights from Piper to Felix, then back again.

The cultist wheezed as if trying to speak.

At his willingness to cooperate, Piper set him down, but kept a hand on his shoulder, preventing an escape should he grow bold. The man gasped and rubbed a hand on his throat. After a brief coughing fit, he recovered.

"Orla," said the cultist. "She planned to lure him from the ball."

"Orla?" Felix said it like he recognized the name.

"You know this person?" Piper asked.

"Well, yeah, she's the sweet old lady who saved Vienna from dyin' of the gray lung. She's a member of Zeal's city council." Felix frowned and scratched his head, sending a shower of dirt from his curls. "No way it's Orla. He's lyin'. Choke him again, Pipes," Felix beckoned, as if she were a trained dog.

The cultist reeled back at Felix's order, but Piper held him firm.

"Stop calling me *Pipes*," she snapped. What once she'd let slide started to sink under her skin. That nickname was reserved for her mother alone. "And don't you dare throw commands at me."

Felix scoffed. "I tell ya, it ain't some old lady out here blowin' up buildins."

"It's true. I swear it." The cultist nursed his broken arm. "The priestess has a chamber under the temple. That's where she summons the wall. It's where she'd take him."

Piper released the man. "Run. Get out of Zeal and don't look back."

The cultist took to his shaking feet and half-hobbled half-sprinted away over the rubble.

"Give me this." Piper tore the weapon from Felix's hands. After a quick inspection, she took it up, aiming the narrow, cylinder-shaped end away from her. Her pointer finger curled easily around the trigger instinctually. The construction told her how to work it—what it needed to come alive. Piper eyed the cultist's fleeing form. Barely more than a shadowed silhouette now in the settling dust. The handprint on the back of the cultist's coat now stood as a mark. With a firm squeeze, she pulled back the trigger, and an explosion rang her ears. A thud came as the fleeing cultist fell and landed in the rubble.

"Thought ya were gonna release him," Felix said quiet at her side.

"I never said that." Piper fiddled with the weapon and managed to open the back part of the barrel. Small pellets filled eight of the nine holes. "Would you rather me release him and risk him returning to his cult? His compliance with us has already proved he's a traitor."

"Well, no, but... have a little mercy. Coulda at least had him fight it out. Somethin' fair."

"It wouldn't be fair against me." Piper snapped the barrel shut and placed the weapon in Felix's hand, holding it there as she looked him straight in his eyes. "His last moments were of hope. That's the most mercy I am capable of right now."

"Yeah, from a demigod and all, right? Guess ya have yer limits. " He scratched his head. "Remind me never ta get on yer bad side, Pipes."

Piper took in Felix for a moment. He had called her demigod as if it were some dooming secret—something he'd scrounged from the bottom of a deep trench. But he was wrong. Her bloodline was merely the surface. Not only to her but to everything. The boy had no idea what horrors had besieged Ohr outside of Zeal... outside of his narrow scope. Socren lay in ruins. Maybe its people, too. Felix's beloved city and home engulfed by flame at Aterus' hand.

At my hand.

No explanation could portray just how dire the situation had become. Piper let her gaze drift away.

"I do take after my father when it comes to patience—the *lack* of it. So, yes, I'm at my limit." Piper leaned in close, but Felix stood his ground. "I'd advise you to stop calling me Pipes." The scent of sweat permeated from her former liberation comrade. Fear. She could smell it on him. But he refused to back down to her presence. Those green eyes held hers. If nothing else, he had courage. *That* she could work with.

"I assume you know where the temple is?"

Felix nodded. That familiar, dumb-looking smile pulled on his mouth.

"Let's find Kole."

"And Vienna," Felix corrected.

"Sure. Her, too."

CHAPTER 38

"You?" Kole gazed the old woman. He shook his head. None of it made sense. "But you shot them. You killed your own people."

"Sacrifices had to be made to keep my position in the council a secret." The smile that Kole had once thought sweet had turned sinister. "I had to gain your trust."

He thought back to all their interactions. She'd saved Kole twice from the hands of the cultists and cured Vienna's gray lung. Now he wondered what sort of concoction ran through Vienna's veins to make that happen. His bones chilled at the thought.

"Then you're the one destroying all the cannons." Kole gripped the door behind him. The situation had changed. He hoped Caradin would find a way to open the door. Whatever Orla wanted him for and why she went through such great lengths to get him alone... well, he didn't need to know the details to know it was the last place he wanted to be right now. "Why would you destroy the one thing protecting the city?"

"The Black Wall is no foe. It is a gift from the gods themselves." Orla pulled a knife from her robes and poised the blade on the thick scars of her palm. Slowly, she pressed on the steel. Blood dripped from the wound. That was when Kole knew Orla had never recruited a blood sorcerer to cure Vienna. She'd done it all on her own.

"The Black Wall cleanses the mortals. Those who prove their worth will drink from me and receive Aterus' blessings."

"Aterus?"

The priestess circled the table, raised her hand over the bowl-like top and let her wound drip freely. "Long ago, before the birth of the wall, the gods walked on Ohr—lived among us, though they remained reclusive. One chose to make himself known to us. Nations worshiped at his feet, asking for blessings. And he gave them." She made a fist, letting the last few drops of the wound fall away. "His blood gave us many powers that manifested in different ways. Some were cured of illness, some lived past their time, and others developed control over the energies of the world."

"Magic," Kole guessed. "He made... sorcerers?"

One side of her mouth lifted in confirmation. Once the blood ceased from her hand, she wrapped the white cloth tightly over the wound. "These gifts were potent. But as the generations continued—mixing with those who had not received blessings—the power diluted. Weaker magic. Shortened lives. A plague was born. One that nearly eradicated all life. It was then Aterus took back his gifts. The plague was cured, but we were left frail and defenseless." She smiled then, a full grin. "The Gray Soul took back his gifts, but only from those he could find. My ancestors hid."

"You still have that original power?" Kole struggled against his shackles. Maybe luck would grant him a rusted link in the chain he could snap with enough effort. He had to get out of here before Orla made her move. When his strength proved useless against the cuffs, he pleaded to Caradin. *"We need to get out now."*

"Our original powers are mostly intact. My ancestors made sure to keep the bloodline pure by merging with suitable partners. But as I see it, why not share the gift, just as Aterus intended?"

A dull light came from the floor. The stones of the Seven Souls symbol embedded in the ground glowed. Had the blood done that?

Orla never so much as looked at the symbol, her eyes remaining firmly on Kole, which gave him the feeling she had done this ritual many times before. Except, what was it used for? The rune's purpose escaped him, but the blood... he'd had too many encounters with the substance to ever forget its power. The fuel of life. The prime component in blood magic. The old warden of Socren had grown drunk with power from it, and Kole himself had experienced the effects when Piper force-fed him a vial. The possibilities of its effect were endless. No doubt, Orla knew this. "You bloodlet," he concluded.

"Just as Aterus let us drink from him a millennium ago, I bestow my blood to my followers. But its use goes far beyond that."

Kole thought back to the deranged man he'd seen on his first day in Zeal. The one who'd called him the "Holy One." The "Burned Savior." Had he been crazed from Orla's blood? "So a bunch of freaks drink your blood. What does that have to do with the Black Wall?"

She sneered at the insult. "The Black Wall cleanses. It chooses the worthy. That is why my followers and I are so enamored with you. All I require is for one to burn themselves in the black flames. If they survive, I share my blood with them. They join the Dark Hand."

"You send them to their deaths. No one survives the Black Wall."

"You're right." Her eyes brightened. "No one survives the *true* touch of the flame. But nearing the inferno... the heat still scorches the skin. A burn like that is enough."

"But you don't tell them that, do you?" A vile twist to her cult. How many had longed to prove their worth and died in the process?

Orla shrugged. "Some become so invigorated, they run straight through. It is a shame to lose a potential member of our cause, but the Black Wall picks the worthy. The smart. Those who survive are provided for. But you...." Orla made her way back around the table and stood over the glowing symbol. "You are wrong."

The dull, pulsing light made her wrinkles appear deeper. Her pointed chin and high cheek bones, lit from beneath, cast eerie shadows over her face. In that moment, Kole wondered how the priestess had ever pulled off the friendly persona he'd fallen for. Orla looked pure evil.

"You survived a full encounter. The flames have touched your skin. I recognized the burns the moment I saw you. But they are far more extreme, yet... healed." She shook her head. "I have lived long beside the Black Wall. Burns like that don't heal on their own. The Souls have chosen you."

They've chosen me all right. Chosen me to die for them. All this time had gone by and Caradin still hadn't responded. *Keep her talking. Bide time.* Every question risked Orla catching on to his plan, but thus far, she seemed oblivious to his intentions. All too eager to share.

Kole puffed up his chest, trying to appear braver than he felt. "What do you want with me?"

"Power runs in your blood." She took a step forward, knife out and ready at her side. "I know not where it came from, but your survival means only one thing: Soul's blood runs in your veins. The potency rivals that of the first drinkers — my ancestors who sipped straight from Aterus' cup." Orla tilted her head. "How is it possible? Generations of offspring, even through selective pairing, have thinned the magic within me. How is it you remain pure as the day of drinking? Have you drunk from Caradin?"

Kole clenched his teeth, holding back a smile. The priestess knew less than he thought. That may prove his saving grace. But she did know of Caradin. His carelessness had outed the Soul on that first day when his stag had transformed into a weasel.

She seethed at his silence. "It matters not how you came to have it. I will take it from you and from the god. Where is he?"

"In the satchel you took," Kole lied. He'd never been so glad for Cardin's shapeshifting powers. The Soul proved cleverer each day.

"It was empty."

"Then it looks like you lost him."

Orla eyed him, stone faced. She dipped her head, looking at him up through her eyebrows. "And I know just the way to find him." With a lunge forward, Orla charged at Kole.

He shoved himself from the door but immediately regretted the quick movement. His vision spun, and his wounded head throbbed with every pulse of his heart. Kole stumbled. He reached out to catch himself on the wall before remembering his hands were still locked in the shackles, and he fell to the cobbles. Without his hands to stop his fall, he landed hard on his face, reagitating the lesion. A groan escaped him.

Soon, Orla's weight pressed into his back. She pulled him by the hands and dragged him backward, toward the table. Rough cobbles scathed his skin. The new pain distracted from the stinging of his face, if only temporarily. In a feat of unusual strength, Orla lifted him back onto his feet. He'd only witnessed brawn like that from Russé. Kole sagged against the altar-like table. Drops of her blood slid to the bottom of the basin and through a tube leading into the depths.

The jingle of keys perked him up. His arms came free and dangled at his sides.

"What do you want with me?" Lips swollen and jaw stiff, his words came out in a slur.

"Your blood, Kole." She lifted one of his hands over the center of the basin, while he used the other to grip the bowl's edge to keep from falling. If only his head would stop spinning.

"Why? Ah!" Cold steel bit his palm. The fragile skin of his scars split at the mercy of the blade.

Warm blood trickled from the cut she'd made, thin but long. Red streamed down his fingers and dripped into the bowl. He swore he could hear each droplet land on the stone in the silence of the chamber, like a deep drum. Or maybe that was his heartbeat thrumming in his inner ear.

"Control," she said. "I feel the Black Wall. I can sense when it moves. But I want to control it. Move it on my own. *That* is true power." Orla thumbed his wound, milking more blood.

Kole winced at the added pressure and cried out.

"I know your blood is the key. Since you stepped foot in Zeal, the flames have been unstable."

Of course it would look that way to an outsider: like he had some connection with the flames. Whenever he'd reached out to Vara, the wall had moved. How could Orla know what Kole truly was? She'd find out who he *wasn't* soon enough, when her whole plan came to a standstill. What would she do with him then? "It's not what you think. I'm not some sorcerer."

"I care not for explanation. I just need your blood." When the stream slowed, she flicked his hand aside. "And Caradin's. I'm sure he won't be long. He won't leave you to die now will he?"

To Kole's horror, the gray light of the symbol before the altar darkened to a deep maroon. His blood had done something, though he knew not what. If it did indeed do what Orla wished... gave her power over the Black Wall... well, he hoped the Hasic and their moonbeam cannons could stand against the oncoming threat. Except, after the explosion, what sort of state was Zeal in?

"Yes," Orla hunched over the table. A thin, giddy smile spread over her features. She spoke again but in a different language: a chant like Kole had heard when he first came to in this underground hold.

Hands free now, Kole crawled to the door, where he'd last seen the beetle. *"Caradin! Where are you?"* He banged on the wood. Someone had to hear him.

"No one will find you down here." Orla's eyes gleamed at him. She'd stopped her chanting to focus back on him. "You are mi—" Orla doubled over as if she'd been punched in the stomach, then fell to her knees. Something rippled beneath the thin skin of her neck. The veins bulged—darkened to an inky black. A screamed ripped from her.

Kole stepped back as the cult leader's skin shifted to an ashen gray. What sort of spell had she performed?

Suddenly, a rumble shook the chamber. Kole gripped the door and pressed himself to the wall as dirt rained down from the packed ceiling. Another explosion? Another crumbling building? But the ground continued shaking long after it should. Memories of Kole's past flashed to the forefront. This had happened before. First came the earthquake, then the winds would rage.

A moan came from the woman, but it twisted in pitch and morphed into a howl of delight. Something about her skin sent an uneasy chill through Kole. The black veins pulsed, and the air around her skin rippled in invisible waves—danced like the air around a hot flame. Orla gasped. A greedy smile overtook her face. "The Black Wall answers my call. It has chosen me." She rose up. When her focus landed on Kole, the room blazed with an oven-like heat. "The wall comes to claim the city as I will claim you."

Panic flooded Kole. His wounds instantly numbed. Fear gripped him, froze him in place. The memories of his first encounter with the Black Wall controlled his every thought. The flames blistering his skin... melting his eyelids and mouth shut.... Kole could hardly breathe. Though he sucked at the air, none made it past his throat. Why couldn't he move?

"Zeal will be cleansed. All will bow to Orla, daughter of Aterus. And you, Kole...." She moved from the altar and closed in. "You are mine." She stood before him, arms open.

Kole shook his head to free himself from the building panic attack. He needed to move.

Too late.

Orla had locked her hand around his wrist below the fresh cut. The pressure around the tender spot made him yelp. Unnatural heat radiated from her grip. Kole knew better than to underestimate her strength now. She may be old, but a blood spell fueled her. Instead, he let her grab him and do what she willed.

"With you, I can bend all of Ohr to my desire. The entire nation under rule of the Dark Hand."

Something tickled Kole's brain. *Caradin.* Kole felt his presence closing in.

"No key, Master."

"Forget the key. It's Orla. She's behind everything. You can't come here. She wants you, too. Leave me and get out of here."

"Protect Master."

"No, Caradin. Go."

Through the quake, Kole heard a distinct set of footsteps. Heavy and tempoed. Instantly, he knew Caradin went against orders.

Kole knew better to stay at the door. Without the strength to overpower Orla, he thought it better to rely on surprise along with a little help from gravity. He threw his body into a roll. The sheer force sent Orla reeling. Kole took advantage of her distracted state and ripped his hand from her grip, then scooted as far as he could from the door in the seconds leading up to Caradin's arrival.

Kole shielded his face when the pounding footsteps sounded outside the door. Wood snapped. Splinters blasted into the chamber. A plank clipped Kole's knee, but despite the initial bruising pain, it had bounced off.

When Kole peeked out, an enraged bull stood over Orla. But not just any bull—a silver-coated beast with glimmering horns as thick as Kole's thighs that came to lethal points. The heft of the great animal's shoulders had cleared portions of the stone wall along with the door and frame, leaving a gaping hole.

Caradin pawed at the floor with his hoof, drool stringing down from his muzzle, nostrils flared and red. The bull snorted and Orla winced, her eyes wider than a full moon.

Kole scrambled to his feet and limped his way over to the animal. "The Black Wall is coming. We have to get out of here."

With the earth shaking, announcing the wall's approach, Kole leaned against the rippling muscles of the bull for support. Though the animal radiated power and danger, Caradin's eyes softened when they landed on Kole.

"I knew he'd come for you." The old priestess stared in awe. Her full attention had gone to the bull. Orla timidly moved to her knees and pressed her palms together in a position of prayer. "I carry the blood of your kin. Daughter of Aterus. Daughter of the Souls. Bless me with your powers. Let me drink from your vein, mighty Caradin."

"He's not interested," Kole barked. "We're trying to save Ohr, not destroy it." Caradin knelt, allowing Kole an easier climb atop his back. Then, he patted his hulking neck and said, "Get us out of here."

Hooves tapped on stone as the bull backed up.

Orla dipped her head, her expression darkening from wonder to ire. Kole caught the change a second too late. Before he could warn Caradin, the priestess lunged for the bull's legs, knife in hand.

A low wail, like the long drone of a shepherd's horn, reverberated from the bull's core. Caradin had been struck. Though Kole sat too high on the animal to see where or how badly, he felt the Soul's agony in his mind.

The muscles in the beast's back rippled and repositioned beneath Kole's seat as Caradin tucked his massive head. Kole wrapped his arms around the animal's neck, anticipating the next move. With a mighty swing, Caradin scooped his horns under Orla's body and launched her into the air. A sickening crunch echoed when her body hit the ceiling and again when she landed limp on the glowing symbol.

The bull snorted and turned to leave. The slight limp in his gait and him favoring his left side told Kole that Orla's knife had struck Caradin's leg.

Movement caught Kole's attention. Orla had lifted to her elbows. She smiled at Kole, blood staining her teeth.

No. Not at Kole.

Her eyes had fixed on the knife in her hand, coated in Caradin's shining, silver blood.

One word from Kole and Caradin would knock it from her hands. They could take it. Prevent her from using it. But as more droplets of silver reflected in the dim room, Kole knew the effort pointless. Caradin continued to bleed. The Soul would leave a trail for her to use wherever they fled. To Kole's disgust, Orla licked the dagger clean, silver staining her lips.

Shouts echoed from the hall where Caradin had busted through. Others were coming. More cultists, no doubt.

Kole settled on getting a head start in this chase.

"Go!" Kole ordered Caradin. The sudden burst of speed shocked Kole. He entangled his fingers in the bull's short coat, gripping tightly, and locked his knees behind the beast's pumping shoulders, hoping it'd be enough to keep him mounted.

"Capture them! Bring them to me." Orla's screech followed Kole and Caradin down the hall.

CHAPTER 39

Piper matched pace with Felix. It had taken him a few minutes to reorientate himself in the wreckage, but now he led true, like a dog stuck on a scent. They ran when they could, bounding over the smaller debris of the fallen tower, but slowed when larger structures forced them to maneuver around.

The farther they distanced themselves from the explosion site, the more the air cleared. Buildings and roads stood before them, untouched by the blast. But the chaos had only just revealed itself.

Those quick pops came from every direction. People stood on the rooftops, their weapons pointed down at the street. Piper recognized the distinguishing red handprint on their garb as they turned to reload.

Small gouges peppered the road where shots had missed their targets. Bodies lay strewn across the scene. Some wore plain clothes—civilians—while others bore similar vested uniforms. Those who escaped the bullets ran screaming into buildings or blindly down backstreets for cover. Women, children, men in all states of disarray.

Despite the havoc, a dozen uniformed men and women fired up at the Dark Hand. The Hasic stood in pairs or groups, taking cover behind walls, carts, and buildings.

Something whizzed by Piper's ear, alerting her. One of the cultists had spotted them emerging from the dust. Piper lifted her gaze, following the line of rooftops until her eyes locked on a man hunched over the wall one building away. His barreled weapon swung straight for her, and his hand cocked back the lever. Piper grabbed Felix by his dust-covered sleeve and yanked him behind the corner of the nearest building.

Felix grunted as he slammed into the brick wall. "Oi, what was that for?"

"They're shooting at us." Piper took a deep breath, then peeked her head around the edge of the building. Her goal wasn't to lay eyes on the cultist but see if he still targeted them. Before she had the chance to blink, a spray of stone showered down on her. She pulled back immediately and spotted a fresh notch in the corner two bricks above her. *Close one.* "He's not going to let up."

Metal flashed to her left as Felix brandished his new weapon. "Then let's shoot back. We got a thingamajig, too."

Piper rolled her eyes. "It's called a pistol." Then she frowned at the sparking excitement in Felix's eyes, as if he could hardly wait to fire it off for himself. Felix barely knew how to use the thing, let alone aim with accuracy. She waved her hand beyond the corner and pulled it back as a test. Another spray of brick, this time right in line where her hand had been. The cultist had them pinned.

"That's a good way ta lose some fingers." Felix flailed the barrel about as he tested each hand for the better grip.

"We can go around the back." Piper leaned around him. The alley between the building ended with a gate only a bit taller than her. An easy climb for both her and Felix.

"I mean, sure, but it'll take a bit longer. I only been here a few days. S'not like I know my way around. Quickest way ta the temple is down that way." Felix pointed the barrel at the road they'd just dove from. "'Sides, the Hasic probably know what's goin' on."

Piper rubbed her temple. "You can shoot that thing?"

When he opened his mouth to answer, she cut him off.

"Properly?"

Felix's mouth scrunched to one side. "I can figure it out."

"Fine. I'll distract him. Make your shot quickly."

"Whatcha gonna do?"

Piper waved him off. "Ready?"

He pulled back that top lever like she'd done before, then nodded.

At that, she turned from him. She usually handled things on her own, whatever the situation. Relying on others meant more room for error. Still, the situation had gone outside of what she could handle. One on one, that cultist never stood a chance. But with other enemies positioned around the buildings, she stood sorely outnumbered. As much as she hated to admit it, help was a welcome relief.

Piper squatted down, readying to sprint. Her demigod nature gave her many advantages over normal humans. Speed being one. Fast enough to beat anyone in a foot race, but not so extreme that someone could pinpoint it as odd. The bullets would easily catch her.

After a deep inhale, Piper bolted. As soon as she passed the corner, a bullet whizzed over her head. She pumped her feet into the road, gaining speed with each step. Soon, she'd reached max speed. More bullets, from other directions, landed at her feet. It seemed she'd pulled attention from more than just the one cultist. But her eyes set firm on her destination: a half wall encasing a small garden on the opposite side of the road.

The rounds went off one after another, like the grand finale of Socren's firework show. Except, the noise came from the ground level as well. Fewer than a dozen paces from her haven, she caught a glimpse of members of the Hasic moving from their cover and entering the road. Bullets clipped the roofs. The assault left the Dark Hand crouching back.

"That's right, hide ya cowards," Felix yelled.

Piper was now in range of diving into the garden. Instead of going for cover, she swerved at the last second and headed for the body of a fallen cultist a few yards off. With the cult distracted by Felix and the Hasic's onslaught, she rummaged through the dead cultist's clothes, patting them down. Her hand passed something hard. Another gun. And ammo, too. Before racing off, she ripped the jacket off the body and pulled her arms through. Warm blood soaked the cloth, making it stick to her skin as she forced it on. Finally, she turned back to where she'd left Felix.

Gone.

She'd *just* heard him. Where had he run off to?

"Not so brave when I got one too, eh?"

Piper followed the voice to where Felix stood in the middle of the road. After one more shot aimed up at the buildings, his gun clicked, empty.

"Felix," she called. "Over here."

He raced to her position. Despite his huffing breaths, his eyes flickered with a new energy—a look Piper recognized from the many Kayetan raids they'd fought together back in Socren under the Liberation. The battle and the adrenaline fueled him as it did herself. That mixture of excitement and fear, never knowing what came next, but ready to react regardless.

Together, they ducked into another alley while the Hasic down the street kept the Dark Hand occupied.

Piper took the pistol from him. "Watch." With a simple pull from her thumb, the cylinder rolled open. Empty metal casings fell to the ground. She pushed the stolen ammo in the holes one by one, set the weapon back, then handed over. "Got it?"

"Ain't no slingshot, but I can handle it." Felix took up his loaded gun and peered around the corner. "Temple's a couple blocks straight down from here."

The shots from the rooftops started back up. It seemed the Dark Hand had reloaded. Piper ground her teeth. It had been five minutes since they'd emerged from the destruction zone, and they'd only made it across the street.

"We need a better way through," she said. "Any ideas?"

"'Sides runnin'? Not really." He turned his head and gave her a once over, pausing on her new bloodied jacket. "That might help ya get by the crazies, but the Hasic will shoot on sight."

"I'll take my chances." Piper was convinced a shot or two would only slow her down. It'd be a pain, for sure, but she could push through.

"*You'll* take yer chances?" Felix squinted. "Leavin' me behind, eh?"

"Nothing personal." Piper moved to the edge, readying for another dead sprint. "Join up with the Hasic. Find your sister. That's what you wanted, anyway. Leave Kole to me."

A prominent wrinkle appeared between his brows. "That's not what—"

The ground shook.

Piper braced herself against the building. She knew better than to blame it on an earthquake, and with Felix's matching, widened gaze, so did he.

The Black Wall.

A whooping siren erupted around Zeal. Felix clamped his ears, but Piper resisted. Something between the short breaks in the wailing sound gave her pause.

Yells? Shouts? No. Not that.

She shouldered past Felix and looked to the rooftops.

Cheering. The Dark Hand had stopped their assault and cheered; their attention fixed west.

"Retreat!"

Piper snapped her head back down the road. The Hasic abandoned their positions and rushed west. She pulled his hands away from his head. "Where are they going?"

"To the cannons. They gotta turn 'em on to push back the wall." Felix snapped his hands back over his ears once she'd loosened her grip.

The cultists moved from the roofs as well, disappearing. If the cannons did what Felix claimed, the Dark Hand would surely try to stop them. This was the diversion she needed. Without a second thought, she took hold of Felix's sleeve. "Keep up."

The street stood clear. Not a Hasic, cultist, or civilian in sight. And up the road gleamed a golden spire. The temple Felix had spoken of.

Hang on, Kole. I'm coming.

CHAPTER 40

Orla's voice had faded behind Kole as he and Caradin bounded further into the Dark Hand's torch-lit lair. Kole squeezed his legs into the bull. They flew through the tunnel-like hallway, cool air hitting his face. Between the ungraceful bounce of Caradin's gait and the bobbing pair of horns, Kole's visibility was shoddy at best.

Shadows moved in the distance. Most leapt from Caradin's charge, but some planted themselves down the hall, weapons raised.

"Watch out," Kole warned the Soul. With no weapons of his own and no knowledge of the layout down here, he clutched helplessly to the bull's back. The rough coat of the animal poked the wound in his palm. He wished to let go, but he feared even the slightest loosening of his grip would leave him sliding off. Kole pressed his cheek into Caradin's beefy neck and squeezed his eyes shut, granting the Soul his full trust.

A shot rang out—so close the sound rattled Kole's eardrum. He winced in pain. Not his own, but through his connection with Caradin. This one had hit squarely in the chest. The bull stood as a great meat shield for Kole, yet the massive size of the animal made for an easy target. The belly beneath Kole roared at the fresh wound. Instead of slowing as Kole expected, a building rage powered the beast faster.

Kole peeked up and immediately regretted it.

Within a few breaths, Caradin had closed the gap between them and their attacker, scooped the cultist up with his horns, and tossed him. The cultist flew up, the fabric of his coat grazing Kole's head, then landed somewhere behind the bull. Kole squeezed his eyes shut again, swearing not to open them until they'd made it out in the open.

Soon, the halls quieted until only the rumble of the quake met Kole's ears. Another sound came to him. A long droning.

Zeal's siren!

"*Caradin, follow the noise of the siren. It'll lead us out of here.*"

The bull followed orders. Every corner they took, the alarm that Kole had once cowered from gave him a sense of building hope. A few more cultists appeared along the way, but they had changed tactics, it seemed, and ran from the path of the charging silver bull. Still, Kole feared what waited for them once they escaped.

A staircase appeared around a corner. Caradin's body bounced higher as he took the steps, rattling Kole further. At the top, the bull lowered his horns, giving Kole a clear view of a metal door. That same, modified, colorless Seven Souls' symbol scrawled out in paint—in grays and blacks.

Realizing Caradin meant to ram through, Kole shifted low in his seat and tucked his chin so he stared at steps racing by below. The sight sent a wave of motion sickness to his gut, but he preferred risking vomiting to staring straight at the nearing door. His fingers wound so tightly around the bull's coarse hair that some pulled free in chunks.

He breathed and closed his eyes. Any second now they'd make contact with the door. He only hoped Caradin blew through it in one go.

Metal whined. Bolts snapped from the hinges of the frame. The noise forced Kole's eyes open, and he glimpsed the massive metal door exploding out from the hall.

The scene ahead made Caradin skid to a stop on polished wooden floors. Kole sat up but kept his blood-soaked fingers curled in the bull's coat.

The door had spit them out in the rear of the nave of the Seven Soul's temple. The chandeliers swung overhead from the Black Wall's quake, but the real chaos lay in the pews.

Maybe a dozen cultists, garbed in their red handprint coats, shot freely at the open double doors of the temple's main entrance. At Caradin's brute charge through the door, though, their heads turned, taking in the giant beast. A moment of recognition flashed on their faces as they narrowed in on Kole. They turned their weapons his way, and the cultists flared their ranks out, circling the bull before slowly moving in.

Caradin had already taken a dagger to the leg and a shot to his chest. How much longer could the animal's rage push through? Kole doubted even a Soul could survive a full-frontal assault of this magnitude. *Even if he can, one shot will bring me down.*

Kole's worry seeped through his connection with the Soul. The bull seemed to agree and made a hesitant step back toward the hall they'd emerged from.

Then he saw it. A rush of movement from the gaping double doors of the temple.

The prominent blonde hair announced her identity.

Vienna.

She slipped inside the nave, something heavy in her hand, like leaden fruit. Their eyes met. Vienna pressed a finger to her lips as a quiet reminder, then jerked her head right.

Kole flicked his eyes to the stone altar at the center of the sanctuary, then back at Vienna, who had started a countdown on her hand.

Three. Two.

Kole passed the plan to Caradin. The bull snorted. The sound made the cultists falter briefly, but their guns trained on the animal.

One.

With a sudden burst of speed, Caradin pounded his hooves into the floor and launched toward the altar. Shots fired out, following the bull's rump.

Kole swung his attention between the altar and Vienna. She threw that strange object at the group of cultists. It arced, barely sweeping below the chandeliers, then plummeted to the floor, bouncing at the enemies' feet.

What happened next, Kole couldn't recall, as Caradin had reached the grand altar. Suddenly, the mount below Kole shrank, leaving nothing but air beneath him. Kole tumbled to the floor behind the cover of the altar.

A ripe explosion rocked the temple. Shards of wood and stone flew past all sides of his stone shield. And blood. Red splattered the temple's walls.

"Kole?" Vienna's voice rose above the quake.

He swiveled his head, searching for Caradin, only to find the god had returned to his weasel form. Blood dripped from one furry paw: only a small cut from his former wound where Orla had sliced. Kole snatched the weasel up in his hands and stood to look out on the nave.

Black soot stained the corner where the cultists had stood a second earlier. Bodies lay in pieces on the floor, pools of blood pouring out from the severed limbs. The pews nearest to the blast had been reduced to no more than tinder.

"Kole!"

Vienna stood in the main aisle. The once radiant green dress she'd worn for the ball had donned a layer of brown soot. The skirt had been shredded. No, not shredded. The cuts' placement appeared too strategic. She'd sliced it herself, exposing her legs so she'd be free to run. Blood stained her arms and legs, though Kole couldn't tell if it belonged to her or the freshly deceased off in the corner.

And her eyes.

That sad disappointment—almost fury—he'd seen in them as they danced had completely vanished.

Relief. That's what lay in her gaze. He knew because he felt it, too. Relief that they were both alive!

She ran to him, her skirt flowing behind her like a waving flag. Arms open wide, she pulled him into a hug.

And he hugged her back.

"I'm so glad I found you," she whispered in his ear.

Kole pulled away, holding her at arm's length. "City Hall... I saw it collapse. I thought you and Felix were...." He lost his words when her expression fell.

"I don't know what came of my brother." She shook her head. "Last I saw of him, we were following you and Orla out of the ballroom. Cultists pinned us down. We split up, wanting to keep an eye on you, and I'm glad I did. I saw her knock you out, Kole. *Orla.*" Vienna's fists clenched around Kole's shoulders. "When the Dark Hand blew up the building I—" Her face scrunched as if holding back tears. "But it's Felix. He knows how to take care of himself," she said as if she'd reassured herself of this a hundred times before.

It felt like Orla had whacked Kole in the head all over again. Where was Felix? A cruel thought bloomed in his head. Kole shot it down immediately. No way he could be dead, buried under the wreckage or hunted down by the Dark Hand. Just as Vienna had said, it was Felix. *Felix.* The slipperiest person he'd ever met. No stone could pin him down. Or so he hoped.

Kole took her by the chin. "We'll find him." The fuzzy body of Caradin squirming in his hand brought Kole back to agency. He wanted to tell her everything, but it seemed time was scarce. The basics would have to do. "The Black Wall. Orla has set it on the city."

Vienna's brows drew together. "What—"

"She's the one behind the Dark Hand. Behind everything in Zeal. And she's done something to herself. We have to stop her."

"Orla will have to wait," a voice boomed over the whooping siren of the city.

Kole peered over Vienna's shoulder. Jax stood a few meters down the aisle. Her body draped over one of her Hasic comrades, her arm around his neck for support. Maroon soaked through her pant leg. An injury from the collapse? Or the aftermath of the shot Kole'd seen her take when the Dark Hand raided the ballroom? She, as well as the other Hasic trickling into the building and surveying the scene in the temple, had streaks of rust-colored muck on them: the blood of their wounds mixing with the dirt from the explosion.

Jax hobbled forward with the help of her comrade. Her attention turned to Vienna. "Now that we've secured Kole, you have to get out of the city. My team can't protect you. I'm sending our numbers to tend to the cannons—or what's left of them. If the Dark Hand has destroyed too many already, all of Zeal will perish tonight. The only hope of survival is outrunning the wall."

How long had Kole been knocked out in that basement? Had the city really gone down so fast? He'd see once he stepped foot outside. "Orla plans to annihilate everything."

Jax shook her head at Vienna. "I had my doubts when you told me she'd taken Kole. But this," she jerked her chin to the aftermath in the temple. "They were right here the whole time. The temple of all places."

"She's the one who called upon the Black Wall," Kole added. "Nothing will stop her. We should evacuate."

"With the attack on City Hall and the Black Wall on the move, the civilians are already vacating." Jax nodded to her people off in the corner of the temple. "We'll hold the wall off for as long as we can. Give you and the city time to leave."

Hold it off. The words burned in Kole's head. The longer the Hasic waited, the smaller chance they had to escape. And with Jax's injured leg... she'd be doomed.

Then it dawned on him.

Jax had never intended to flee. The grim sense weighing on him must've shown on his face clear as the cracked stained glass of the temple because Jax dipped her head and said, "As Leader of the Hasic, my fate lies with the city. It's my oath."

The man keeping Jax on her feet nodded in solidarity. All the Hasic sided with their commander. They'd follow her to the end to defend Zeal. Or perhaps it was more about making a last stand against the black flames they'd long battled. Either way, they showed no sense of fear at the chance of death. Instead, it seemed as if Jax were proud to make such a sacrifice.

With an unheard command, the Hasic man helped Jax turn back toward the door. The other members fell in line behind them.

"Wait. What about Orla?" Kole pointed to the empty archway leading to the Dark Hand's hidden lair. "There's more cultists down there."

"I don't have the numbers to spare. Not when the wall draws near. Let Orla burn down there. It's more than she deserves." She signaled to one of her soldiers, who approached Kole and Vienna, then pulled out a round object from his satchel, identical to the one that Vienna had used on the cultists. "Cave in the tunnel. Trap them down there so at least those traitors can't interfere with any more of my weapons. Souls know we already have a big enough mess on our hands."

Vienna carefully clutched the explosive and cradled it against her stomach, keeping one hand free. With it, she put her hand to her mouth, then lifted her palm to Jax and the Hasic. "May the lost find their way," she said solemnly.

Jax dipped her head. When a few of the Hasic started to return the gesture, Jax stopped them with a wave. "You will run. Understand?"

The Hasic leader gave Kole a once over, passed him a half smile, then turned for the door, her people closing ranks behind her.

As he watched them leave, Kole realized why Jax had refused to reciprocate Vienna's gesture. She never questioned his and Vienna's survival. She banked on them escaping. Returning the phrase would pose as a bad omen, anticipating the chance of their death—anticipating her own failure. Not just for Kole and Vienna but all of Zeal. Jax planned on saving everyone.

A deep, sinking feeling gnawed on Kole's core.

"Can Caradin carry us out of here?" Vienna's words drew him from his thoughts. She fidgeted with the explosive.

"Uh, sure." He set the weasel on the ground. "You heard her."

The weasel enlarged. The legs grew long and lean while Caradin's snout thickened. Behind the weasel's ears sprouted nubs, which split at the base like grasping fingers. Within seconds, the grand elk Kole had first met back in the swamp stood before him. That crown of antlers, nearly twice the animal's size, amplified the ethereal nature of the beast. At least this time the Soul had opted for a more subtle-colored coat: white. Though a bit ostentatious, it would draw less attention than a silver glow.

The Soul's wounds had enlarged with the new form as well. Instead of bloody gashes on the animal's legs, half-healed pink skin encased the wound. The deep circular hole in the stag's chest concerned Kole most. Thick, congealed blood stained the surrounding fur. The deeper wound needed far greater time to stitch itself up.

When Kole had been a hunter back home, removing an arrow would cause his prey to bleed out faster. He wanted to help Caradin, but he knew little about the ammo of the strange weapons and feared digging it out may cause greater pain and blood loss.

As if answering Kole's concern, Caradin snorted then knelt to his good leg, inviting Kole to his back. Kole grabbed the antler and flung himself over the stag. The seat proved more comfortable than the bull, now that the animal's shoulders had slimmed. He waited for the Soul to flinch under his weight, but it never came. Either Caradin purposefully put on a good show to quell Kole's concerns, or the animal was really this resilient. *He is a god, after all.*

"Ready?" Vienna asked.

Kole moved to offer her a hand up then stopped mid-reach and returned his grip to the elk's neck. She was fully capable of mounting on her own. "Ready when you are."

As Kole expected, Vienna easily leapt atop the stag, despite one hand securing the explosive. Her warm body pressed up behind his, and she wrapped her free arm around his waist to secure herself. Even with the combined danger of the Black Wall and the Dark Hand, his heart still found a way to flutter. Kole shook his head, dissipating the fogginess her touch gave him. Focus. He had to focus.

"When I say, run him for the exit," she said.

Some clicks sounded behind Kole. Though he peeked over his shoulder, he couldn't quite tell what she was doing. Before he knew it, she held a linchpin in her hand. Had it come from the explosive?

"Go!" Vienna shouted.

The sphere flew through the air on the cusp of Kole's sight. He wanted to watch it soar, but his job lay with their escape.

Kole ushered Caradin forward, and the elk sprang into action. Five vaulting strides and they'd made it out the temple's door. A boom thundered from the nave, but they had gone too far to feel the concussion.

"It'll slow them down if nothing else," Vienna said next to his ear.

Caradin paused on the temple's steps, awaiting the next command.

Out in the open city, with no walls to dilute the siren, the volume blared along with the rumbling of the creeping Black Wall. And creep it had. Kole had no way of knowing how much time had passed since Orla had used his blood to call on it, but what once was a shadow in the distance had doubled — maybe tripled — in size. Worse still, the moonbeam cannons atop the city wall lay dormant as the black flames charged ahead.

To Kole's left, hundreds of people flooded the street, all running east. Bodies lay here and there in the open road. Some wore civilian clothes, others the vest of the Hasic. To Kole's horror, more buildings had fallen like City Hall. His ignorance of the city left him only guessing what buildings they were, but the skyline had drastically changed. Some structures lay half crumbled, while others had disappeared altogether, scattered on the streets of Zeal.

To his right, the shrinking figures of Jax and her team of Hasic ran down the street. Even at full speed, it'd take her group ten minutes to reach the city limits. The Black Wall might beat them. In that case, all of Zeal would burn.

When, one at a time, Jax's companions split off from the group, things started to click. The Hasic never intended to beat back the wall. Jax knew the chances of making it that far stood slim. Her goal, after all, was to ensure escape, not to save the city, as she'd said. Jax sent her comrades to the few buildings which housed moonbeam cannons. City Hall had been one of them. During his short while in the city, Kole had seen more but never thought to memorize where. As he looked out now, his heart sank.

At first, the destroyed buildings seemed random. Not the case. They'd been targeted. The Dark Hand had sabotaged as many moonbeam cannons as possible.

"We have to keep moving." A sadness lined Vienna's voice.

Left, toward escape. Or right.

Kole knew from where Vienna's glum tone originated: a place of worry. "Where did you last see Felix?"

A beat passed. When she stayed silent, Kole glanced over her shoulder. Tears ran down her face. Her bottom lip paled between her teeth. She shook her head. "You need to get out of Zeal." As she said it, she leaned forward, trying to slide off the stag.

Kole grabbed her before she could. "You are *not* going alone."

A flash of anger swept over her eyes. "Someone has to find him, and I'll be damned if I lose you in the process." She held his gaze.

A horse whinnied. Kole's head snapped to the sound.

The horse bore a rider with a black coat, whose gaze fell on Kole. A red handprint lay on the man's breast pocket. Had Orla sent him? The cultist slammed his heels into the horse and the animal bolted for the elk.

CHAPTER 41

Piper ran at full speed, one arm on Felix, half-dragging him along. If Felix meant to tag along, he'd need to keep pace. Her grip on his arm kept him from stumbling to the ground when he tripped over his own feet.

Two more blocks down the street, closing in on the temple, she spotted a group of people exiting the doors of the grand structure. She ducked behind the corner of a building, Felix in tow.

"You're fast, mate," Felix huffed.

Piper shushed him. Her eyes narrowed on the group's clothing. Vests. The Hasic.

"Oi, that's Jax!" Felix pointed to the woman hobbling at the center of the group, leaned against another for support. "Glad she made it out...," he paused as if only now noting her lame gait, "... alive."

But Piper's eyes flicked on what emerged from the building after them. A gleaming elk bearing two riders. Even from a distance, Piper could recognize the fragile frame.

"Kole," she whispered. The girl seated behind him could only be Vienna. "They're safe. Both of them." Piper flinched as Felix gripped her arm, peeking around the corner. She almost snapped at him, but the wave of relief radiating from his body made her hold her tongue.

"'Course they are. We're the Liberation, am I right? Can't keep us down."

After a split second, the stag bounded down the steps of the temple and darted across the street. They fled from a cultist on horseback. The handprint on the coat told Piper everything she needed to know.

"Wait, V!" Felix called, but the cacophony of the Black Wall drowned him out.

Piper cursed under her breath. *So close.* Even with her gifted speed, she never hoped to catch up. But she could follow. Felix proved a nuisance now. He'd only slow her down. But she'd grown too fond of

Felix to ditch him. She growled. This "keeping people alive" thing made everything more difficult. *I was better off working alone.*

Then, a wisp of smoke behind Felix washed her concern away. All this time she'd been distracted — oblivious to daylight fleeing the city. Streetlamps flickered on, marking the day's end.

Night had fallen.

Finally.

"Felix," Piper called. Maybe she could ditch him after all, without the added guilt trip. And with a little extra help.

As he looked at her, the Kayetan materialized behind him.

"I need you to trust me." Piper drew her nail down the side of her forearm. Blood blossomed up in a thick bead. She hated to do it — stoop to her father's level and use her blood as a power source. Truth was, Felix could turn the tides of this battle with his Kayetan, but she had no clue how far he'd progressed with his shadow. They needed to utilize every advantage at their disposal. "Take it. I'm only half god, but it will make you stronger."

He stared at her for a moment, mouth drooped in disgust. With the shaking ground, the screams bellowing from every direction in the city, and the Black Wall pulling closer, that frown evened out. Though Felix never said yes, he waved her over.

Piper stepped forward and placed her wrist in his grip.

"How much?"

"Just until you feel it."

He hesitated. Black smoke wisped from the scars on his wrists.

"It'll wear off within a couple hours," she added, hoping to soothe his doubts.

Then, he pressed his lips to her skin.

Each passing second, Felix's Kayetan grew more defined. An aura of darkness rimmed the shadow's silhouette. It was working. Whatever power manifested in her blood transferred to Felix and his Kayetan.

Finally, Felix dropped her arm. When his eyes met hers, they had grown completely black, and the seeping shadow from his wrists swirled.

"I know you want to come with me — follow after your sister and Kole — but there's more to saving them than just finding them. Their lives lay in constant danger with the Black Wall approaching." Piper glanced up as the first moonbeam flooded out from a nearby building. "Help the Hasic secure the cannons. Then come find us."

A yearning held in Felix's face. Then his jaw locked, hardening his features. Like any true Liberation member, he knew how to take orders.

"You know what to do," said Piper.

Felix turned to his Kayetan and opened his arms as if welcoming it in. When the shadow siphoned into Felix's body, Piper stepped back.

Out of all her encounters with these shadow demons and their maker, she'd never witnessed such a thing: a Kayetan merging with its master. It seemed Felix knew exactly how to use his shadow.

Smoking claws grew from Felix's fingers, and his whole body faded to a mirage-like state. Something between shadow and smoke.

"Go," Piper ordered.

Felix's legs moved normally into the first few strides of his run, then his body swelled with shadow, lifted off the ground, then streaked through the air like the Kayetans Piper had once fought. His silhouette disappeared into the night, leaving her alone behind the building.

Interesting. Though the urge to study Felix's new form gnawed at Piper's thoughts, she pushed her curiosity away. Kole. She had to get to Kole.

CHAPTER 42

"Caradin, go!"

The elk bounded down the steps. At the edge of the temple, another horse and rider burst from the alley.

Caradin turned faster than Kole realized what was going on. The stag carried them south down the road, though Kole doubted even Caradin knew where he was heading. *Anywhere but here.*

Vienna's arms looped tightly around Kole's waist. "There's another ahead."

Kole lifted his gaze. A third horse and rider came down the road.

"Where do we go?" Kole asked.

"An elk can take turns quicker. Lose them through the alleys."

"Right." He should've thought of that. A quick message to Caradin, then the stag swerved right into the narrow path between the buildings.

The cultists followed.

Kole nudged Caradin down every new alley. Though he'd lost his bearings two turns ago, the last whirl around a building gave them relief. The horses had fallen behind.

Just when Kole thought they'd reached safety, something whistled by his ear. The stone of the road sprayed up at Caradin's hooves. Another shot hit the nearby building.

"The rooftops!" Vienna shouted.

A force weighed down on Kole's back. His face pressed firmly against the stag's neck. Golden hair swept by his cheek. Vienna pinned him down, covering his body with her own. Before he could protest, a sharp pain clipped his upper arm. Like a bite. The hot, searing bite of a striking snake. He felt the blood swell and pour over the wound, but Vienna had his face smashed to the side, unable to see it.

Rushing wind swept over Kole's face as Caradin found new speed.

"We have to get inside," Vienna said. She must've noticed the blood on Kole's arm because her voice dropped an octave. "Hang on. I'll get us out of here."

More shots peppered the road at Caradin's feet, but the god charged on.

The pain of his arm would worsen after the adrenaline faded, but for now, he could manage. Kole lifted his gaze to a familiar sight. *This road....* He'd been through here before. They traveled close to Jax's workshop.

"I know a place close by. We can hide there." Kole reminded Caradin of their meeting with Jax, and the elk set on the path.

Here, at the heart of the city, the streets had long been evacuated. The growing claim of night revealed the distant glow of fires. No happy bonfires but buildings up in flames. The dusty scent of smoke and pulverized rock filled the air.

The cultists atop the buildings ceased fire as the animal bounded out of range. With the enemy eye off them and the pursuing horses nowhere in sight, Kole directed Caradin straight to the white stone building a block down the road.

Vienna slid off Kole's body and dismounted the stag at the door. The entrance swung free and Caradin carried Kole through the threshold, Vienna quick on his tail.

The vast building gave off an eerie vibe in the darkness. Only the light of a burning building nearby carried through the glass ceiling and bestowed an orange glow overhead. Metal rattled. The grated, see-through hanging floors above swayed precariously with the quake of the Black Wall.

"They won't find us here." Kole swung off the elk and inspected his arm. Blood glazed his skin. To his relief, a swipe or two revealed a shallow nick on his bicep. It looked worse than it felt.

"That's not the problem." Vienna lingered by a window, peering out. "We need to get you out of Zeal. Away from the wall, away from the cult."

"We need to find Felix first."

"Leave that up to me." She stayed pressed against the wall. A gasp escaped her. "Look!"

Kole rushed to the window. Between the line of buildings, a ray of white light shot out of the city. Another and another lit up.

The Hasic had made it to their posts. He wondered which one Jax was manning.

Hope, however slight, bloomed in Kole. "That'll give us more time. It'll hold off the flames until we find —"

His voice caught in his throat as one of the moonbeam lights cast toward the Black Wall extinguished. He waited for it to relight. *A malfunction. Nothing more.* But deep in his marrow, he knew the truth.

The Dark Hand had taken the cannon out along with the Hasic who manned it.

Kole set his sights west. The wall surged forward undeterred by the miniscule force of the cannons.

Cannons. That's what they needed. More cannons.

Kole flipped around to the main factory. The cannons here were in development and unusable. But *one* worked. Jax had brought back their special weapon. It had to be here somewhere.

"What are you doing?" Vienna asked when he jogged around the main floor.

Around the back of the room, near a wide door, sat the custom piece, hooked up to Jax's vehicle.

"We have to help. For everyone's sake, including Felix." Kole rushed to the weapon. The click of hooves and pattering of Vienna's steps followed him. "This is the one Jax made to get me through the wall."

"You want to use it?"

"It's a moonbeam cannon. It can help defend the city. The Hasic are out there fighting, the least we can do is utilize all their equipment."

"It'll put a target on our backs," Vienna warned.

"Orla's already put a target on my back." Kole stared at the mechanism securing the cannon to the vehicle. The iron lock seemed to have a pull handle. He gripped it and leaned back, using his weight to inch it open. The effort tormented his arm, but he clenched his teeth and pushed through it. Only when Vienna came to his aid did the contraption release. "Thanks," he mumbled.

"We should wrap your arm."

Kole circled her, avoiding eye contact. If he played it casual, she might let up on him. "I'll be fine. Only nicked the skin is all."

With the cannon detached, he could roll it into the road. But first he needed to figure out how to turn it on. No use fiddling with it in the open street for the Dark Hand to spot them. He thought back to Jax — tried to remember the steps she'd taken.

The moonstone crystal sat in its proper place. Kole gave the tank a pat. The slosh from within told him the thing was filled to the brim.

Moonstone... fuel... just have to start it up. Two buttons sat atop the fuel tank beside one lever. Kole pushed one.

Nothing.

He tried the other.

The lack of ignition prompted Vienna to ask, "Do you know how to work it?"

"No," Kole confessed. "All I know is not to open the fuel tank while it's running, or it'll explode."

Vienna took a giant step back at that. "My brother is rubbing off on you."

Kole replayed the brief memory of Jax starting up the cannon during their test. He'd been so focused on the proximity of the wall and in awe of seeing the contraption up close. Why hadn't he paid more attention?

The lever had to do something. He gave it a pull down. A ticking sound came from the fuel tank.

He was on to something.

While keeping the level pulled, he pushed the buttons one at a time. The second one sent the cannon purring.

"It's on." Kole assumed the last button would initiate the beam. He'd wait to test it out on the road. "Help me push it out."

"Hang on." Vienna rushed to the window, scanned the road, then returned. "All clear for the moment." She joined Kole at the rear of the cannon and braced to push.

Their combined strength creaked the wheels forward. After a few paces, Kole found himself exhausted.

"A little help?" Kole called to the Soul.

Caradin shifted to his bull form and stepped up. The bulky animal made for an easy undertaking. Kole and Vienna moved to the sides of the cannon, steering it for the door as Caradin pushed.

Once at the door, Vienna looked one final time before they shoved the cannon onto the road.

The winds had picked up in the few minutes they'd taken refuge in the factory. Kole's open shirt pulled at the seams. A sudden gust nearly knocked him off his feet.

The wall was close, but the night sky concealed just *how* close.

No sky of navy or silver stars above—only black as far as Kole could see. This had to work. Time had run out. Soon the very buildings, swaying and groaning to the max against their bolts and nails in the raging winds, might fall on their own accord. Like a vacuum, the wind pulled west toward the creeping flames.

Light it up, then get out of here. Or else I'll... I'll....

Or else what happened in Solpate would happen again. Kole had been lucky the first time and managed to survive. The chances of that happening again... impossible. Not only had he lost his fully functioning body then, but Niko, too. Kole side-eyed Vienna. He would never allow that to happen again.

A half-dozen beams from cannons throughout the city still burned. Their wide light slammed into the Black Wall. Slowed it. Yet those flames had crept well within Zeal's walls, maybe a mile out from Kole's location now.

A squeeze to Kole's hand broke his concentration.

Vienna had turned to him. Her lips moved, but the wind, quake, and roar of the Black Wall drowned out even his own heartbeat.

One thing he recognized.

Her body flinched and her eyes held a terror like he'd only seen in her when she'd thought Felix had been taken by Savairo those long weeks ago.

The Black Wall must've scared her as much as it did him. His brows furrowed, and he moved to touch her shoulder, offering what comfort he could at the moment.

A discoloration in the bottom of his vision pulled his attention downward. The bodice of Vienna's green dress darkened. Liquid spread out from a dot under her chest and bloomed over her abdomen.

Blood.

Vienna clutched her stomach and hunched over.

"Caradin! Help us," Kole screamed through their connection, then looped his arms under hers and caught her before she dropped to the ground. She leaned into him. Warm blood soaked into his clothes. Her head fell limp on his shoulder in the hug-like embrace. He squeezed her tight, then looked up.

Down the road stood a line of horses. Atop the lead animal sat a white-haired woman.

Orla.

Her arm stretched out, a hand-cannon in her grip, pointed at Kole.

She'd shot Vienna.

Orla lowered her gun and smiled. Her free hand beckoned him to her.

The deepest of hatred ignited his core, shook his bones, gripped his being. His hands ached to close in around Orla's neck. Squeeze and watch her struggle for air. Squeeze until life's luster fled her eyes.

A hot snort on his face announced Caradin's presence.

"Heal her. Use your power." He cared not if it weakened the god or compromised his pact with Aterus. In the moment, staring at the open wound, Kole only knew he needed to save her. *"Master commands it."*

The bull bowed his massive head and set the tip of his nose on Vienna. A warm orange light built around the Soul's horns.

A hand against Kole's chest simmered his anger.

Vienna pushed away from the bull and Kole. She gripped the cannon for support, unsteady from the wound and the building wind. She stared at Kole. Fear still plagued her gaze, but they held a command in them. Her mouth opened in a single syllable—one all too easy to read. "No."

"Take it Vienna. It's the only thing that will save you." Even if the wind muffled his words, he knew she heard him.

Still, she shook her head. And with that second refusal, Caradin snuffed the energy from his horns. "Go," she said.

Kole stood there, mouth ajar, and shook his head. He'd never leave her here. Not like this. Not when he could make this right.

At his hesitance. Vienna slammed her hands on the buttons.

Radiant light erupted from the cannon.

"Go!" she said again.

Kole glanced right.

Orla urged her steed forward into a strenuous gallop. The Dark Hand cultists followed the charge, their horses spreading out to cover any chance of escape.

And to his left?

The only possible way to avoid them now... the door through the flames. A door that would only stand open for a mere moment. A one-way road to the only place Orla couldn't follow.

Another shove to his shoulder. Hard this time.

Vienna's face, lit up by the moonbeam, held a palpable pain with lines deep on her forehead and trembling, thin lips. She laced her fingers in his one last time and squeezed. Her other hand went to his cheek. Vienna rubbed his scars with her thumb.

The sensation sent a numbing wave through Kole. The finality of it. It hit him like a wave breaking on the shore. It was a goodbye.

Then, Vienna's shoulders lifted as she took in a deep breath. She dropped her hands, then she turned her back on him, facing Orla head on.

Helpless. All Kole ever felt was helpless.

Without a rambler, Kole was just... a burned boy. Weak. Vulnerable. And doomed. Always needing saving.

But he heeded Vienna's last word. One final look at her back, putting her wavy hair to memory, then he ran straight for Caradin and flung himself on the bull's back.

"*Speed. Give us speed,*" Kole urged the Soul.

The bull pushed off with powerful legs. Under Kole's weight, the animal's back thinned, and the silver elk emerged beneath him once again, the grand antlers shining like beacons in the moonbeam.

He refused to look back for fear of what he'd see.

Vienna face down on the road? Orla gaining? Kole couldn't bear any of it.

The roaring winds deafened him. The air warmed the farther they followed the moonbeam. Flashbacks of his last close encounter left his body quivering. Violent shakes now. He very well may be racing to his death.

Closer and closer they ran. Caradin pumped his hooves hard into the quaking earth, with an unwavering stride. A small shift left and they galloped into the conduit of the beam.

Instantly, the noise vanished. The winds calmed. Cool air flourished here. Like the eye of a hurricane, the moonbeam provided safe haven from the surrounding chaos. An eerie peace set on Kole. He wondered if he still stood in the city, or if the flames had lashed out and killed him. Maybe this was some dream or roadway to the afterlife.

He spotted the dull blur of buildings outside the moonbeam. *Not dead yet.*

Kole had faith in Jax's creation. Despite his head telling him to turn around, his heart settled on trust in the Hasic leader. Even with all his confidence set in Jax, his body continued protesting with convulsions.

Then, a voice. Not Russé reaching out, nor Caradin, who focused on maintaining top speed.

Vara.

She called to him, saying his name over and over in desperate pleas. "*Save me.*"

Black fire appeared on the edge of the moonbeam. The flames lashed at the radiant light, but the beam held true. They were leaving the city. About to cross the barrier between Ohr and lands long lost.

No longer did the buildings of Zeal edge the tunnel of light. Instead, ash, as piece by piece the fire of the wall touched the elegant structures and reduced them to particles. Zeal disappeared one building at a time, claimed by the vicious power of the ever-burning flames.

The destruction was unbearable to watch. Kole set his sights forward. He focused on his task. On Vienna's last word to him. On Vara's pleas for freedom.

The portal lay ahead.

Within reach now.

Caradin jumped.

Kole's last thoughts hovered on Vienna and Felix. He prayed to the Souls — prayed with every breath and heartbeat — that they would make it out of Zeal. *Make it true. Please, make it true.*

Then they passed, boy and elk, through the portal.

Beyond the flame.

CHAPTER 43

Piper panted in the backstreets of Zeal. She'd managed to follow the horse and rider, pursuing Kole for a short time before falling behind. Now she wandered aimlessly, hoping each new turn would offer a clue.

Everything looked the same. Glowing streetlamps lined every road, casting the alleys in deepened shadow. It'd been no more than ten minutes since she'd sent Felix on his mission, and yet only a few more beams had lit. Maybe she'd set him up for too much.

The looming Black Wall to the west prevented her from becoming completely lost. Yet time worked against her. Even now, the wind strengthened. If she lingered too long, the gale of the moving wall would grow powerful enough to knock down the more fragile towers. If it came to that, anyone left out here may perish before the flames ever got to them.

A horse whinnied behind her.

Piper spun and crouched behind the stone base of a streetlamp.

"Where is he?!" A voice boomed between the droning evacuation sirens. The disdain in the woman's tone told Piper this was the enemy. The Dark Hand.

The scent of horses floated to Piper's nose. They had to be close.

"We lost him on Rayet Street," another responded.

A pause. Piper brought her eyes to the brim of the thick stone base of the light. The lips of the old woman moved, but they'd gone too far from her position to hear. Piper sprinted for the next lamp for cover.

"I know where he's heading." Blood dripped from the old woman's mouth, and red streaked her white outfit. Too much blood for a mere mouth wound. The cultist had gone through major trauma, yet her posture said otherwise. Tall and poised, she sunk her heels into her steed, and the horse sprang ahead.

Piper tailed them. Before they pulled too far ahead, she fell in line behind the rider at the rear. She lunged at the animal's rump, grabbed hold of the cultist's jacket, and yanked the rider backward off the horse. A quick kick to the cultist's head rendered them unconscious.

She raced to the slowing horse. One jump had her leg swung halfway over its back. Piper heaved herself into the saddle, then pulled the hood of her stolen Dark Hand coat low over her face. She scanned the group ahead. No one so much as glanced her way. The quake and siren had concealed her attack.

The group rounded the block ahead.

Come on. I can't lose them now. As long as the enemy lay in her sight, she need not worry for Kole. Piper tapped her heels into the animal, but the horse had reached peak speed. Not ten seconds later, she whirled around the same corner, and the sight had her jerking hard on the reins.

The blood-stained woman had halted her horse. She held up a weapon, pointed down the road. Just as Piper's eyes focused on the target, a *bang* sounded.

No time to respond. No time to fix it or take it back. All Piper had was now. She urged her horse on, coming up on the last line of cultists.

Piper tucked her feet beneath her and leapt from the saddle to the closest cultist. The man crumbled beneath her weight. The horse tossed its head at the impact and veered right, splitting from the group. She squeezed her arm around the cultist's neck until a snap marked her kill, then shoved the body off, settled in, and took hold of the new reins to find the cultists had begun a charge toward Kole and Vienna.

If only Piper could get to the leader. Subduing the old woman may halt her followers. Piper pulled a dagger from her belt and held the blade between her fingers, while her other hand secured her to her horse. The gallop made for a difficult aim. But she pulled back, ready to throw, when a radiant light blinded the space.

She'd been so focused on Kole and the cultists, Piper had overlooked the cannon. Now it cast a ray toward the wall. The brilliance made her eyes ache and washed out the scene. Her hand barely lay visible in front of her face.

A sudden surge lifted her in the air. Her horse had bucked. She flew off, unsure when or where her body would land. Rough stone bit her right side, and she rolled in the white luminescence. For a moment her concerns fell away; she knew the temporary blindness would affect everyone. It meant Kole was safe for the moment.

Piper felt the ground around her. The smooth surface meant she had landed somewhere on the road rather than the cobbled sidewalks.

She climbed to her feet and pushed forward, toward the source of the light—where she'd last seen Kole.

She fumbled on, arms outstretched and waving in case she ran into another. The dagger had been knocked out of her hand, but she had other means of fighting.

Then, just as abruptly as it had appeared, the beam deactivated.

White orbs floated in Piper's vision. Her eyes took a long moment to adjust. In the meantime, other sounds perked her ears. A cry of pain, and a heated voice on the ever-building wind.

"No! Where is he?"

Shapes in the night formed as her vision stabilized. Other figures surrounded her. Some cultists had been thrown off their steeds like Piper and crawled up from their hands and knees, regaining their bearings, while two lay pinned and motionless under their horses, bodies broken.

There, by the cannon, stood the Dark Hand's leader. Her foot stomped on Vienna's chest, who lay writhing on the ground. She grasped fiercely at Orla's ankle, trying to pry free, but to no avail.

"Find him!" Orla screamed at her comrades. "I need the boy. Bring me the boy and his god." On command, the surviving cultists dispersed around the area. Orla's rage turned on Vienna. "Where is he? Tell me." Her weight shifted further onto Vienna.

Piper broke into a sprint. She'd tear every one of them down with her bare hands if she had to, but Orla would go first.

With all the noise, the priestess never saw her coming. Piper tackled the old woman and drew her to the ground by the waist. She expected Vienna to join in the attack, but when she remained still on her back, Piper guessed her afflictions were worse than she'd initially thought.

Finish the hag quick. Piper could heal Vienna as long as she still clung to life.

Atop Orla, Piper clamped her hands around the woman's neck and squeezed. She stared into the woman's eyes, waiting for the moment death took her. But a hot pain scorched Piper's hands like she'd plunged them into a river of lava. Piper pulled away and sucked through her teeth at the pain. Blisters covered her skin all the way up to her wrists. While she nursed her wounds, the cult leader grabbed her by the shoulders and threw her off.

Piper landed on her back. *What in Soul's name...?* She inspected her hands in the meager light from the lampposts. Slowly, the skin began to itch, and blisters faded back to her unblemished skin. Blood sorcery.

That was obvious. Though the exact nature of spell eluded her. She rolled to her feet and studied Orla, who had already risen and held her eyebrows high at Piper, interest glinting in her eyes. No doubt the old woman had seen her heal.

"What a gift I've been given. Two of my long-lost kin in one day."

"Kin?"

"Can you not see? Can you not feel it?" Orla stepped toward her, and Piper readied her fists. The old woman may be fueled by blood magic, but Piper refused to back down—show weakness. A broad smile grew on the cultist's lips. "I sense it in you. In your blood. We share the heritage of the gods. Of Aterus himself." Orla tilted her head. "I do not wish to harm you."

"What the hell are you talking about?" Piper's fists tightened.

"I am daughter of Aterus. And I know what you are." Orla reached out to her. "Sister."

Sister? The old woman was delusional. Aterus bore no other heir. Had he? Not with Evangeline, that was for sure. Her mother would've told her if she had a sibling. With another mortal perhaps?

At Piper's hesitation, Orla said, "Let me show you." Orla turned and raised her hand to the Black Wall. "With our brother's blood, I can call upon the flames of destruction—of cleansing. And with you—another daughter of Aterus—we can control it together and purify this world. What was once blessed upon my ancestors, diluted with each passing generation, is revived within me."

The wind around Piper picked up, and the temperature spiked. Orla called upon the Black Wall. And it obeyed. A stroke of flame siphoned off from the wall, blocks away in the distance, like a thin, fiery twister. The dark fire shot to Orla's beckoning hand, where it swirled around her flesh like a tamed snake. The woman's skin remained intact despite the flame's presence.

Piper shielded her face from the sweltering heat. Yet Orla withstood it. Reveled in it.

Blessed ancestors. Those words triggered a memory in Piper's head. Research she'd done back in Socren. The years leading up to Piper's birth, Aterus' had granted power to those who worshiped him. Her father never spoke of his doings before her, but Piper had learned from her time with the Liberation—from Leo—that those blessings had been revoked as an attempt to appease Aterus' kin and prevent them from forcing his ascension. It seemed one worshiper had been neglected.

But it didn't explain this boost in power. Unless when Orla said "with our brother's blood" she meant Kole's. That would explain the cult's interest in him. They wanted to use him like the Souls wished to use him. And it seemed Orla already had. Piper wouldn't allow that again. She was here now. She could protect him. But where was the blasted boy? If the wall continued its advance, the entire city, including Kole, would be swallowed whole.

"Call off the Black Wall," Piper said. "You've proven your power. You have your followers—ones who gladly join you. Why force the others into your cult?"

"Only the strong may live in the new era. Those worthy of Aterus' gifts. You can be one of them. Imagine a world where everyone is like us?"

A lunatic? The more Orla spoke, the more Piper believed her to be what she claimed: Aterus' daughter. Not by conception, but by blood all the same. They certainly shared an interest in running Ohr with a vice-like grip.

"You mistake my intentions with your own." Piper looked past Orla's shoulder at the oncoming wall of black, licking flames. Dust of perishing buildings thickened the air. "The only things I wish to rid the world of are the Souls and everything they've tainted."

Lines of confusion riddled Orla's face. "But that is a self-destructive wish."

"I know."

Orla's demeanor changed at that. Darkness seemed to emanate from her eyes. "Then die along with the others." A wave of her hand and the black fire in her possession lashed out like a whip.

Piper ducked behind the cannon for cover. The flame lashed at the wheel, a mere arm's reach from where she hid. That small touch initiated a chain reaction. The wheel dissolved into ash. Piece by piece, the cannon fell away under her weight, reduced to nothing more than bitter dust. Piper stood exposed in the street with only a cloud of swirling ash remaining of the cannon between her and Orla.

The deep pit in Piper's stomach expanded. For the first time in decades, she felt true fear. Orla's control over the wall was one thing, but wielding its power to her own personal will made this a one-sided battle. Even for a demigod.

Only one option left.

Run.

She dove for Vienna. Her bloodied body made for a slippery mess—a worrisome amount puddled on the road—but Piper slugged her over her shoulder and forced her feet faster than she ever thought she could. The horse she'd rode in on had long fled. A glance over her shoulder showed the other cultists had returned to Orla.

"Kill Vienna, save the girl for me," said Orla.

The cultists seem unfazed by their leader's new powers and charged Piper on command. She pushed on, urging her feet as fast as Vienna's extra weight allowed.

Only a block down the road with the cultists gaining, a streak of darkness lashed out at Piper's side. Black fire crossed her mind. She flinched as it passed. Yet the temperature hadn't spiked as it had when Orla last used her power. She veered away, regardless, unwilling to risk herself or Vienna burning to nothingness like the cannon.

But the strange dark cloud came again. This time in a familiar, curly-headed shape. Within a blink, Felix had appeared, his body still in that shadowed state, merged with his Kayetan.

"Need a hand?" He must've just realized who lay in Piper's arms, because the sides of his smirk did a nosedive.

"She's alive. Don't worry, I can fix her. Just get those cultists off my tail. And stay away from—"

Felix phased away before she could finish.

Idiot.

Screams pierced over the sounds of the roaring fires of the Black Wall. Piper hoped it meant Felix was making fodder of the cultist and not the other way around.

Then, on Piper's next stride, Vienna heaved in a struggled breath, and her body fell limp. "Hold on." Piper squeezed her arms tighter, but Vienna gave no response, and her waist, slick with blood, slowly began slipping from Piper's shoulder. "Shit." If she pushed on to the edge of the city—to safety—Vienna may be too far gone to revive. She had to do it now.

Piper tucked into a small alcove where a fountain nestled. The curved structure provided minimal shelter from the strong winds carrying a thickening ash, but it was the best she could do for now. If nothing else, it kept them out of sight.

She propped Vienna up against the stone base of the water feature. Mist cooled her face. Piper cupped some of the water and splashed it on Vienna, hoping the coolness would spark her awake, but the girl's chest had since stopped moving.

A bit of silver skin marked where Felix had drank. With a drag of her nail, Piper opened the skin on her other forearm, then pressed the wound to Vienna's mouth. Blood smeared over Vienna's lips and entered her mouth, but she made no moves to swallow.

"You're not dying like this," Piper raged at her. "Drink it!" She held her arm there a bit longer.

Nothing.

But the blood pooled in Vienna's mouth. Piper grabbed the girl's chin and tilted her head back. The blood must've triggered some sort of reflex, because Vienna sprung to life, coughing and gagging.

"Good girl." Piper anxiously tapped her fingers on her thighs as she stared, hyper-focused on the wounds, waiting for them to start mending. The moment felt like it lasted forever. She knew her blood held the same properties as her father's—as any of the Souls—but her half-human ancestry lessened the potency. Where a god could bring someone back from even true death if done at the right moment, Piper's had its limits; ones she herself had never really explored beyond tending to minor cuts and bruises. She'd only really ever used it as a tool to strengthen, like she had with Felix. Would it even work? The longer she stared, the more doubt plagued her mind.

The streak of darkness came as no surprise this time. Felix knelt next to his sister. Even in his shadowed form, his face held the utter shock of worry. "Is she...?"

"I've done all I can. We have to wait it out. But we can't stay here, or we'll all get burned. Either by the wall or that crazy hag." Piper moved to lift Vienna when a voice came loud on the wind.

"If you will not meet the fire willingly, I will bring it to you." Orla stood in the road. Her white hair whipped around her face. The swirling ash and rings of inky flames circled her body, making her look like she'd come straight out of some nightmare.

"Take your sister and run," Piper commanded.

"I ain't runnin' from no one." The wisping shadows around Felix flared at his new anger. He stood and faced Orla. "Ain't scared of her."

"You should be. She's not some old woman, she's done something to herself. That fire around her is straight from the wall. Whatever it touches is dust." Piper reached to tug Felix back, but her hand passed through his arm.

Felix looked over his shoulder at her as if he felt her touch, then returned his anger to Orla. "I saw what she can do."

"Dammit, Felix, we have to get Vienna out before the wall annihilates everything."

"The Black Wall is dealt with." He pointed to the sky, where new rays of pale light washed out the stars. Piper had been too focused on Vienna to notice before. Even now, as she watched, more rays ignited — one high atop the building across the street. Felix had secured the cannons for the Hasic. If the wall had been stabilized, Orla proved the only danger.

Orla lifted a hand their way. Piper knew what came next. Without a second thought, she looped her arms under Vienna's shoulders, shoved her body to the back of the alcove, then dove over her unconscious form.

The temperature on Piper's back spiked. The smell of singed rock caught her nose before the pain registered. Piper flipped around to a vacant spot where the fountain had stood. Water gurgled up from the pipe in the ground and puddled in the empty space. Piper's back prickled as it healed over, but fear took her when her comrade had vanished.

"Felix?" she called out.

A streak of shadow zipped down from the top of the alcove. Felix reformed beside her.

"How the hell are we suppose ta fight against that?"

Powered by Soul's blood or blood magic, it mattered not. The woman before them stood mortal. Even Orla's deepest wishes would never change that. She could be defeated. They just needed an opening. *How do you fight when she's surrounded by the Black Wall's energy?* Piper's eyes focused back on the cannon six stories up. "There may be a way."

He followed her gaze. "Gotcha." Then he sped away like a streaking black comet up the side of the building.

Stall. You need to stall her. Piper cautiously stepped up. One deep breath in, then she held her hands high over her head and exited the alcove.

Orla's arms swelled up, ready to attack.

"Kill me if you must. Just know your spell will fade in a matter of hours when the power of Kole's blood wanes. The Black Wall won't answer to you. It'll burn you like everyone else." At that, Orla's twitching fingers paused. It seemed Piper had caught her attention. She needed to keep her calm until Felix enacted the plan. "You're nothing without his link to the Souls. That's why you wanted him captured isn't it? To tap him? Use him as your own personal power source?"

"Kole's blood gave me a boost. But the real power came from the Soul."

Well shit. If Orla got her hands on Kole *and* Caradin's essence, they had little chance of overpowering her save for waiting for the blood to leave her system. The longer she stalled, the better. Piper walked forward. "And that, too, will diminish. The only way to keep a power like that is to be blessed with it. Your ancestors knew that better than anyone. You need a source. Something to sustain you. And the closest thing you have right now is me."

Orla's eyes glinted as Piper neared, but her featured remained calculated. "Sister...."

"True heir to the Gray Soul," Piper said through clenched teeth. Never in her entire existence had she expected to say those words aloud. They lingered on her tongue like bitter poison. The twist of persuasion so easily came to her. Piper had her father to thank for that. "Take me until you find Kole and the god."

As the final act of surrender, Piper kneeled at Orla's feet. The fire swirling around the cult leader made Piper's skin shrivel and peel, which itched and ached as her bloodline healed her wound, but the constant exposure left it in a state of rawness. Piper arched her head back so that the light of the moonbeam cannons might illuminate her face and allow Orla to witness the proof of her lineage.

While Orla studied her, Piper lifted her eyes to the rooftop. *Right on time.*

The moonbeam cannon swung its light down. If Orla so much as noticed it, their only weapon against her would be reduced to dust within the blink of an eye. Piper forced her muscles still. One small twitch might give it all away.

Pale light flooded the road. Orla sent her gaze upward.

Time to strike.

Piper launched from her knees and sent a kick to Orla's legs. The cult leader went down, slamming hard on her back. Scrambling up, Piper gaped in horror as the black flames swirling around Orla's arms lashed out.

In that moment, time froze. She'd messed up—underestimated her opponent. And worse, nothing could stop it. Once the fire touched her, she'd become filth in the wind.

Piper tensed, waiting for the pain to come.

CHAPTER 44

Despite the fall of darkness, the city shown clear and bright, as if the moon had taken on the brilliancy of the sun. The Kayetan did that to Felix. Each time he merged with his shadow his eyes became something more. Felix imagined this was how an owl felt hunting in the night. Every movement caught his attention — hypersensitive and aware of the tiniest things going on around him. But *this* merge felt more severe. Amplified by Piper's blood.

Felix soared to the rooftop to the moonbeam cannon. The weightlessness and pure energy coursing through his shared body gave him a boost of adrenaline as he defied gravity and left the ground far below. One of these days, he swore to himself he'd fly all night. It was hard to imagine ever getting used to the new powers bestowed upon him.

"Choose death. Together as one." A voice hissed within Felix's head. Normally the voice came quiet — on the edge of Felix's mind, calling from a distance. Ever since drinking Piper's blood, the Kayetan seemed stronger. Right in his ear. Insistent.

"Oh, bugger off," Felix replied. His Kayetan was at it again, whispering strange things to him. Where at first, the voice had frightened him, now Felix shrugged it off as more of a nuisance than anything. "Always with the ominous omens, aren't ya? Ain't ya got somethin' useful for me?"

The shadow said nothing, but the whistle-like hiss rang in Felix's ears.

Felix shot straight up along the last two floors of the building. When he emerged next to the cannon, he spotted a Hasic woman at the base of the weapon. Her arms clutched tightly to the handles at the rear, fighting to keep the beam focused on the Black Wall. Not even Felix's presence distracted her.

"'Fraid I'm gonna need that for a hot second."

She flinched at his sudden arrival. "You'll have to pry it from my hands," she said through gritted teeth, and clutched tighter.

Felix glanced down to Piper, who knelt in the middle of the road before Orla. Time grew short. "I can do that, but ya ain't gonna like it."

Immediately, the Hasic shot her hand to her side, where her pistol waited.

"No need for that. We're on the same side, mate." The shadow within him swelled. He let the Kayetan take hold. Felix only had to imagine where he wanted to go and his Kayetan obeyed. The weight of his body evaporated, and, in a blink, his body left the space where he floated. He'd only done this trick a handful of times in the last two days. The first few times had left him dizzy, but the more he practiced, the more he just got used to it.

Before the Hasic woman could draw her pistol, Felix reappeared behind her, a streak of smoke trailing his body.

"Just work with me a second here." Felix wrapped one arm around her torso, locking her arms in place, while the other grasped the handle of the cannon. One swift pull dragged the floodlight of moonbeam away from the flames encroaching on Zeal and swung it into the street below. "See this ain't so bad, is it?" he soothed when her body trembled within his hold.

Felix held her in place, all the while fixing a keen eye on Piper and Orla below. He expected something grand to happen, telling him the beam had extinguished the priestess' power source. Yet nothing came.

Those flames still burned around Orla's wrists. And the old woman's hands....

They stretched out toward Piper.

"*Strike.*" Came his Kayetan's command again.

An alarm went off in Felix's shadowy core. The Kayetan's urge to move sent his hands shaking. Felix gave in to the need. He willed to be at the base of the building, down at Piper's side. The vertigo set in. A great swirling of his brain. The jump was far. Farther than he'd ever attempted, but he had to try. The Kayetan granted his wish and took him from the rooftop.

A moment of darkness.

Then a new scene surrounded him. Wobbly. Rippling, almost. As if the street stood at the base of the ocean. Through his warped vision, Felix anchored his eyes on flaming auburn hair. His target. One push off his heel gave him the speed of the wind. He flashed toward her with arms open wide and stole her from the earth. Together they soared from Orla's wrath.

Felix pushed off to fly, but her weight kept him grounded. He'd lose speed this way. So he swerved and brought her back the short distance to the alcove where Vienna lay and released her.

"It didn't work." The direness of the situation hung over him like growling storm clouds.

After a quick scrutiny over him, Piper said, "No. It didn't."

A groan came from the floor. Vienna had woken.

"V!" Felix knelt beside her.

"What's going on?" she mumbled. Her hand scratched at her stomach.

Piper pulled up a flap in the destroyed boning of Vienna's corset. "The blood is working. Look."

The edge of bloodied skin moved. It seemed to thread itself back together. The wound shrunk before his eyes until the healing slowed to a stop. The fresh wounds appeared as if they'd had a week to mend.

Piper must've read the worry on Felix's face, because she put a hand on his shoulder. "She's going to be fine. But we need to get her out of here."

"How the hell we gonna do that? Ask the demon lady over there for a timeout?" If only it were that easy. Seeing Vienna on the mend gave Felix hope, but that hope was devoured by the doom that was Orla. Piper's weight in his arms had all but tethered him. Vienna would be no different. Worse, he doubted his sister could walk yet. If his strength failed him, they'd be stranded on the streets. "I can only fly on my own. I won't get her outta here any faster than you."

The normally stoic mask Piper put on cracked a bit, allowing a glimmer of fear to peek through. She was out of ideas.

"Orla's human. She can be killed. That fire is too quick for me." Piper's attention turned back to his sister. "Vienna? Listen to me. Where is Kole?"

"Kole is...." Tears flooded her eyes at the name. Vienna shook her head, her next words drenched in guilt. "I had to get him out of here. I had to keep him safe."

Piper and Felix locked eyes with matching curiosity.

"What did ya do, V?"

"I let him go. Made him."

Piper's voice trembled with impatience. "Where did you make him go?"

"Through the fire." Vienna reached out and grabbed Felix's shadowed hand. He twitched at the touch, afraid his claws might hurt her, but she held strong and sure. "He went through the portal with Caradin."

"Impossible," was all Piper said.

"'Fraid it ain't."

"But how?"

"These people make strange things. The cannons. They—"

A sudden flame burst from the road cut Felix short. To his horror, the building he'd just climbed with the moonstone cannon went up in a flash. The Hasic, the cannon, the entire building turned to dust in an instant. The ash hovered there for a moment, keeping the former shape of the structure before the gale cast it west. Without the moonbeam's protection, Orla could draw the wall in closer.

Piper cursed, but her words were drowned out by a guttural pain. The Kayetan inside Felix swelled at the sight of the demolished building. The Kayetan roared within.

The pure, animalistic feeling of his shadow sent clarity through Felix. A clarity he feared.

Orla had to be stopped. Whether the priestess realized it or not, Zeal's and Kole's fates were linked. The cannons provided the only way to Kole. Without them, and the Hasic to operate them, Kole would be stranded. The outcome of this night may well decide the survival of Ohr.

Piper had been right: she was too slow for Orla's powers. But *he* wasn't. Not with his Kayetan—these new powers. Without Kole. Without the gods. He and he alone could take on Orla. In the past, he'd fling himself into battle. Craved the chance to fight and cause a little mischief. But this time....

Felix gazed at his sister. He took in her face. Memorized it. The dimple on her chin reminded him of his ma. The feature had always been on his sister's face, but he only connected the resemblance now. And the freckles their faces shared had come from their pa.

His heart weighed heavy, as if it had hardened into iron. He gulped, then reached around his waist for the pouch at his side. It jingled like sweet bells as the metal pellets within shifted around. The familiar navy canvas held his old stitching: stars, a sun and moon, the Seven Souls symbol, and one new motif he'd done in haste that morning. A red hand clasped in a handshake with a black, clawed one. The work was sloppy—rushed—but it turned out well enough to convey the meaning.

Felix held out the slingshot and bag of pellets to Vienna. "Makes sure he gets this, will ya?"

The second turned long with the pouch hanging in the space between Felix and Vienna. Her face paled to a color only corpses held. "Don't you dare."

The tone of her voice pulled on his heart—shattered him. He shoved the slingshot into her hands. If he didn't go now, he feared he may not have the will a moment later. "I love ya, Sis."

Something snapped in Vienna. She lunged at him, fingers clawing at anything she could hold: his hair, his clothes, his belt. The onslaught cut short as Piper dove in and pinned her against the building. Still Vienna fought like a cornered beast, shouting, "No! Felix, no!" over and over.

Unspoken words passed between him and Piper, whose eyes held firm on him. She nodded as if she understood what he needed from her and what he was about to do.

Before doubt could creep in, Felix cast one last look at his sister, still writhing in Piper's hold, tears pouring down her cheeks, then he bit his bottom lip and tore away in a jet of smoke.

His sister's screams of agony chased him until the roaring of the Black Wall drowned her out.

For how insistent his Kayetan had been before, his shadow remained silent. Perhaps Felix had done exactly what the Kayetan had intended. No thinking. He couldn't. Every thought that popped up—worries if this were the right answer—Felix shoved aside. His mind was made up.

Felix flew toward the silhouette of the priestess standing in the middle of the road, her fire readying to annihilate another building. In hopes of catching her off guard, he took a rounded path, then swerved in for her back. He lifted his claws, ready to strike.

But the priestess turned.

A stream of black flame arced from her hands at Felix. One deep breath, then he clenched his teeth, bracing for the vertigo that bubbled in his core. Felix reappeared on the opposite side of the street at Orla's back once again. An arm's reach away. As his claws arced toward her back, a rush of flame burst up from the ground.

Like a shield, the black flames encased Orla.

The sheer heat overwhelmed Felix. Though he wanted to strike her down, here and now, his instincts made him back off. And thank the Souls it did. One touch of the fire would turn him to ash like the building.

Felix reappeared a dozen paces away. With each jump he made in his Kayetan form, he grew more and more dazed. Two in the last few seconds had him bumbling to stand. And what to show for it? The old woman had bested him. If only he'd practiced more. Gotten used to his new abilities. Why had he resisted against his shadow for so long? Especially when this power may be the one thing that could save Zeal.

He waited for Orla to drop her fiery defense for another shot at her. It never came.

Instead, the crazy old woman beckoned him with a hand. That smile plastered on her face gave him the creeps. *I'll knock it right off yer face, old timer.*

"*Decide.*" The Kayetan called to him.

"Whaddya think I'm doin' out here?" Felix whispered back. He'd decided to save Zeal. What more did the blasted demon want from him?

He tried to think it through. But that was what Vienna did, not him. He was the action. The doer. The muscle, as he liked to believe. Clearly, throwing himself at Orla wouldn't cut it. He needed a distraction. One could feign while the other went for the kill. Like back in his days with the Liberation. Him and Boogey and Criz always did the switch and bait. *The bait and switch? Whatever it's called.*

"Decide, eh?" Felix had his plan. "Yeah, I've decided. We do it my way."

Felix shot forward, straight for Orla.

The frontal charge sent a hint of confusion over Orla's face. She smiled and lowered her shield. The dome of fire condensed into a stream at her hands, which she pushed out at Felix.

He waited until the last possible moment. The fire growing ever nearer.

Then, Felix shoved his Kayetan out of his body.

Felix tumbled to the ground. He rolled in a somersault to his feet and closed the distance. From the corner of his eye, his Kayetan veered off in the opposite direction, the flames fast on its tail, luring the fire away.

It took Orla a beat to react. Felix had banked on her choosing between the two of them to send her flame after first. Instead, she bisected the fire with a signal from her hands, a thinner rope of pyre honing in on each of them.

With the fire sent out, Orla had no more circling her hands. Defenseless. Not exactly what he intended, but he could work with it.

It came down to a racing game. Felix would make it to his prey first and kill the witch, or the fire would catch him.

Felix knew the odds. Still, he ran. Even with Piper's blood coursing through him, his legs felt lethargic. And the dizziness had only heightened from the rushed disconnect with his shadow.

This was the moment. The choice.

The Kayetan easily outran the flame Orla cast its way. It rushed in toward her and Felix. One command and his Kayetan could teleport to him—merge with him and get Felix away to safety.

Or.

The shadow could take her down.

A growl rumbled in Felix's head. The Kayetan had caught on to his intentions, and the animalistic need to flee filled Felix from head to pumping feet. But that need came from the demon, not Felix. Self-preservation.

"No." The shadow echoed in Felix's head. "Run."

"Not this time."

To his anger, the shadow resisted Felix's will and shifted his flight path to his master. Felix focused his mind like Kole had taught him—calmed it as best he could despite his racing heart—then harnessed all his will into one final command. "Death to the blood witch."

A tension released. Felix felt it in his bones. No longer did he fight for control with his shadow. The demon submitted. Fully. That sensation gave Felix the confidence to continue. He knew his Kayetan would obey.

Felix found his voice bubbling up in his throat. He let out a war cry. No weapon needed. He'd fulfill his role as the bait. And his Kayetan would do something miraculous. Something *good*.

He thought of Kole braving the Black Wall alone, guilty he wasn't by his friend's side. He replayed Vienna's face, twisted in agony, screaming and crying. But he morphed that image into her warm smile. Thought of the good times they'd had side by side growing up in the Liberation.

Yeah. Those would be his last thoughts. Of the good times. Of the things he'd miss. Of seeing Ma and Pa again.

The Kayetan stayed true to course. The shadow's claws struck down on Orla. Slashed from her throat, across her chest and down to her hips. Ribbons of flesh gave way at the fatal attack. The shock of death registered on the priestess' face.

That same moment when blood sprayed out from the Kayetan's blow, the tickle of heat closed in on Felix. The burning touch on his back came so hot his brain mistook it for ice.

That feeling snared him. He looked down to see his stomach dissolving away. Up his chest and down his legs.

Someone shrieked his name in the distance.

Then the fire consumed him.

THE END

ACKNOWLEDGEMENTS

Thank you to all my beta readers and my writing group buddies, who helped me forge this book. To my mother and Dad, who continuously encourage me to follow my dreams no matter how impossible they may seem. I never would've started writing to begin with if it hadn't been for your early support.

I give all the thanks in the world to the amazing editor, Darren Todd. You continue to help me grow in this profession and challenge my story by asking all the questions I never thought to answer, and for laughing with me when my brain has me write ridiculous things.

And finally, a great big thank you to David Lane (aka Lane Diamond), who is responsible for this story in your hands. I will forever be grateful for the chance you've given me and for welcoming me into the Evolved Publishing family.

ABOUT THE AUTHOR

Parris lives in Mesa, Arizona with her husband and two golden retrievers. She discovered her love for reading when a middle-school reading assignment led her to the fantasy section of the library. This passion sparked stories of her own imagination, yet she never put pen to paper until after college. When she's not consumed in her writing, she enjoys Olympic weightlifting, playing Dungeons & Dragons, and coaching color guard.

For more, please visit Parris online at:
Website: www.ParrisSheetsAuthor.com
Facebook: @AuthorParrisSheets
Twitter: @Parris_Sheets

MORE FROM EVOLVED PUBLISHING

We offer great books across multiple genres, featuring high-quality editing (which we believe is second-to-none) and fantastic covers.

As a hybrid small press, your support as loyal readers is so important to us, and we have strived, with tireless dedication and sheer determination, to deliver on the promise of our motto:
QUALITY IS PRIORITY #1!

Please check out all of our great books,
which you can find at this link:
www.EvolvedPub.com/Catalog/

Thank you!